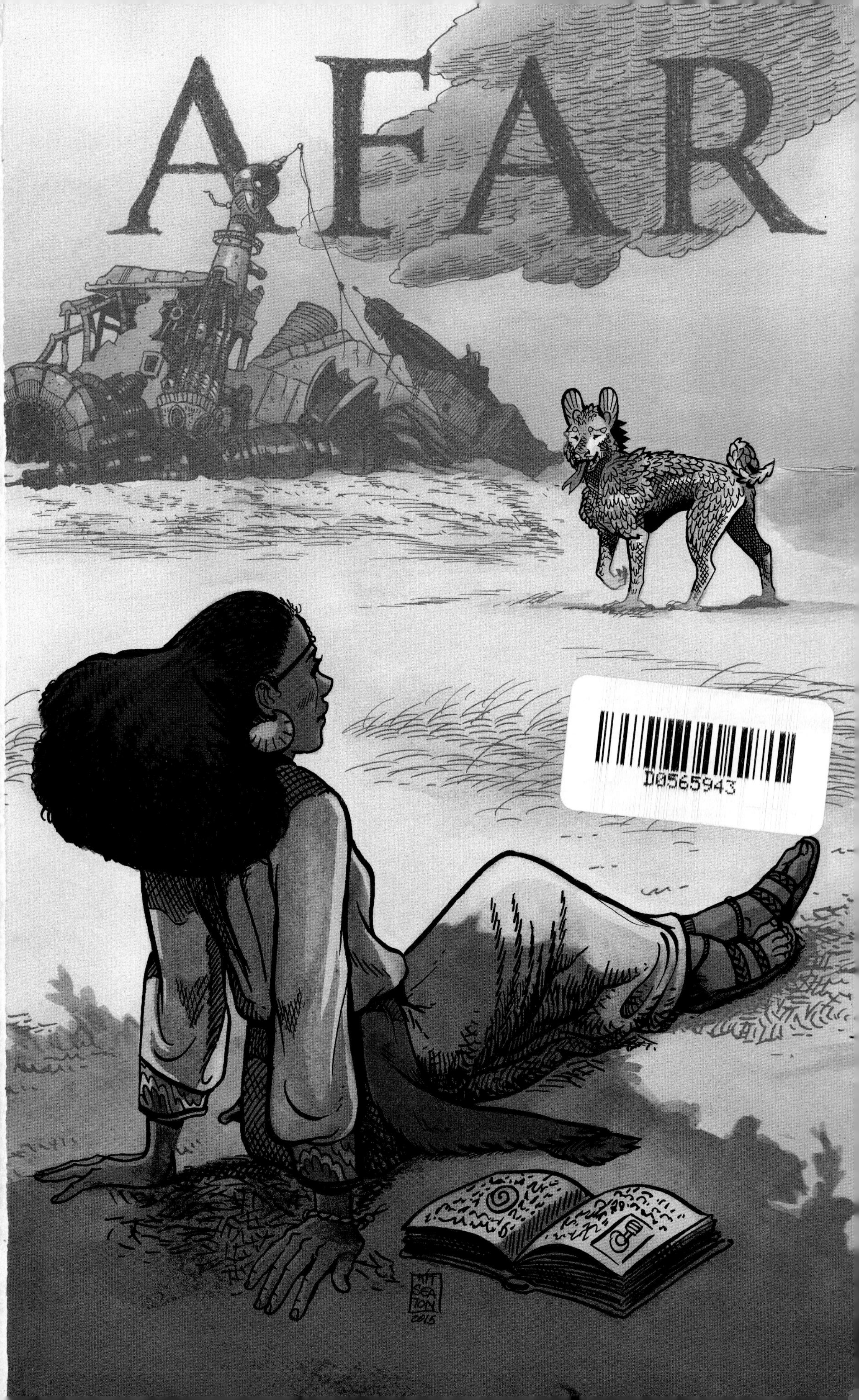
AFAR

Special thanks to William Thomas, Rosa del Duca, Emi Lenox and Joe Keatinge for the early feedback and the encouragement, to my family and friends for your unyielding support, and to my wonderful readers for making my dreams possible.
— Leila del Duca

My deepest thanks to my sister Cat Seaton, and my folks, for their constant love and support. Special thanks to the teachers, and mentors who helped shape my artistic identity, especially Murray and Carol Tinkelman, with remembrance and gratitude.
— Kit Seaton

AFAR. First printing. March 2017. Published by Image Comics, Inc. Office of publication: 2701 NW Vaughn St., Suite 780, Portland, OR 97210. Printed in the USA. For information regarding the CPSIA on this printed material call: 203-595-3636 and provide reference #RICH–729815. For international rights, contact: foreignlicensing@imagecomics.com. ISBN: 978-1-63215-941-0.

AFAR

WRITTEN BY **Leila del Duca**
ART BY **Kit Seaton**
EDITED BY **Taneka Stotts**

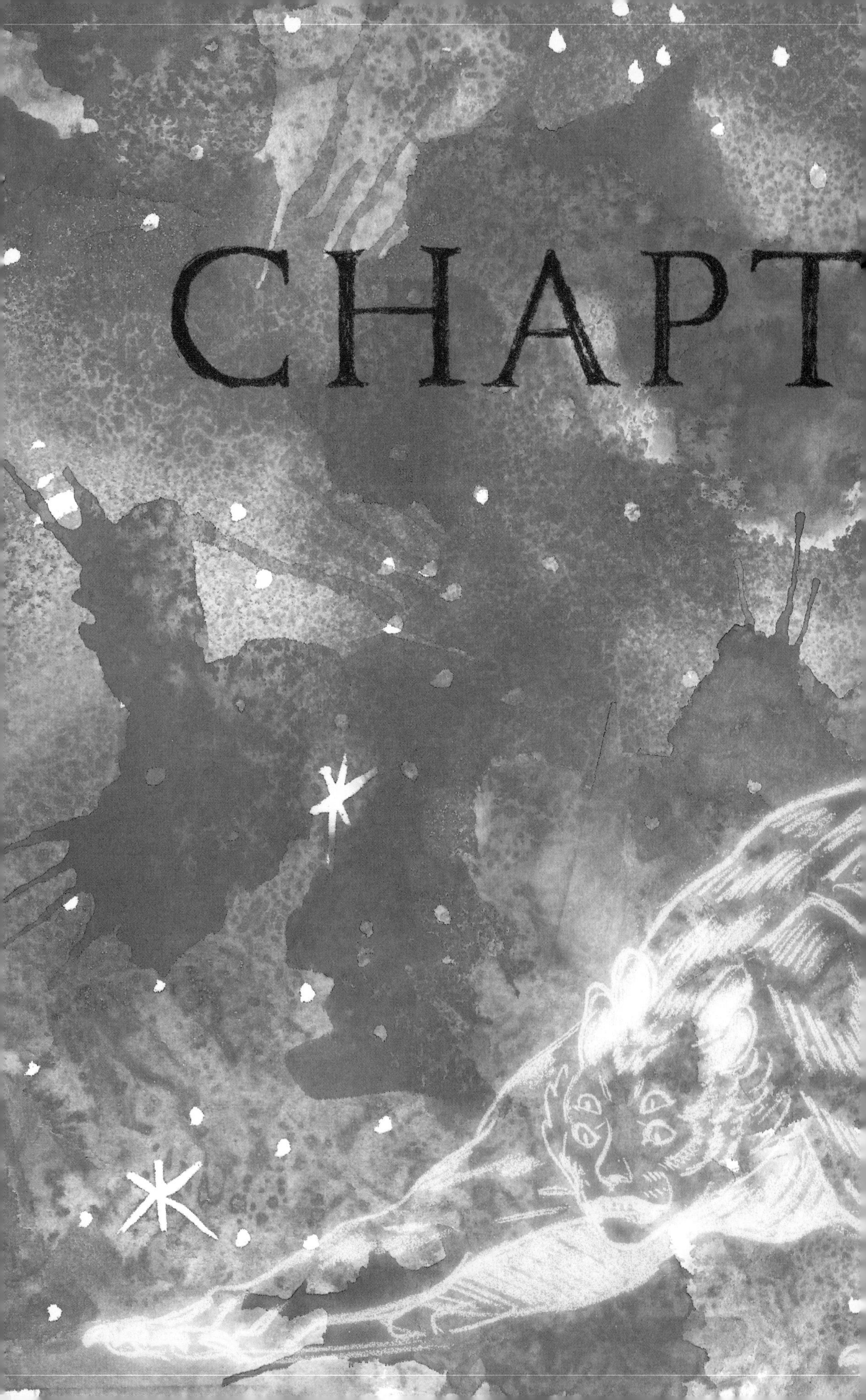
CHAPT

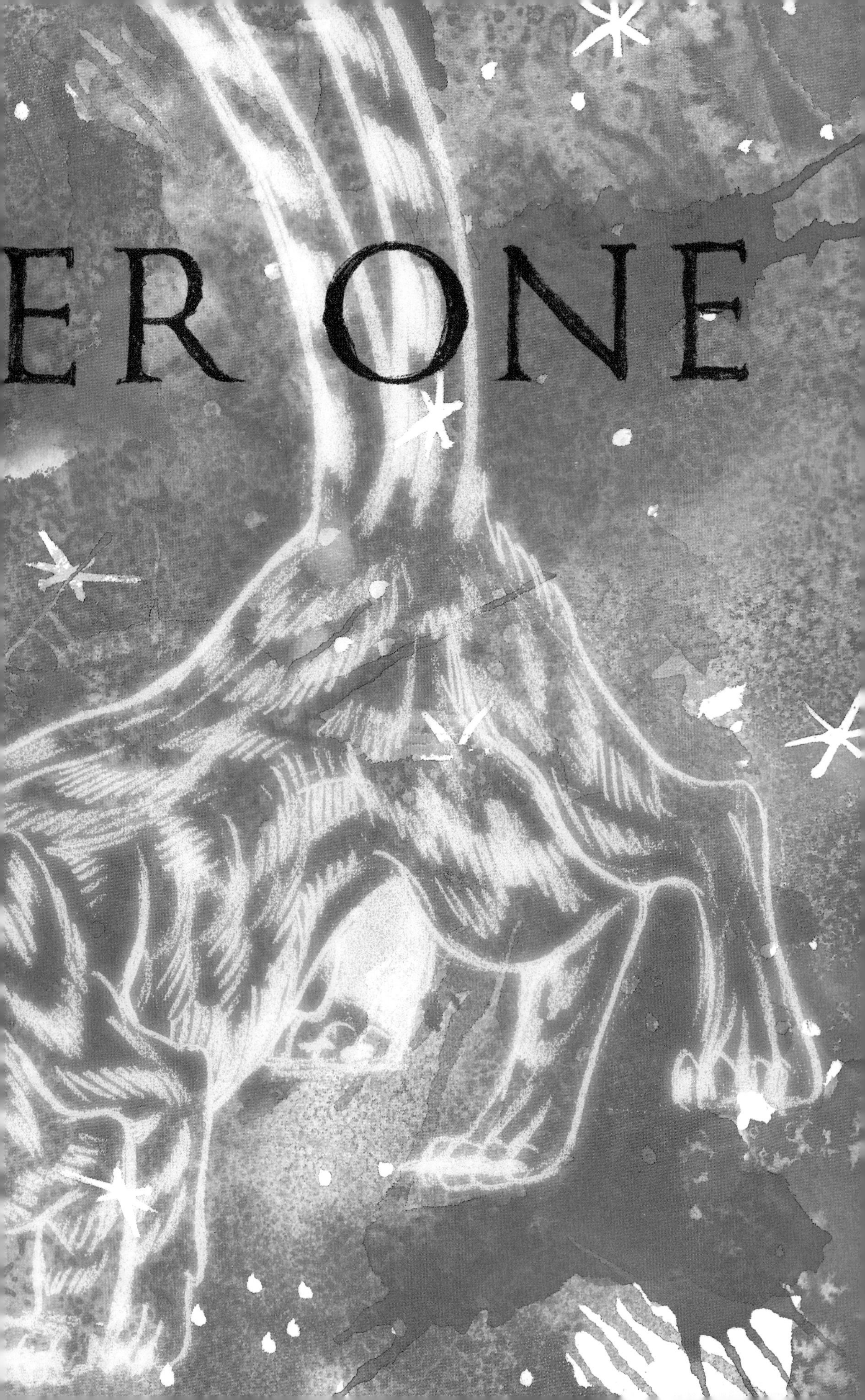
ER ONE

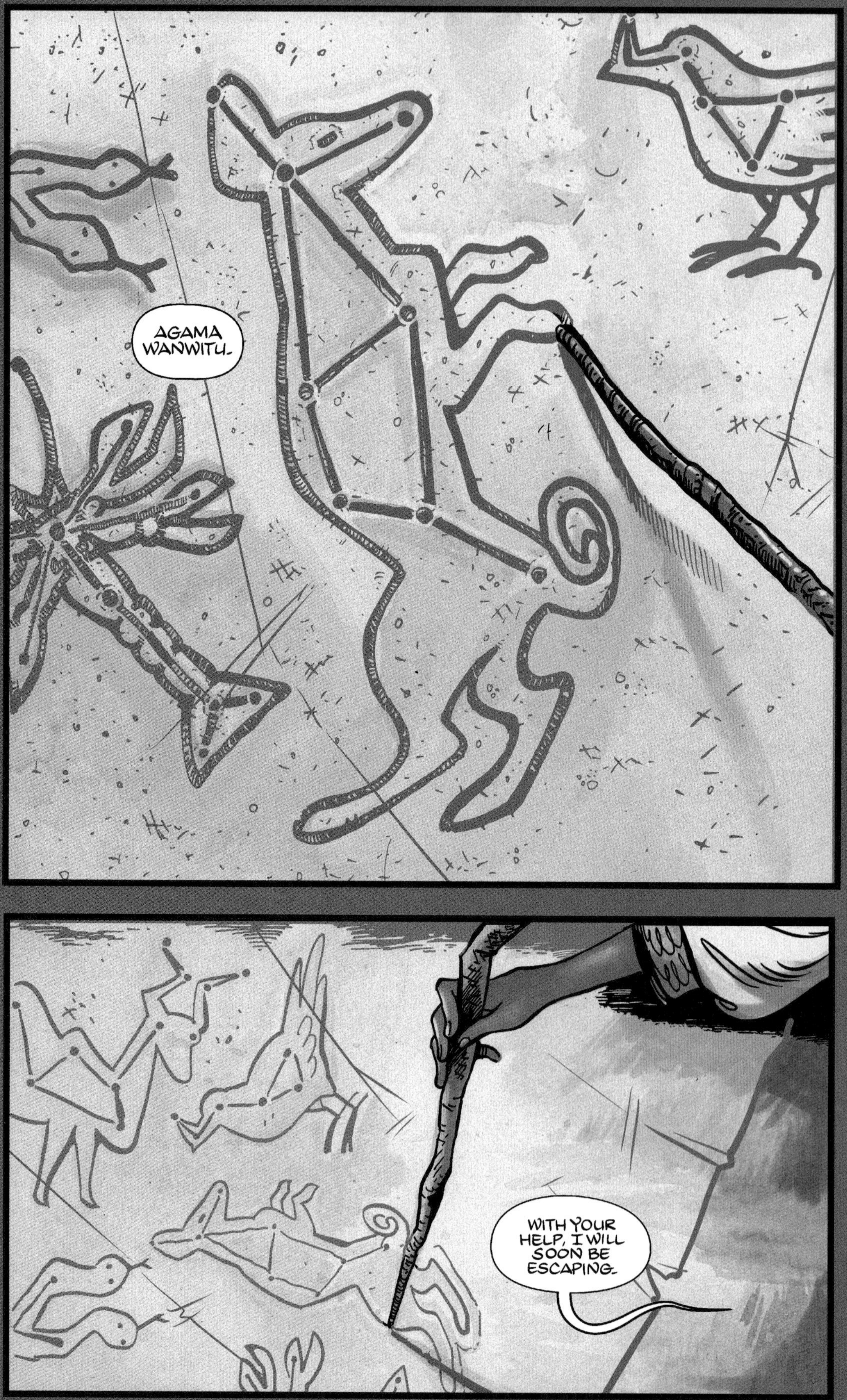
AGAMA WANWITU.
WITH YOUR HELP, I WILL SOON BE ESCAPING.

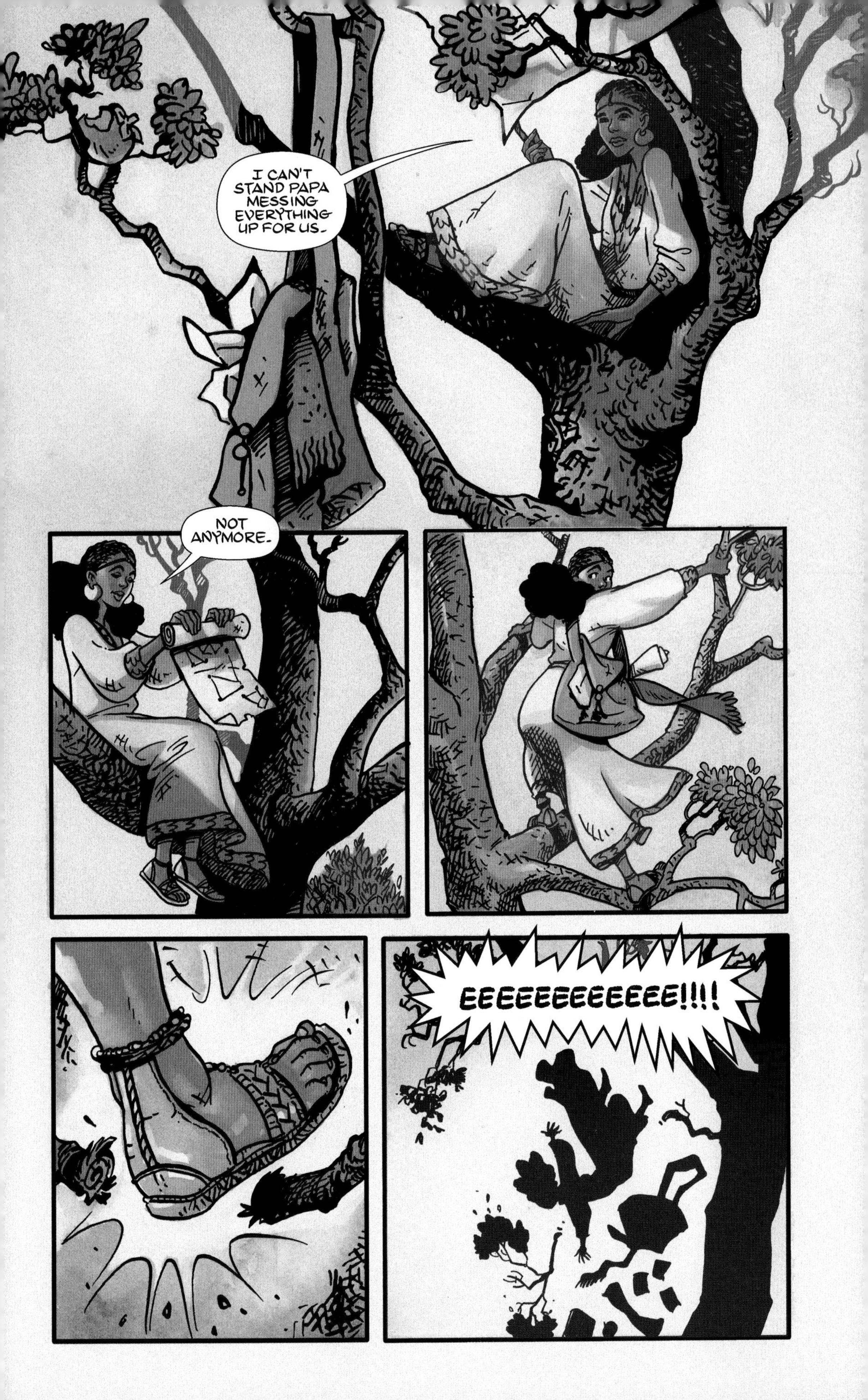
I CAN'T STAND PAPA MESSING EVERYTHING UP FOR US.
NOT ANYMORE.
EEEEEEEEEEEEE!!!!

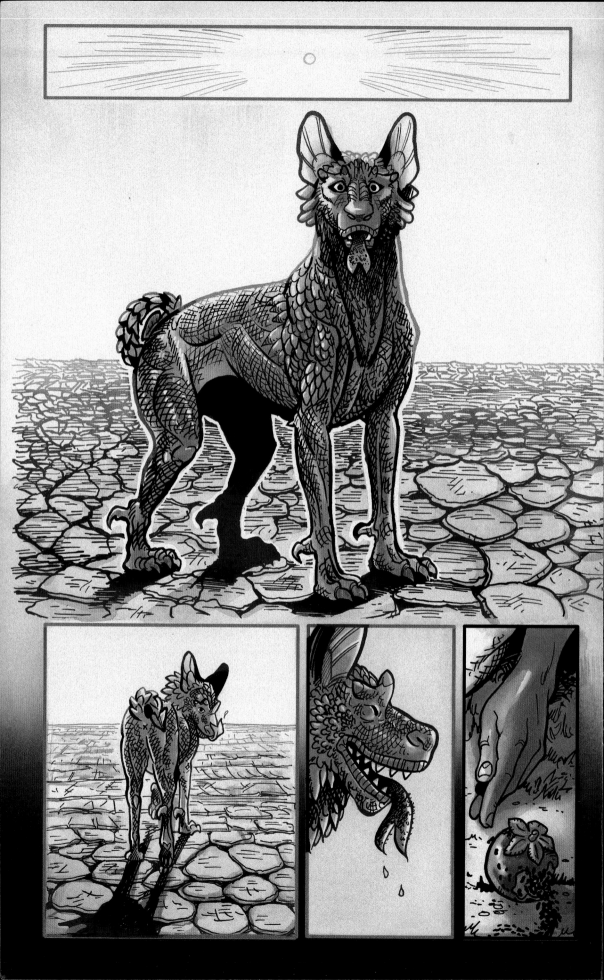

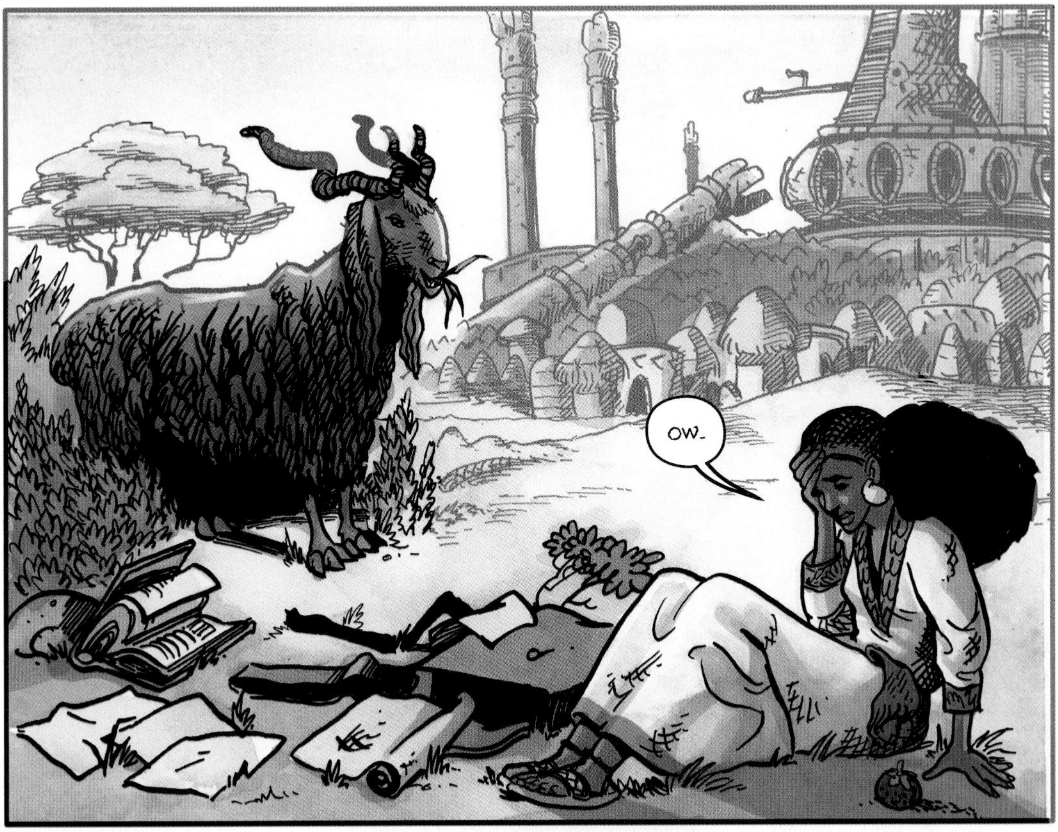
OW.

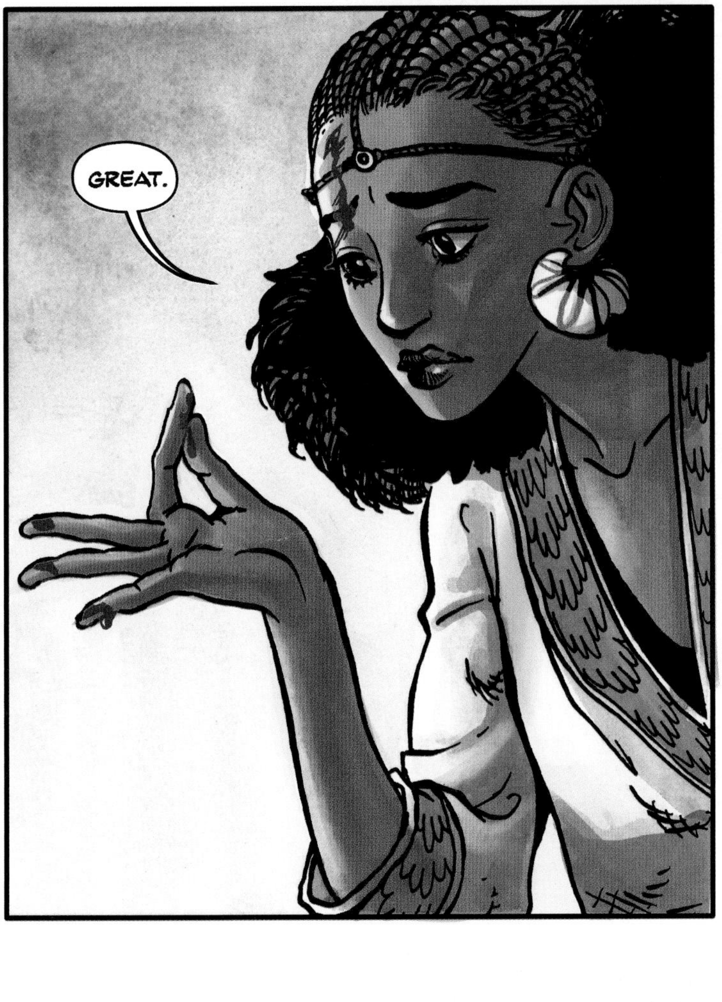
GREAT.

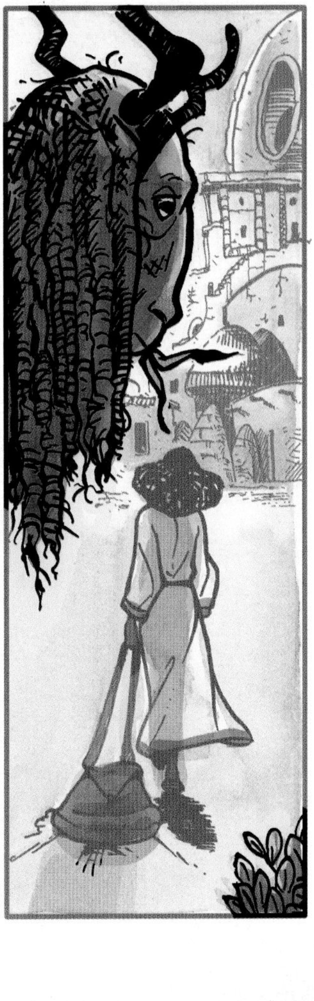

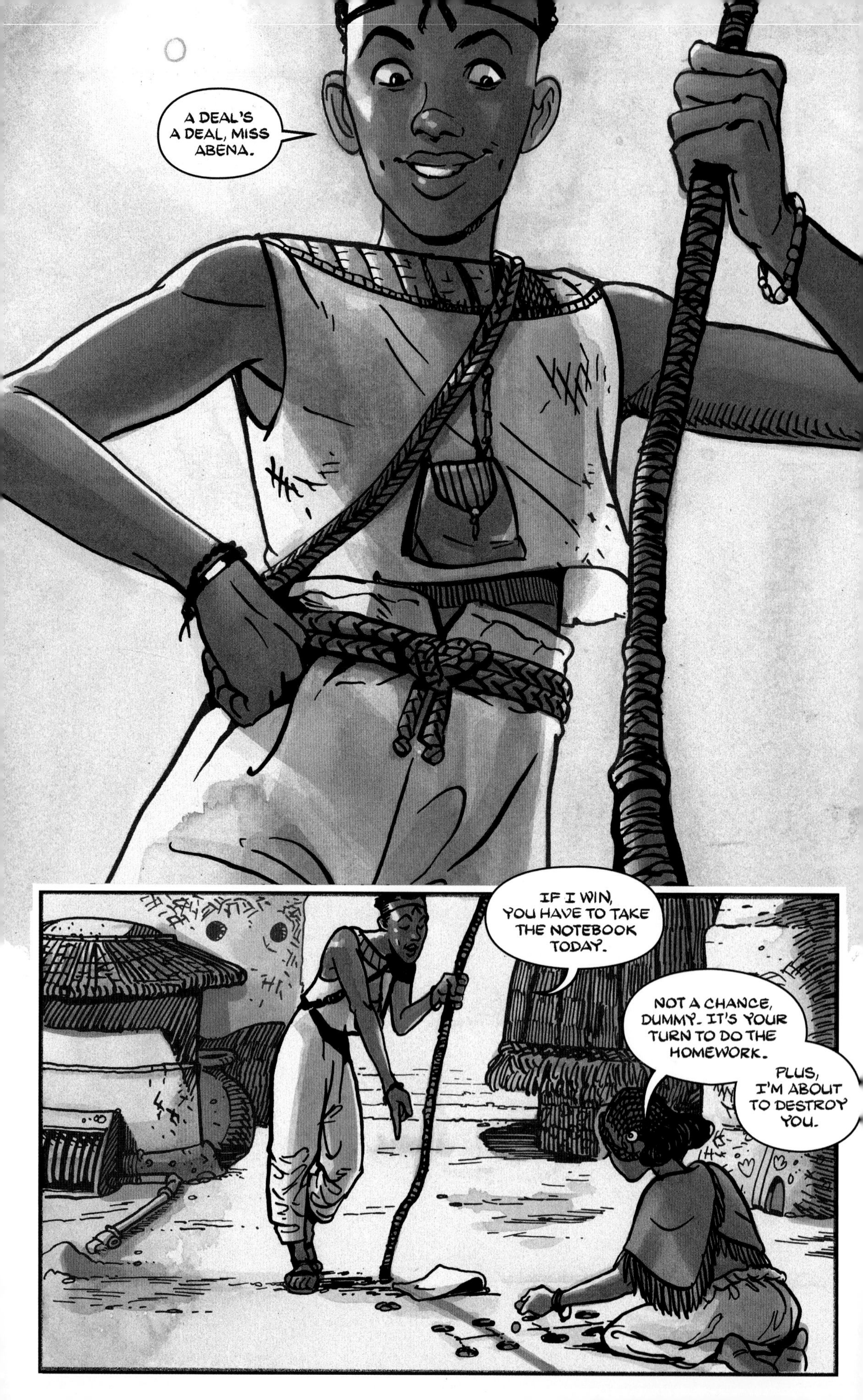
A DEAL'S A DEAL, MISS ABENA.
IF I WIN, YOU HAVE TO TAKE THE NOTEBOOK TODAY.
NOT A CHANCE, DUMMY. IT'S YOUR TURN TO DO THE HOMEWORK.
PLUS, I'M ABOUT TO DESTROY YOU.

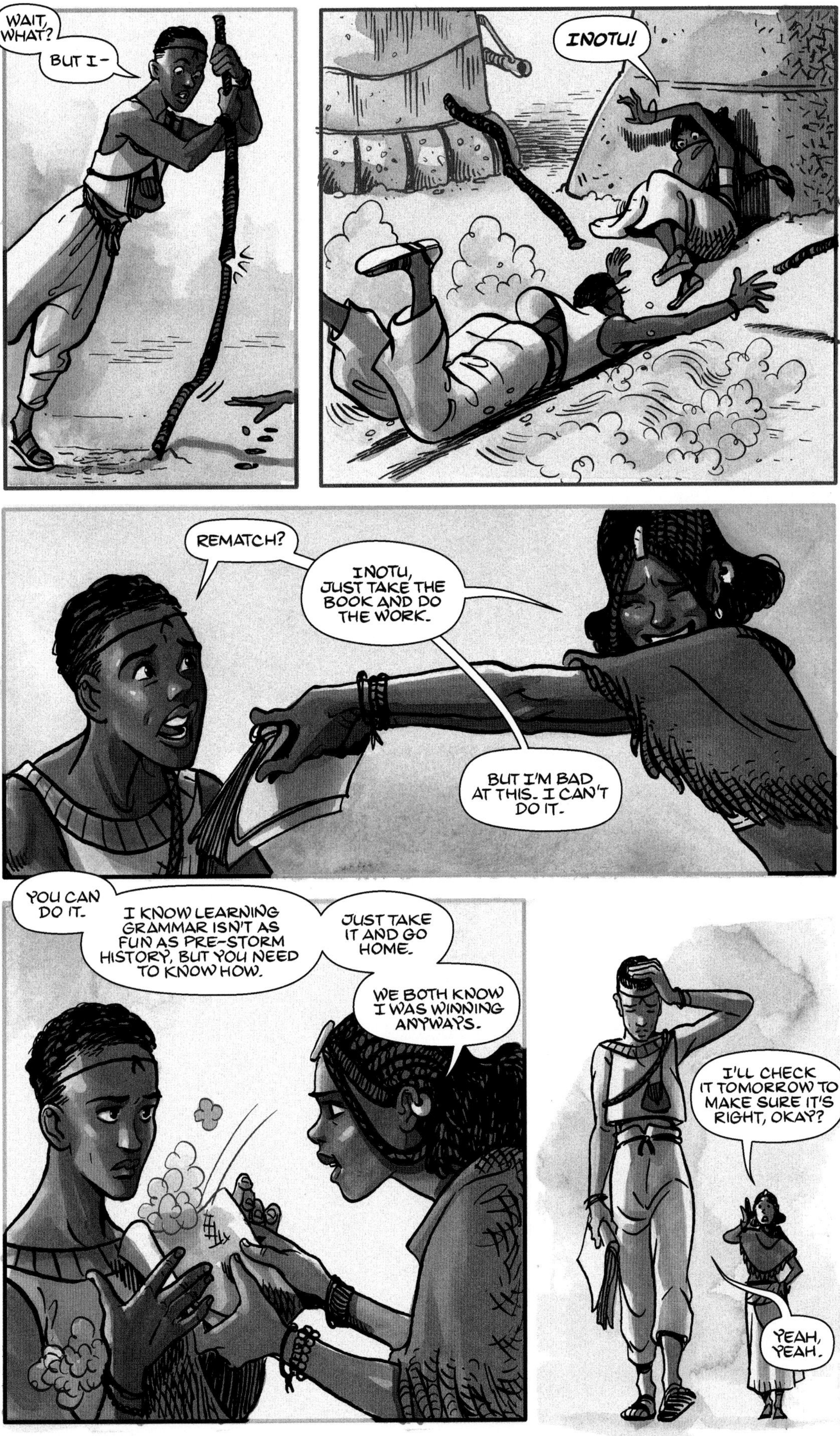
WAIT, WHAT?
BUT I-
INOTU!
REMATCH?
INOTU, JUST TAKE THE BOOK AND DO THE WORK.
BUT I'M BAD AT THIS. I CAN'T DO IT.
YOU CAN DO IT.
I KNOW LEARNING GRAMMAR ISN'T AS FUN AS PRE-STORM HISTORY, BUT YOU NEED TO KNOW HOW.
JUST TAKE IT AND GO HOME.
WE BOTH KNOW I WAS WINNING ANYWAYS.
I'LL CHECK IT TOMORROW TO MAKE SURE IT'S RIGHT, OKAY?
YEAH, YEAH.

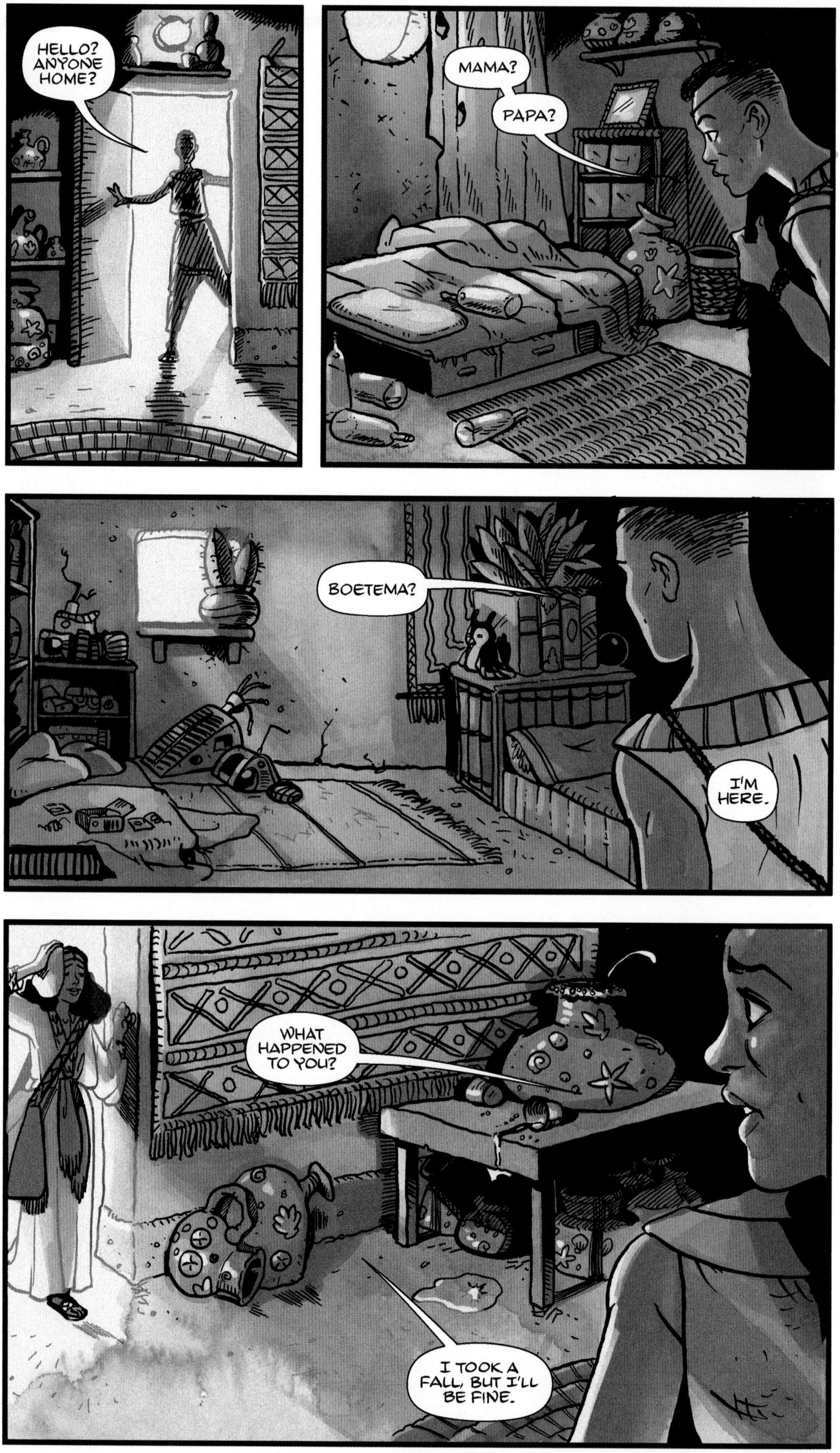
HELLO? ANYONE HOME?
MAMA?
PAPA?
BOETEMA?
I'M HERE.
WHAT HAPPENED TO YOU?
I TOOK A FALL, BUT I'LL BE FINE.

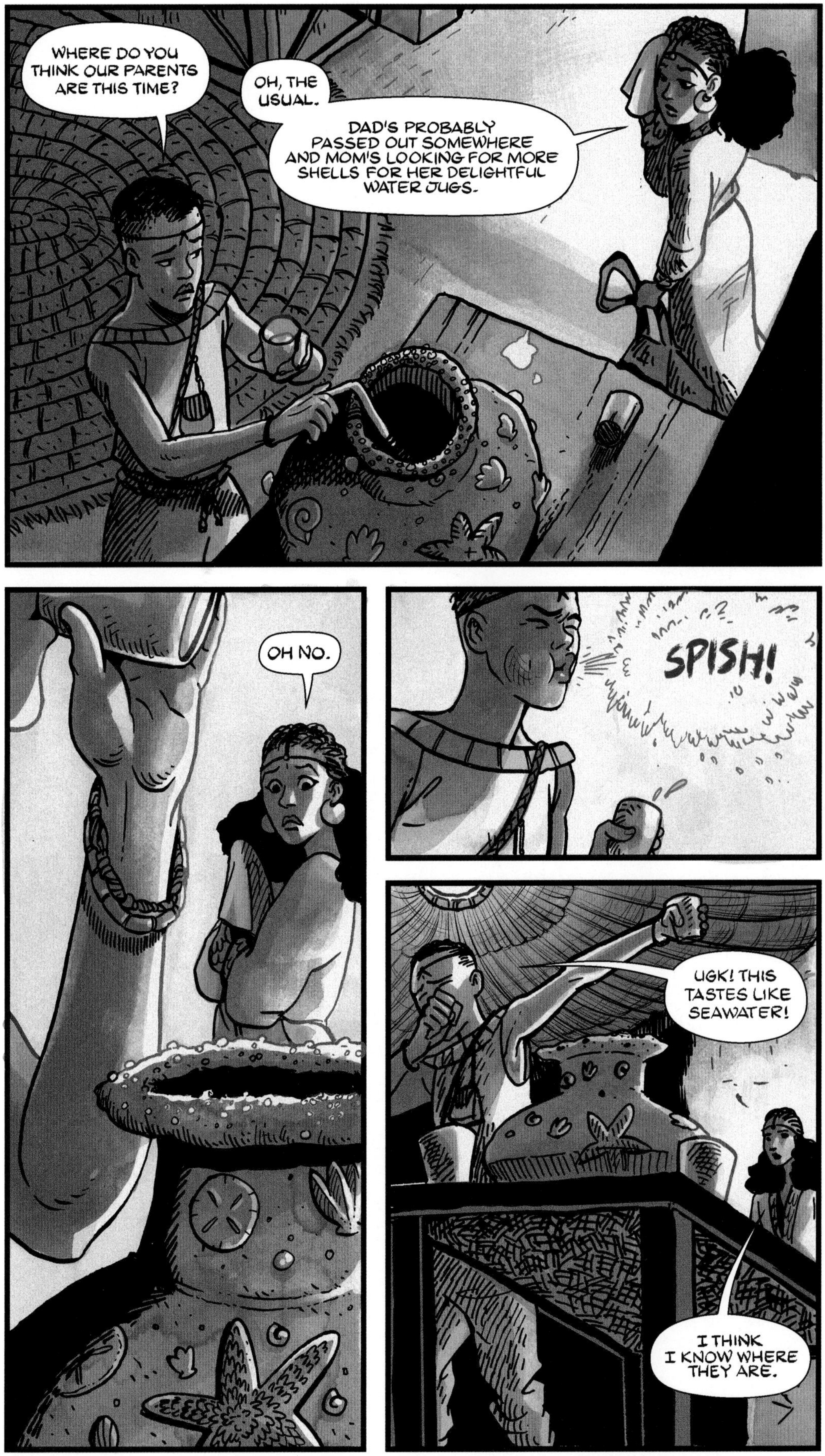
WHERE DO YOU THINK OUR PARENTS ARE THIS TIME?
OH, THE USUAL.
DAD'S PROBABLY PASSED OUT SOMEWHERE AND MOM'S LOOKING FOR MORE SHELLS FOR HER DELIGHTFUL WATER JUGS.
OH NO.
SPISH!
UGK! THIS TASTES LIKE SEAWATER!
I THINK I KNOW WHERE THEY ARE.

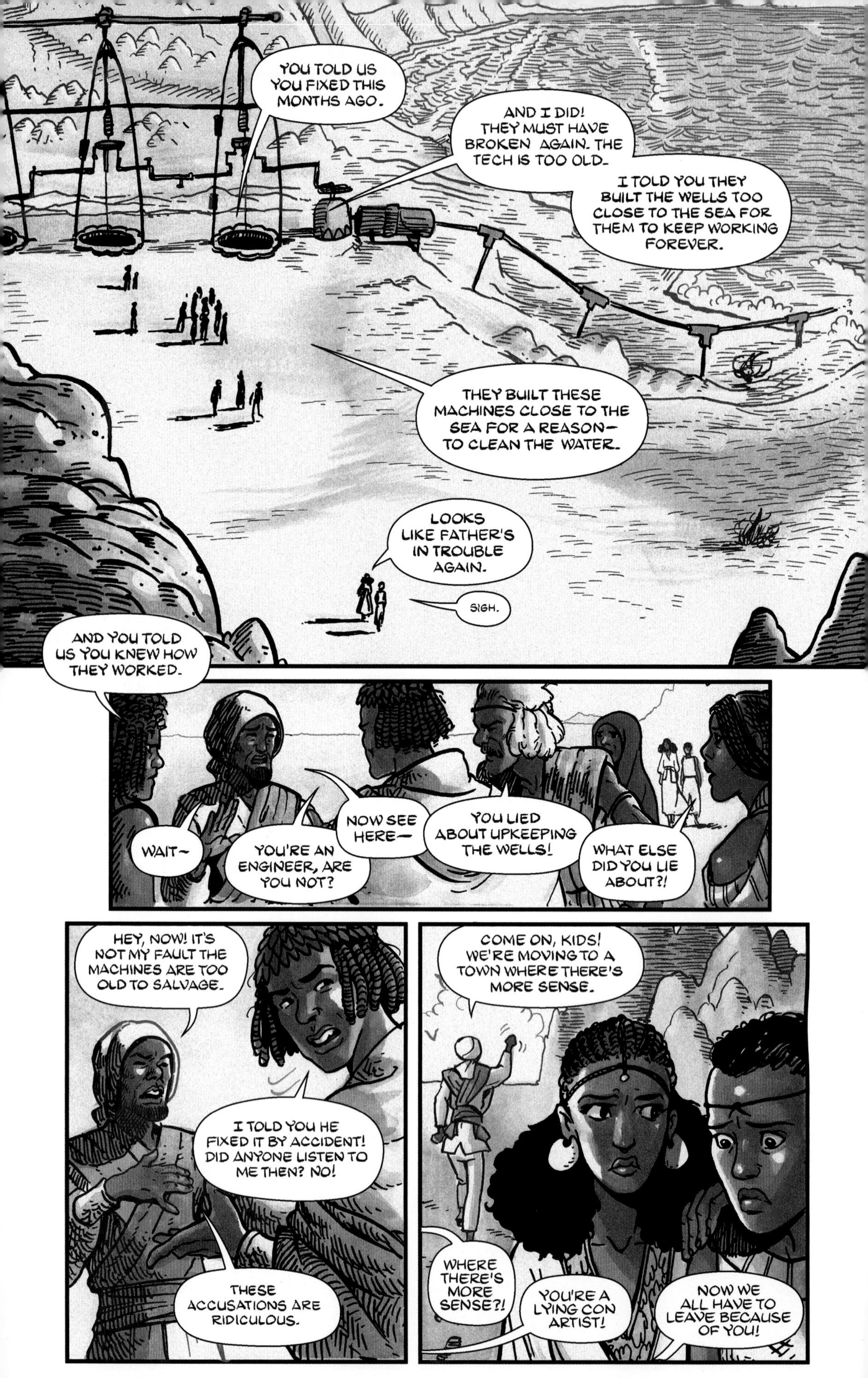
YOU TOLD US YOU FIXED THIS MONTHS AGO.
AND I DID! THEY MUST HAVE BROKEN AGAIN. THE TECH IS TOO OLD.
I TOLD YOU THEY BUILT THE WELLS TOO CLOSE TO THE SEA FOR THEM TO KEEP WORKING FOREVER.
THEY BUILT THESE MACHINES CLOSE TO THE SEA FOR A REASON— TO CLEAN THE WATER.
LOOKS LIKE FATHER'S IN TROUBLE AGAIN.
SIGH.
AND YOU TOLD US YOU KNEW HOW THEY WORKED.
WAIT~
YOU'RE AN ENGINEER, ARE YOU NOT?
NOW SEE HERE—
YOU LIED ABOUT UPKEEPING THE WELLS!
WHAT ELSE DID YOU LIE ABOUT?!
HEY, NOW! IT'S NOT MY FAULT THE MACHINES ARE TOO OLD TO SALVAGE.
I TOLD YOU HE FIXED IT BY ACCIDENT! DID ANYONE LISTEN TO ME THEN? NO!
THESE ACCUSATIONS ARE RIDICULOUS.
COME ON, KIDS! WE'RE MOVING TO A TOWN WHERE THERE'S MORE SENSE.
WHERE THERE'S MORE SENSE?!
YOU'RE A LYING CON ARTIST!
NOW WE ALL HAVE TO LEAVE BECAUSE OF YOU!

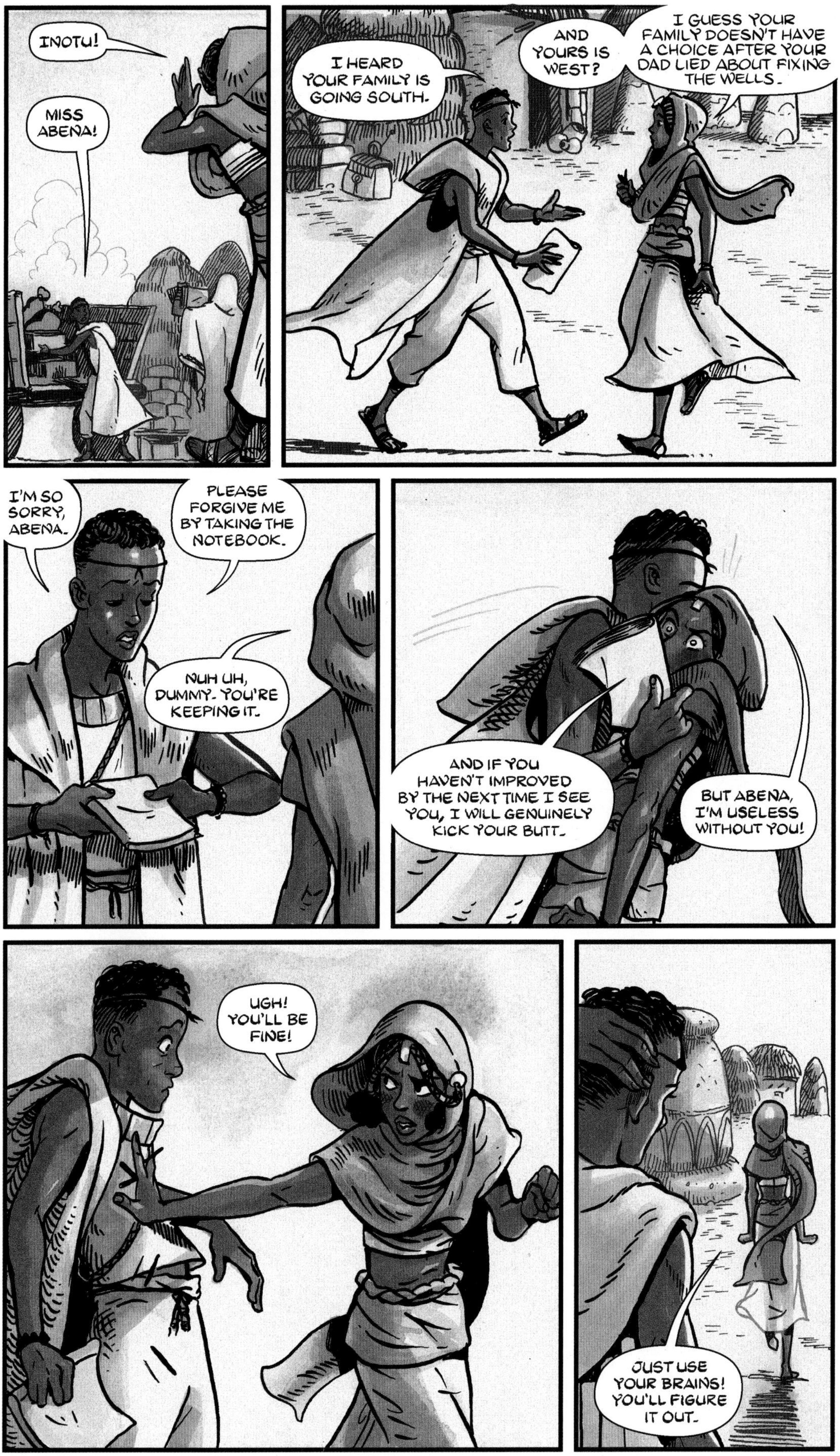
INOTU!
MISS ABENA!
I HEARD YOUR FAMILY IS GOING SOUTH.
AND YOURS IS WEST?
I GUESS YOUR FAMILY DOESN'T HAVE A CHOICE AFTER YOUR DAD LIED ABOUT FIXING THE WELLS.
I'M SO SORRY, ABENA.
PLEASE FORGIVE ME BY TAKING THE NOTEBOOK.
NUH UH, DUMMY. YOU'RE KEEPING IT.
AND IF YOU HAVEN'T IMPROVED BY THE NEXT TIME I SEE YOU, I WILL GENUINELY KICK YOUR BUTT.
BUT ABENA, I'M USELESS WITHOUT YOU!
UGH! YOU'LL BE FINE!
JUST USE YOUR BRAINS! YOU'LL FIGURE IT OUT.

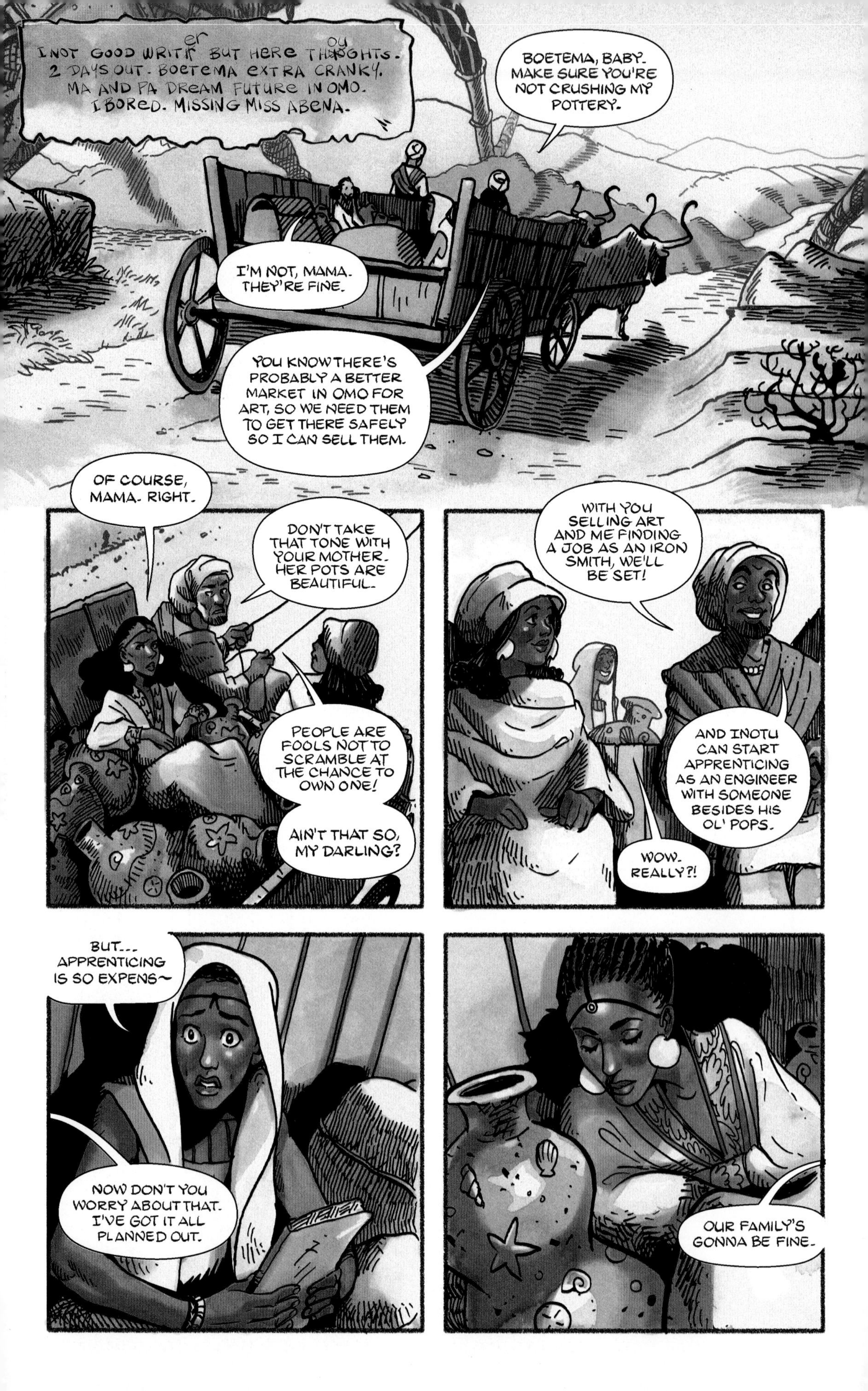
I NOT GOOD WRITER BUT HERE THOUGHTS. 2 DAYS OUT. BOETEMA EXTRA CRANKY. MA AND PA DREAM FUTURE IN OMO. I BORED. MISSING MISS ABENA.
BOETEMA, BABY. MAKE SURE YOU'RE NOT CRUSHING MY POTTERY.
I'M NOT, MAMA. THEY'RE FINE.
YOU KNOW THERE'S PROBABLY A BETTER MARKET IN OMO FOR ART, SO WE NEED THEM TO GET THERE SAFELY SO I CAN SELL THEM.
OF COURSE, MAMA. RIGHT.
DON'T TAKE THAT TONE WITH YOUR MOTHER. HER POTS ARE BEAUTIFUL.
PEOPLE ARE FOOLS NOT TO SCRAMBLE AT THE CHANCE TO OWN ONE!
AIN'T THAT SO, MY DARLING?
WITH YOU SELLING ART AND ME FINDING A JOB AS AN IRON SMITH, WE'LL BE SET!
AND INOTU CAN START APPRENTICING AS AN ENGINEER WITH SOMEONE BESIDES HIS OL' POPS.
WOW. REALLY?!
BUT... APPRENTICING IS SO EXPENS~
NOW DON'T YOU WORRY ABOUT THAT. I'VE GOT IT ALL PLANNED OUT.
OUR FAMILY'S GONNA BE FINE.

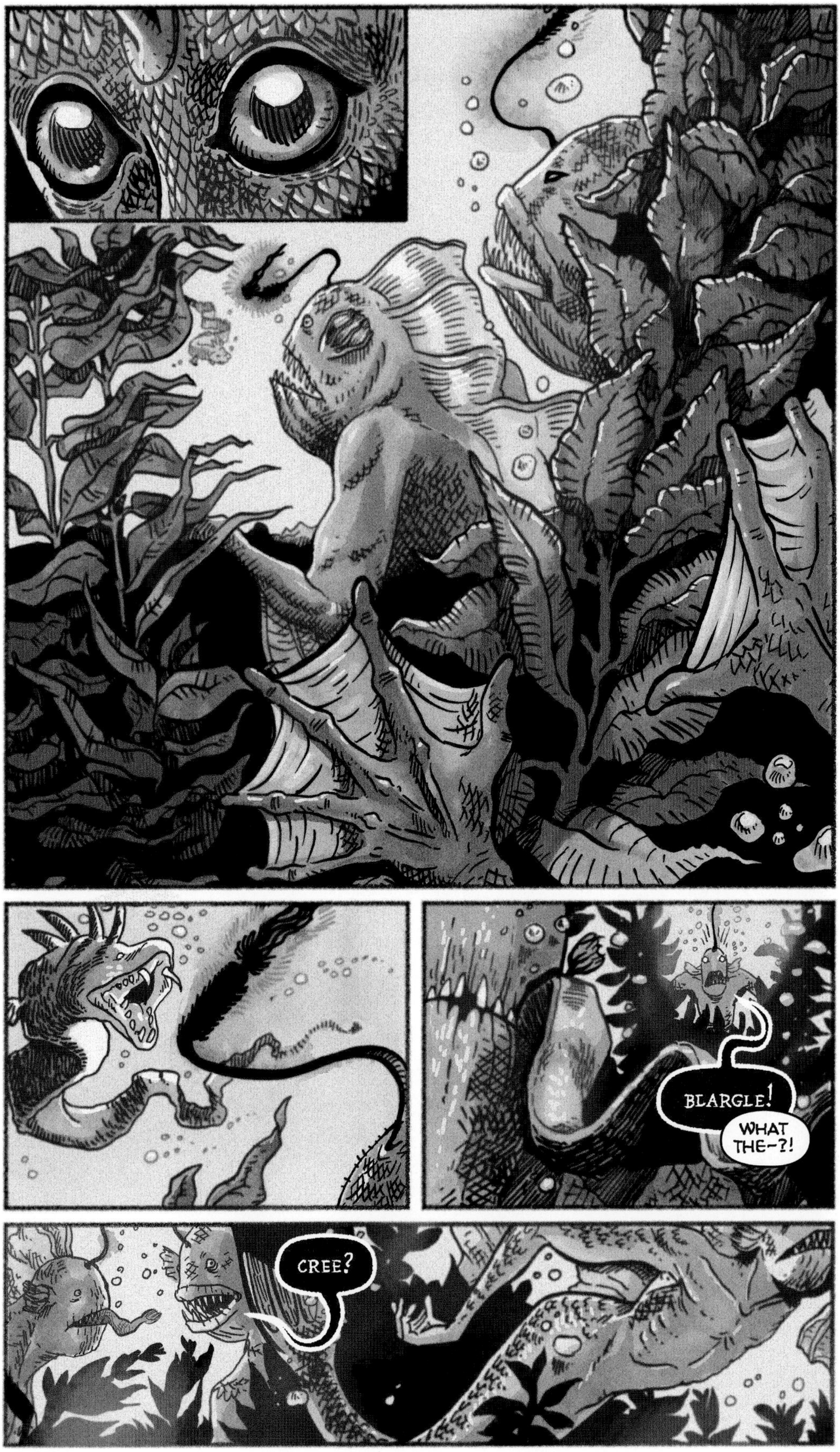
BLARGLE!
WHAT THE-?!
CREE?

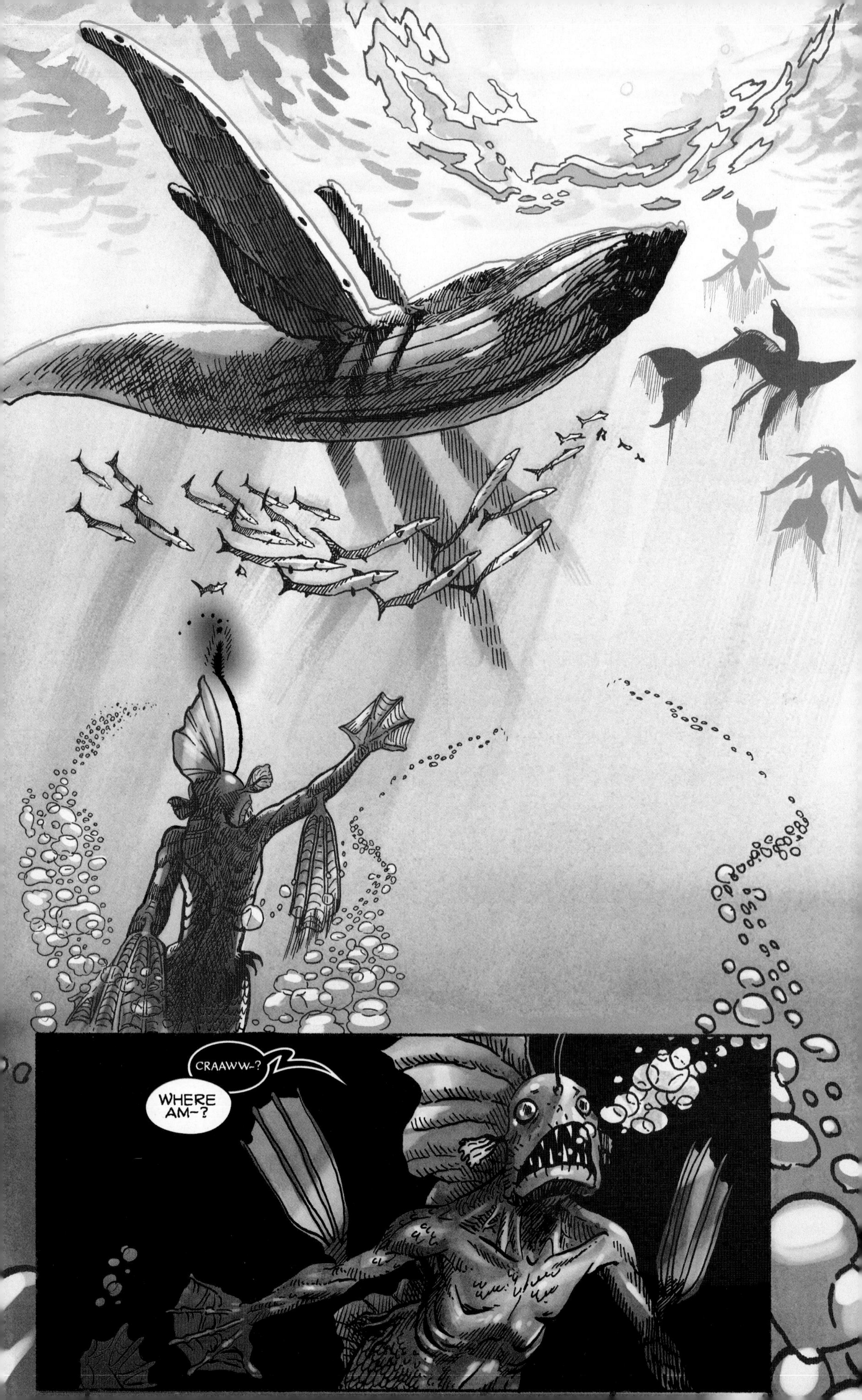
CRAAWW-?
WHERE AM-?

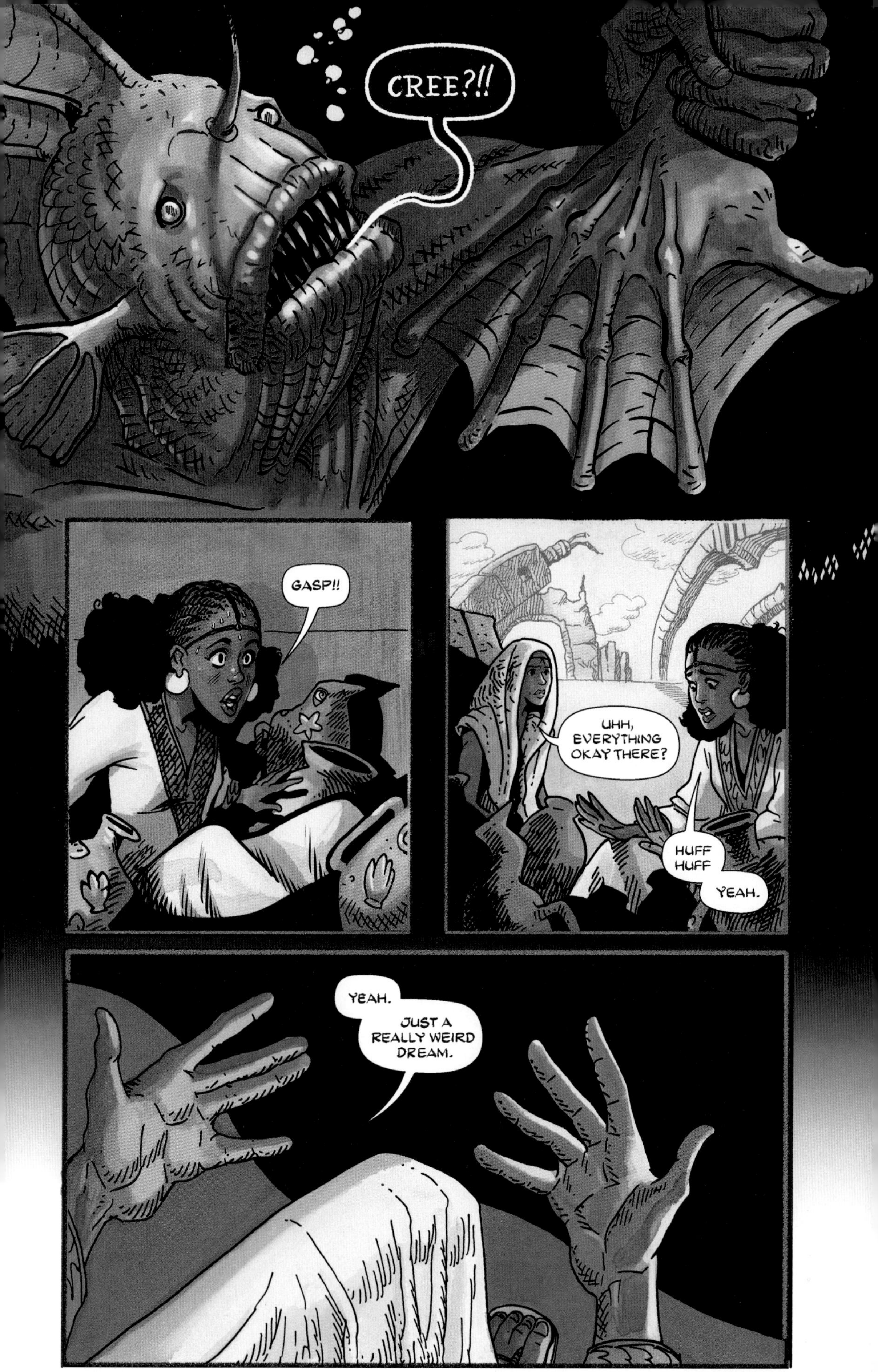
CREE?!!
GASP!!
UHH, EVERYTHING OKAY THERE?
HUFF HUFF
YEAH.
YEAH.
JUST A REALLY WEIRD DREAM.

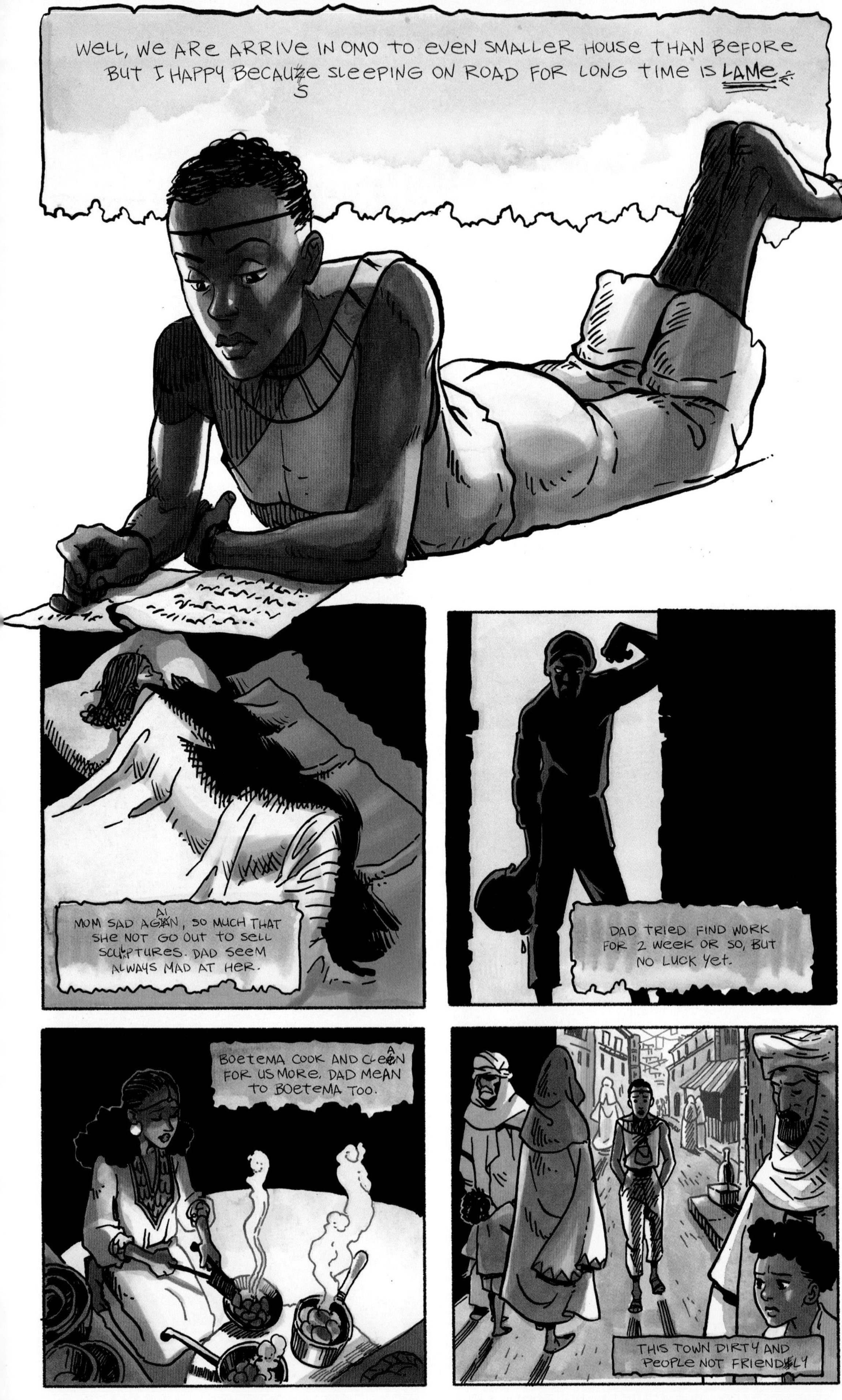
WELL, WE ARE ARRIVE IN OMO TO EVEN SMALLER HOUSE THAN BEFORE BUT I HAPPY BECAUSE SLEEPING ON ROAD FOR LONG TIME IS LAME
MOM SAD AGAIN, SO MUCH THAT SHE NOT GO OUT TO SELL SCULPTURES. DAD SEEM ALWAYS MAD AT HER.
DAD TRIED FIND WORK FOR 2 WEEK OR SO, BUT NO LUCK YET.
BOETEMA COOK AND CLEAN FOR US MORE. DAD MEAN TO BOETEMA TOO.
THIS TOWN DIRTY AND PEOPLE NOT FRIENDLY

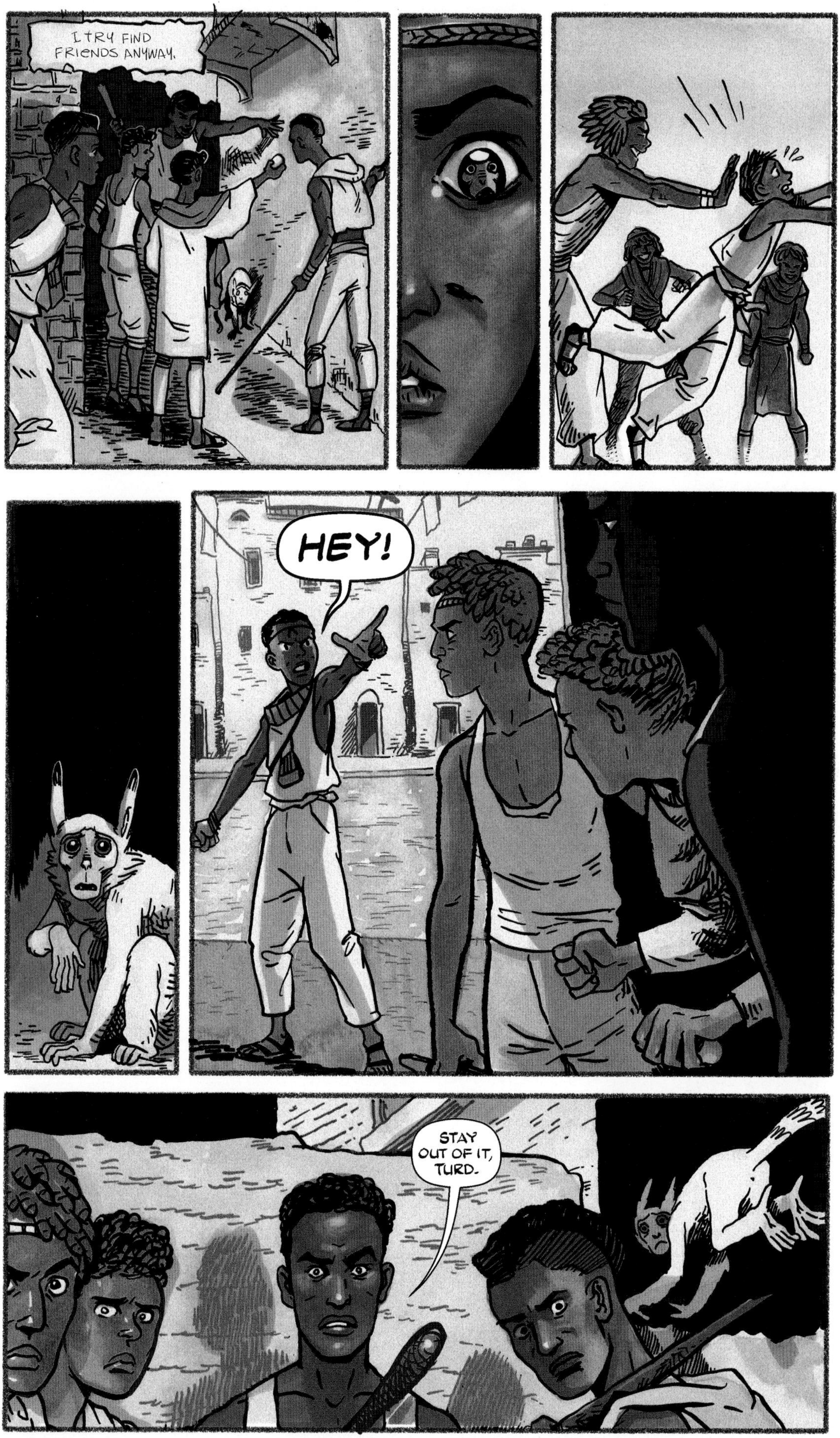
I TRY FIND FRIENDS ANYWAY.
HEY!
STAY OUT OF IT, TURD.

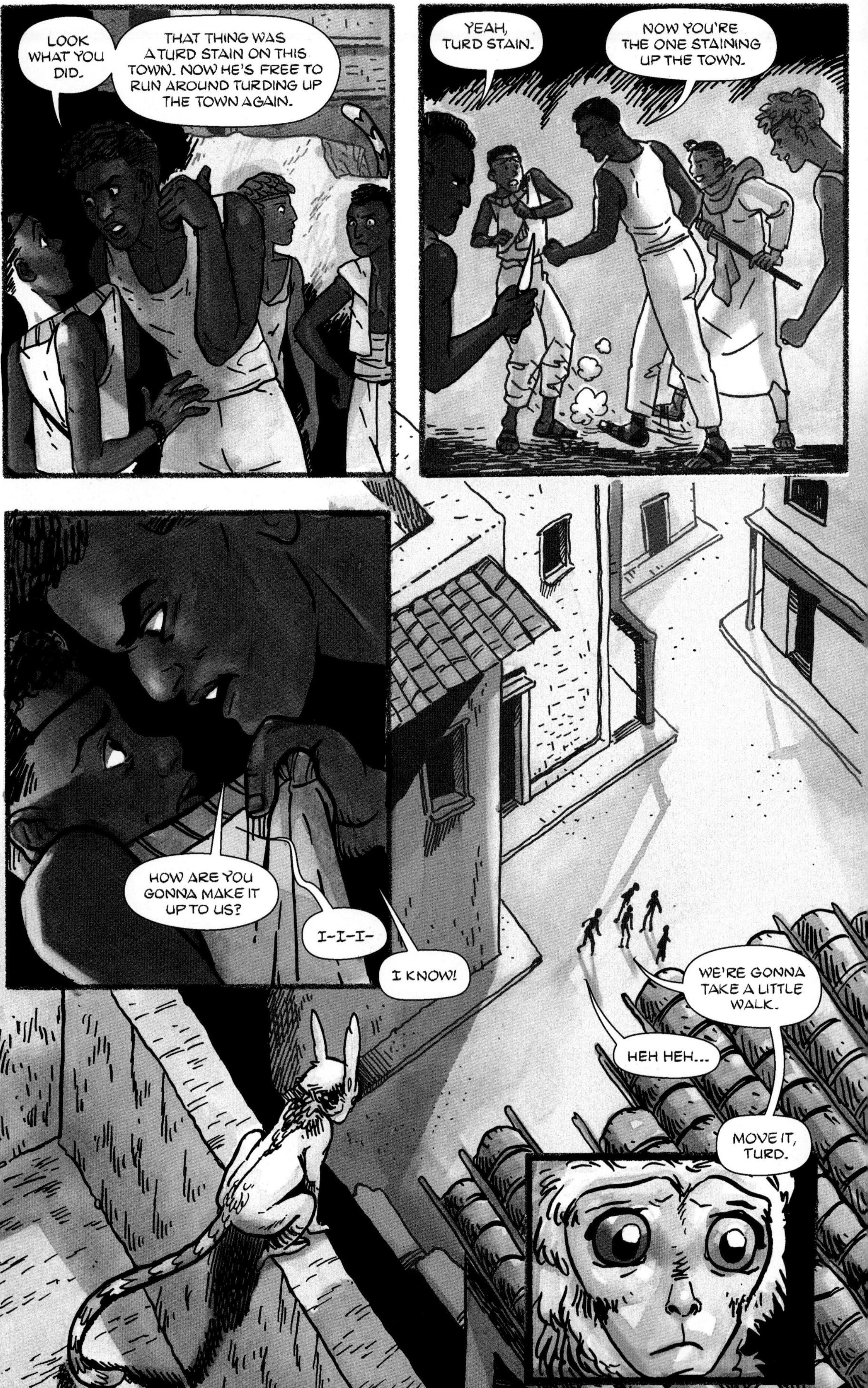
LOOK WHAT YOU DID.
THAT THING WAS A TURD STAIN ON THIS TOWN. NOW HE'S FREE TO RUN AROUND TURDING UP THE TOWN AGAIN.
YEAH, TURD STAIN.
NOW YOU'RE THE ONE STAINING UP THE TOWN.
HOW ARE YOU GONNA MAKE IT UP TO US?
I-I-I-
I KNOW!
WE'RE GONNA TAKE A LITTLE WALK.
HEH HEH...
MOVE IT, TURD.

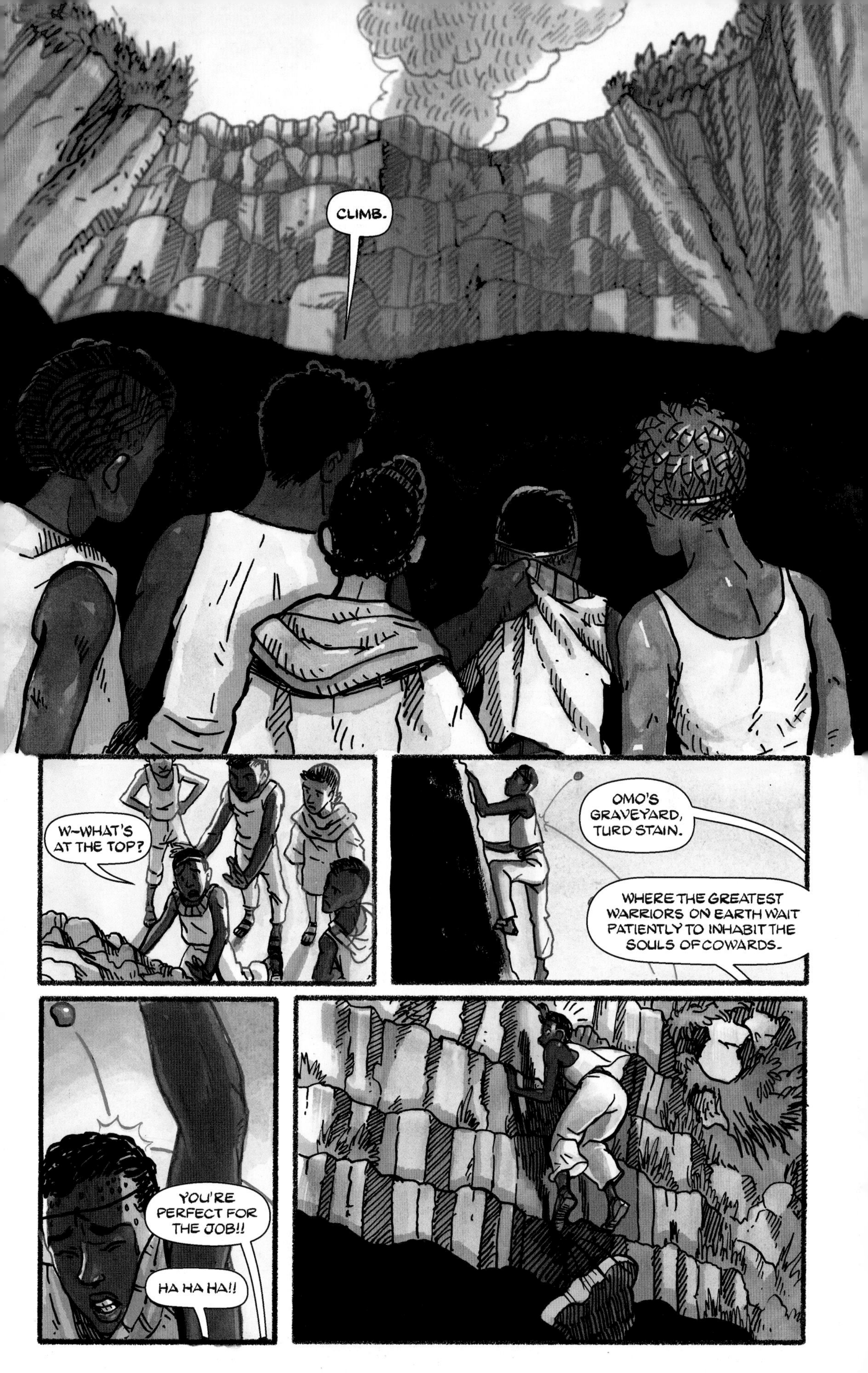
CLIMB.
W-WHAT'S AT THE TOP?
OMO'S GRAVEYARD, TURD STAIN.
WHERE THE GREATEST WARRIORS ON EARTH WAIT PATIENTLY TO INHABIT THE SOULS OF COWARDS.
YOU'RE PERFECT FOR THE JOB!!
HA HA HA!!

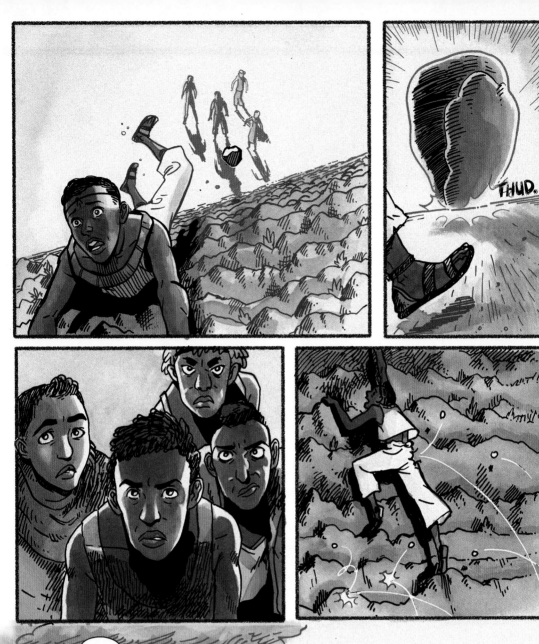

THUD.

HUFF
HUFF

CONSIDER
IT DONE.

COME NEXT WEEK,
YOU'LL BE ON THE BOARD
OF CURRENCY REGULATION
AND WE'LL BE ABLE TO MOVE
FORWARD FROM THERE.

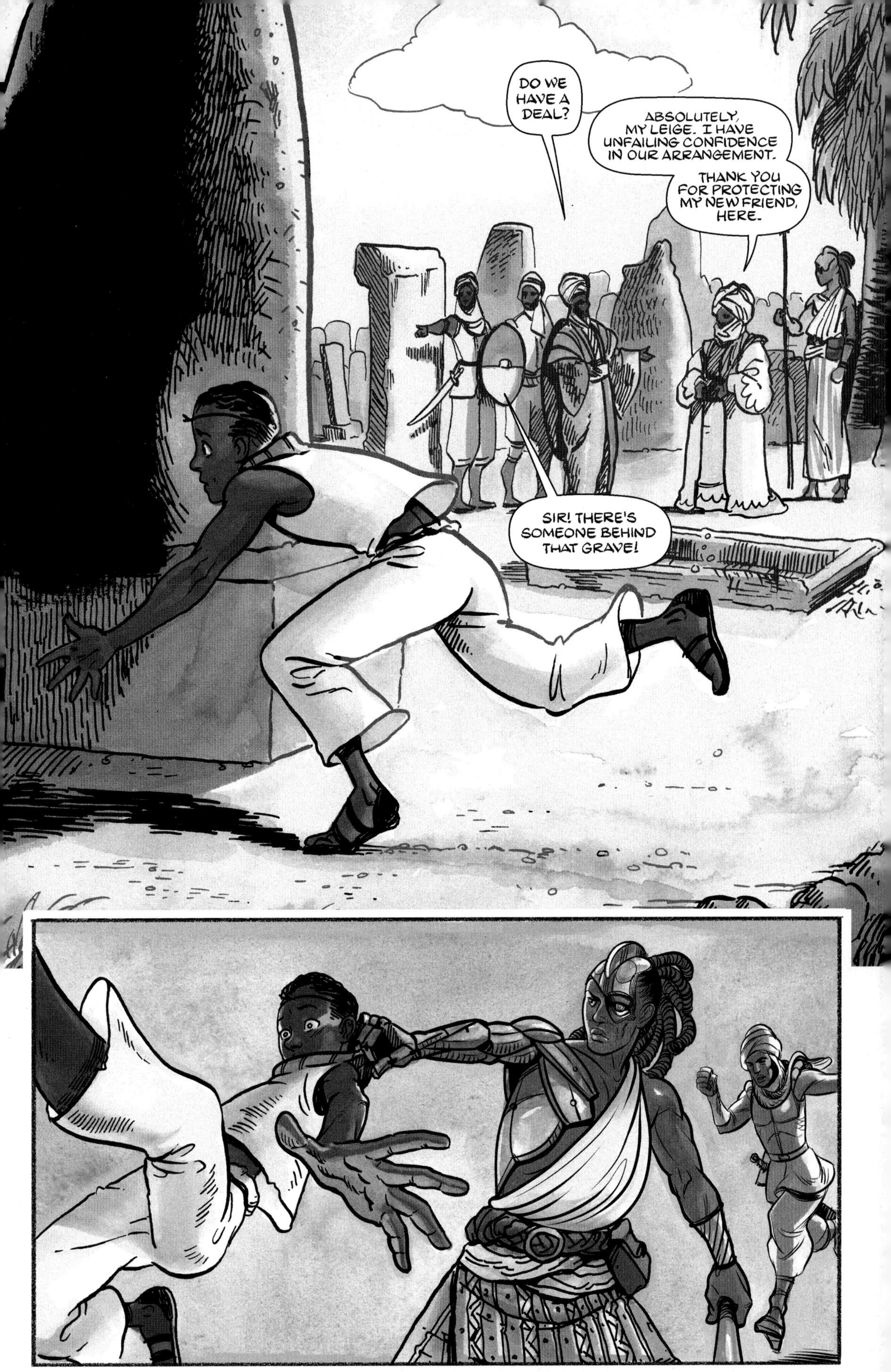
DO WE HAVE A DEAL?
ABSOLUTELY, MY LEIGE. I HAVE UNFAILING CONFIDENCE IN OUR ARRANGEMENT.
THANK YOU FOR PROTECTING MY NEW FRIEND, HERE.
SIR! THERE'S SOMEONE BEHIND THAT GRAVE!

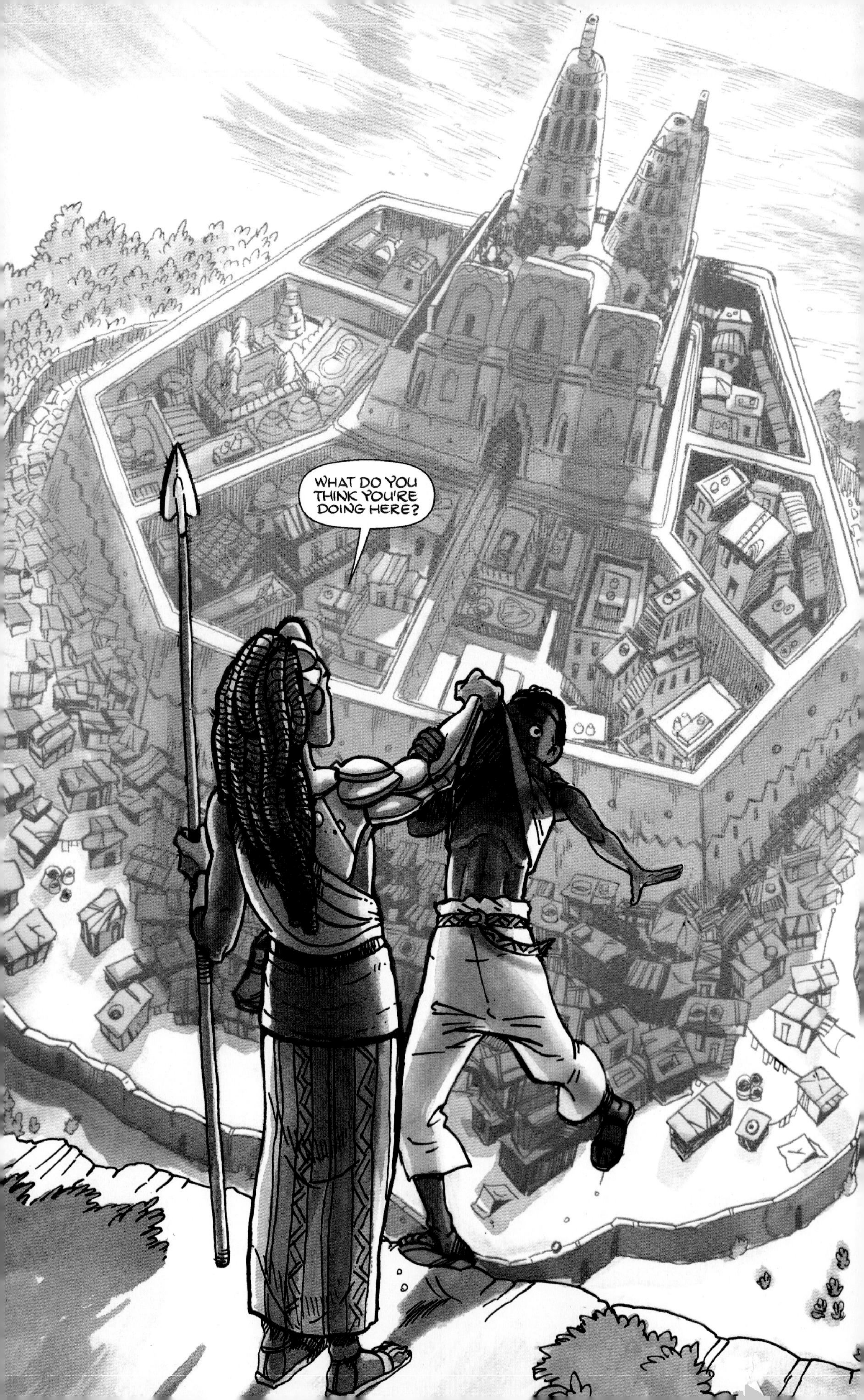
WHAT DO YOU THINK YOU'RE DOING HERE?

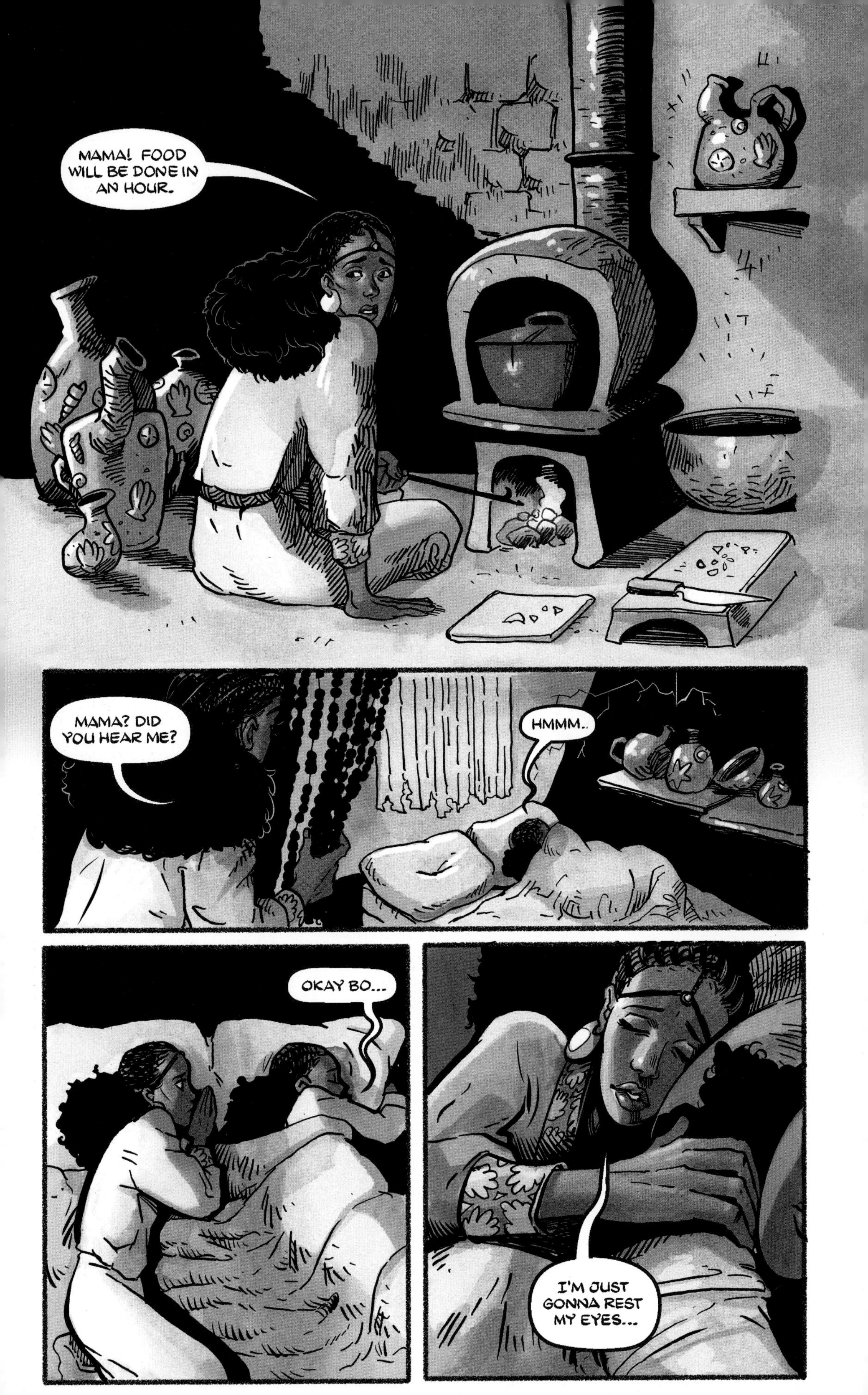
MAMA! FOOD WILL BE DONE IN AN HOUR.
MAMA? DID YOU HEAR ME?
HMMM..
OKAY BO...
I'M JUST GONNA REST MY EYES...

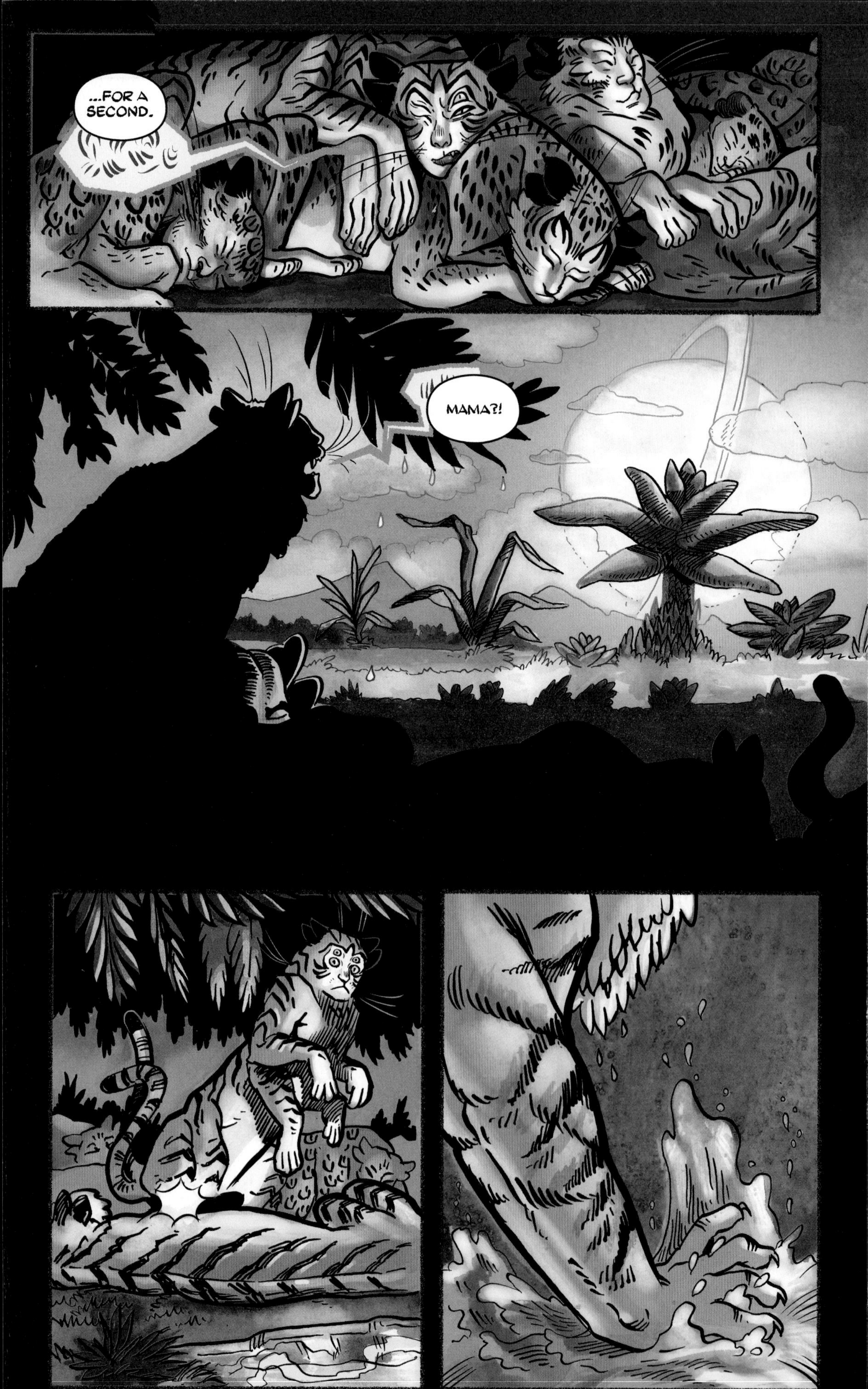
...FOR A SECOND.
MAMA?!

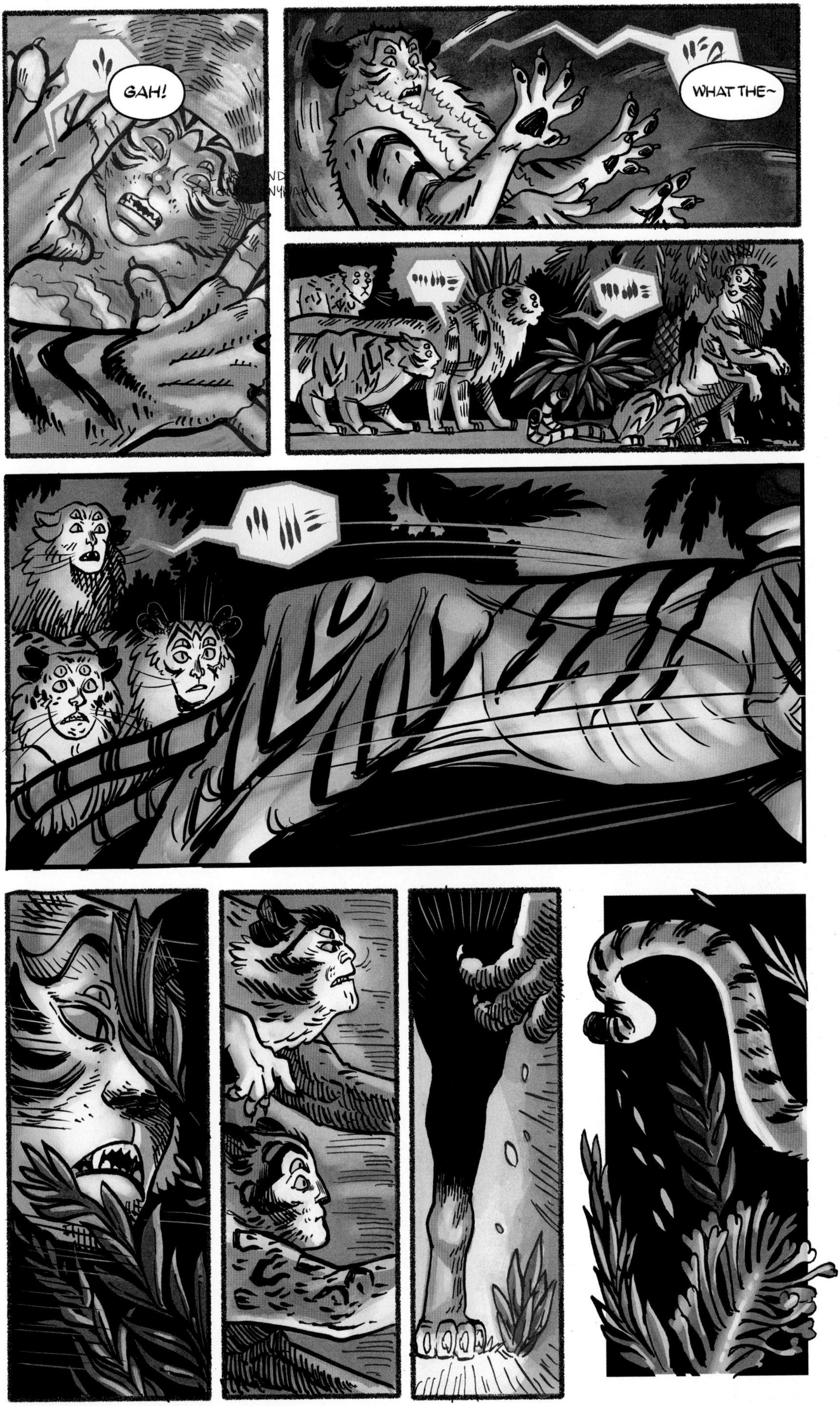
GAH!
WHAT THE~

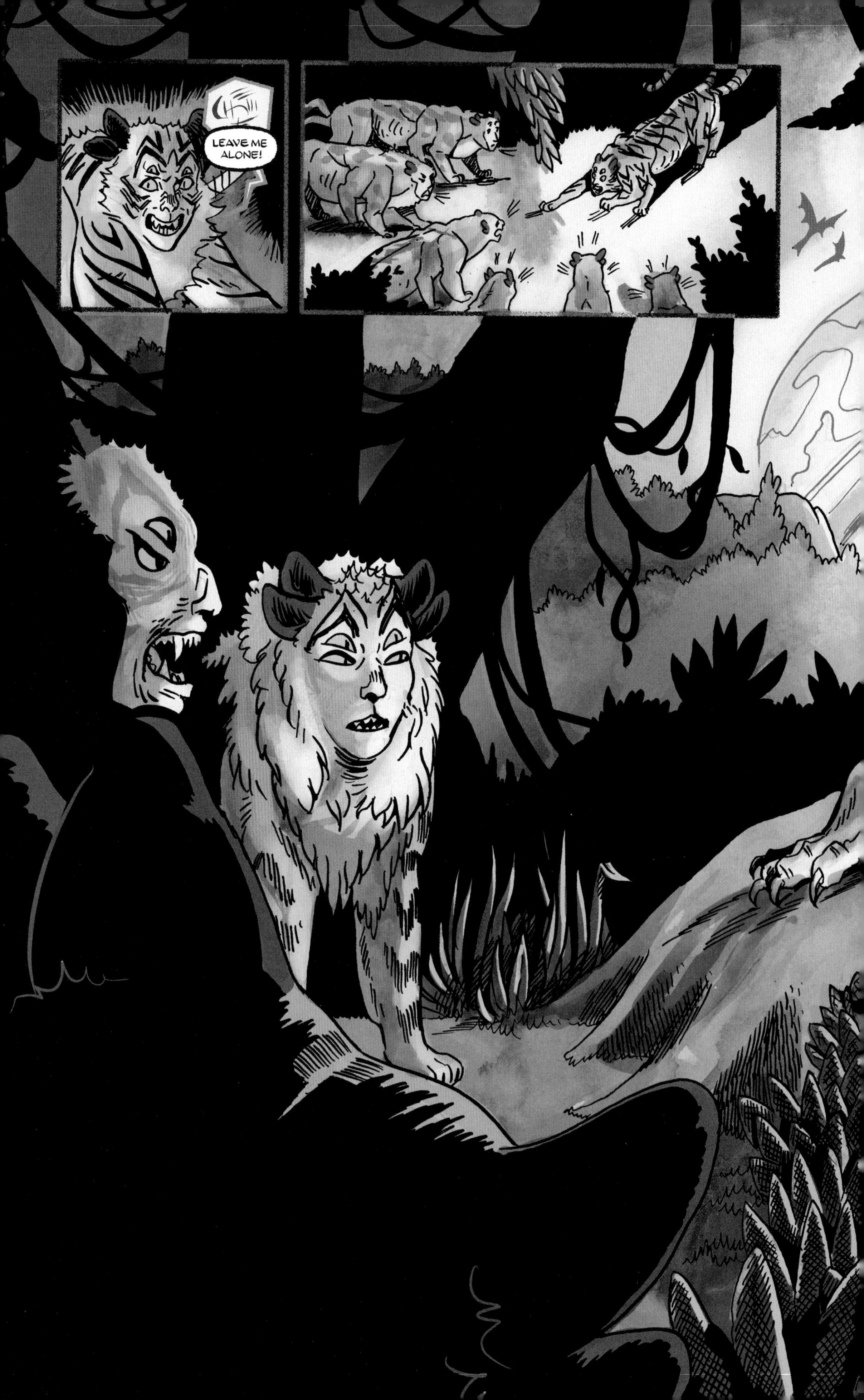
LEAVE ME ALONE!

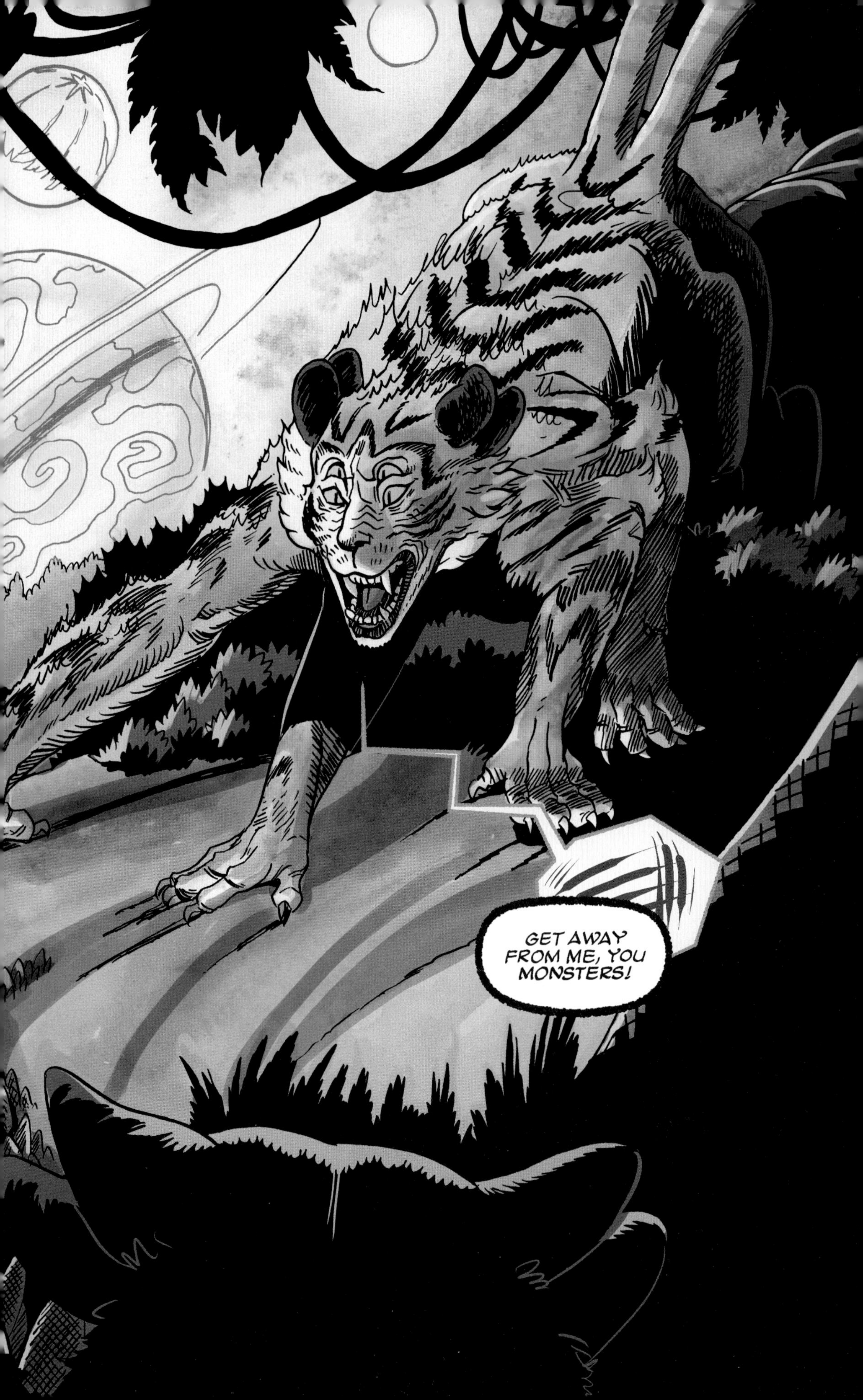
GET AWAY FROM ME, YOU MONSTERS!

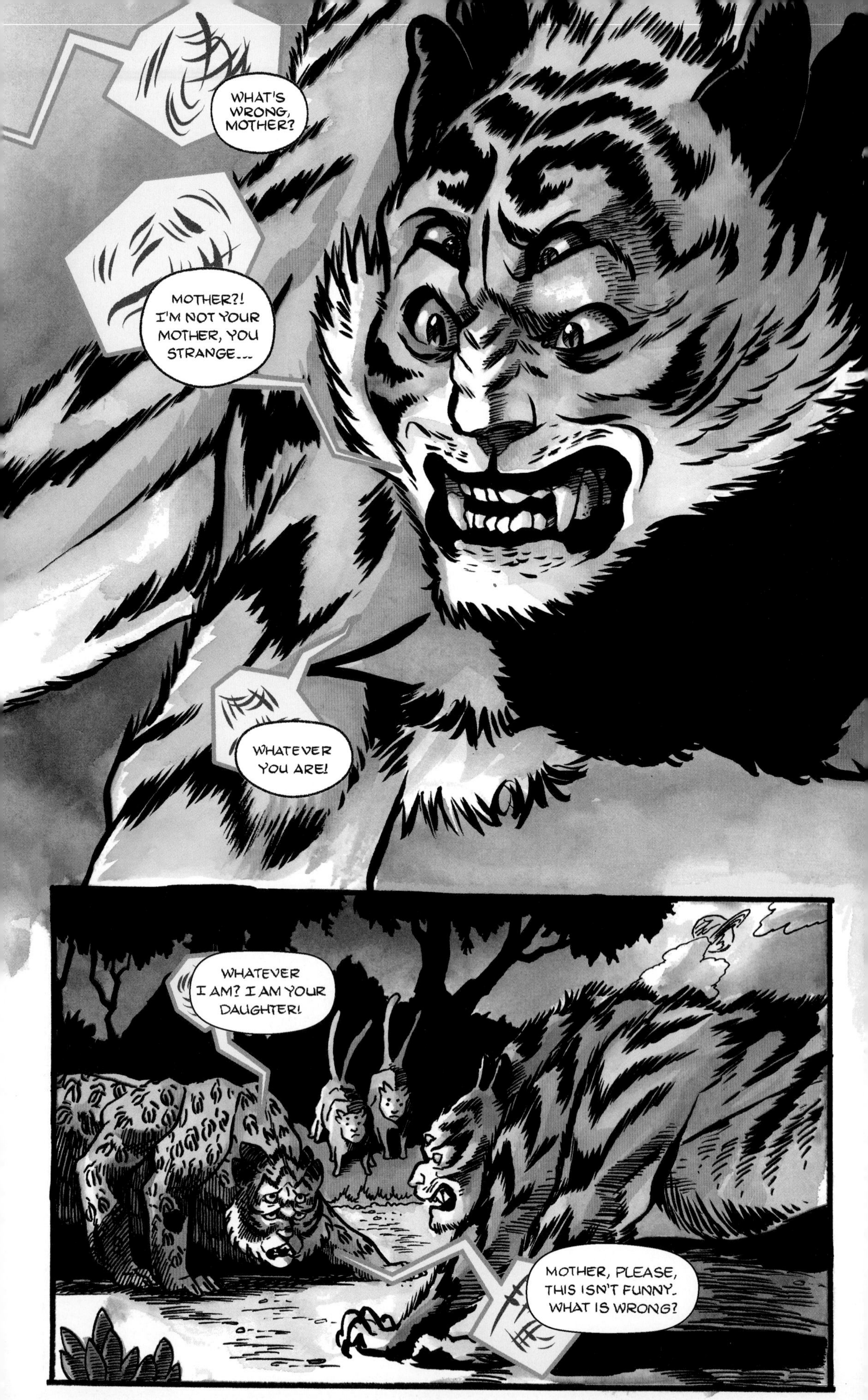
WHAT'S WRONG, MOTHER?
MOTHER?! I'M NOT YOUR MOTHER, YOU STRANGE...
WHATEVER YOU ARE!
WHATEVER I AM? I AM YOUR DAUGHTER!
MOTHER, PLEASE, THIS ISN'T FUNNY. WHAT IS WRONG?

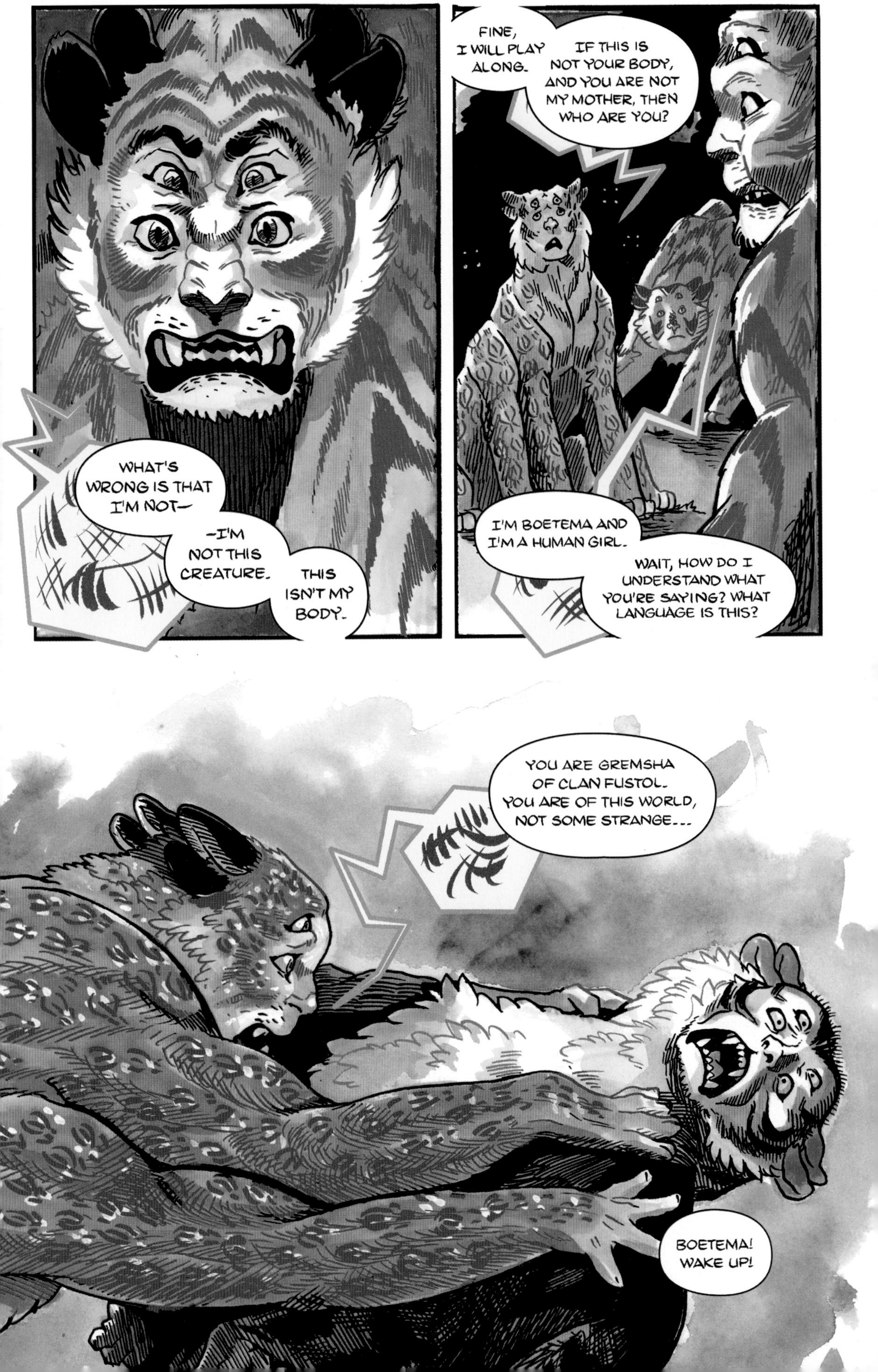
WHAT'S WRONG IS THAT I'M NOT—
—I'M NOT THIS CREATURE.
THIS ISN'T MY BODY.
FINE, I WILL PLAY ALONG.
IF THIS IS NOT YOUR BODY, AND YOU ARE NOT MY MOTHER, THEN WHO ARE YOU?
I'M BOETEMA AND I'M A HUMAN GIRL.
WAIT, HOW DO I UNDERSTAND WHAT YOU'RE SAYING? WHAT LANGUAGE IS THIS?
YOU ARE GREMSHA OF CLAN FUSTOL. YOU ARE OF THIS WORLD, NOT SOME STRANGE...
BOETEMA! WAKE UP!

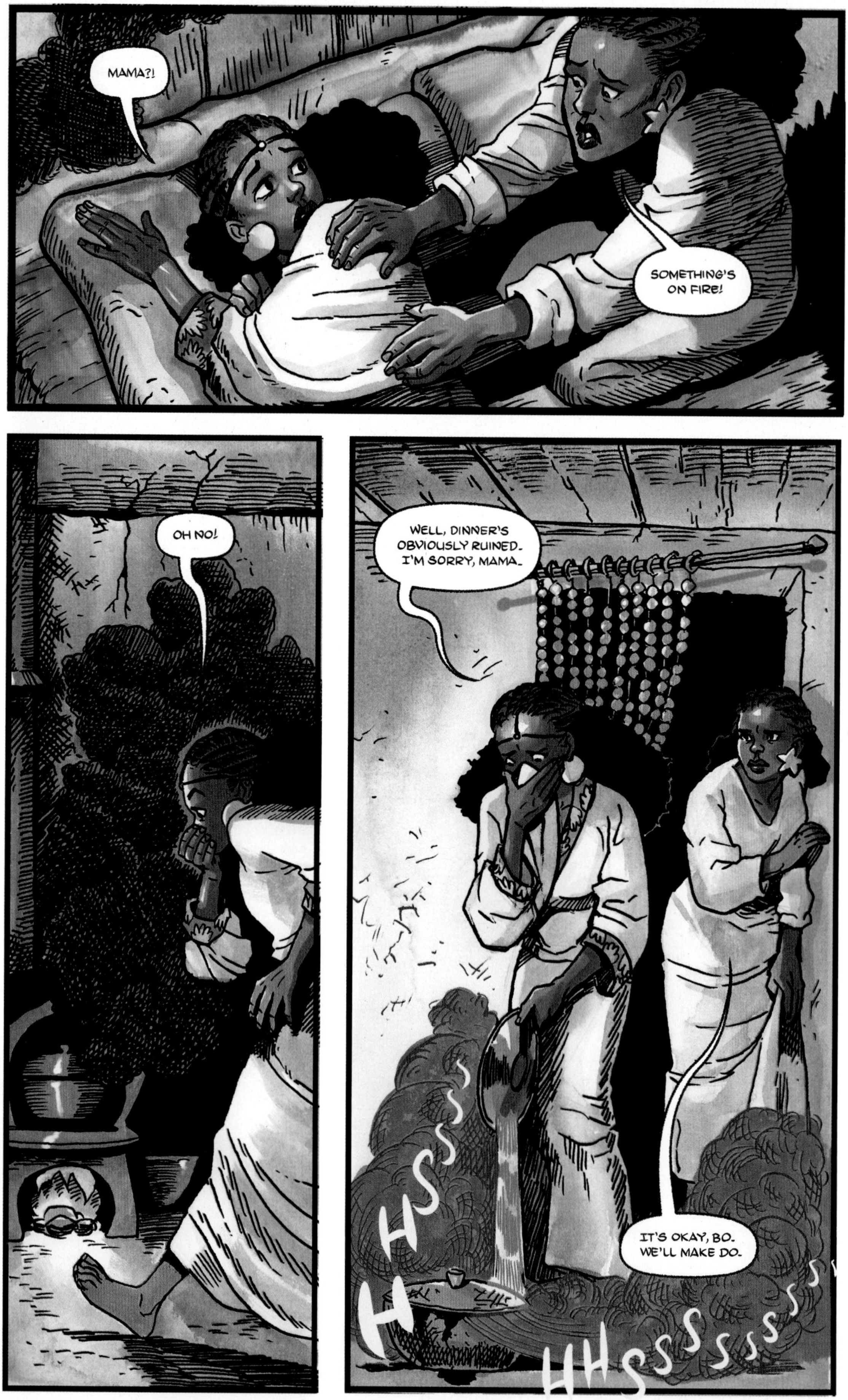
MAMA?!
SOMETHING'S ON FIRE!
OH NO!
WELL, DINNER'S OBVIOUSLY RUINED. I'M SORRY, MAMA.
HSSS
IT'S OKAY, BO. WE'LL MAKE DO.
HHSSSSSSS

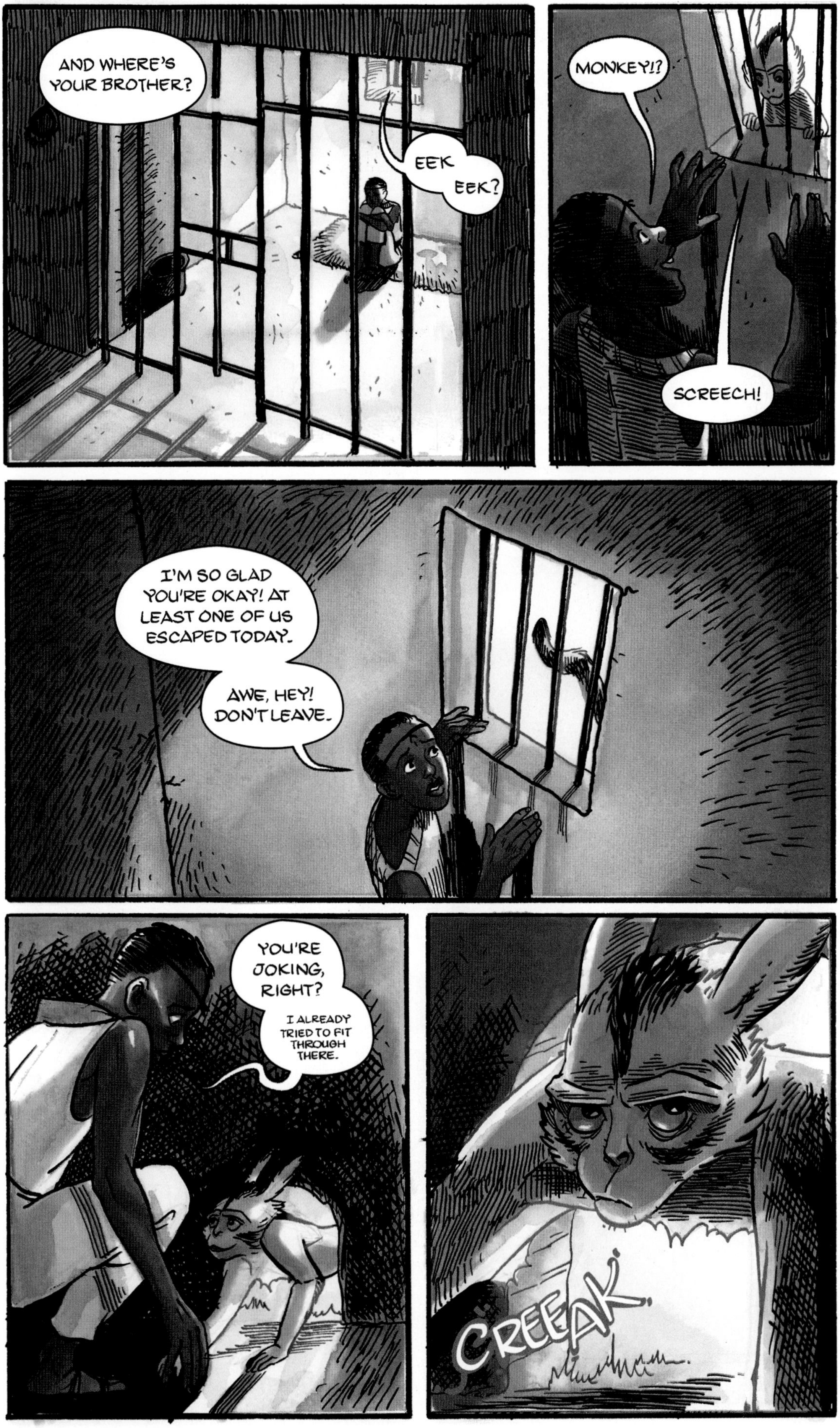
AND WHERE'S YOUR BROTHER?
EEK EEK?
MONKEY!?
SCREECH!
I'M SO GLAD YOU'RE OKAY! AT LEAST ONE OF US ESCAPED TODAY.
AWE, HEY! DON'T LEAVE.
YOU'RE JOKING, RIGHT?
I ALREADY TRIED TO FIT THROUGH THERE.
CREEAK

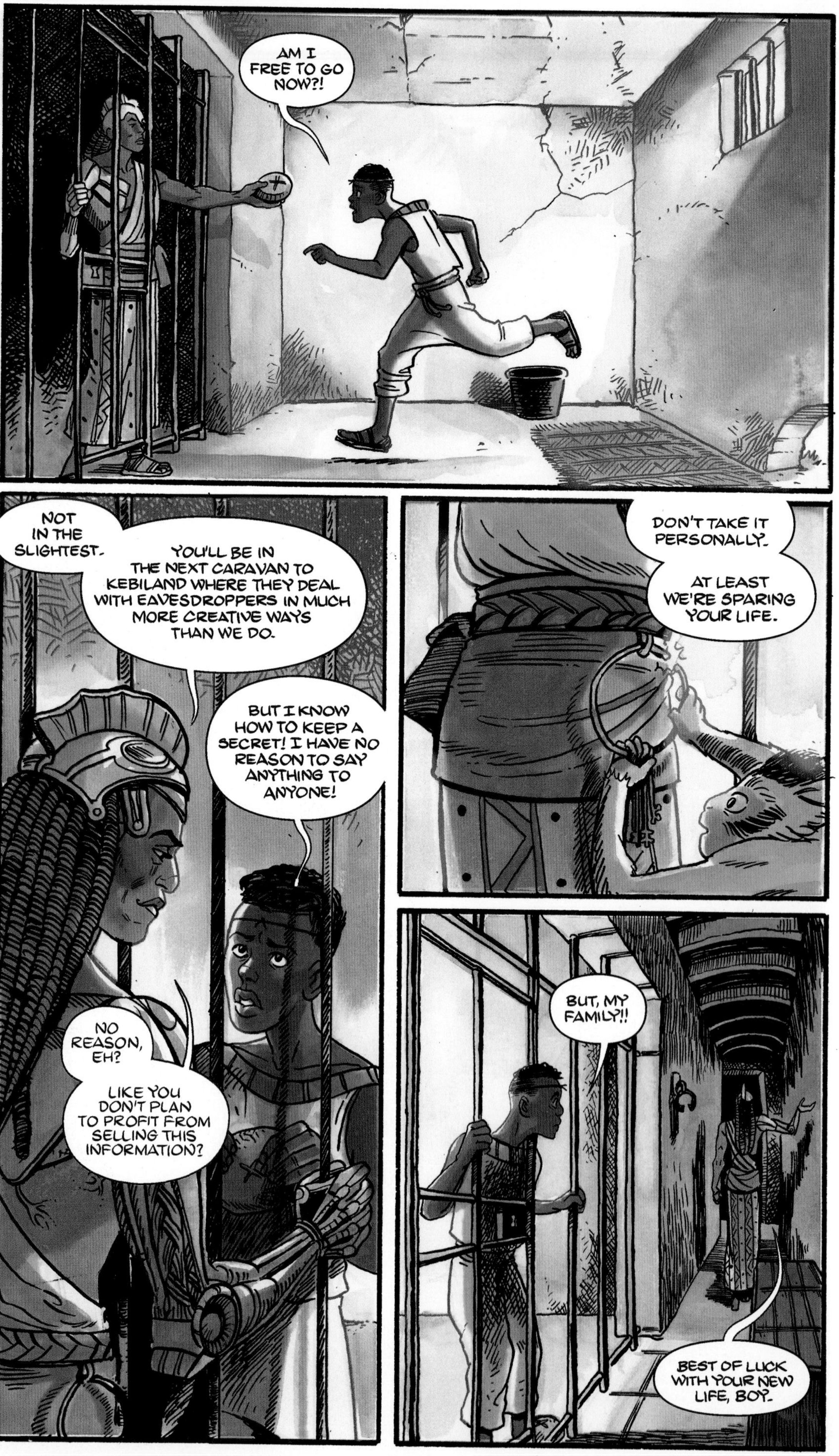
AM I FREE TO GO NOW?!
NOT IN THE SLIGHTEST.
YOU'LL BE IN THE NEXT CARAVAN TO KEBILAND WHERE THEY DEAL WITH EAVESDROPPERS IN MUCH MORE CREATIVE WAYS THAN WE DO.
BUT I KNOW HOW TO KEEP A SECRET! I HAVE NO REASON TO SAY ANYTHING TO ANYONE!
NO REASON, EH?
LIKE YOU DON'T PLAN TO PROFIT FROM SELLING THIS INFORMATION?
DON'T TAKE IT PERSONALLY.
AT LEAST WE'RE SPARING YOUR LIFE.
BUT, MY FAMILY?!
BEST OF LUCK WITH YOUR NEW LIFE, BOY.

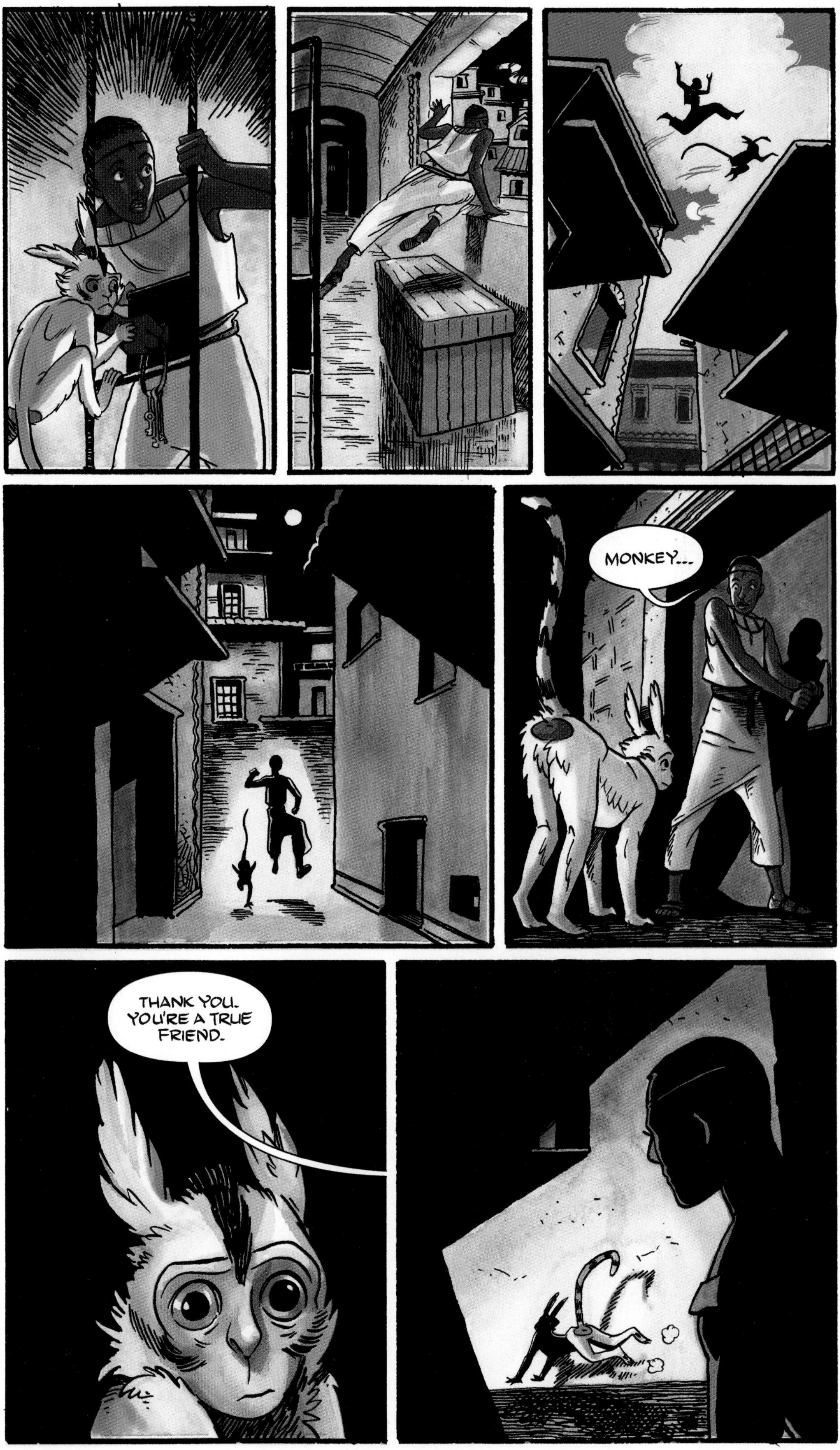
MONKEY...
THANK YOU. YOU'RE A TRUE FRIEND.

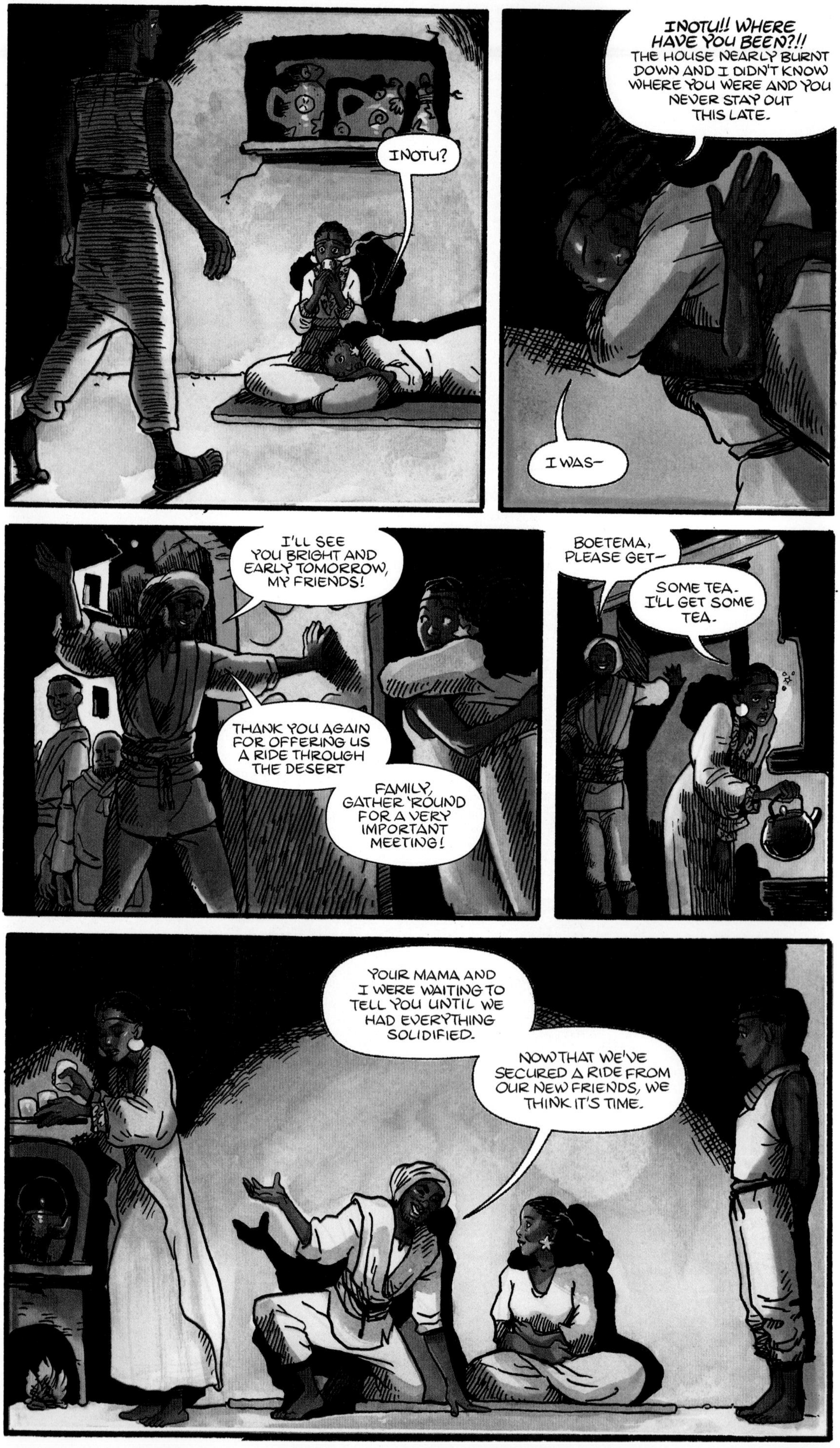
INOTU?
INOTU!! WHERE HAVE YOU BEEN?!! THE HOUSE NEARLY BURNT DOWN AND I DIDN'T KNOW WHERE YOU WERE AND YOU NEVER STAY OUT THIS LATE.
I WAS—
I'LL SEE YOU BRIGHT AND EARLY TOMORROW, MY FRIENDS!
THANK YOU AGAIN FOR OFFERING US A RIDE THROUGH THE DESERT
FAMILY, GATHER 'ROUND FOR A VERY IMPORTANT MEETING!
BOETEMA, PLEASE GET—
SOME TEA. I'LL GET SOME TEA.
YOUR MAMA AND I WERE WAITING TO TELL YOU UNTIL WE HAD EVERYTHING SOLIDIFIED.
NOW THAT WE'VE SECURED A RIDE FROM OUR NEW FRIENDS, WE THINK IT'S TIME.

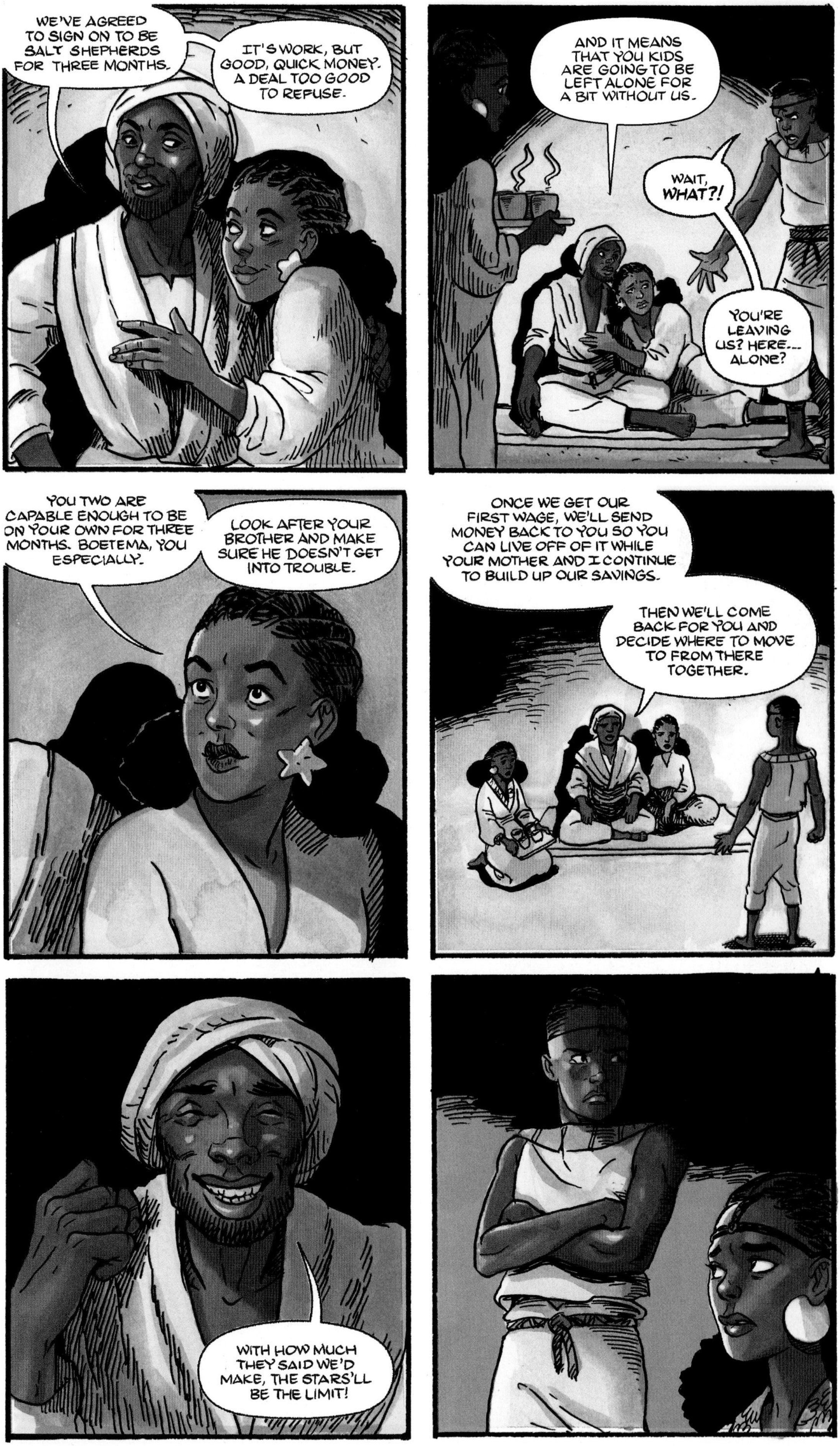
WE'VE AGREED TO SIGN ON TO BE SALT SHEPHERDS FOR THREE MONTHS.
IT'S WORK, BUT GOOD, QUICK MONEY. A DEAL TOO GOOD TO REFUSE.
AND IT MEANS THAT YOU KIDS ARE GOING TO BE LEFT ALONE FOR A BIT WITHOUT US.
WAIT, WHAT?!
YOU'RE LEAVING US? HERE... ALONE?
YOU TWO ARE CAPABLE ENOUGH TO BE ON YOUR OWN FOR THREE MONTHS. BOETEMA, YOU ESPECIALLY.
LOOK AFTER YOUR BROTHER AND MAKE SURE HE DOESN'T GET INTO TROUBLE.
ONCE WE GET OUR FIRST WAGE, WE'LL SEND MONEY BACK TO YOU SO YOU CAN LIVE OFF OF IT WHILE YOUR MOTHER AND I CONTINUE TO BUILD UP OUR SAVINGS.
THEN WE'LL COME BACK FOR YOU AND DECIDE WHERE TO MOVE TO FROM THERE TOGETHER.
WITH HOW MUCH THEY SAID WE'D MAKE, THE STARS'LL BE THE LIMIT!

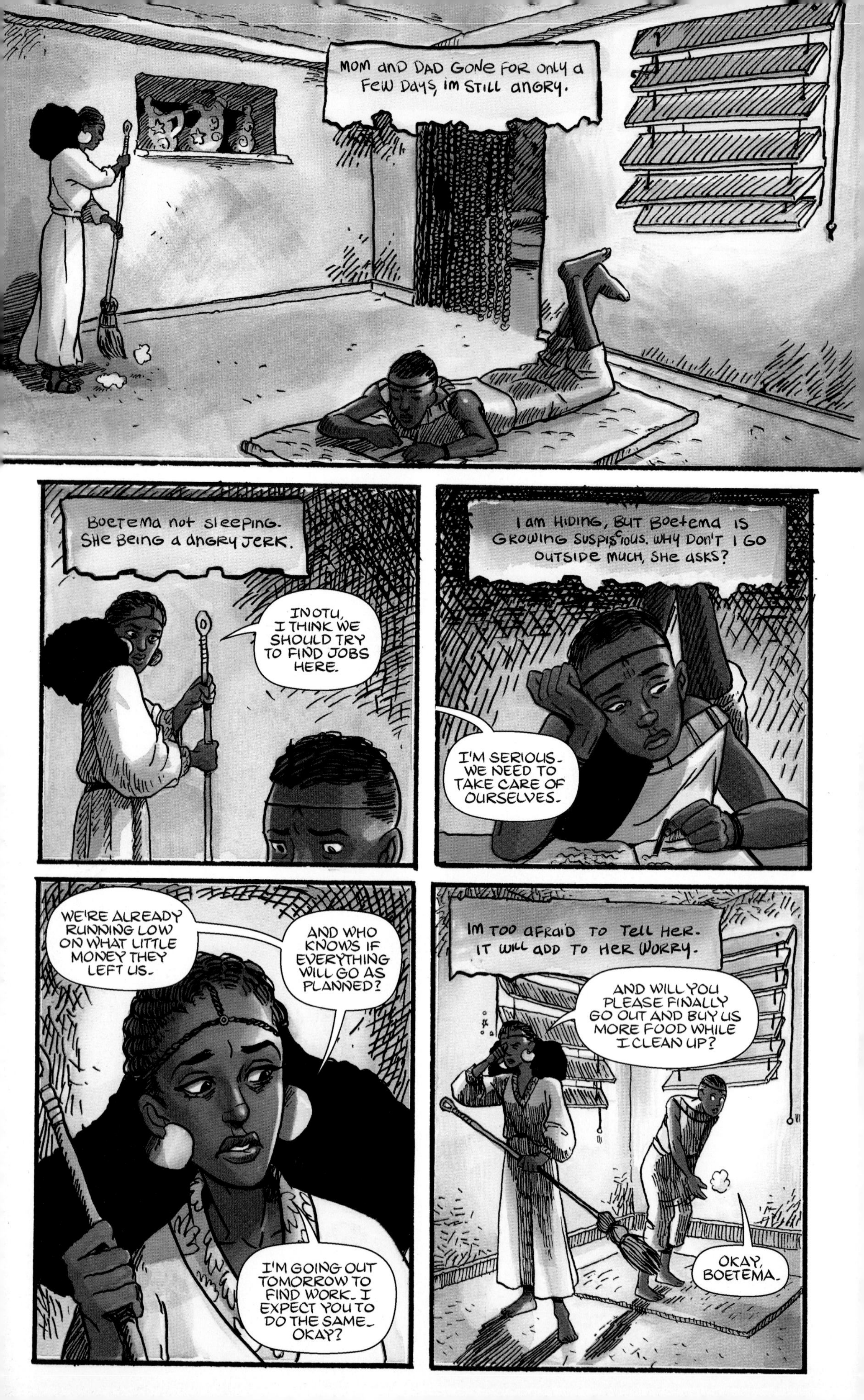
MOM AND DAD GONE FOR ONLY A FEW DAYS, IM STILL ANGRY.
BOETEMA NOT SLEEPING. SHE BEING A ANGRY JERK.
INOTU, I THINK WE SHOULD TRY TO FIND JOBS HERE.
I AM HIDING, BUT BOETEMA IS GROWING SUSPICIOUS. WHY DON'T I GO OUTSIDE MUCH, SHE ASKS?
I'M SERIOUS. WE NEED TO TAKE CARE OF OURSELVES.
WE'RE ALREADY RUNNING LOW ON WHAT LITTLE MONEY THEY LEFT US.
AND WHO KNOWS IF EVERYTHING WILL GO AS PLANNED?
I'M GOING OUT TOMORROW TO FIND WORK. I EXPECT YOU TO DO THE SAME. OKAY?
IM TOO AFRAID TO TELL HER. IT WILL ADD TO HER WORRY.
AND WILL YOU PLEASE FINALLY GO OUT AND BUY US MORE FOOD WHILE I CLEAN UP?
OKAY, BOETEMA.

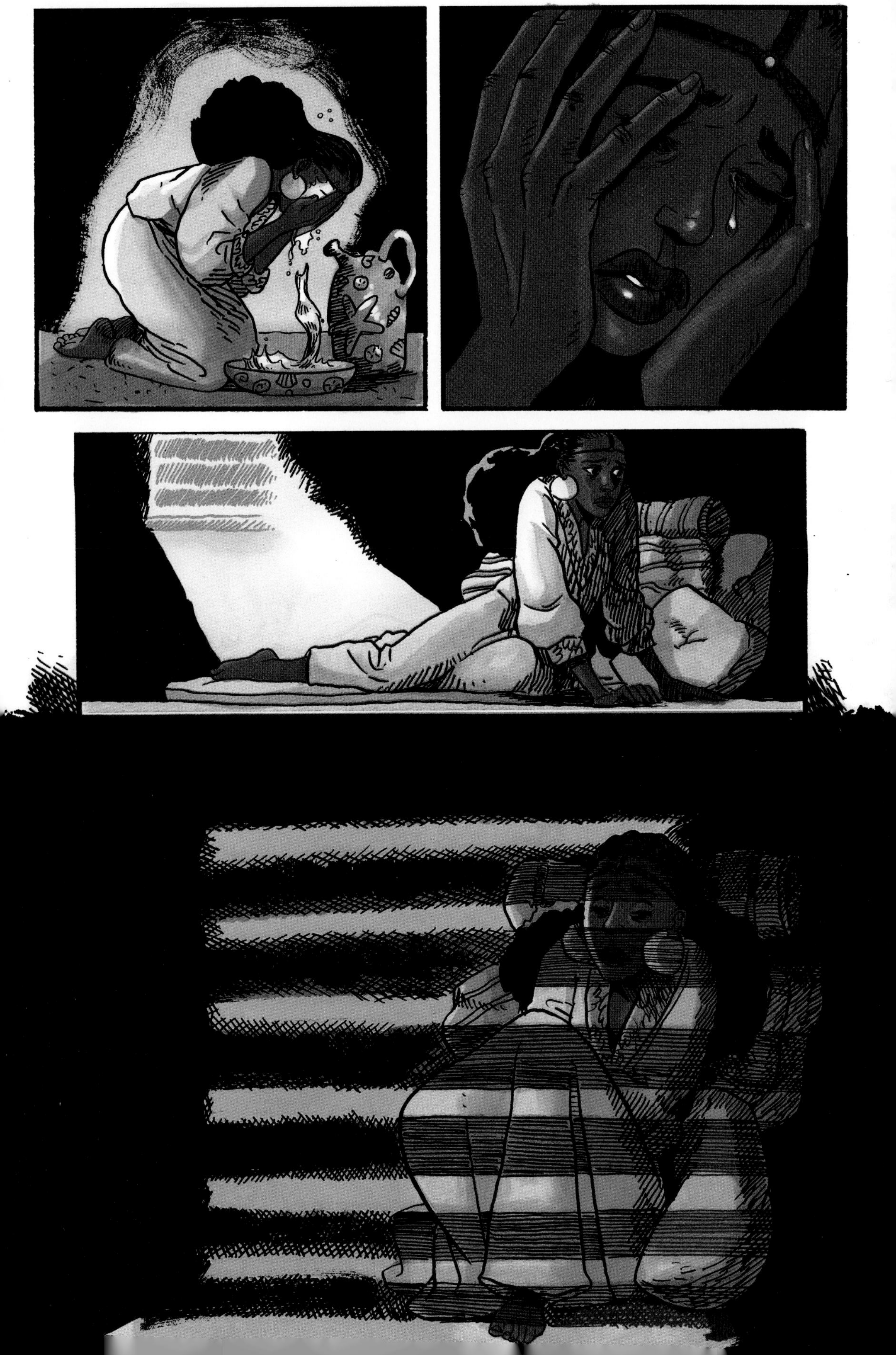

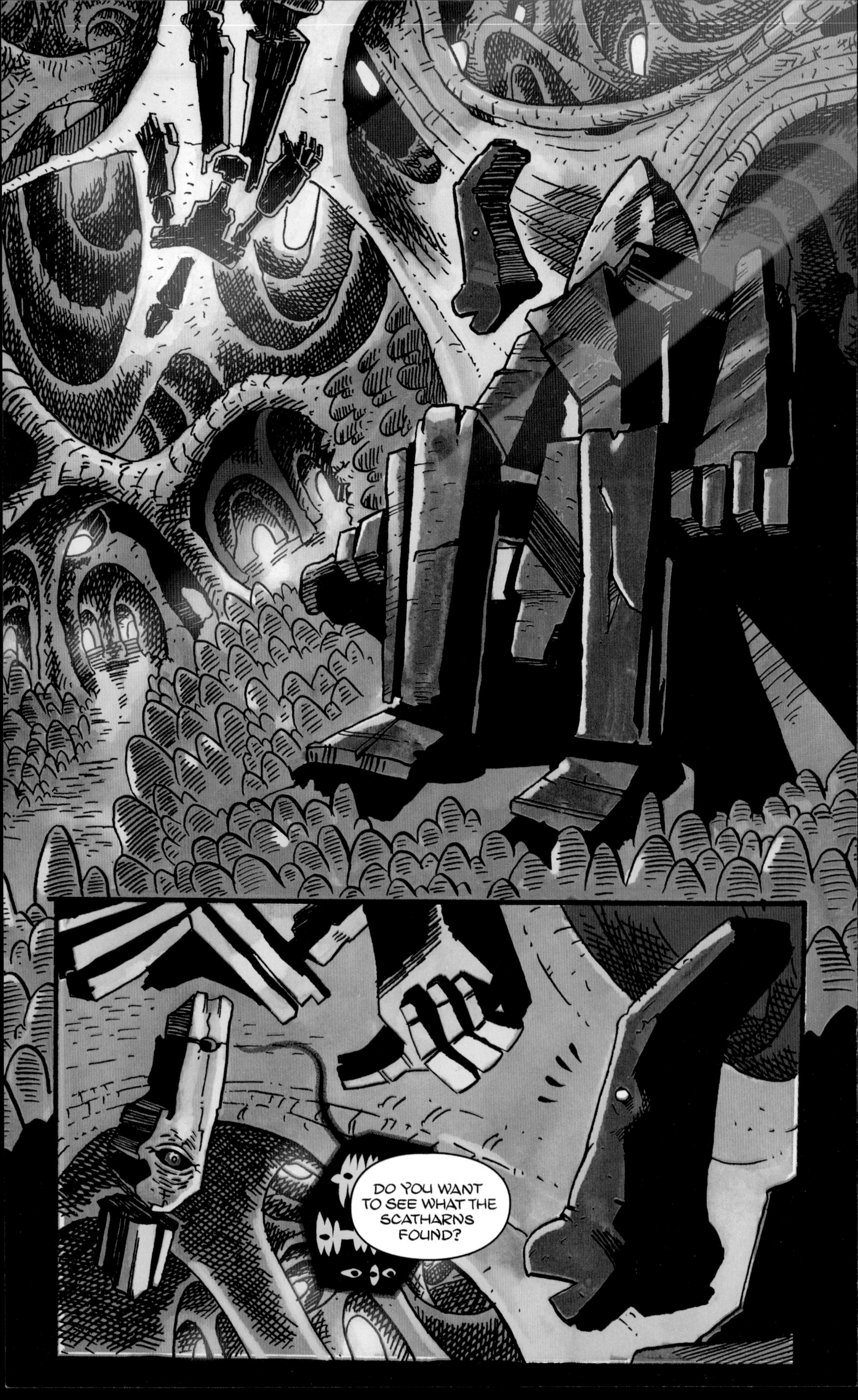
DO YOU WANT TO SEE WHAT THE SCATHARNS FOUND?

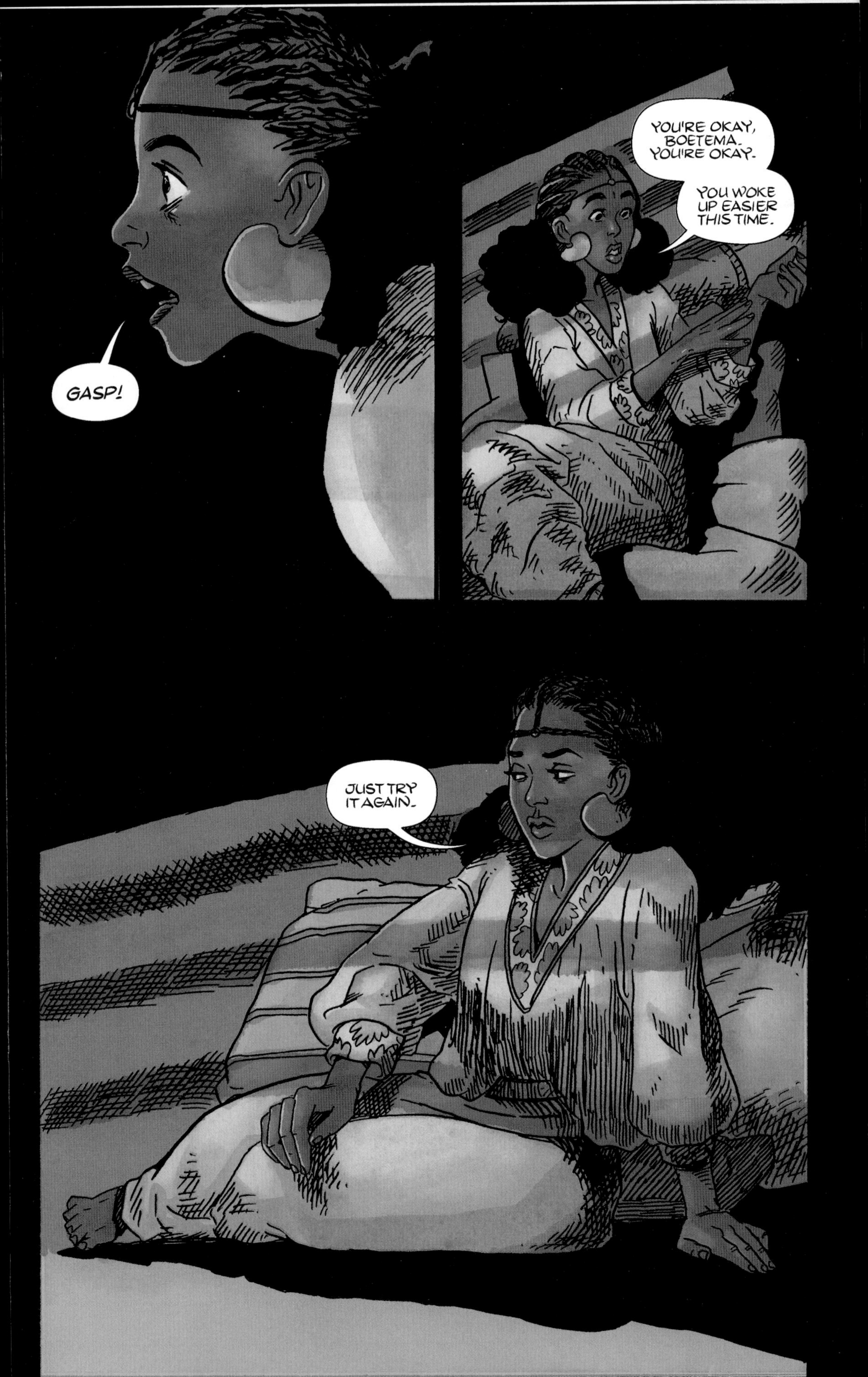
GASP!
YOU'RE OKAY, BOETEMA. YOU'RE OKAY.
YOU WOKE UP EASIER THIS TIME.
JUST TRY IT AGAIN.

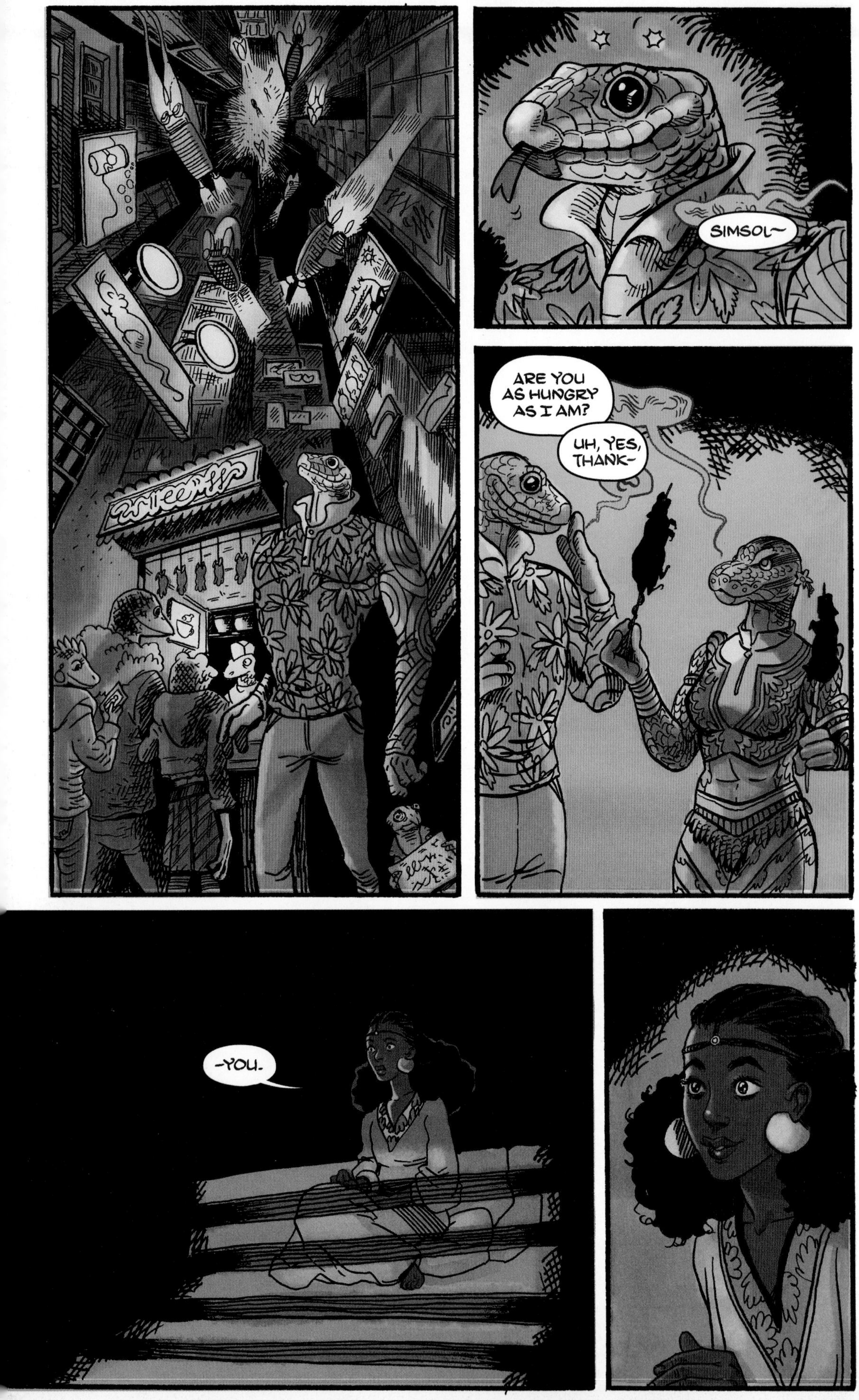
SIMSOL~
ARE YOU AS HUNGRY AS I AM?
UH, YES, THANK-
-YOU.

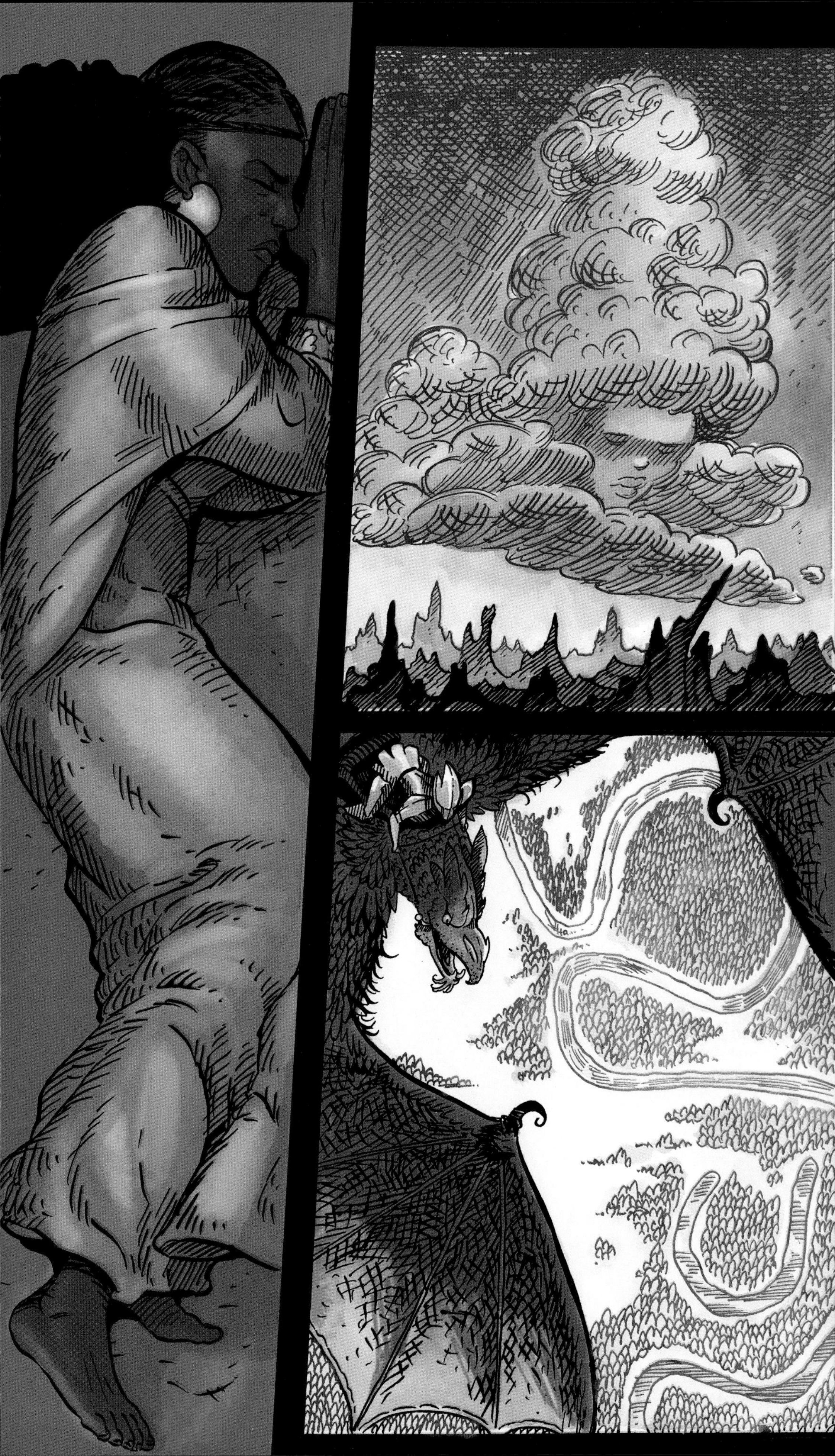

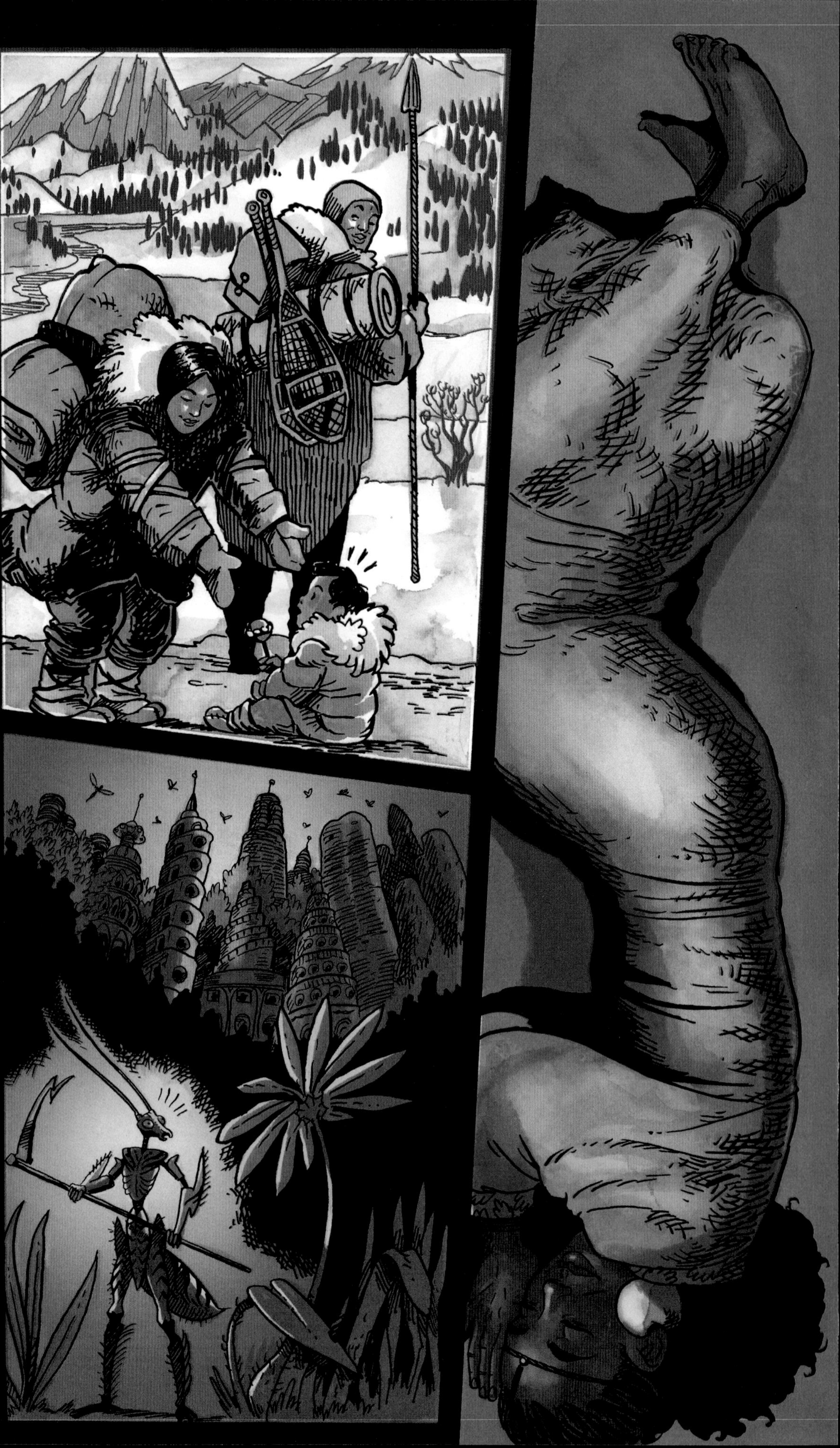

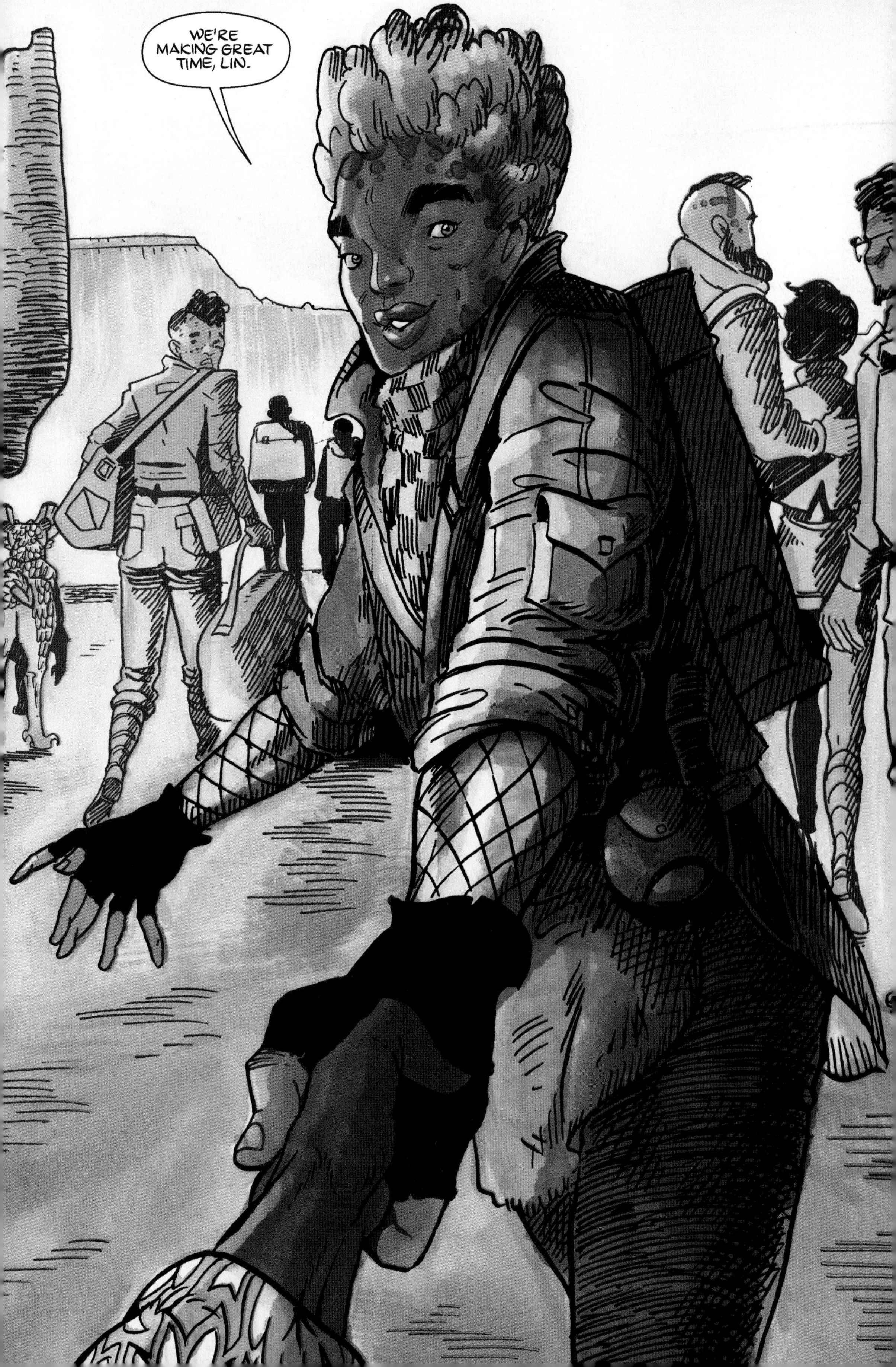
WE'RE MAKING GREAT TIME, LIN.

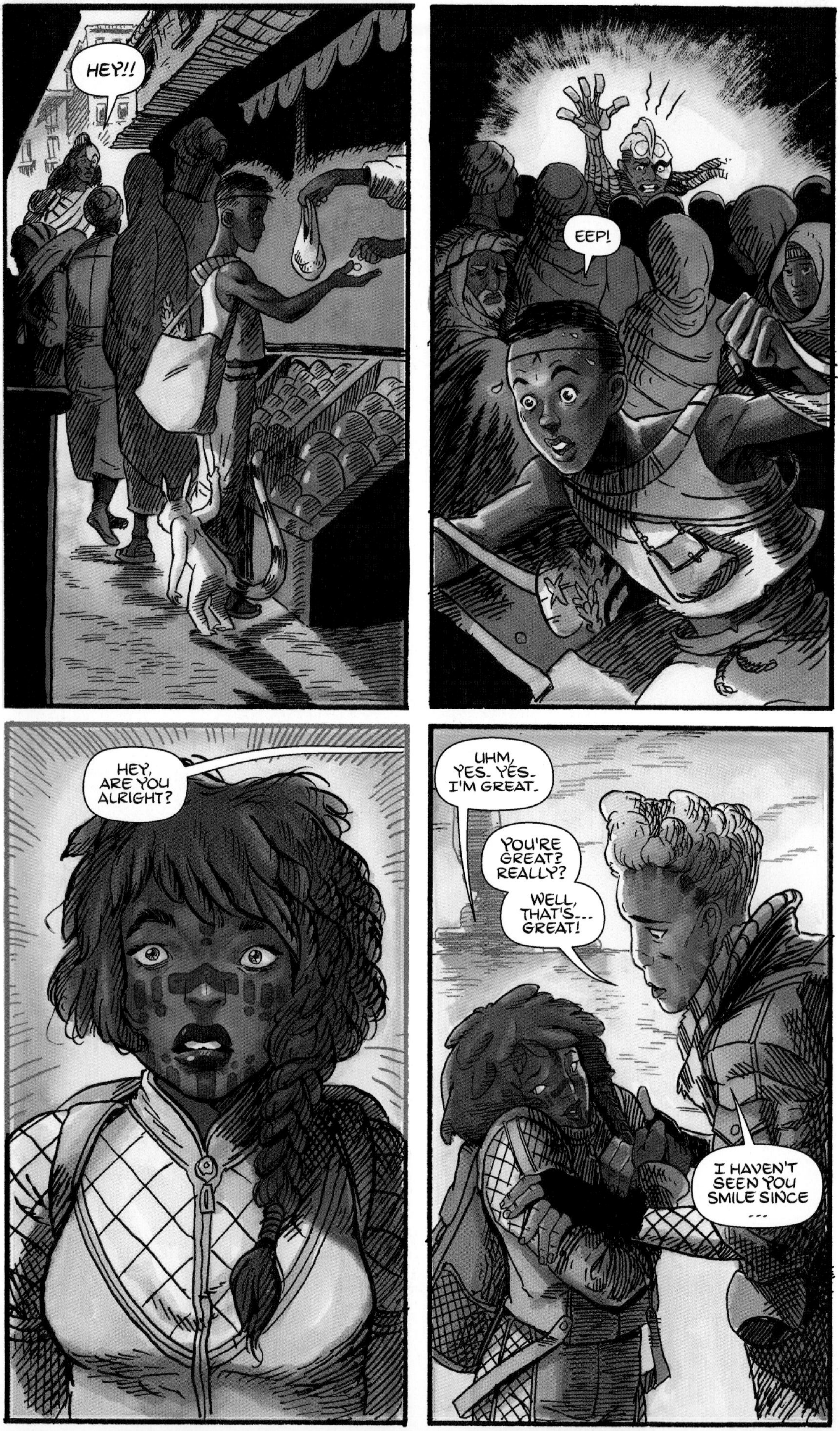
HEY?!!
EEP!
HEY, ARE YOU ALRIGHT?
UHM, YES. YES. I'M GREAT.
YOU'RE GREAT? REALLY?
WELL, THAT'S... GREAT!
I HAVEN'T SEEN YOU SMILE SINCE ...

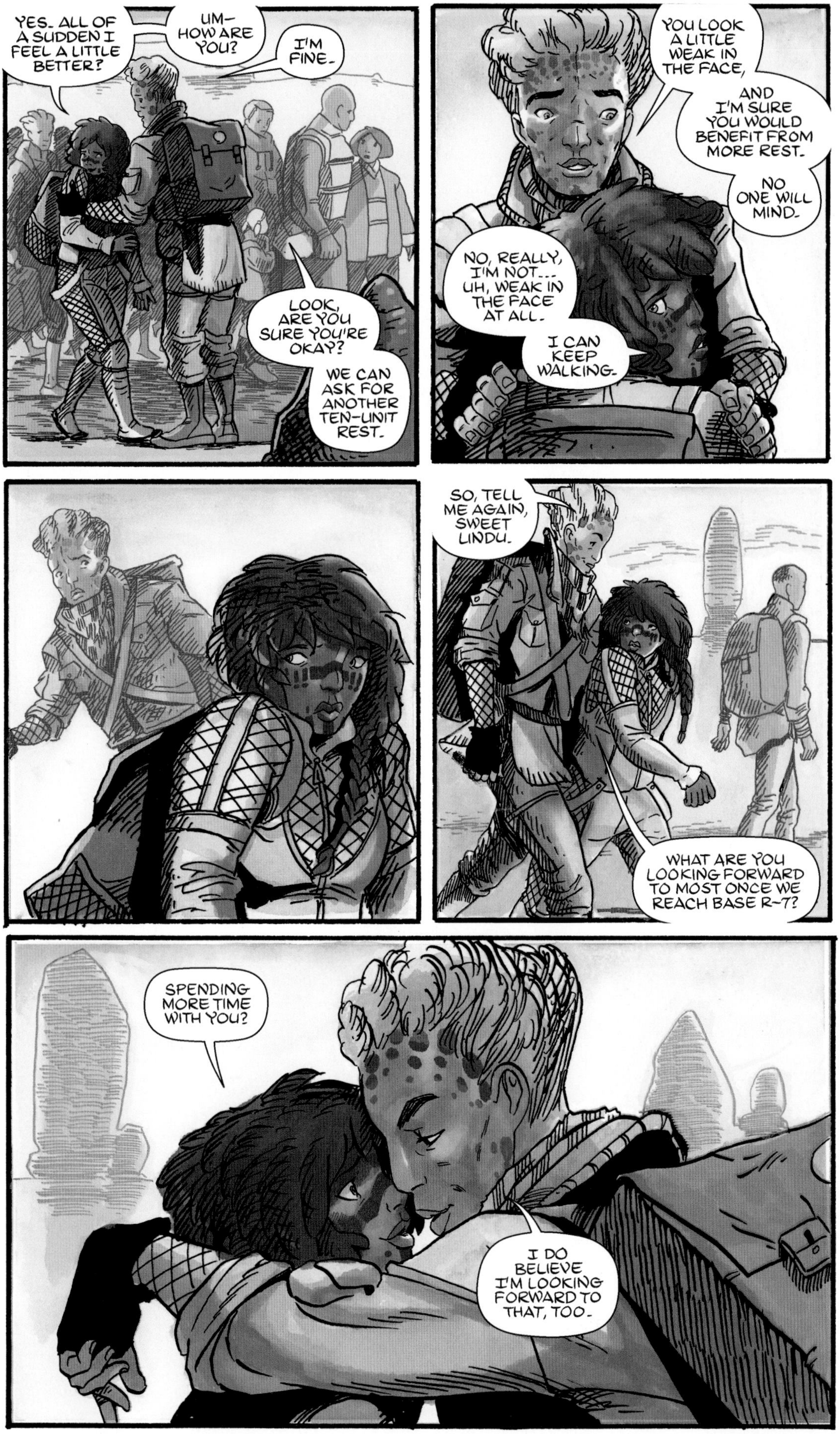

YES. ALL OF A SUDDEN I FEEL A LITTLE BETTER?
UM— HOW ARE YOU?
I'M FINE.
LOOK, ARE YOU SURE YOU'RE OKAY?
WE CAN ASK FOR ANOTHER TEN-UNIT REST.
YOU LOOK A LITTLE WEAK IN THE FACE,
AND I'M SURE YOU WOULD BENEFIT FROM MORE REST.
NO ONE WILL MIND.
NO, REALLY, I'M NOT... UH, WEAK IN THE FACE AT ALL.
I CAN KEEP WALKING.
SO, TELL ME AGAIN, SWEET LINDU.
WHAT ARE YOU LOOKING FORWARD TO MOST ONCE WE REACH BASE R-7?
SPENDING MORE TIME WITH YOU?
I DO BELIEVE I'M LOOKING FORWARD TO THAT, TOO.

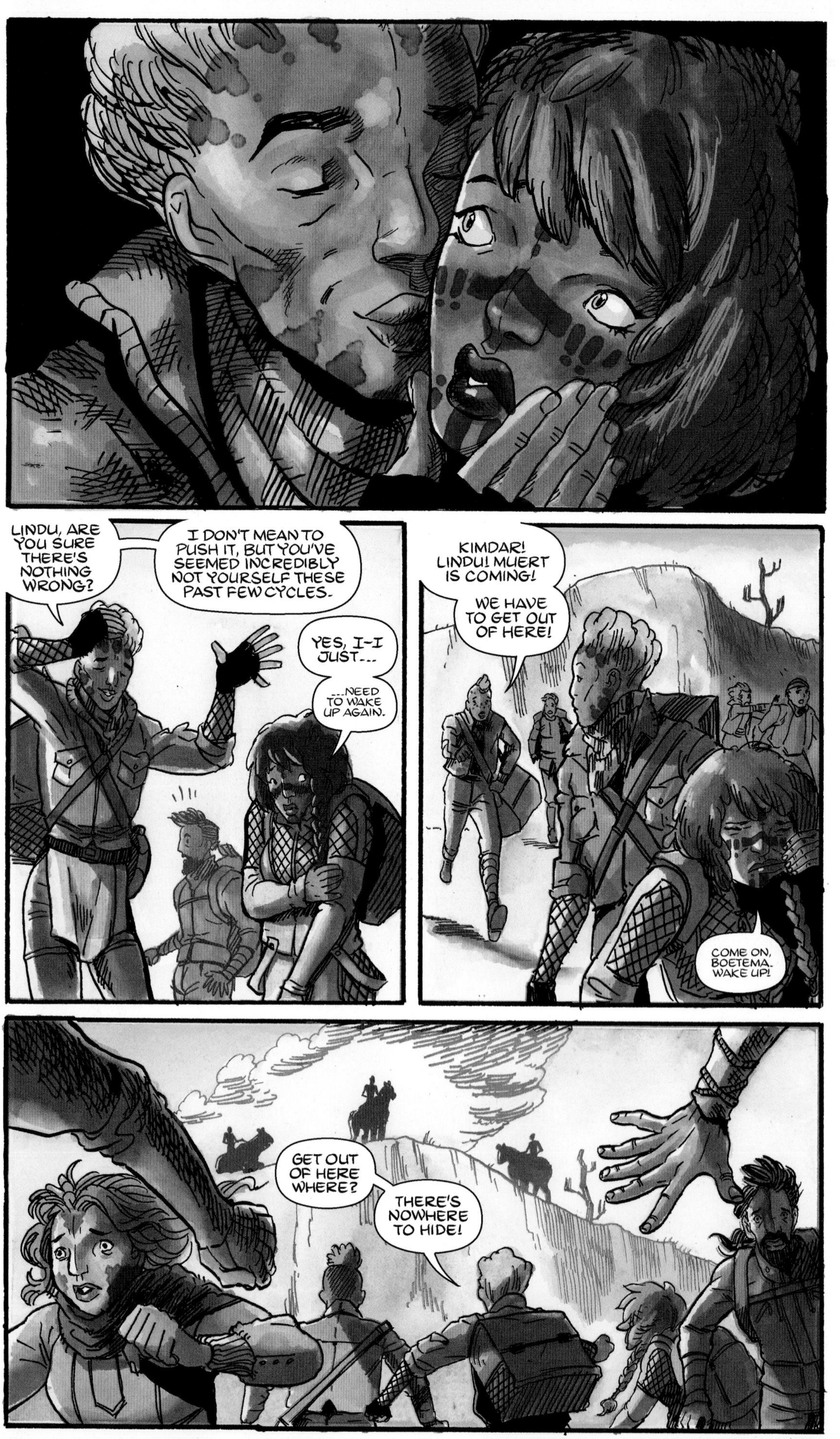
LINDU, ARE YOU SURE THERE'S NOTHING WRONG?
I DON'T MEAN TO PUSH IT, BUT YOU'VE SEEMED INCREDIBLY NOT YOURSELF THESE PAST FEW CYCLES.
YES, I-I JUST...
...NEED TO WAKE UP AGAIN.
KIMDAR! LINDU! MUERT IS COMING!
WE HAVE TO GET OUT OF HERE!
COME ON, BOETEMA. WAKE UP!
GET OUT OF HERE WHERE?
THERE'S NOWHERE TO HIDE!

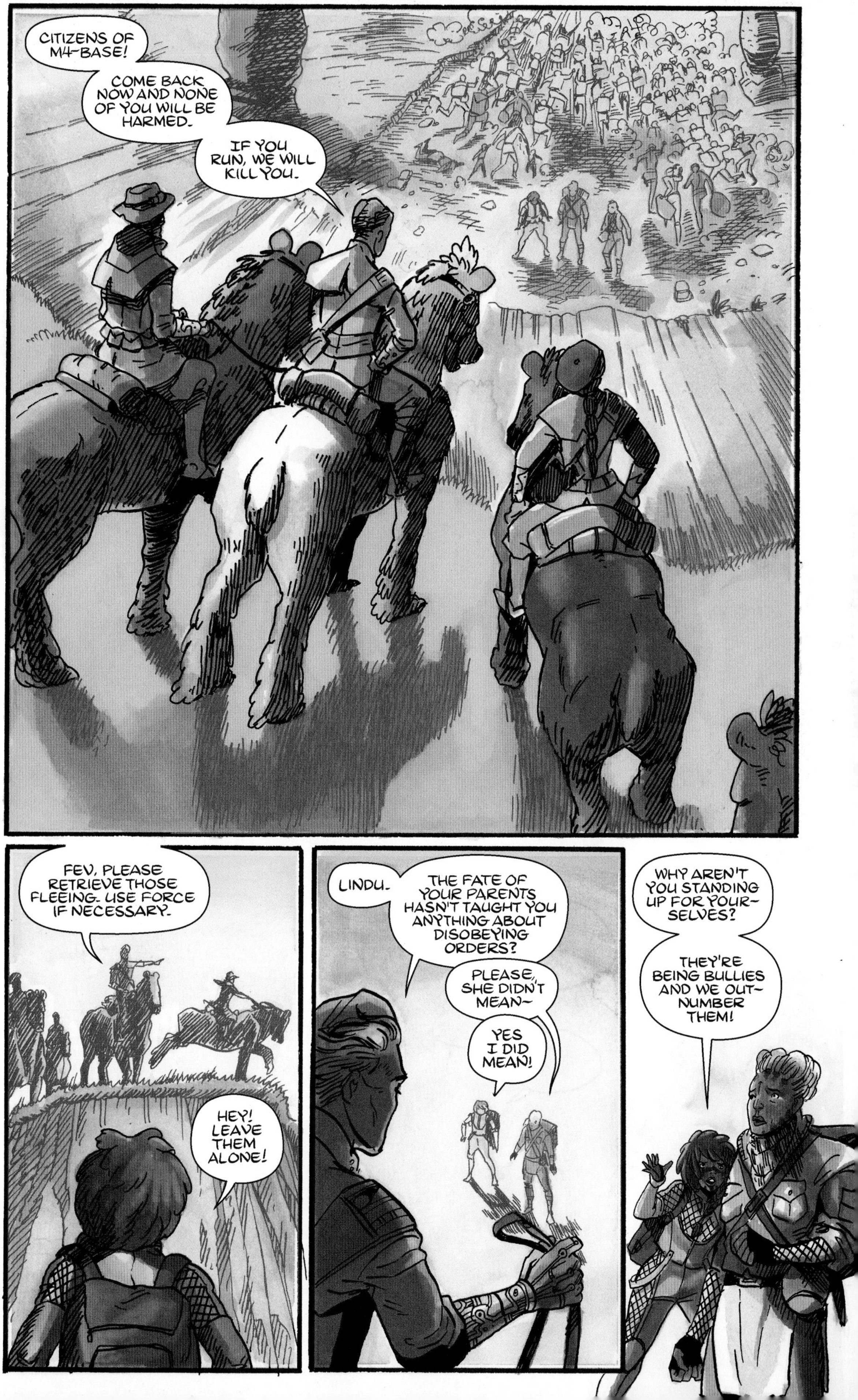
CITIZENS OF M4-BASE!
COME BACK NOW AND NONE OF YOU WILL BE HARMED.
IF YOU RUN, WE WILL KILL YOU.
FEV, PLEASE RETRIEVE THOSE FLEEING. USE FORCE IF NECESSARY.
HEY! LEAVE THEM ALONE!
LINDU.
THE FATE OF YOUR PARENTS HASN'T TAUGHT YOU ANYTHING ABOUT DISOBEYING ORDERS?
PLEASE, SHE DIDN'T MEAN~
YES I DID MEAN!
WHY AREN'T YOU STANDING UP FOR YOUR-SELVES?
THEY'RE BEING BULLIES AND WE OUT-NUMBER THEM!

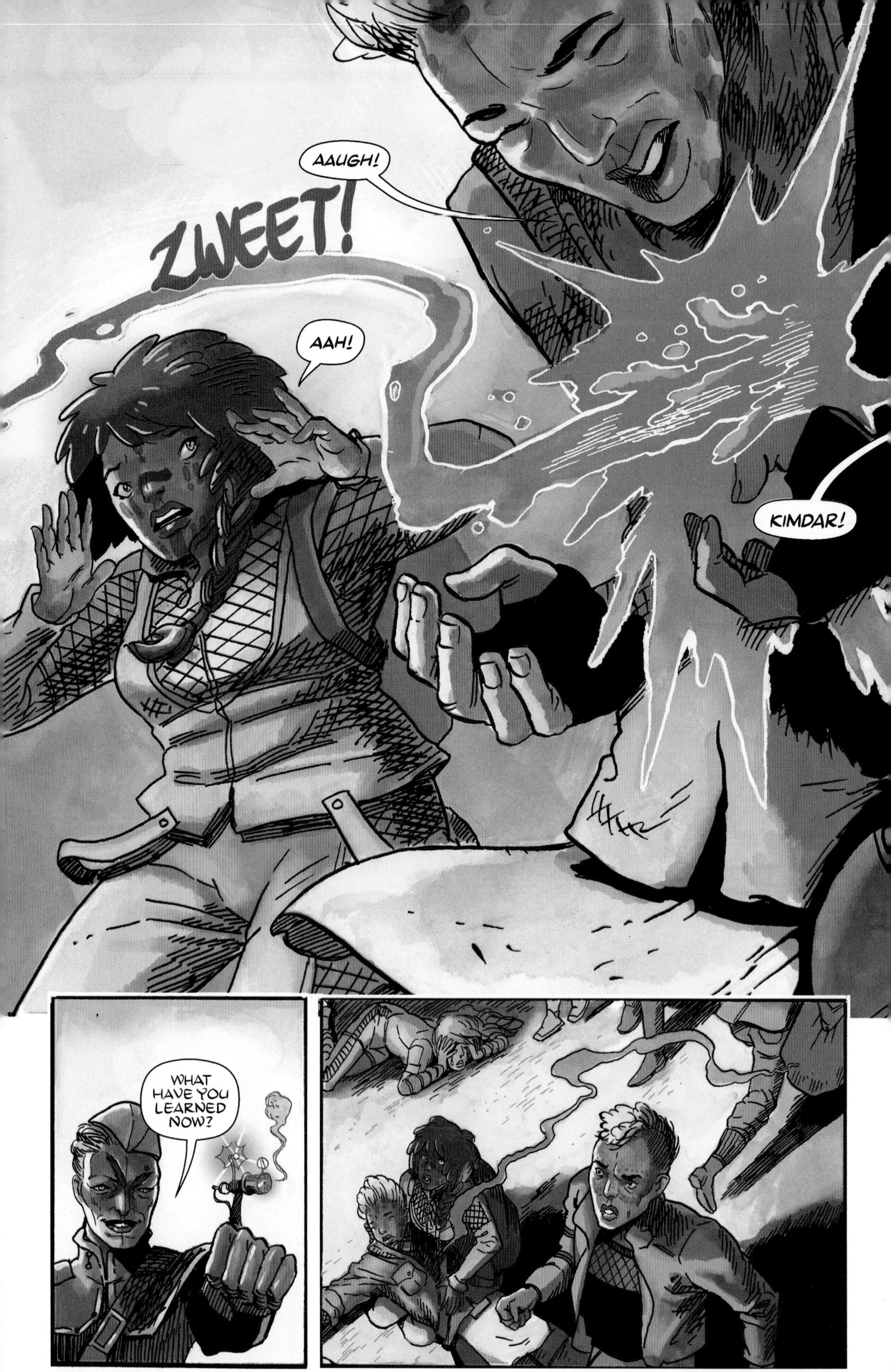
ZWEET!
AAUGH!
AAH!
KIMDAR!
WHAT HAVE YOU LEARNED NOW?

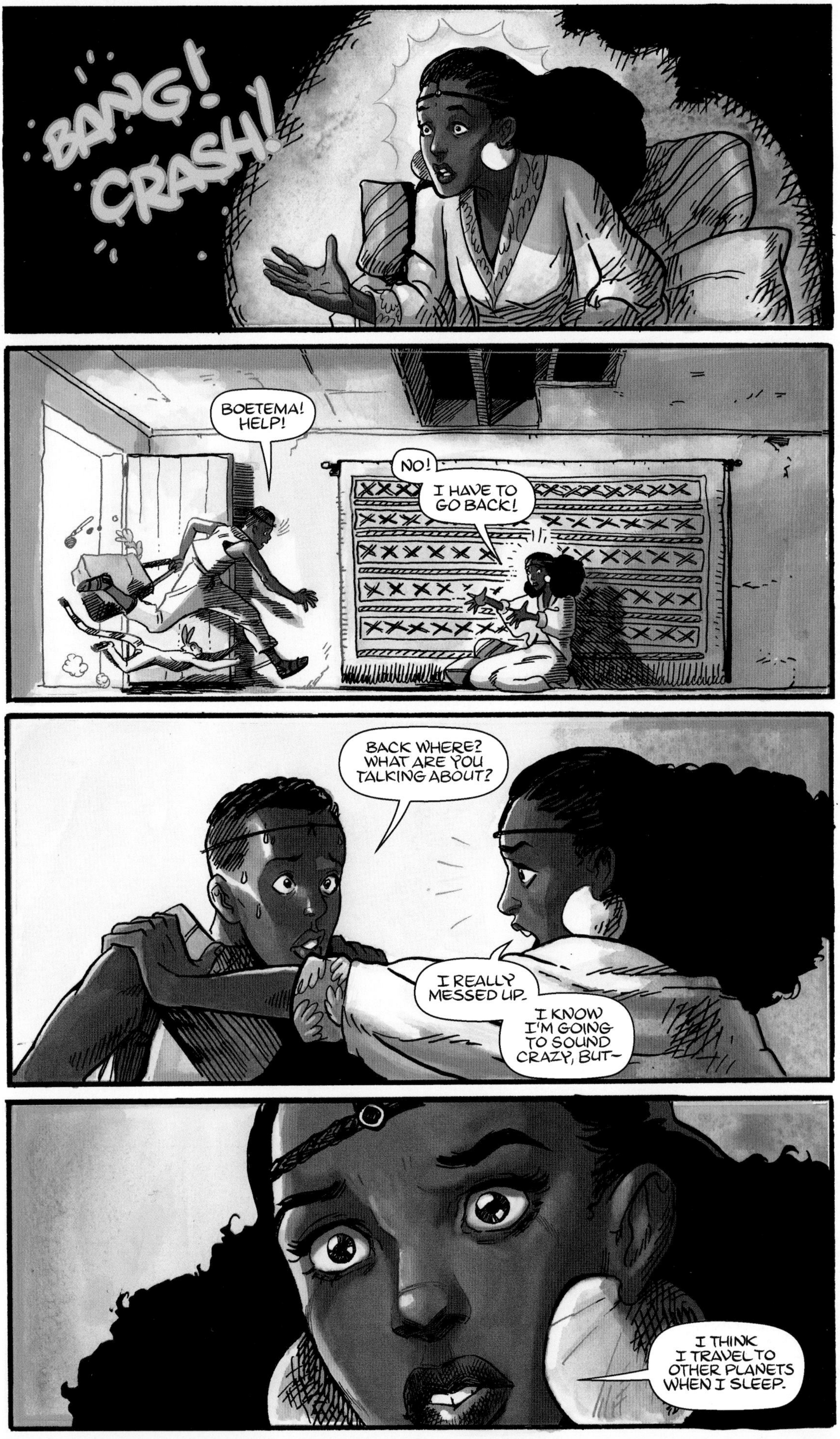
BANG! CRASH!
BOETEMA! HELP!
NO!
I HAVE TO GO BACK!
BACK WHERE? WHAT ARE YOU TALKING ABOUT?
I REALLY MESSED UP.
I KNOW I'M GOING TO SOUND CRAZY, BUT—
I THINK I TRAVEL TO OTHER PLANETS WHEN I SLEEP.

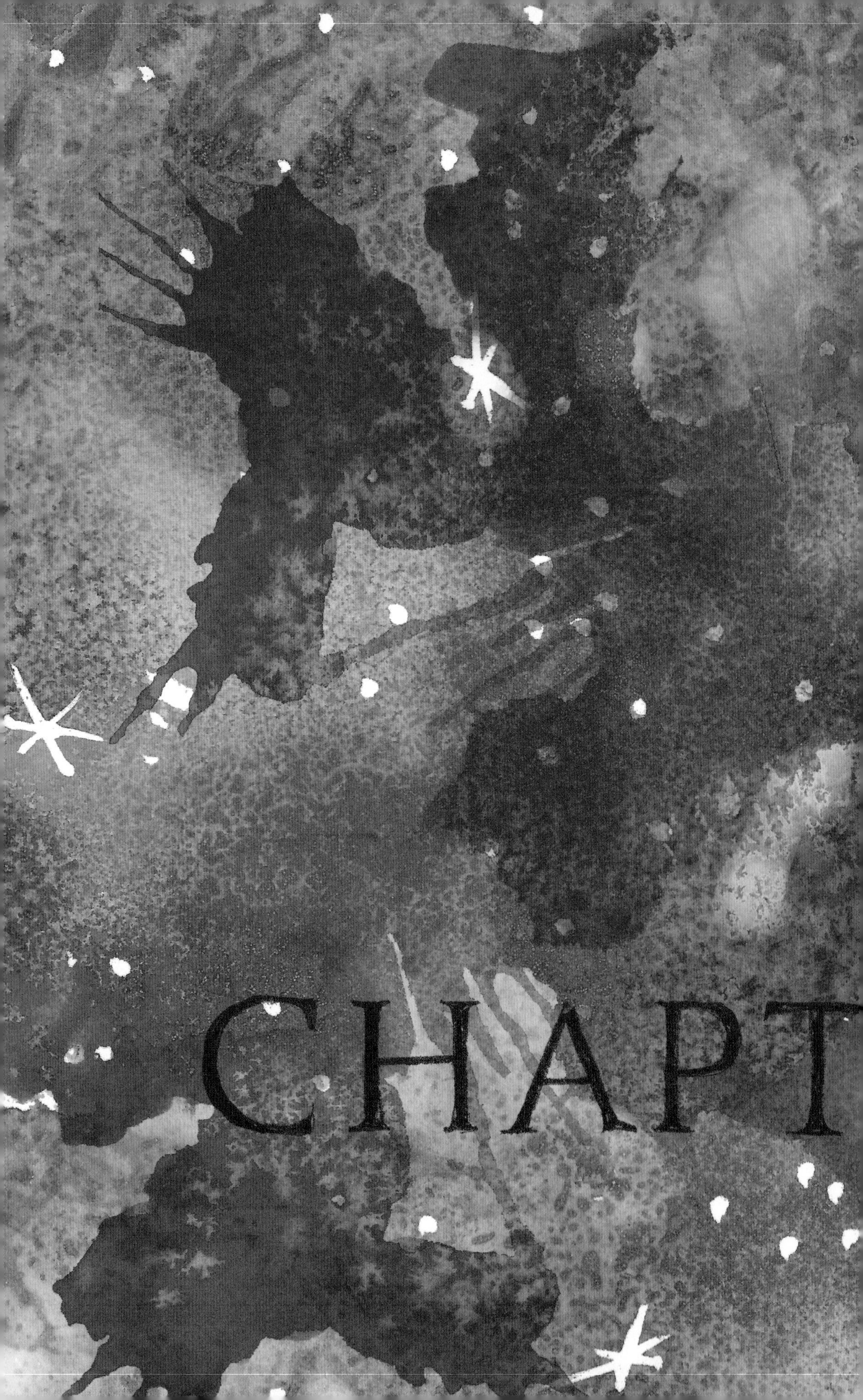
CHAPT

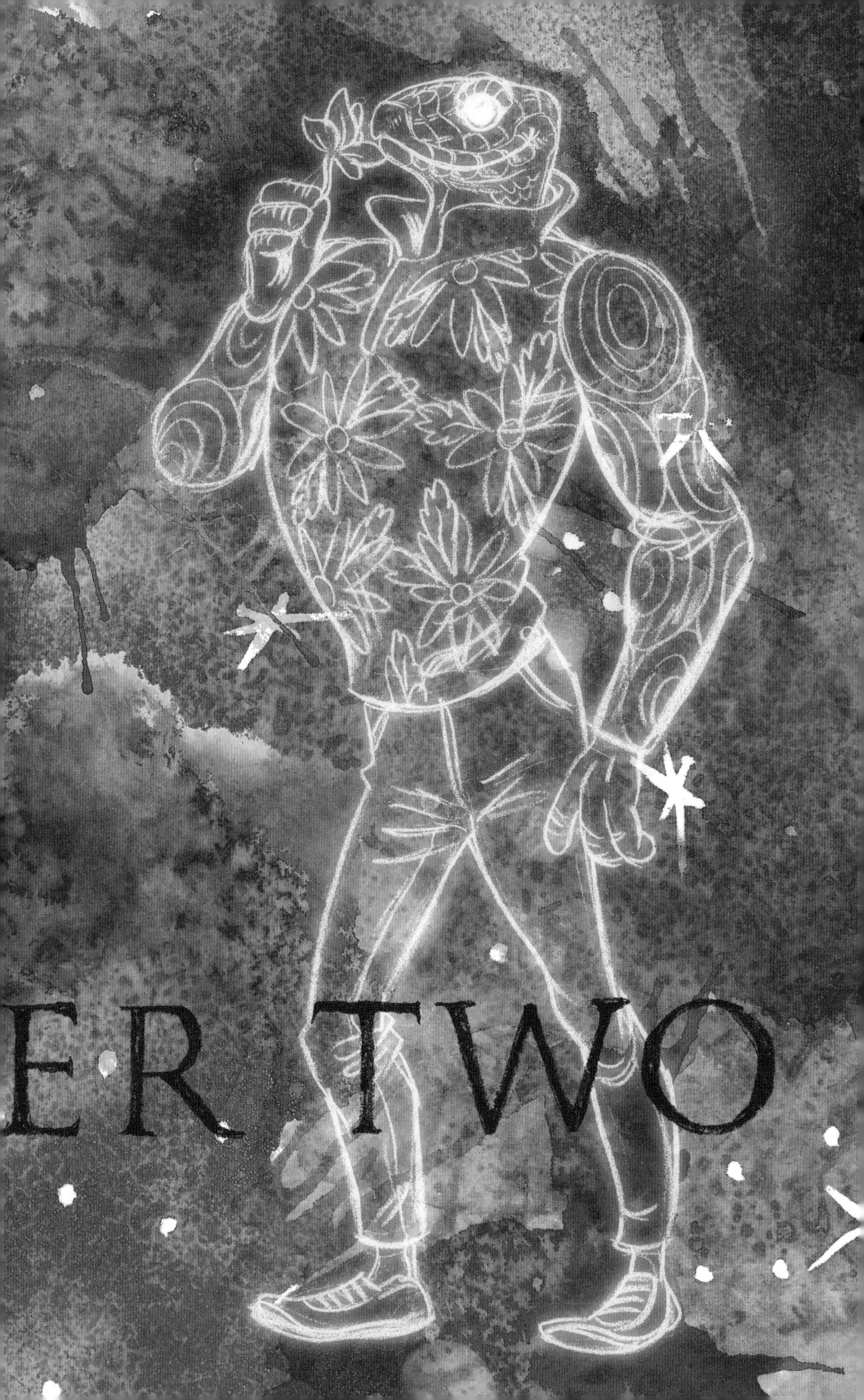
ER TWO

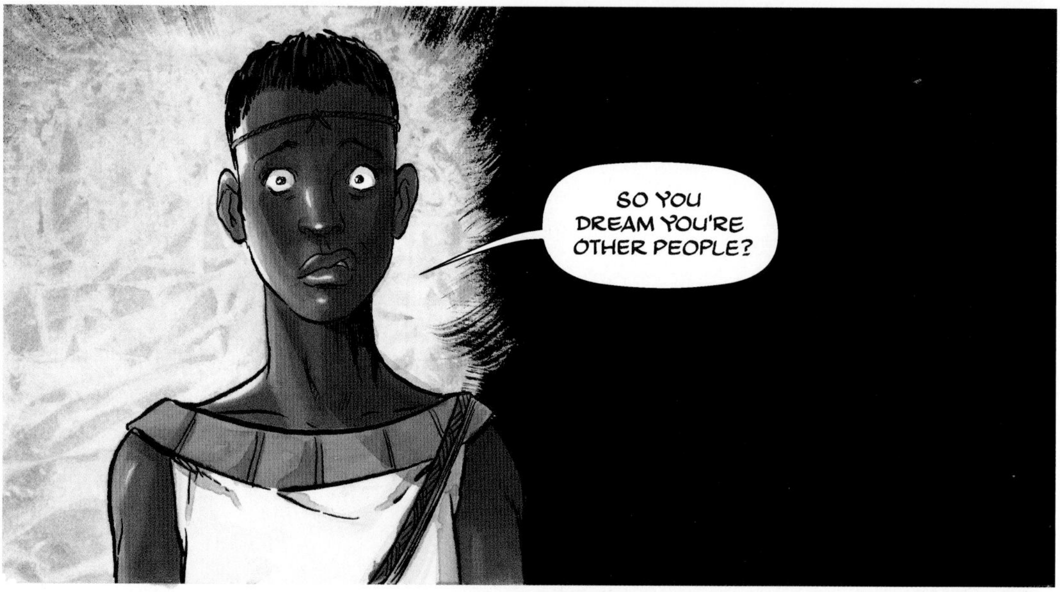
SO YOU DREAM YOU'RE OTHER PEOPLE?

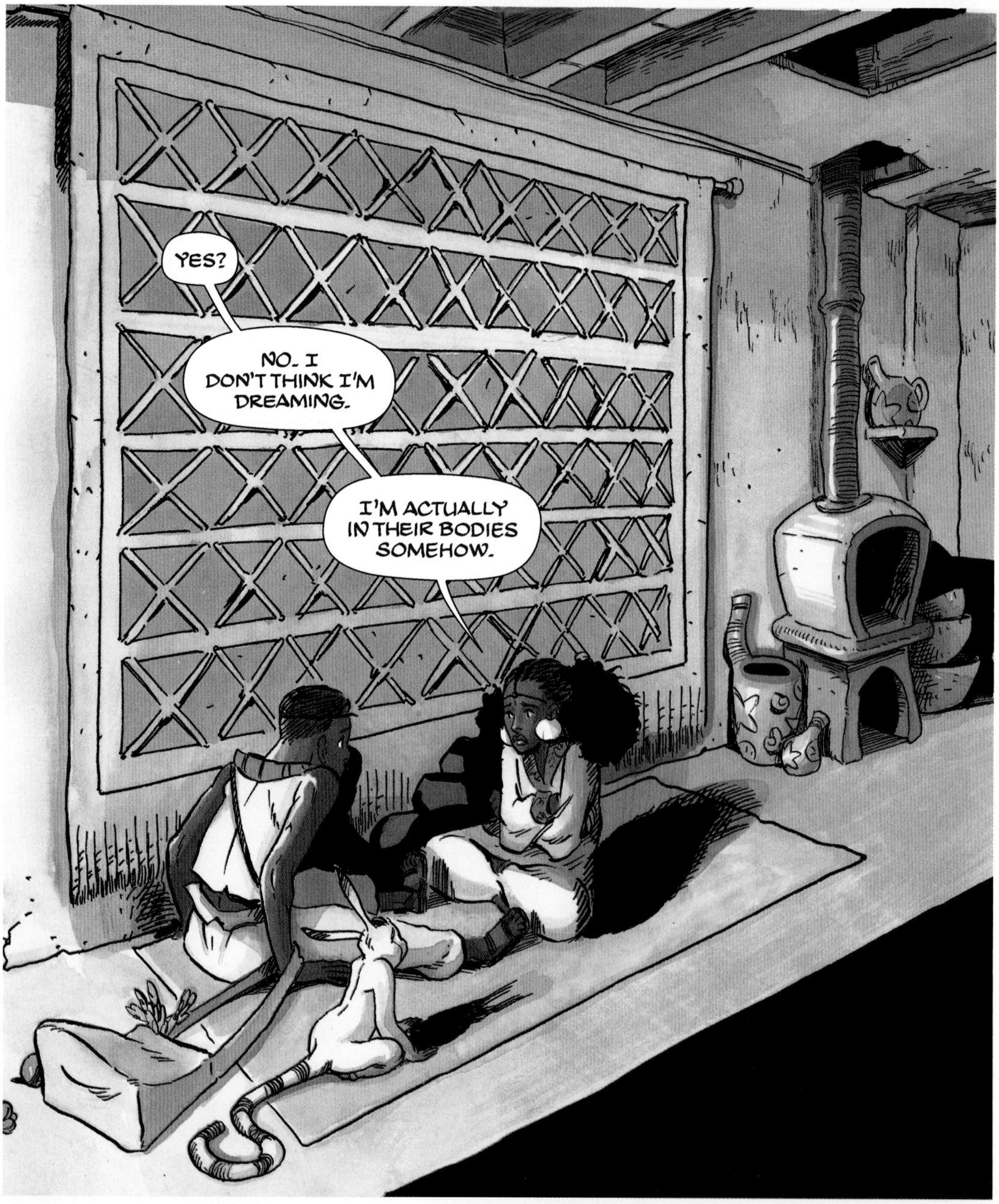
YES?
NO. I DON'T THINK I'M DREAMING.
I'M ACTUALLY IN THEIR BODIES SOMEHOW.

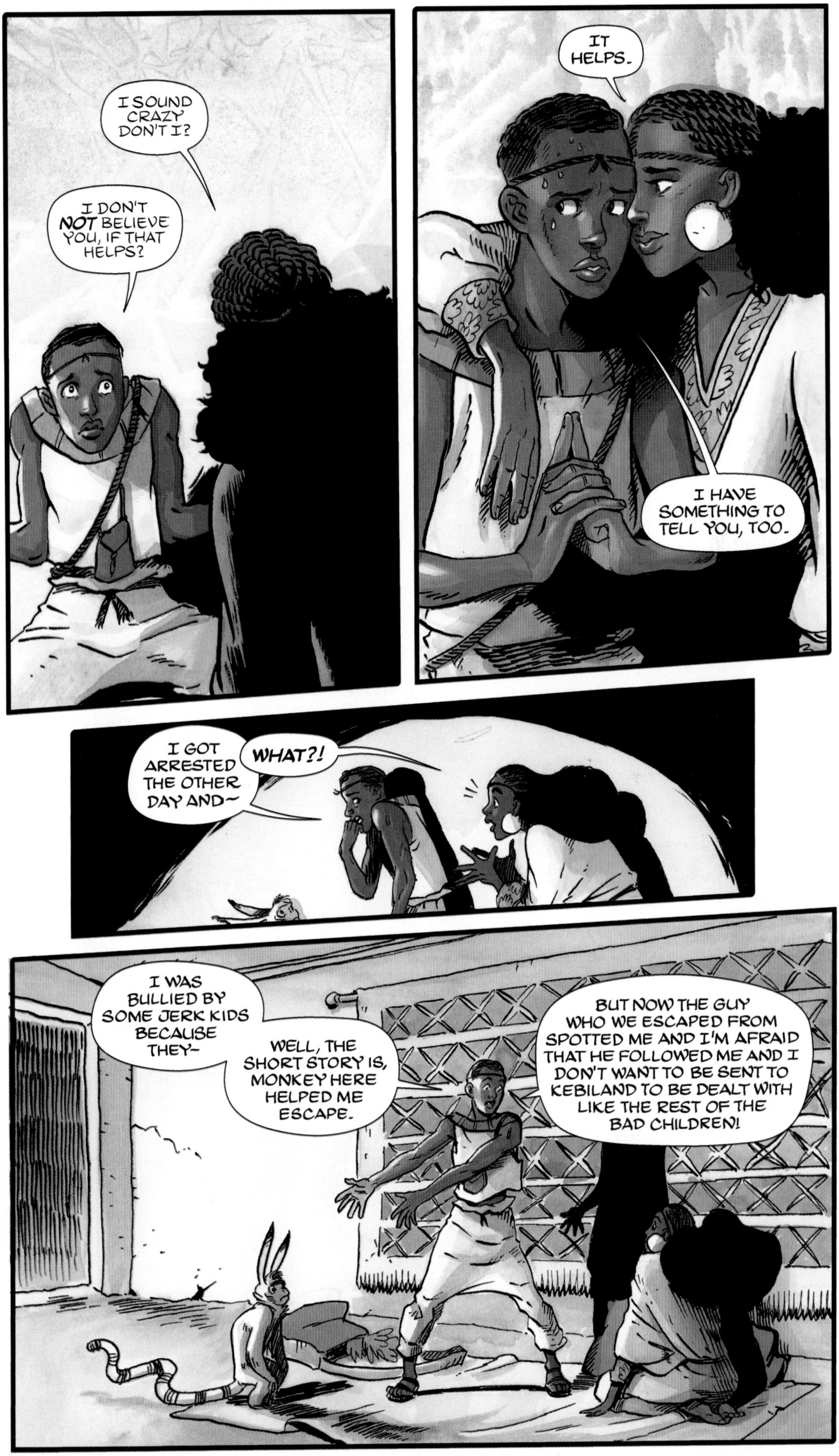
I SOUND CRAZY DON'T I?
I DON'T NOT BELIEVE YOU, IF THAT HELPS?
IT HELPS.
I HAVE SOMETHING TO TELL YOU, TOO.
I GOT ARRESTED THE OTHER DAY AND~
WHAT?!
I WAS BULLIED BY SOME JERK KIDS BECAUSE THEY~
WELL, THE SHORT STORY IS, MONKEY HERE HELPED ME ESCAPE.
BUT NOW THE GUY WHO WE ESCAPED FROM SPOTTED ME AND I'M AFRAID THAT HE FOLLOWED ME AND I DON'T WANT TO BE SENT TO KEBILAND TO BE DEALT WITH LIKE THE REST OF THE BAD CHILDREN!

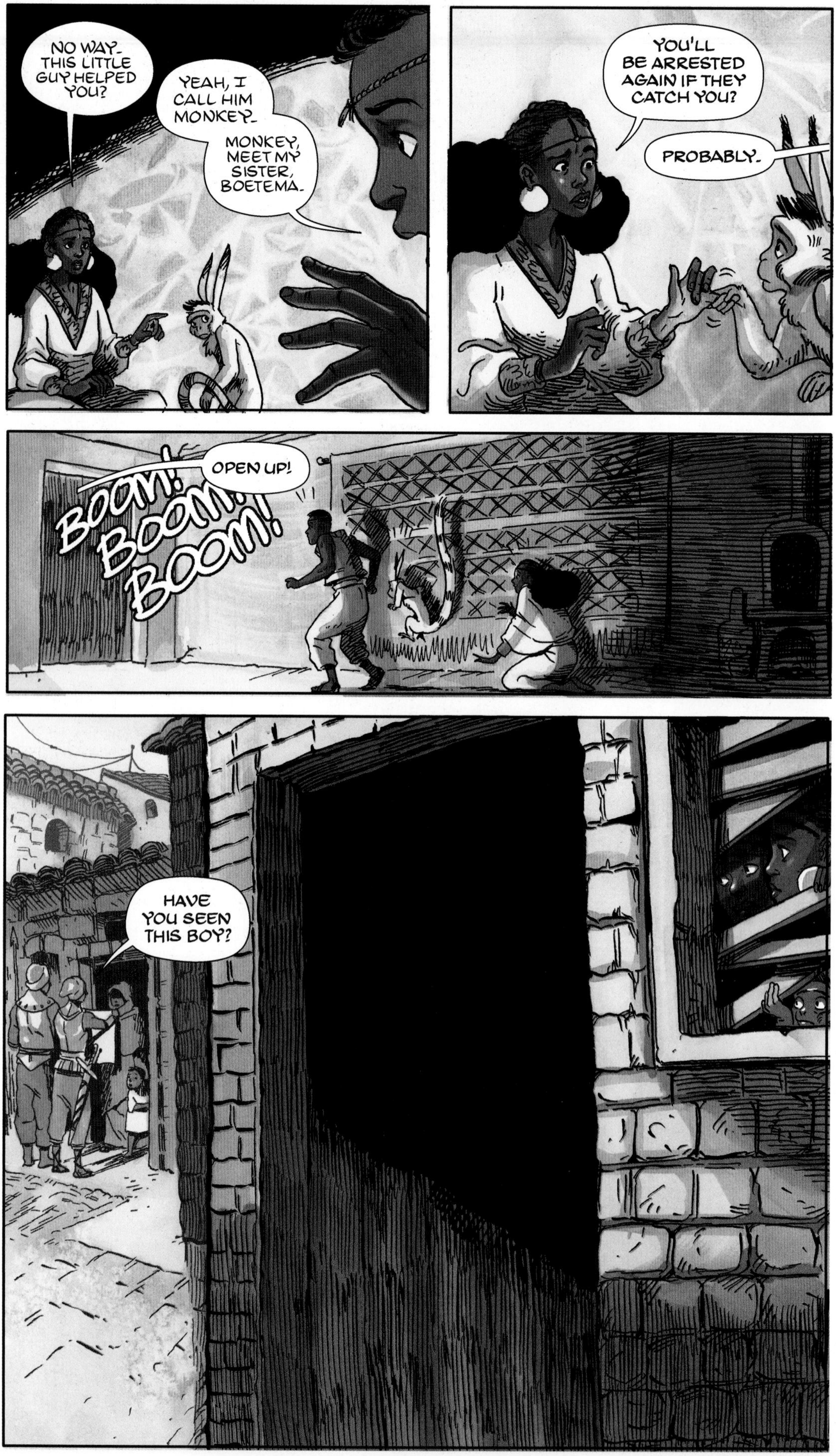
NO WAY. THIS LITTLE GUY HELPED YOU?
YEAH, I CALL HIM MONKEY.
MONKEY, MEET MY SISTER, BOETEMA.
YOU'LL BE ARRESTED AGAIN IF THEY CATCH YOU?
PROBABLY.
BOOM! BOOM! BOOM!
OPEN UP!
HAVE YOU SEEN THIS BOY?

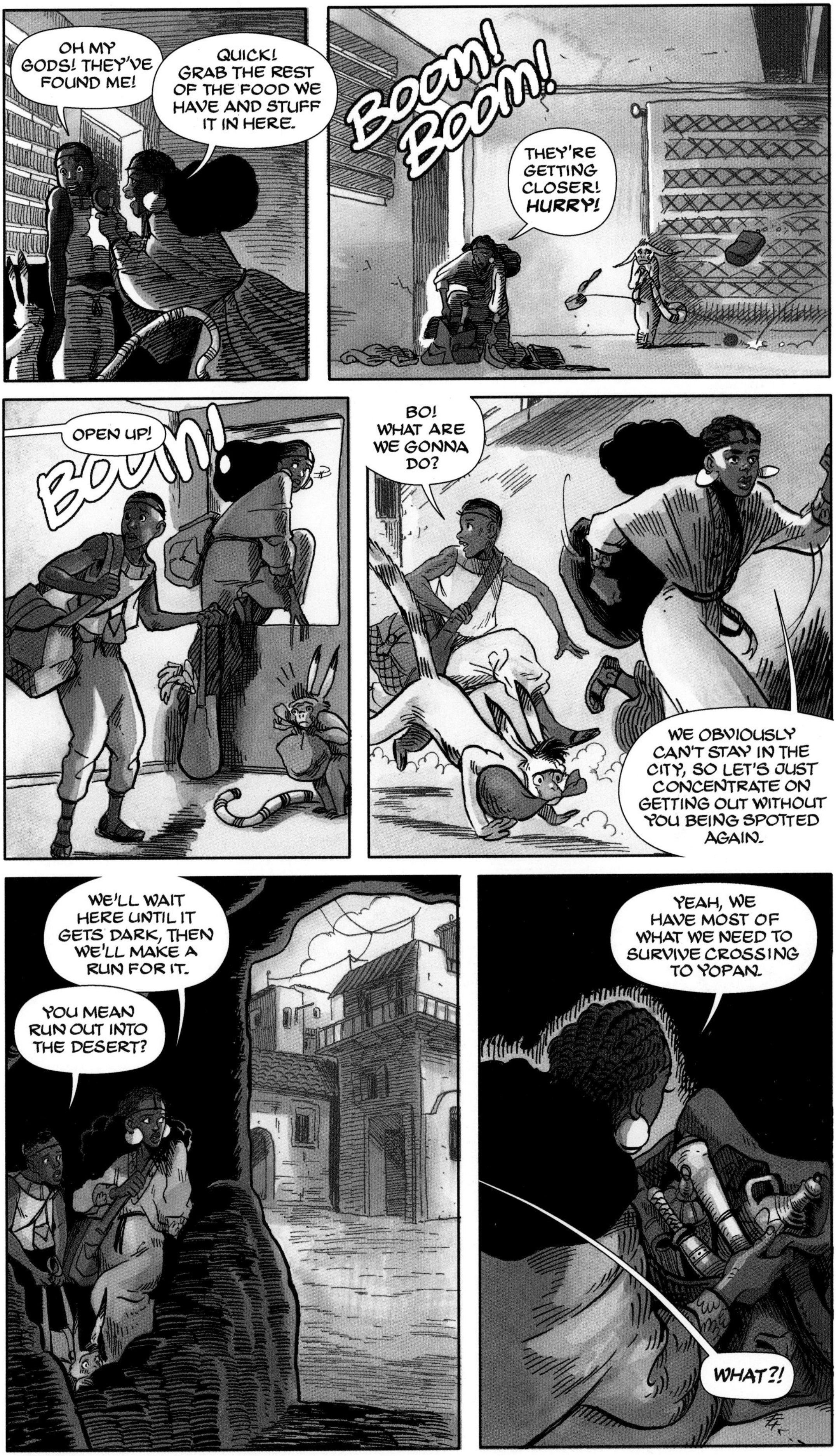
OH MY GODS! THEY'VE FOUND ME!
QUICK! GRAB THE REST OF THE FOOD WE HAVE AND STUFF IT IN HERE.
BOOM! BOOM!
THEY'RE GETTING CLOSER! HURRY!
OPEN UP!
BOOM!
BO! WHAT ARE WE GONNA DO?
WE OBVIOUSLY CAN'T STAY IN THE CITY, SO LET'S JUST CONCENTRATE ON GETTING OUT WITHOUT YOU BEING SPOTTED AGAIN.
WE'LL WAIT HERE UNTIL IT GETS DARK, THEN WE'LL MAKE A RUN FOR IT.
YOU MEAN RUN OUT INTO THE DESERT?
YEAH, WE HAVE MOST OF WHAT WE NEED TO SURVIVE CROSSING TO YOPAN.
WHAT?!

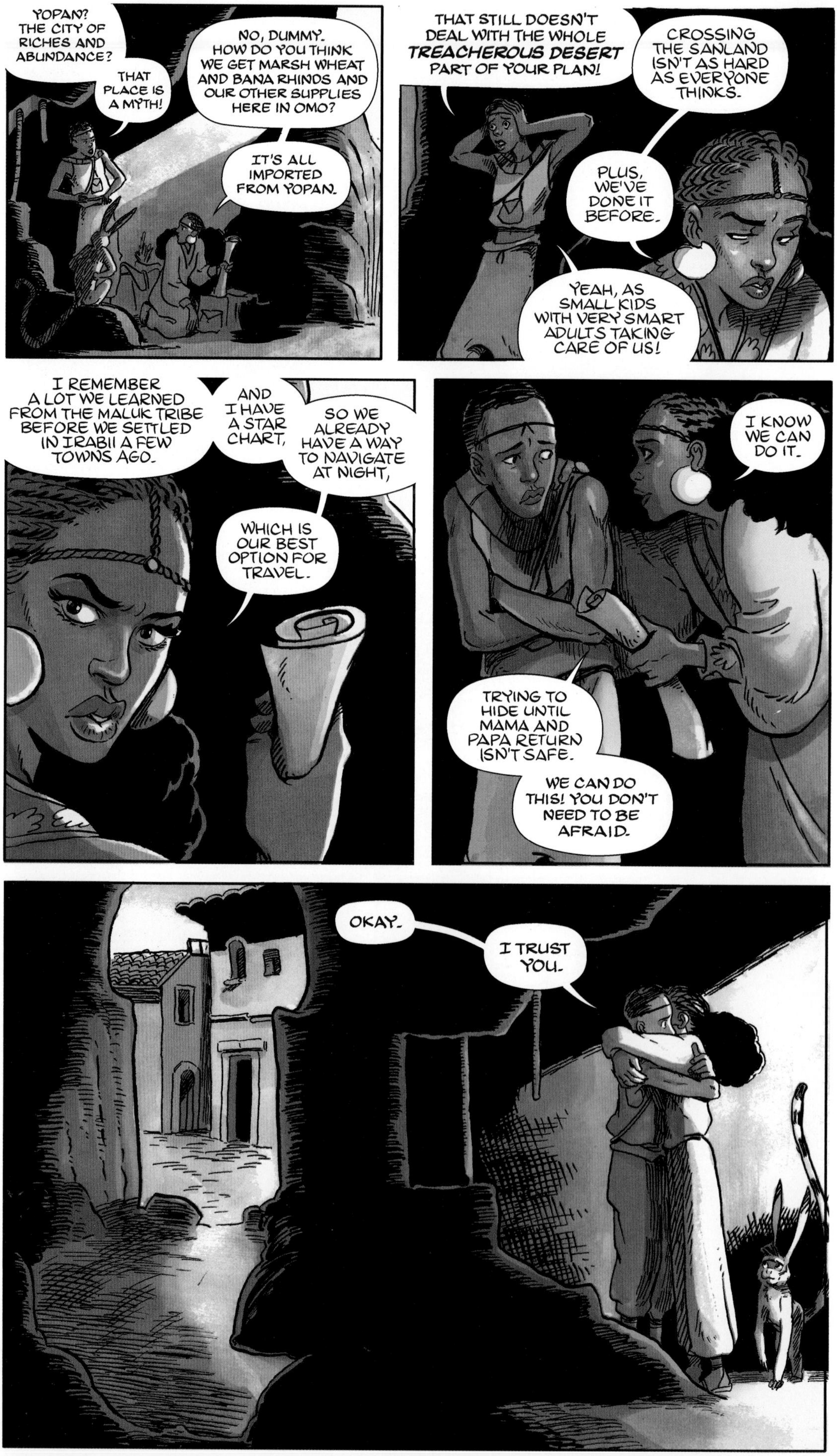
YOPAN? THE CITY OF RICHES AND ABUNDANCE?
THAT PLACE IS A MYTH!
NO, DUMMY. HOW DO YOU THINK WE GET MARSH WHEAT AND BANA RHINOS AND OUR OTHER SUPPLIES HERE IN OMO?
IT'S ALL IMPORTED FROM YOPAN.
THAT STILL DOESN'T DEAL WITH THE WHOLE TREACHEROUS DESERT PART OF YOUR PLAN!
CROSSING THE SANLAND ISN'T AS HARD AS EVERYONE THINKS.
PLUS, WE'VE DONE IT BEFORE.
YEAH, AS SMALL KIDS WITH VERY SMART ADULTS TAKING CARE OF US!
I REMEMBER A LOT WE LEARNED FROM THE MALUK TRIBE BEFORE WE SETTLED IN IRABII A FEW TOWNS AGO.
AND I HAVE A STAR CHART,
SO WE ALREADY HAVE A WAY TO NAVIGATE AT NIGHT,
WHICH IS OUR BEST OPTION FOR TRAVEL.
I KNOW WE CAN DO IT.
TRYING TO HIDE UNTIL MAMA AND PAPA RETURN ISN'T SAFE.
WE CAN DO THIS! YOU DON'T NEED TO BE AFRAID.
OKAY.
I TRUST YOU.

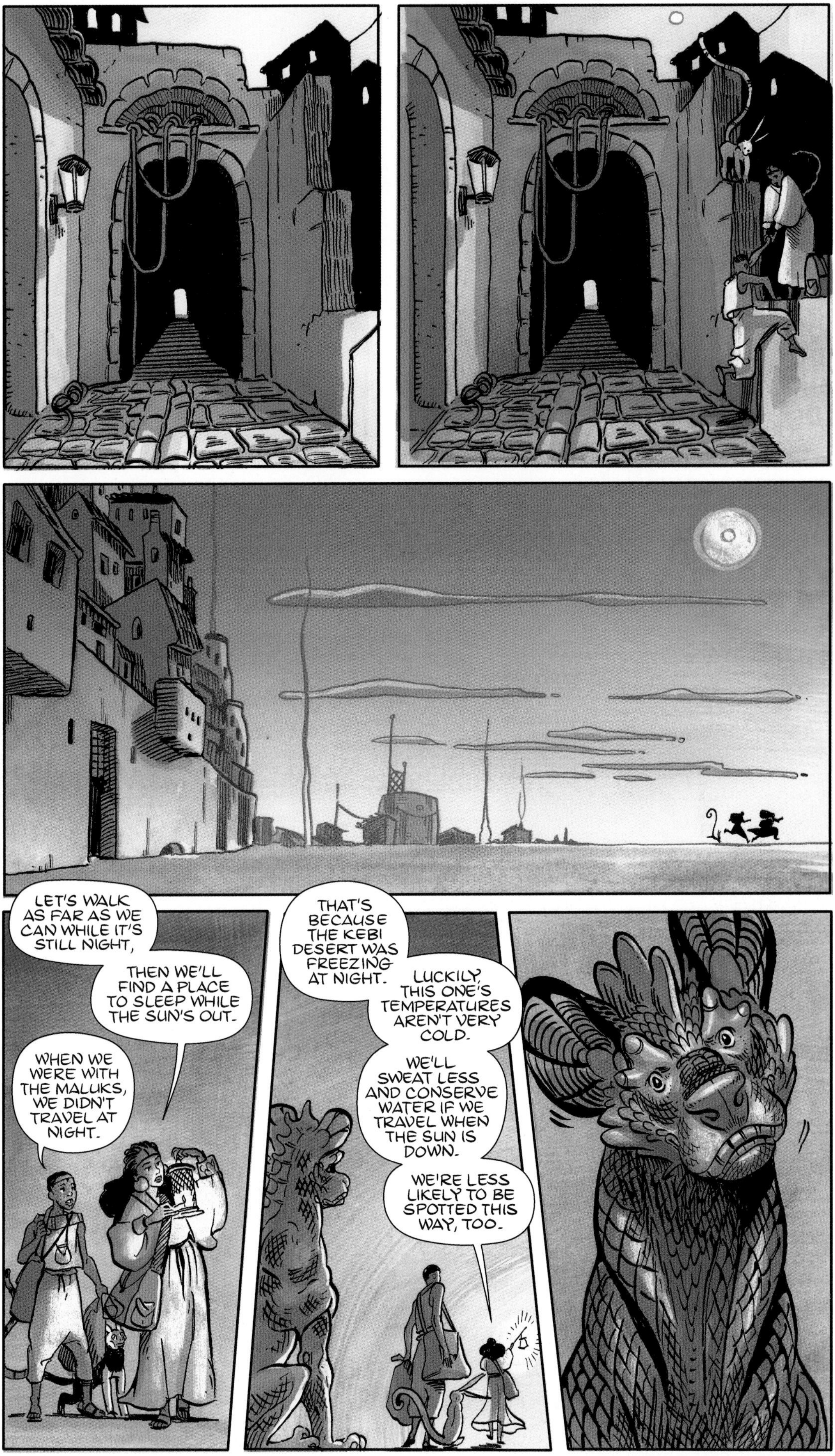
LET'S WALK AS FAR AS WE CAN WHILE IT'S STILL NIGHT,
THEN WE'LL FIND A PLACE TO SLEEP WHILE THE SUN'S OUT.
WHEN WE WERE WITH THE MALUKS, WE DIDN'T TRAVEL AT NIGHT.
THAT'S BECAUSE THE KEBI DESERT WAS FREEZING AT NIGHT.
LUCKILY, THIS ONE'S TEMPERATURES AREN'T VERY COLD.
WE'LL SWEAT LESS AND CONSERVE WATER IF WE TRAVEL WHEN THE SUN IS DOWN.
WE'RE LESS LIKELY TO BE SPOTTED THIS WAY, TOO.

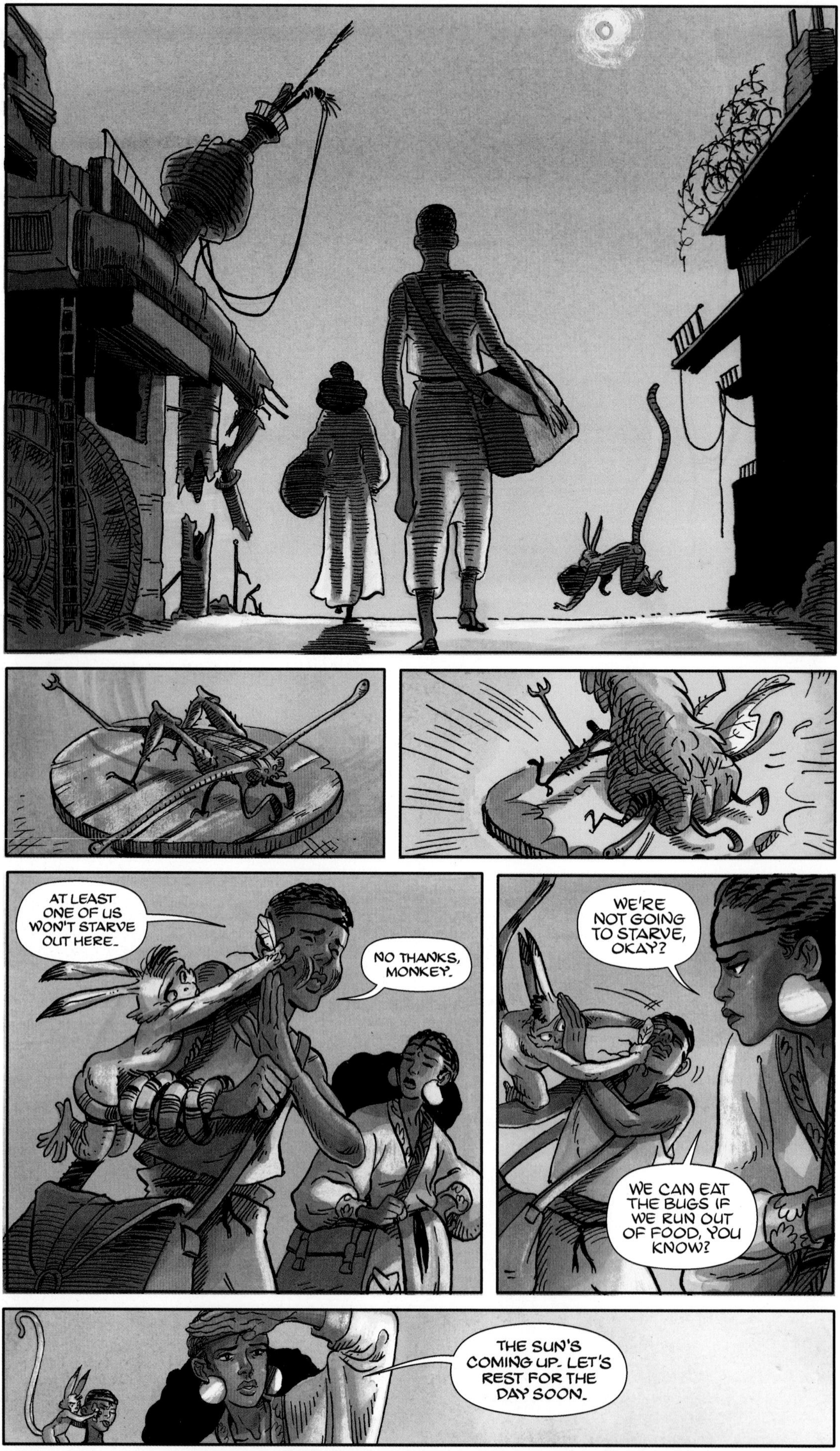
AT LEAST ONE OF US WON'T STARVE OUT HERE.
NO THANKS, MONKEY.
WE'RE NOT GOING TO STARVE, OKAY?
WE CAN EAT THE BUGS IF WE RUN OUT OF FOOD, YOU KNOW?
THE SUN'S COMING UP. LET'S REST FOR THE DAY SOON.

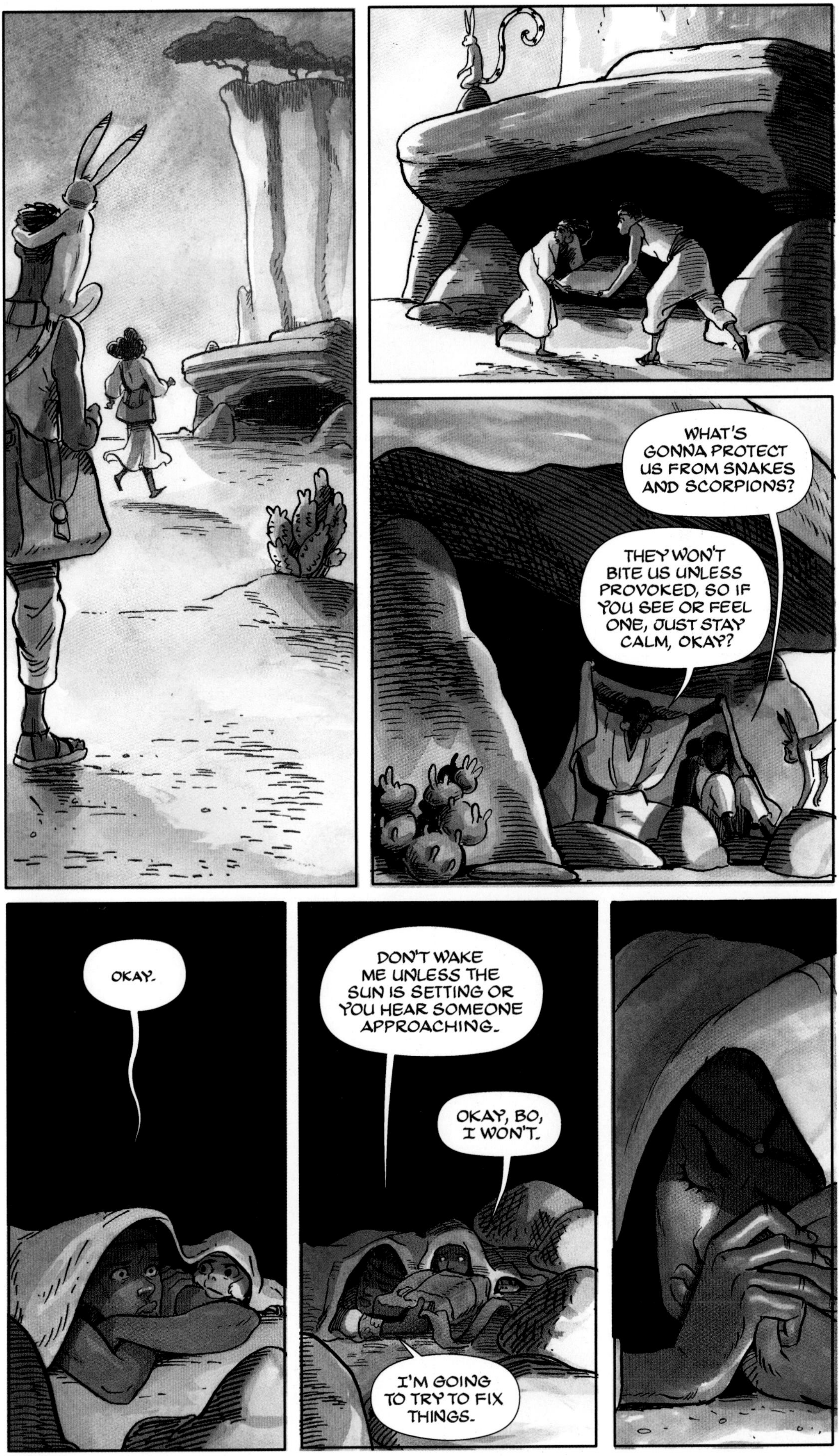
WHAT'S GONNA PROTECT US FROM SNAKES AND SCORPIONS?
THEY WON'T BITE US UNLESS PROVOKED, SO IF YOU SEE OR FEEL ONE, JUST STAY CALM, OKAY?
OKAY.
DON'T WAKE ME UNLESS THE SUN IS SETTING OR YOU HEAR SOMEONE APPROACHING.
OKAY, BO, I WON'T.
I'M GOING TO TRY TO FIX THINGS.

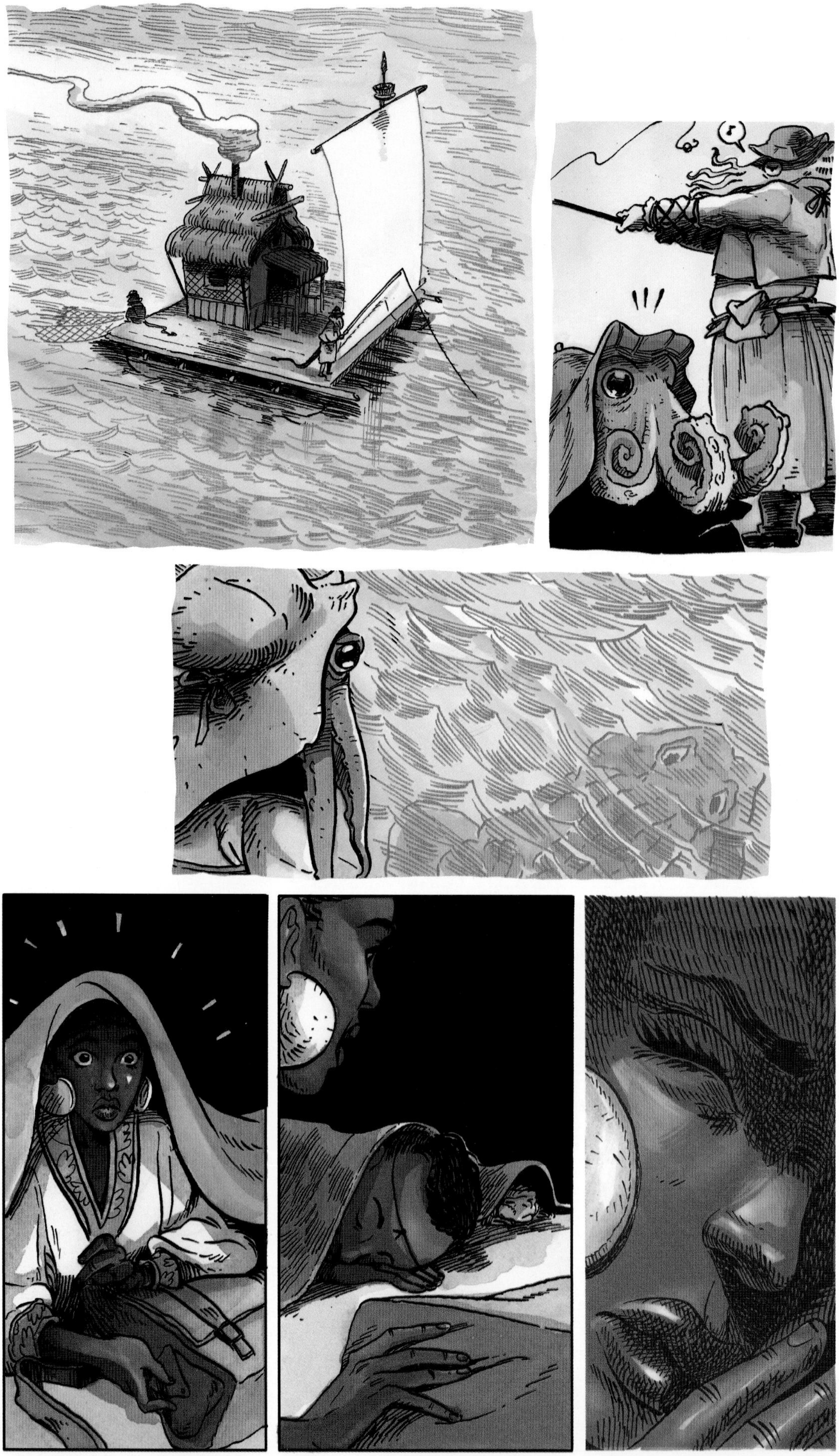

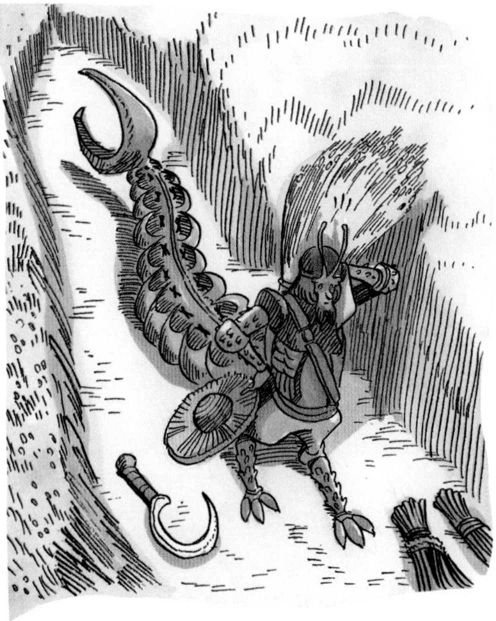

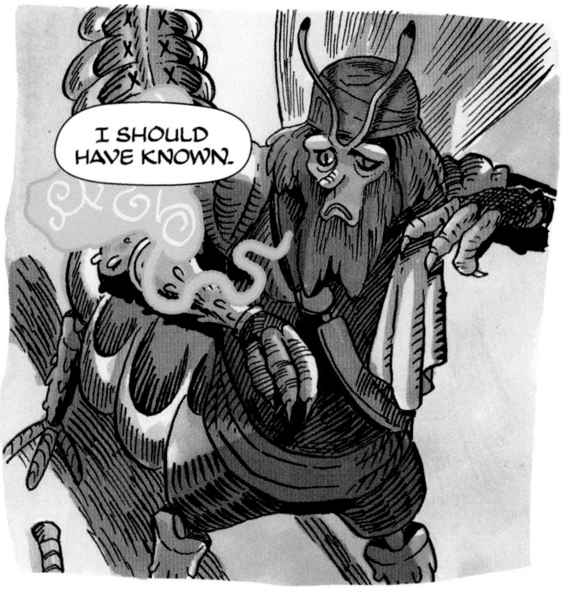
I SHOULD HAVE KNOWN.

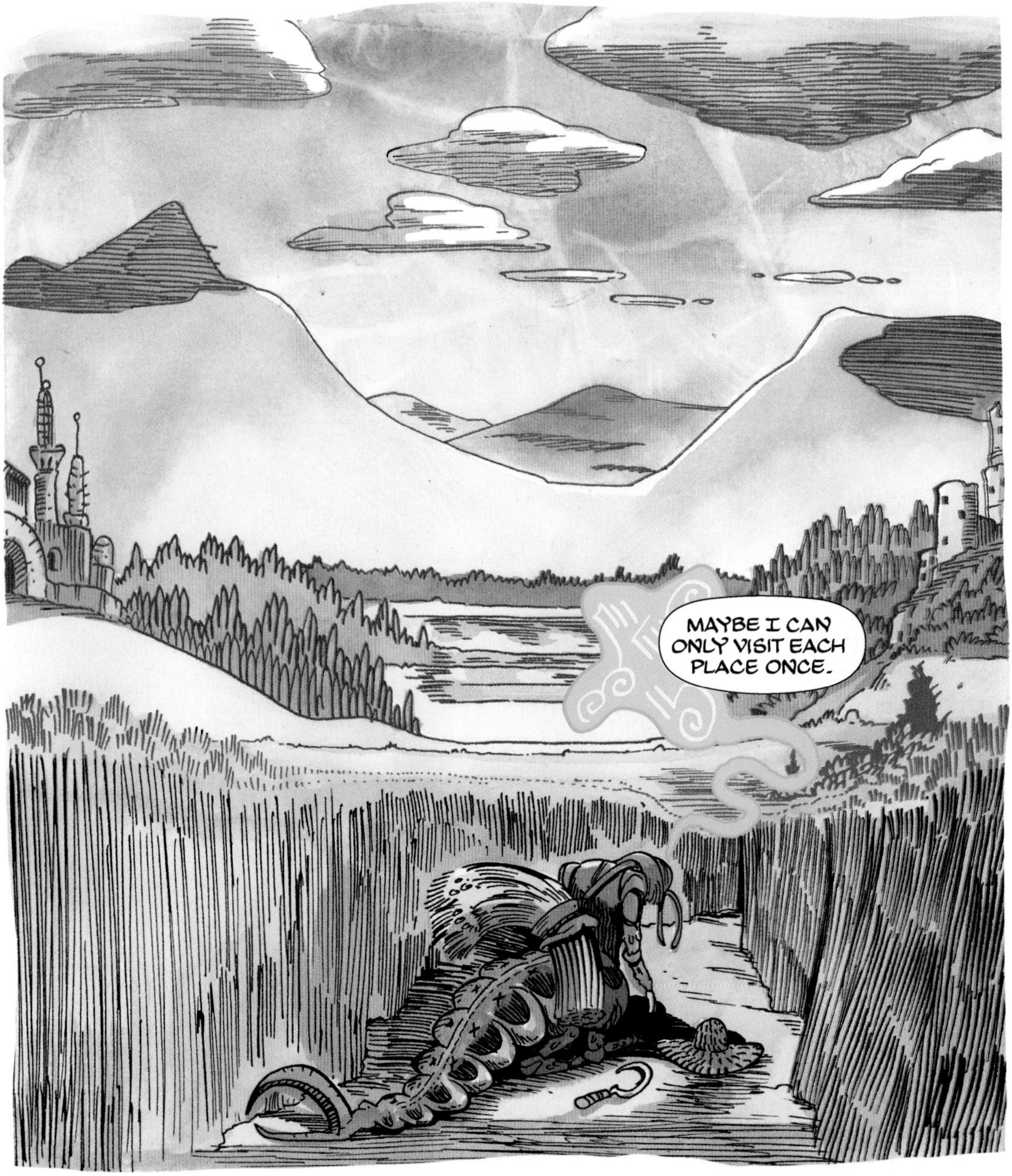
MAYBE I CAN ONLY VISIT EACH PLACE ONCE.

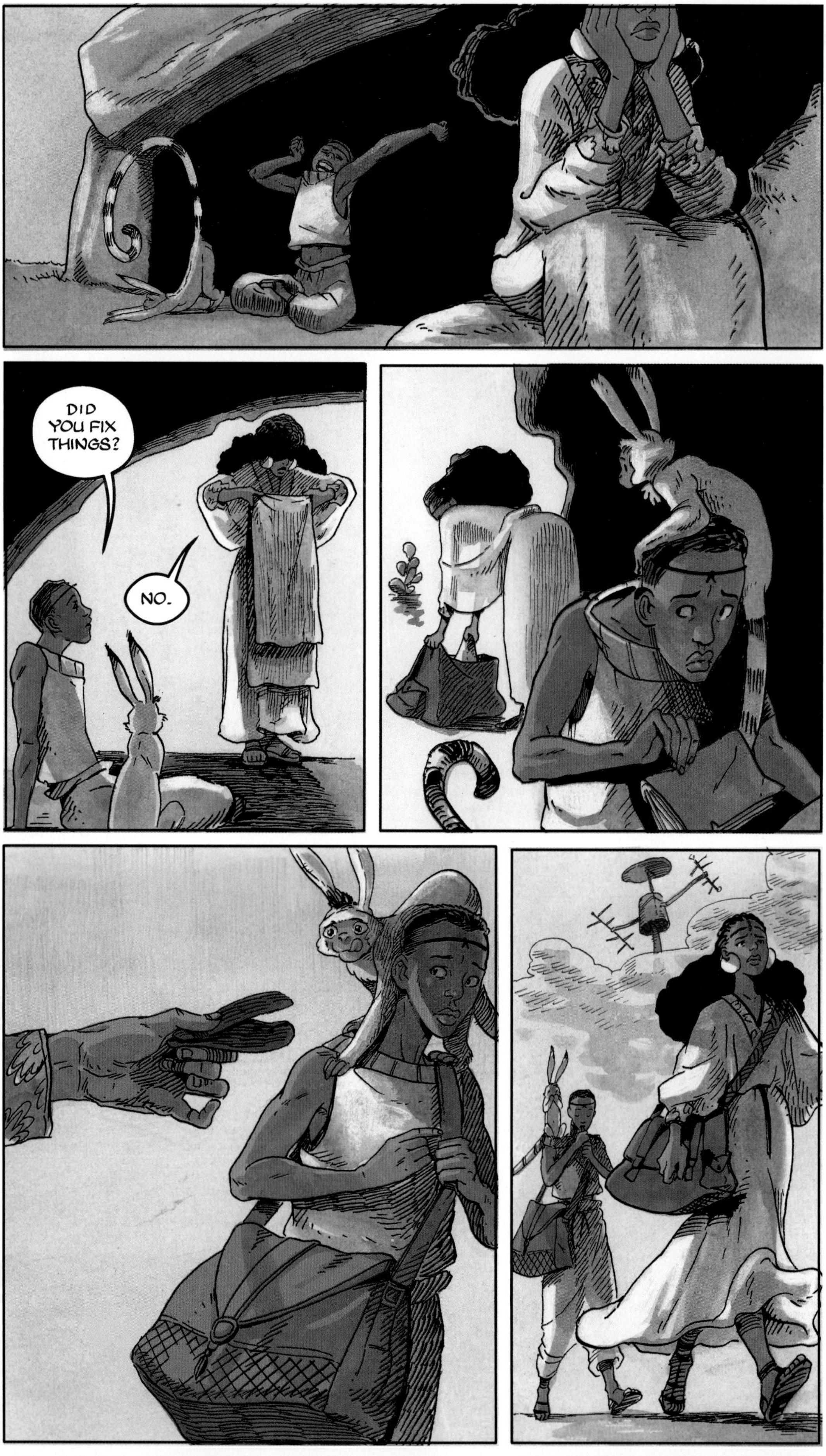
DID YOU FIX THINGS?
NO.

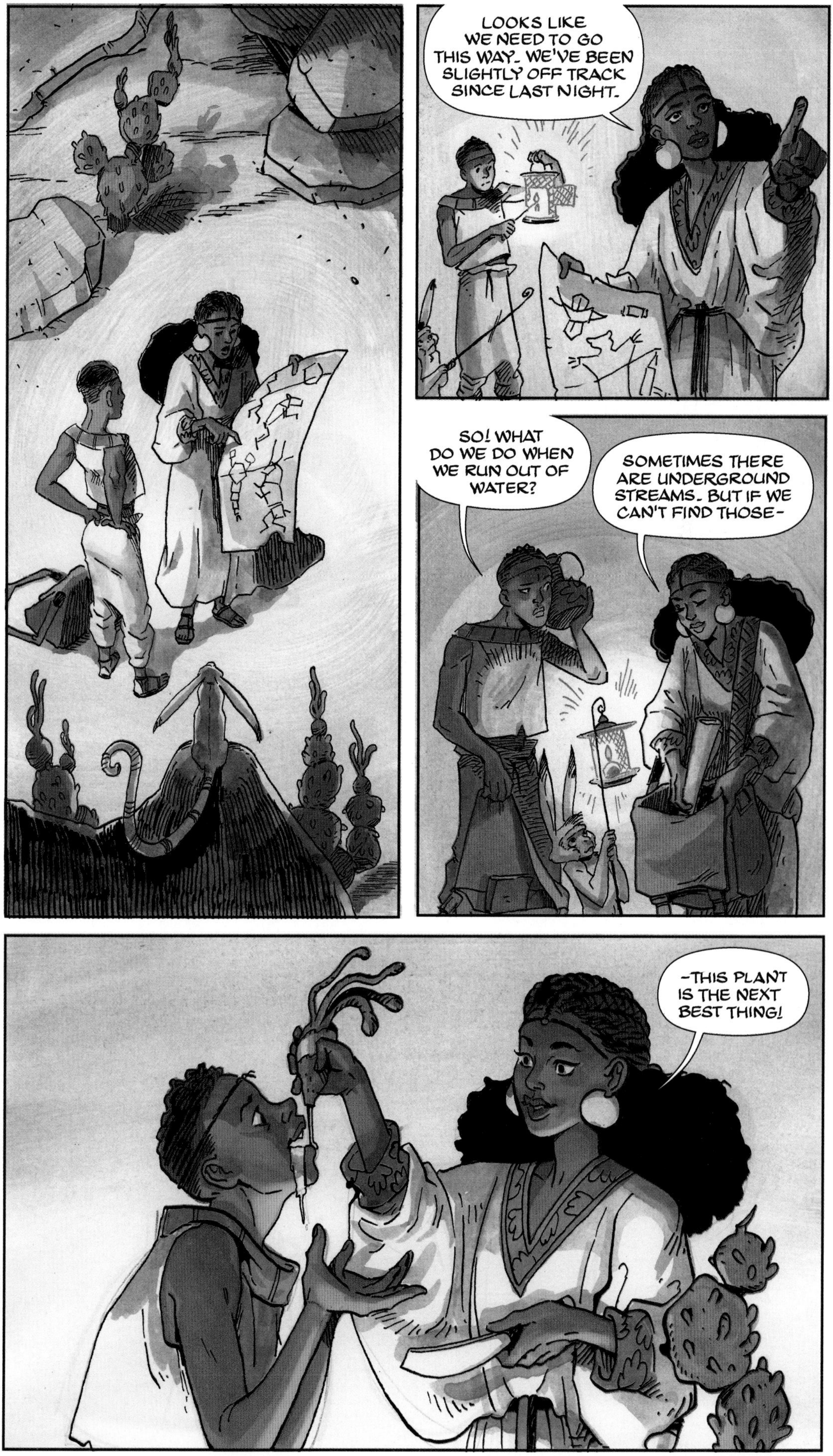
LOOKS LIKE WE NEED TO GO THIS WAY. WE'VE BEEN SLIGHTLY OFF TRACK SINCE LAST NIGHT.
SO! WHAT DO WE DO WHEN WE RUN OUT OF WATER?
SOMETIMES THERE ARE UNDERGROUND STREAMS. BUT IF WE CAN'T FIND THOSE-
-THIS PLANT IS THE NEXT BEST THING!

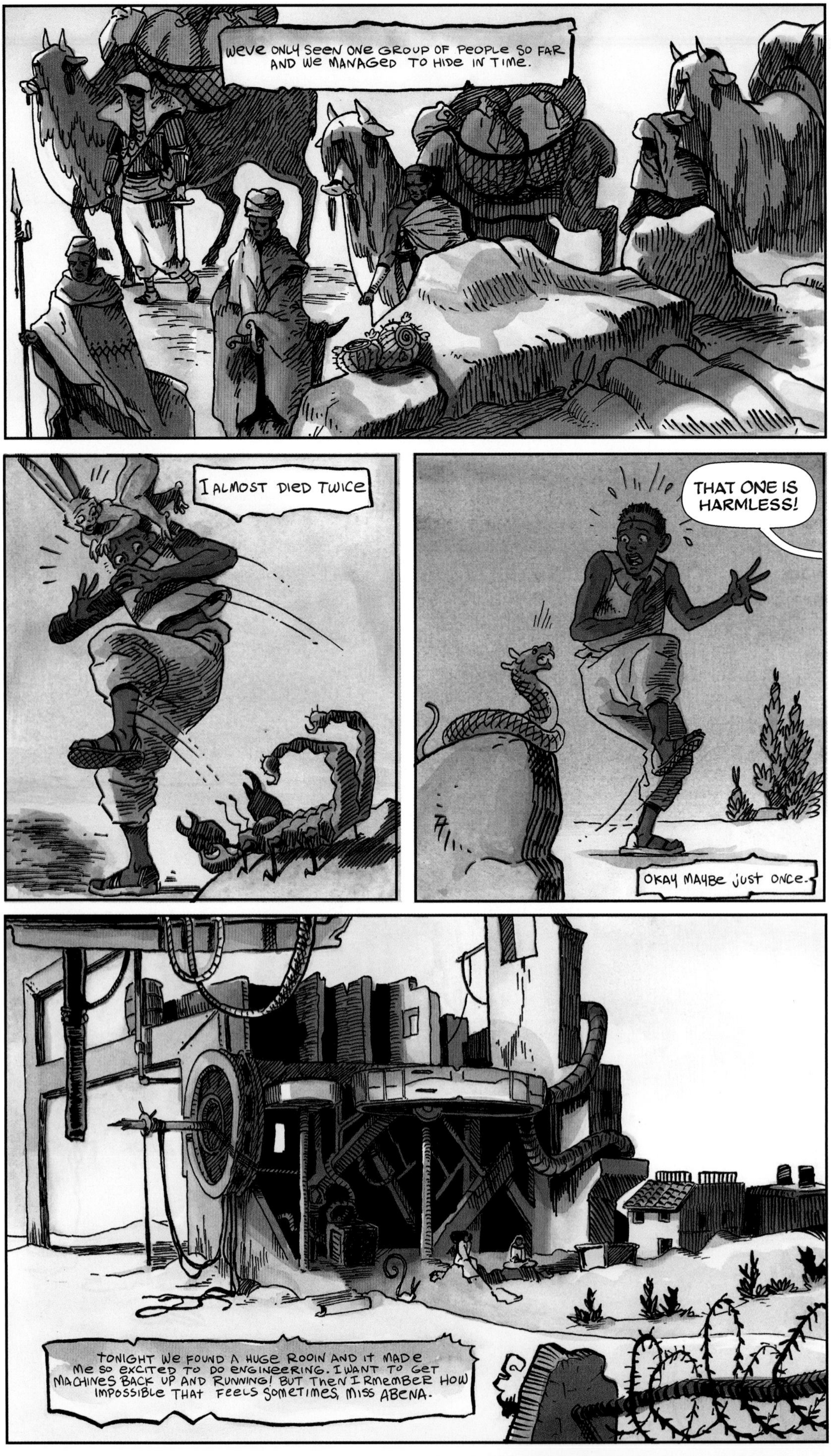
WEVE ONLY SEEN ONE GROUP OF PEOPLE SO FAR AND WE MANAGED TO HIDE IN TIME.
I ALMOST DIED TWICE
THAT ONE IS HARMLESS!
OKAY MAYBE JUST ONCE.
TONIGHT WE FOUND A HUGE ROOIN AND IT MADE ME SO EXCITED TO DO ENGINEERING. I WANT TO GET MACHINES BACK UP AND RUNNING! BUT THEN I RMEMBER HOW IMPOSSIBLE THAT FEELS SOMETIMES, MISS ABENA.

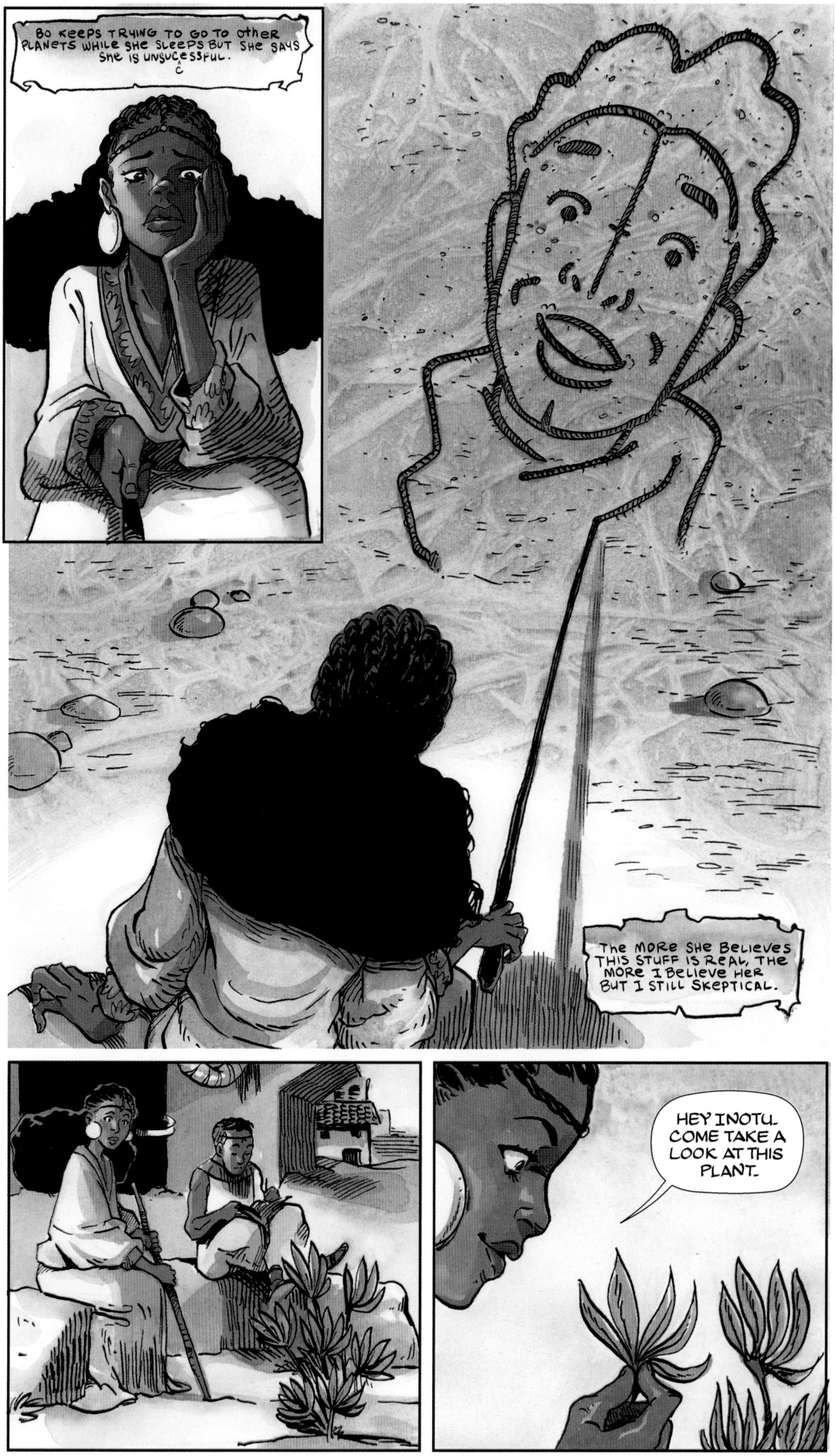
BO KEEPS TRYING TO GO TO OTHER PLANETS WHILE SHE SLEEPS BUT SHE SAYS SHE IS UNSUCESSFUL.
THE MORE SHE BELIEVES THIS STUFF IS REAL, THE MORE I BELIEVE HER BUT I STILL SKEPTICAL.
HEY INOTU. COME TAKE A LOOK AT THIS PLANT.

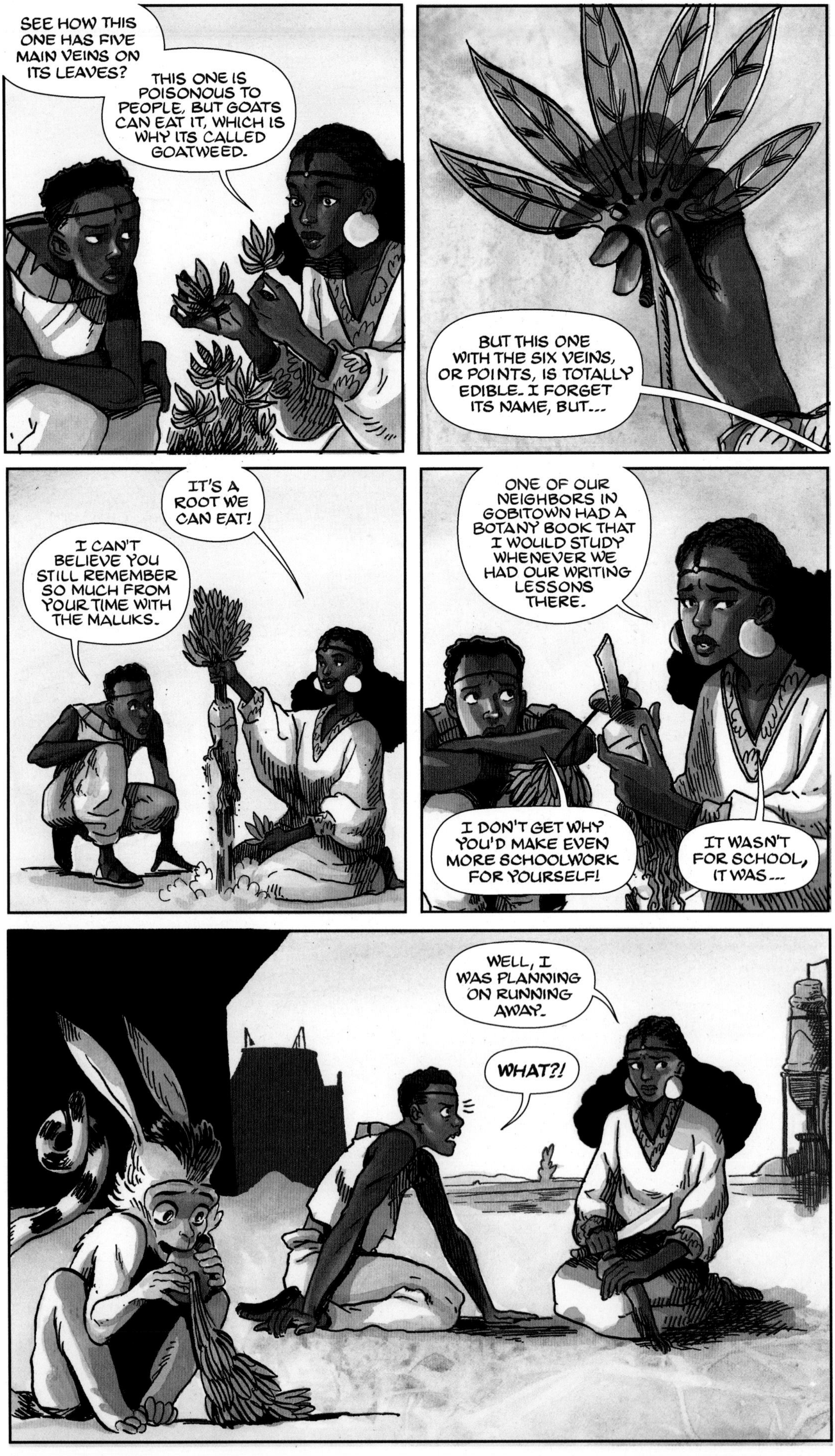

SEE HOW THIS ONE HAS FIVE MAIN VEINS ON ITS LEAVES?
THIS ONE IS POISONOUS TO PEOPLE, BUT GOATS CAN EAT IT, WHICH IS WHY ITS CALLED GOATWEED.
BUT THIS ONE WITH THE SIX VEINS, OR POINTS, IS TOTALLY EDIBLE. I FORGET ITS NAME, BUT...
IT'S A ROOT WE CAN EAT!
I CAN'T BELIEVE YOU STILL REMEMBER SO MUCH FROM YOUR TIME WITH THE MALUKS.
ONE OF OUR NEIGHBORS IN GOBITOWN HAD A BOTANY BOOK THAT I WOULD STUDY WHENEVER WE HAD OUR WRITING LESSONS THERE.
I DON'T GET WHY YOU'D MAKE EVEN MORE SCHOOLWORK FOR YOURSELF!
IT WASN'T FOR SCHOOL, IT WAS...
WELL, I WAS PLANNING ON RUNNING AWAY.
WHAT?!

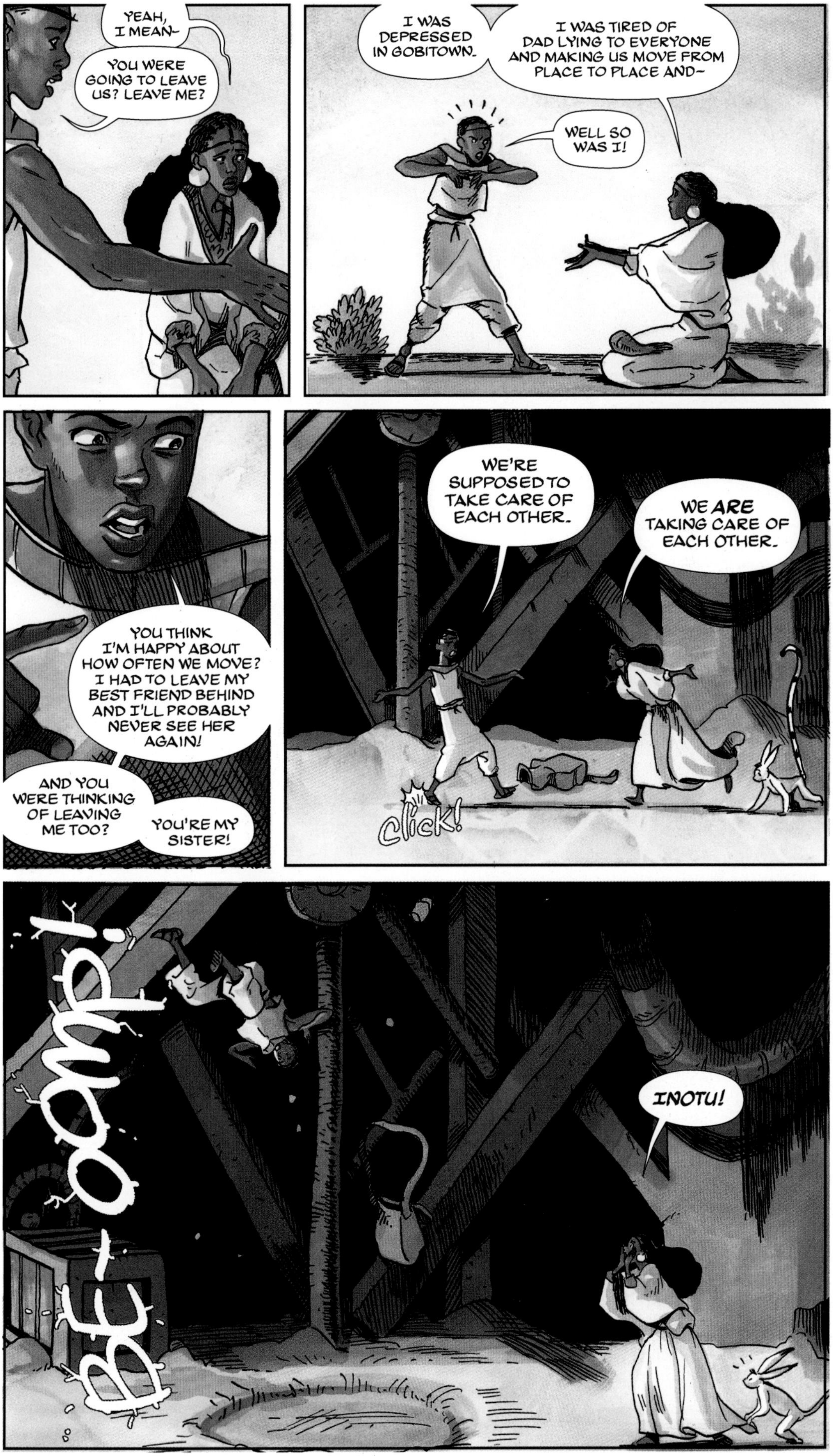
YEAH, I MEAN-
YOU WERE GOING TO LEAVE US? LEAVE ME?
I WAS DEPRESSED IN GOBITOWN.
I WAS TIRED OF DAD LYING TO EVERYONE AND MAKING US MOVE FROM PLACE TO PLACE AND-
WELL SO WAS I!
YOU THINK I'M HAPPY ABOUT HOW OFTEN WE MOVE? I HAD TO LEAVE MY BEST FRIEND BEHIND AND I'LL PROBABLY NEVER SEE HER AGAIN!
AND YOU WERE THINKING OF LEAVING ME TOO?
YOU'RE MY SISTER!
WE'RE SUPPOSED TO TAKE CARE OF EACH OTHER.
WE ARE TAKING CARE OF EACH OTHER.
CLICK!
BE-OOMP!
INOTU!

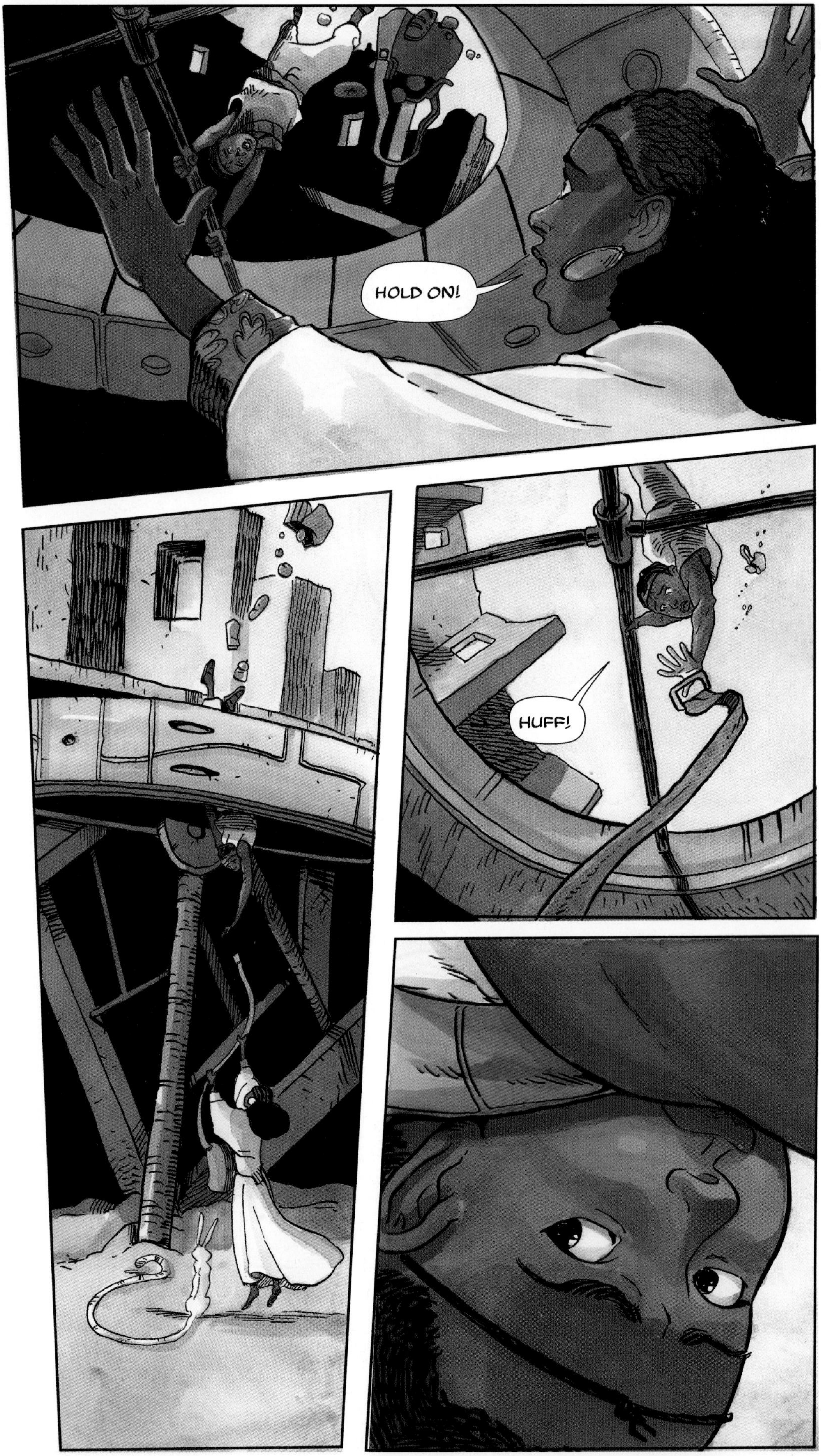
HOLD ON!
HUFF!

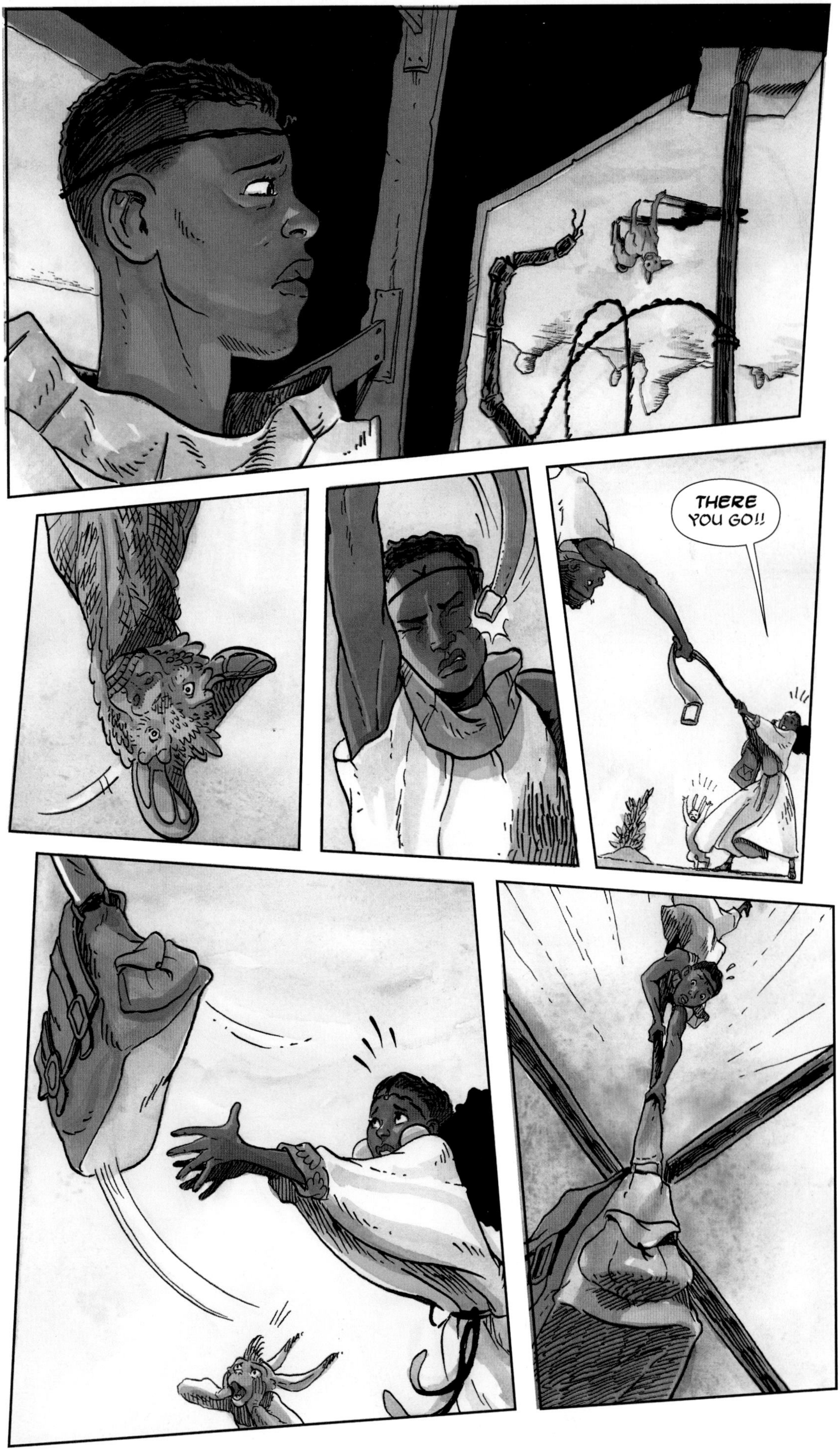
THERE YOU GO!!

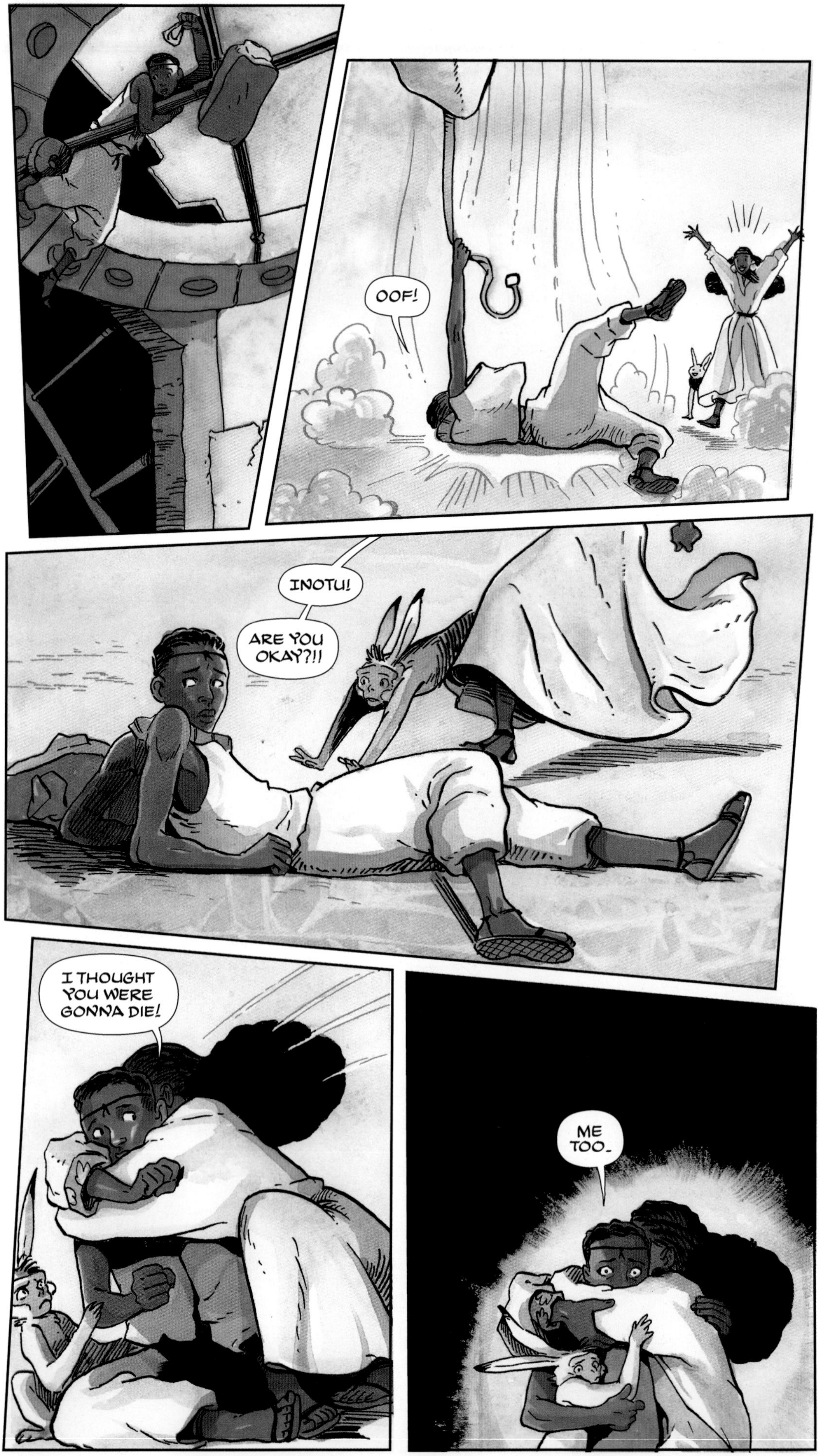
OOF!
INOTU!
ARE YOU OKAY?!!
I THOUGHT YOU WERE GONNA DIE!
ME TOO.

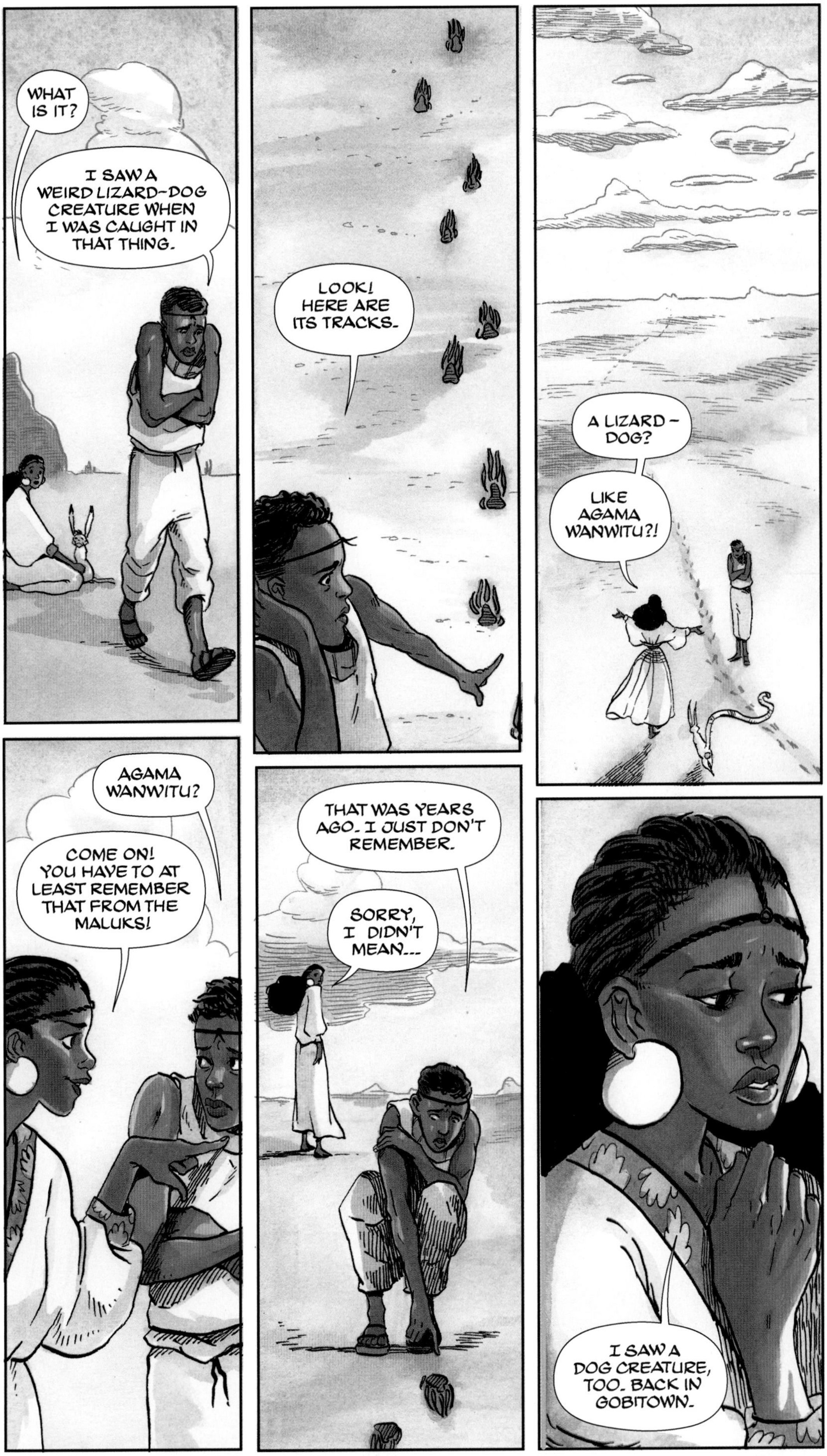
WHAT IS IT?
I SAW A WEIRD LIZARD-DOG CREATURE WHEN I WAS CAUGHT IN THAT THING.
LOOK! HERE ARE ITS TRACKS.
A LIZARD-DOG?
LIKE AGAMA WANWITU?!
AGAMA WANWITU?
COME ON! YOU HAVE TO AT LEAST REMEMBER THAT FROM THE MALUKS!
THAT WAS YEARS AGO. I JUST DON'T REMEMBER.
SORRY, I DIDN'T MEAN...
I SAW A DOG CREATURE, TOO. BACK IN GOBITOWN.

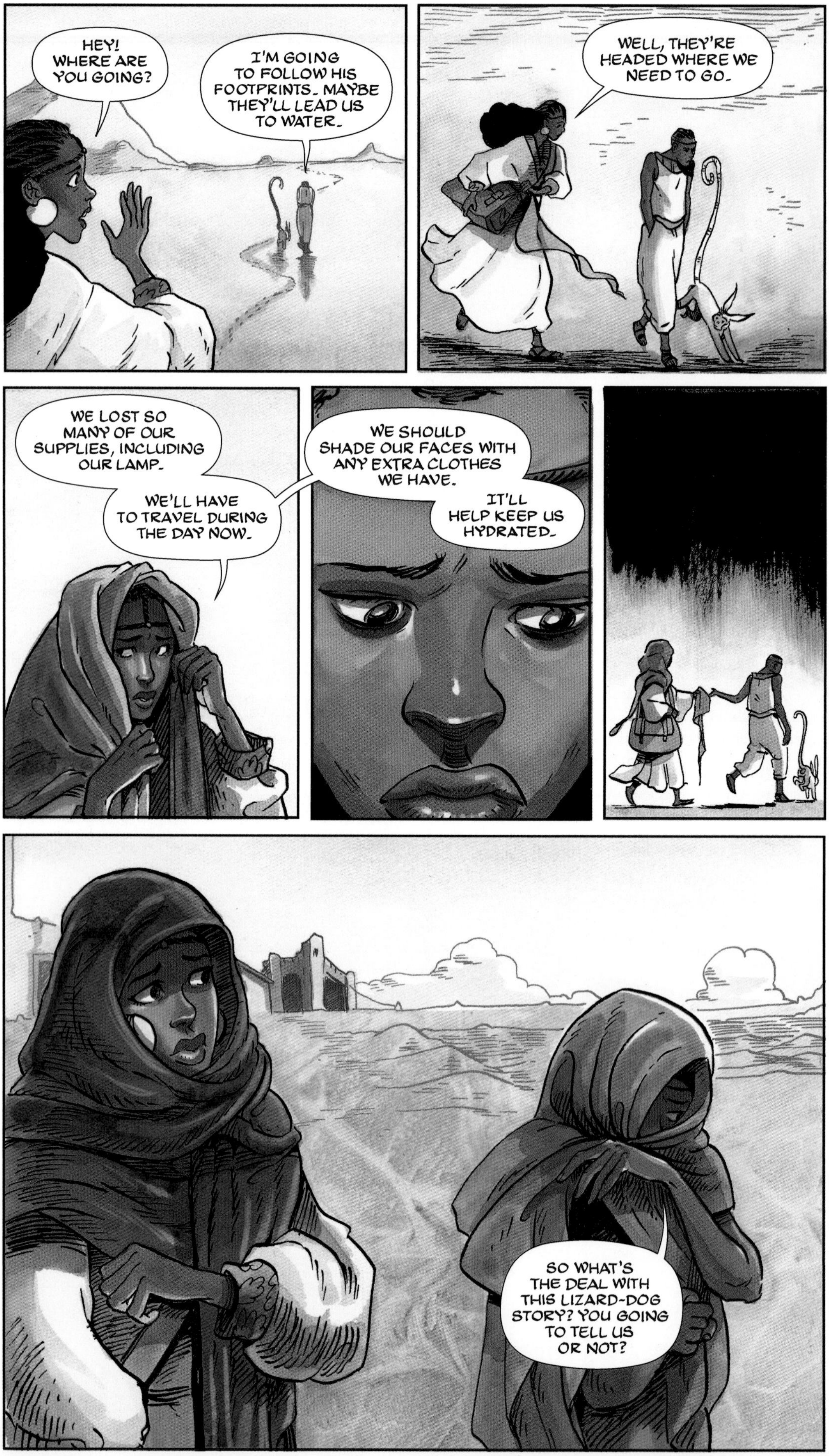
HEY! WHERE ARE YOU GOING?
I'M GOING TO FOLLOW HIS FOOTPRINTS. MAYBE THEY'LL LEAD US TO WATER.
WELL, THEY'RE HEADED WHERE WE NEED TO GO.
WE LOST SO MANY OF OUR SUPPLIES, INCLUDING OUR LAMP.
WE'LL HAVE TO TRAVEL DURING THE DAY NOW.
WE SHOULD SHADE OUR FACES WITH ANY EXTRA CLOTHES WE HAVE.
IT'LL HELP KEEP US HYDRATED.
SO WHAT'S THE DEAL WITH THIS LIZARD-DOG STORY? YOU GOING TO TELL US OR NOT?

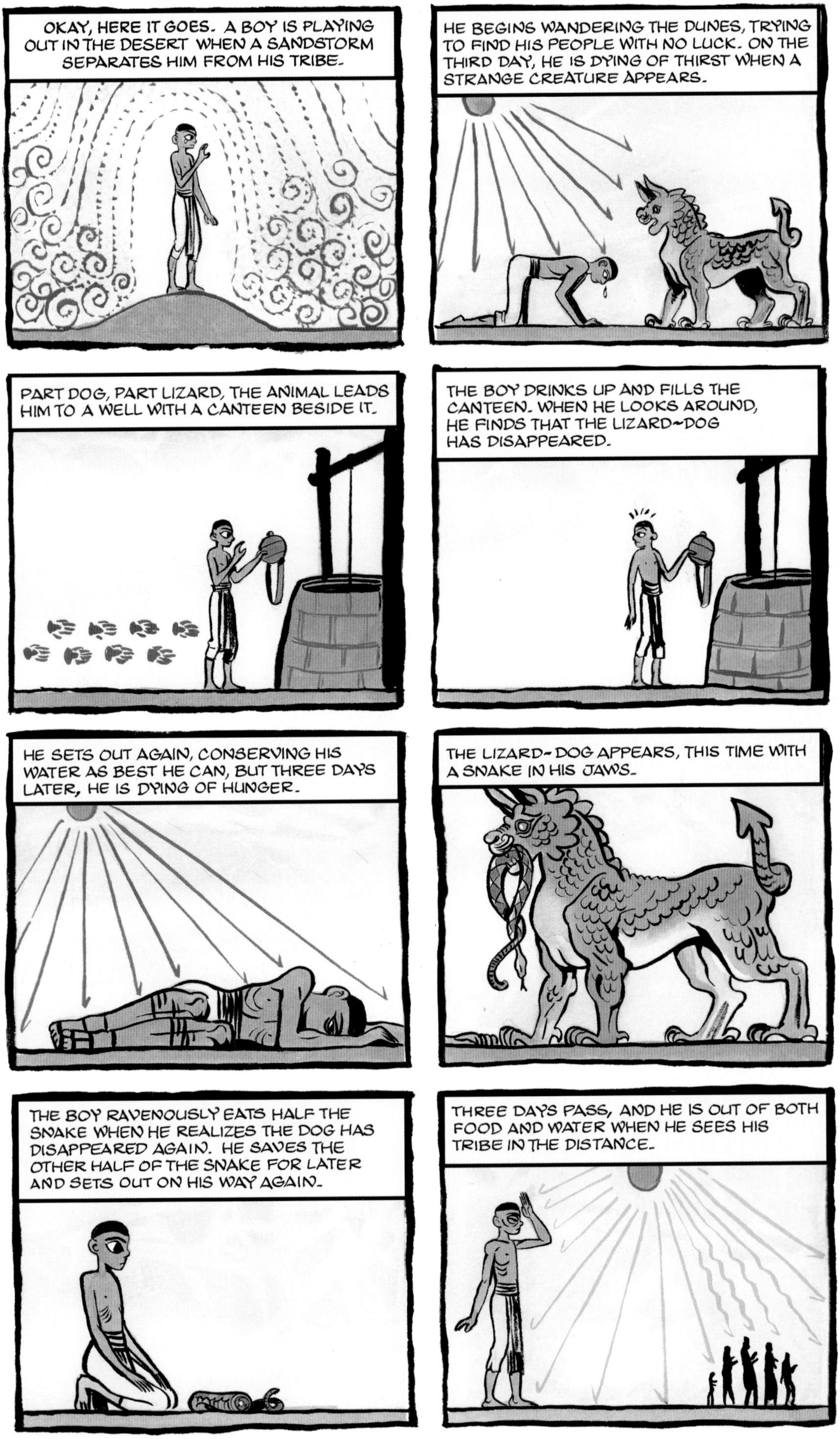
OKAY, HERE IT GOES. A BOY IS PLAYING OUT IN THE DESERT WHEN A SANDSTORM SEPARATES HIM FROM HIS TRIBE.
HE BEGINS WANDERING THE DUNES, TRYING TO FIND HIS PEOPLE WITH NO LUCK. ON THE THIRD DAY, HE IS DYING OF THIRST WHEN A STRANGE CREATURE APPEARS.
PART DOG, PART LIZARD, THE ANIMAL LEADS HIM TO A WELL WITH A CANTEEN BESIDE IT.
THE BOY DRINKS UP AND FILLS THE CANTEEN. WHEN HE LOOKS AROUND, HE FINDS THAT THE LIZARD-DOG HAS DISAPPEARED.
HE SETS OUT AGAIN, CONSERVING HIS WATER AS BEST HE CAN, BUT THREE DAYS LATER, HE IS DYING OF HUNGER.
THE LIZARD-DOG APPEARS, THIS TIME WITH A SNAKE IN HIS JAWS.
THE BOY RAVENOUSLY EATS HALF THE SNAKE WHEN HE REALIZES THE DOG HAS DISAPPEARED AGAIN. HE SAVES THE OTHER HALF OF THE SNAKE FOR LATER AND SETS OUT ON HIS WAY AGAIN.
THREE DAYS PASS, AND HE IS OUT OF BOTH FOOD AND WATER WHEN HE SEES HIS TRIBE IN THE DISTANCE.

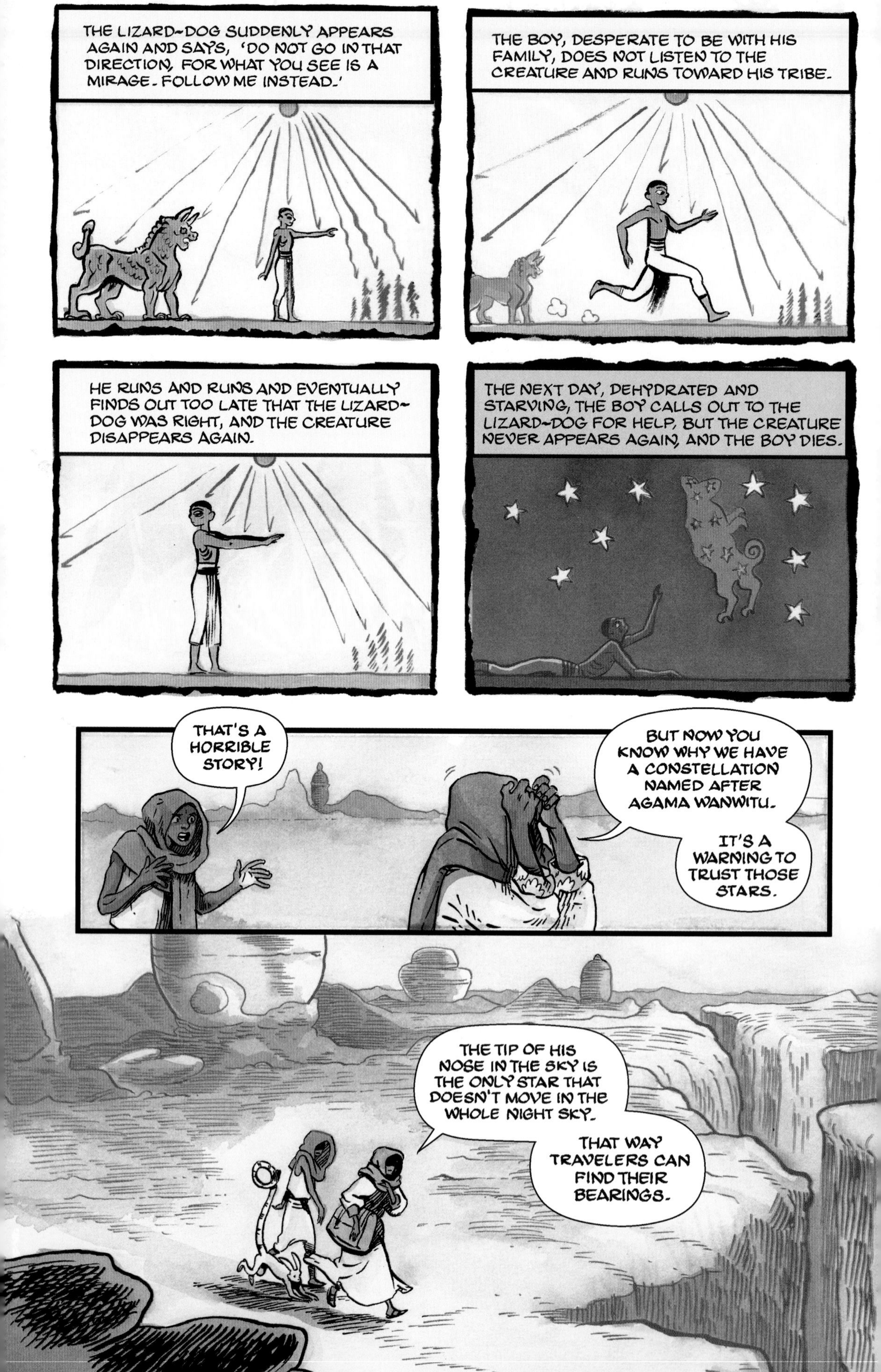
THE LIZARD-DOG SUDDENLY APPEARS AGAIN AND SAYS, 'DO NOT GO IN THAT DIRECTION, FOR WHAT YOU SEE IS A MIRAGE. FOLLOW ME INSTEAD.'
THE BOY, DESPERATE TO BE WITH HIS FAMILY, DOES NOT LISTEN TO THE CREATURE AND RUNS TOWARD HIS TRIBE.
HE RUNS AND RUNS AND EVENTUALLY FINDS OUT TOO LATE THAT THE LIZARD-DOG WAS RIGHT, AND THE CREATURE DISAPPEARS AGAIN.
THE NEXT DAY, DEHYDRATED AND STARVING, THE BOY CALLS OUT TO THE LIZARD-DOG FOR HELP, BUT THE CREATURE NEVER APPEARS AGAIN, AND THE BOY DIES.
THAT'S A HORRIBLE STORY!
BUT NOW YOU KNOW WHY WE HAVE A CONSTELLATION NAMED AFTER AGAMA WANWITU.
IT'S A WARNING TO TRUST THOSE STARS.
THE TIP OF HIS NOSE IN THE SKY IS THE ONLY STAR THAT DOESN'T MOVE IN THE WHOLE NIGHT SKY.
THAT WAY TRAVELERS CAN FIND THEIR BEARINGS.

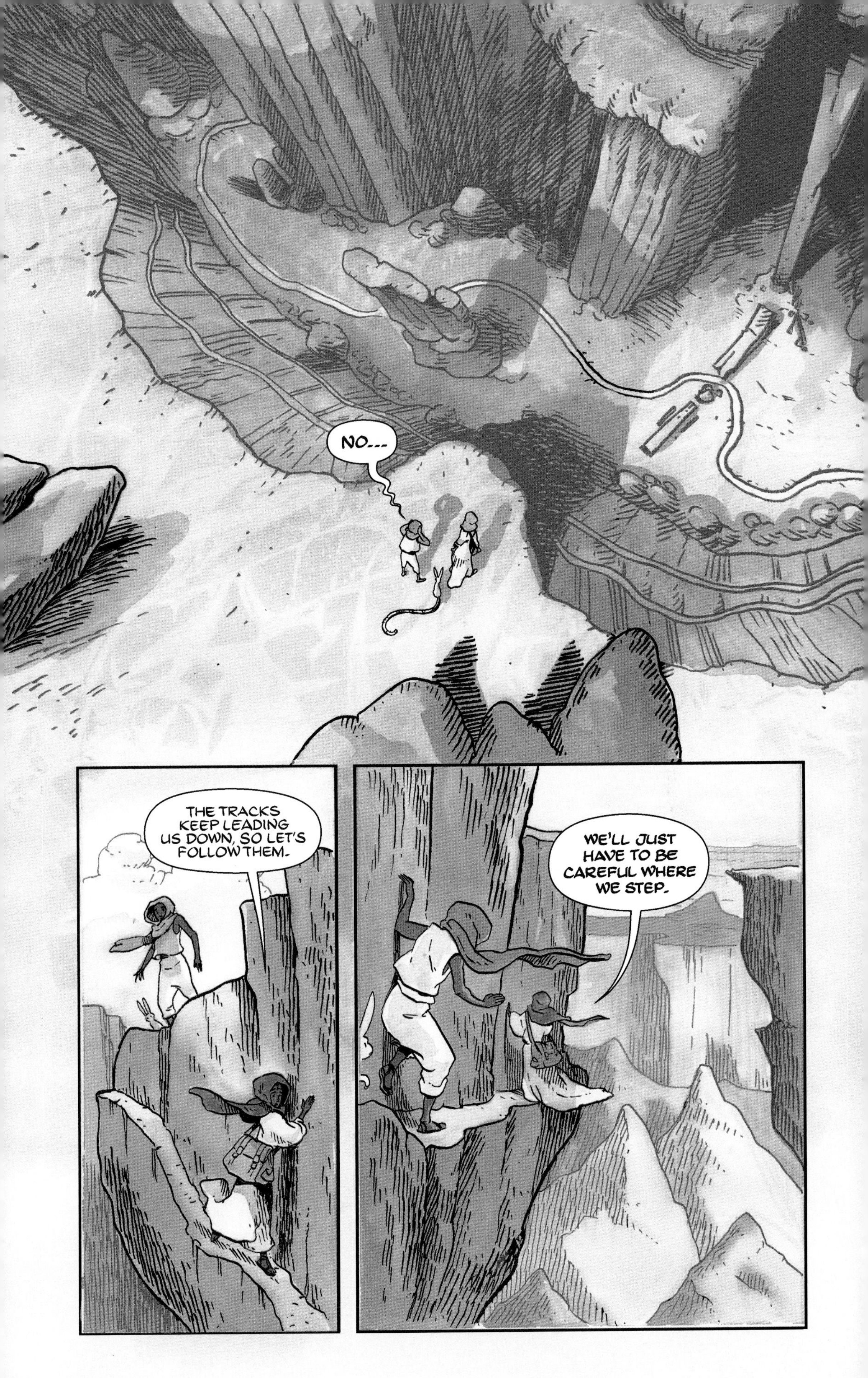
NO...
THE TRACKS KEEP LEADING US DOWN, SO LET'S FOLLOW THEM.
WE'LL JUST HAVE TO BE CAREFUL WHERE WE STEP.

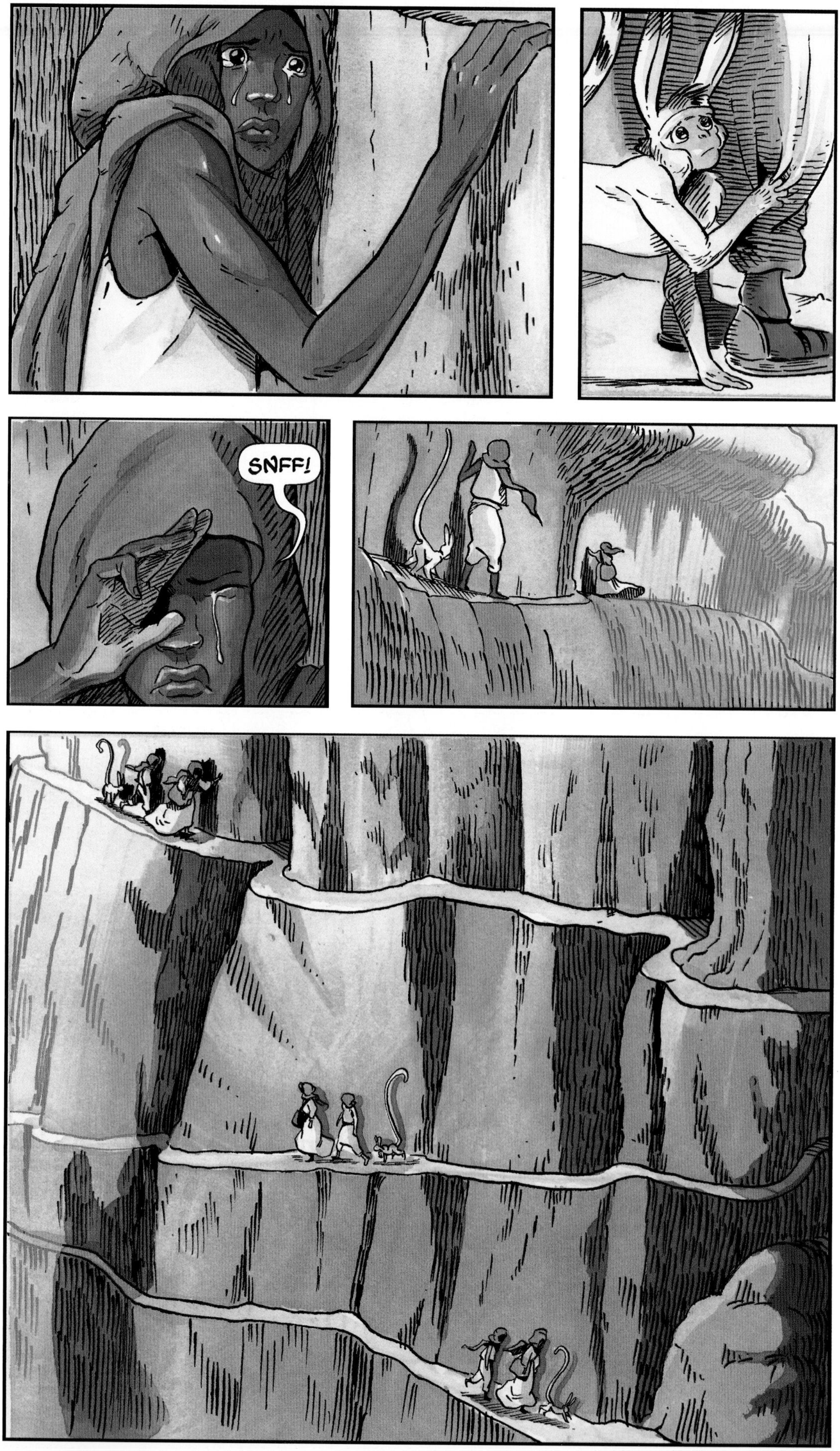
SNFF!

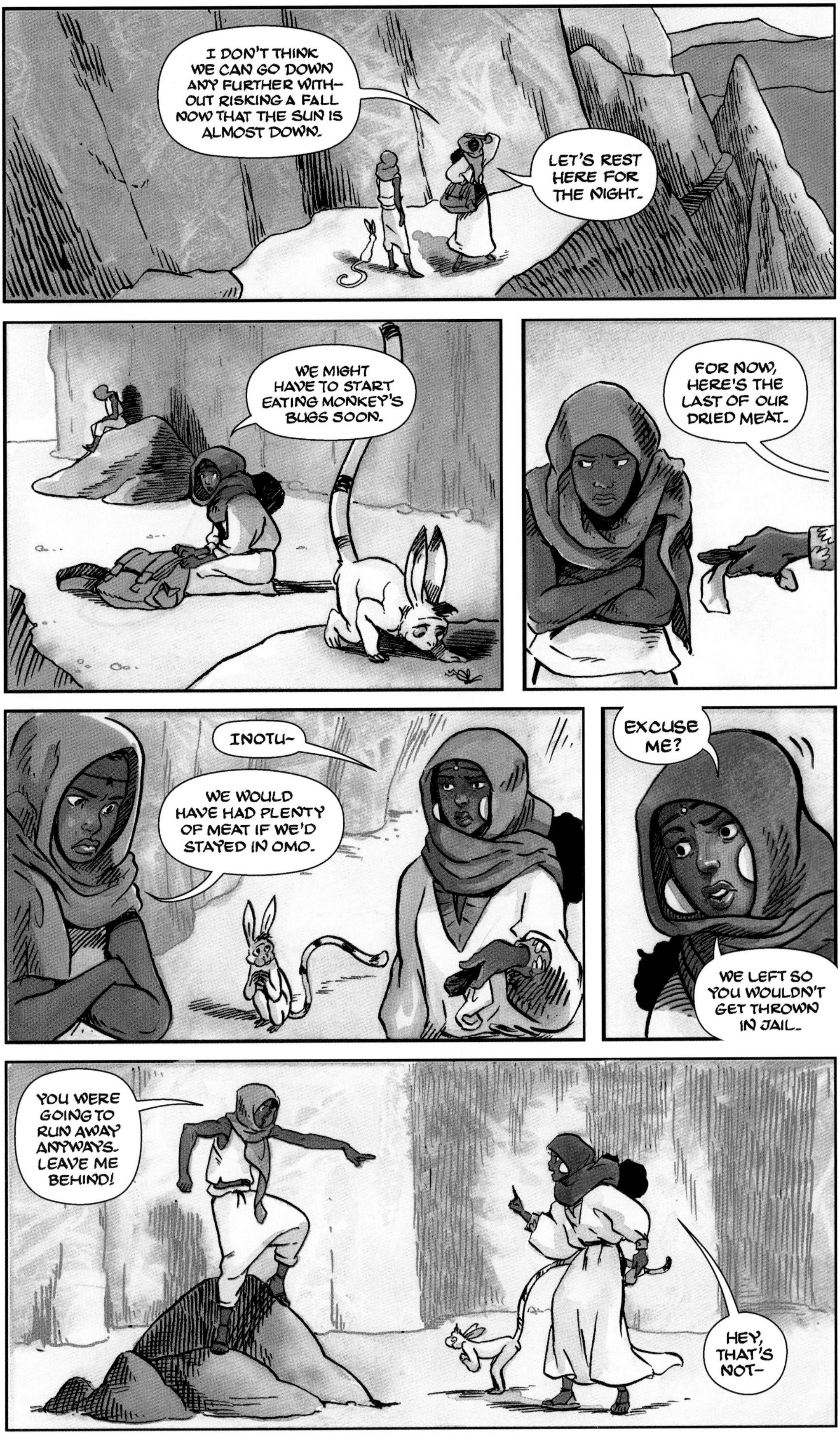
I DON'T THINK WE CAN GO DOWN ANY FURTHER WITH-OUT RISKING A FALL NOW THAT THE SUN IS ALMOST DOWN.
LET'S REST HERE FOR THE NIGHT.
WE MIGHT HAVE TO START EATING MONKEY'S BUGS SOON.
FOR NOW, HERE'S THE LAST OF OUR DRIED MEAT.
INOTU-
WE WOULD HAVE HAD PLENTY OF MEAT IF WE'D STAYED IN OMO.
EXCUSE ME?
WE LEFT SO YOU WOULDN'T GET THROWN IN JAIL.
YOU WERE GOING TO RUN AWAY ANYWAYS. LEAVE ME BEHIND!
HEY, THAT'S NOT-

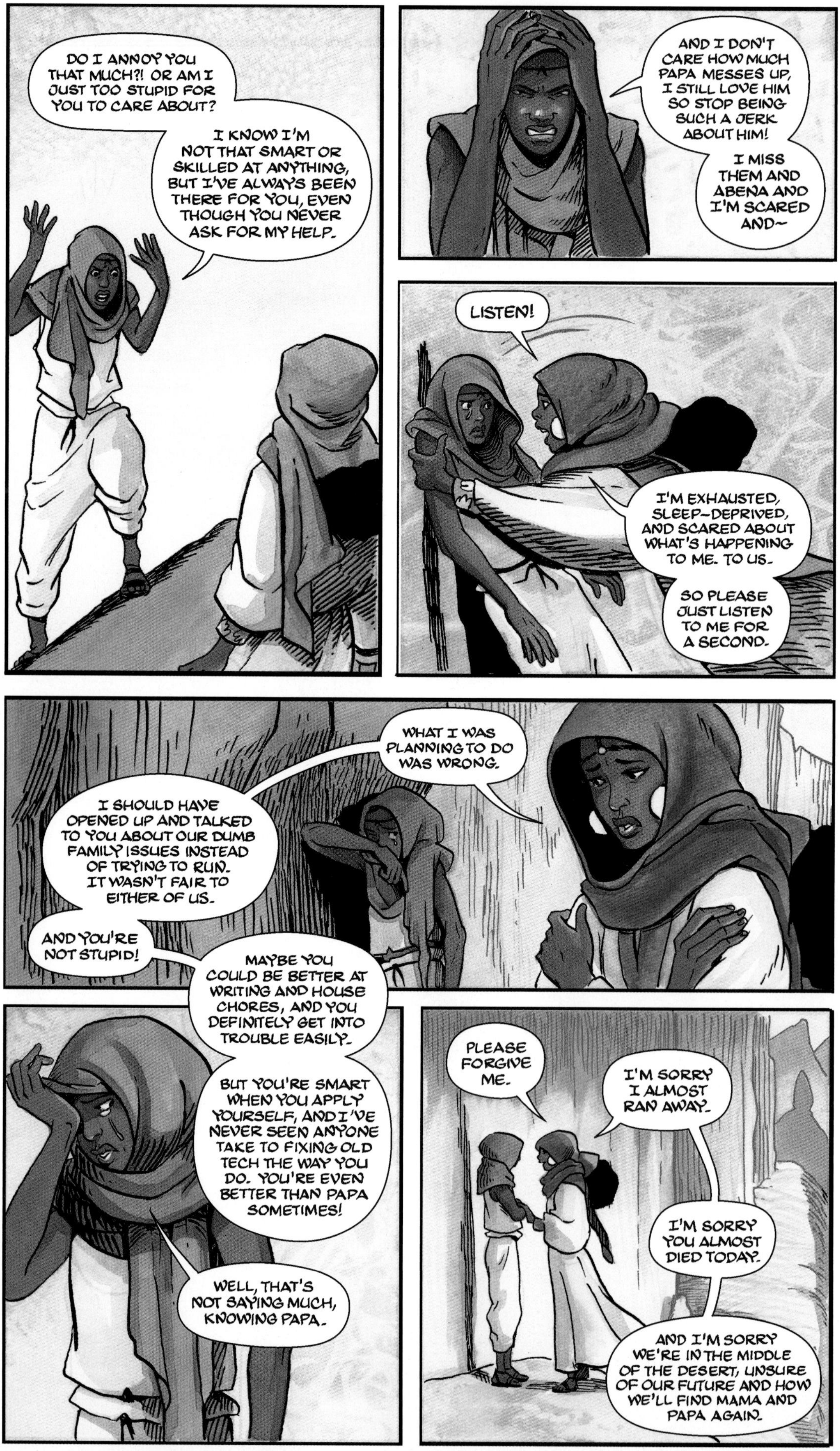
DO I ANNOY YOU THAT MUCH?! OR AM I JUST TOO STUPID FOR YOU TO CARE ABOUT?
I KNOW I'M NOT THAT SMART OR SKILLED AT ANYTHING, BUT I'VE ALWAYS BEEN THERE FOR YOU, EVEN THOUGH YOU NEVER ASK FOR MY HELP.
AND I DON'T CARE HOW MUCH PAPA MESSES UP, I STILL LOVE HIM SO STOP BEING SUCH A JERK ABOUT HIM!
I MISS THEM AND ABENA AND I'M SCARED AND~
LISTEN!
I'M EXHAUSTED, SLEEP-DEPRIVED, AND SCARED ABOUT WHAT'S HAPPENING TO ME. TO US.
SO PLEASE JUST LISTEN TO ME FOR A SECOND.
WHAT I WAS PLANNING TO DO WAS WRONG.
I SHOULD HAVE OPENED UP AND TALKED TO YOU ABOUT OUR DUMB FAMILY ISSUES INSTEAD OF TRYING TO RUN. IT WASN'T FAIR TO EITHER OF US.
AND YOU'RE NOT STUPID!
MAYBE YOU COULD BE BETTER AT WRITING AND HOUSE CHORES, AND YOU DEFINITELY GET INTO TROUBLE EASILY.
BUT YOU'RE SMART WHEN YOU APPLY YOURSELF, AND I'VE NEVER SEEN ANYONE TAKE TO FIXING OLD TECH THE WAY YOU DO. YOU'RE EVEN BETTER THAN PAPA SOMETIMES!
WELL, THAT'S NOT SAYING MUCH, KNOWING PAPA.
PLEASE FORGIVE ME.
I'M SORRY I ALMOST RAN AWAY.
I'M SORRY YOU ALMOST DIED TODAY.
AND I'M SORRY WE'RE IN THE MIDDLE OF THE DESERT, UNSURE OF OUR FUTURE AND HOW WE'LL FIND MAMA AND PAPA AGAIN.

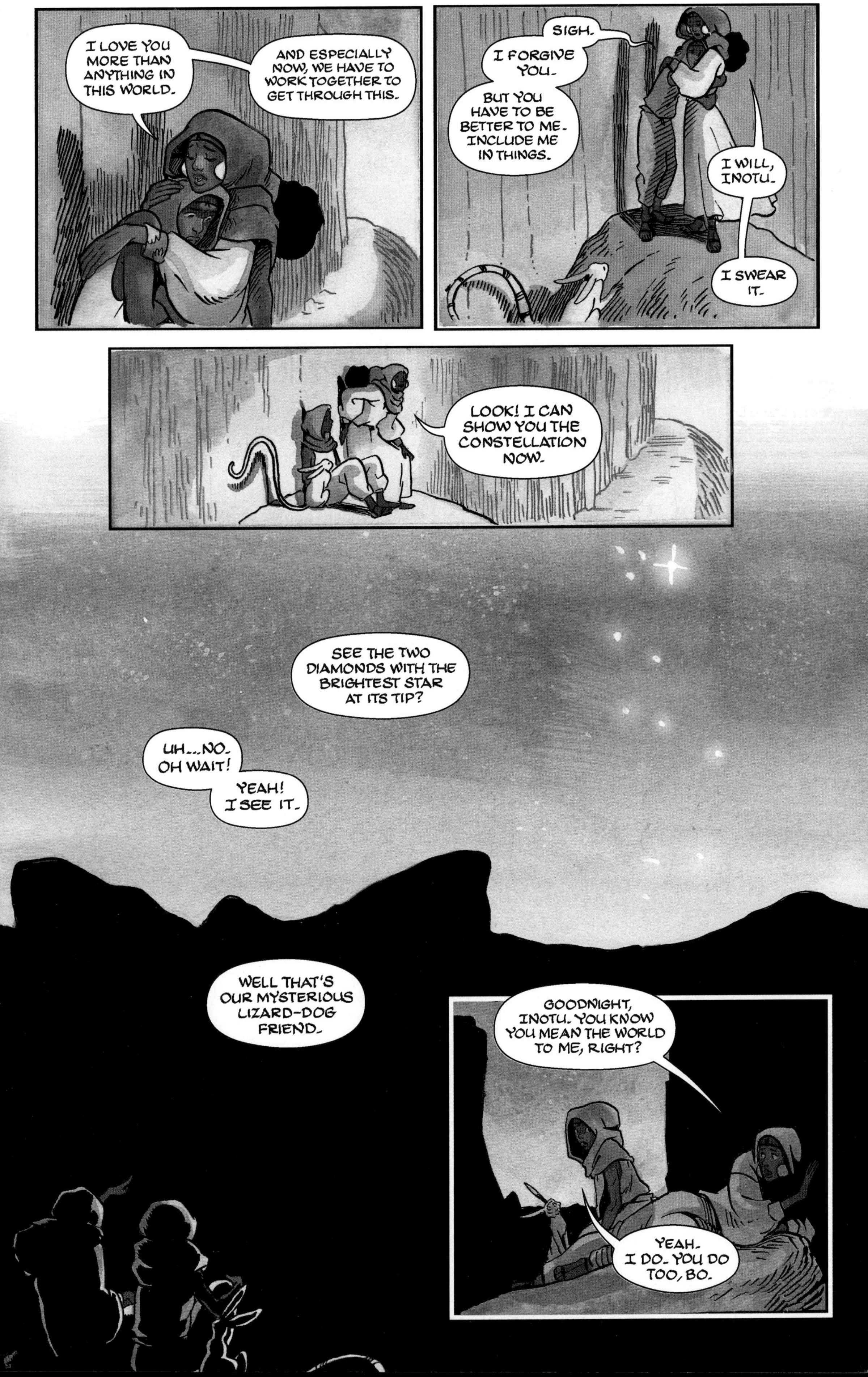
I LOVE YOU MORE THAN ANYTHING IN THIS WORLD.
AND ESPECIALLY NOW, WE HAVE TO WORK TOGETHER TO GET THROUGH THIS.
SIGH.
I FORGIVE YOU.
BUT YOU HAVE TO BE BETTER TO ME. INCLUDE ME IN THINGS.
I WILL, INOTU.
I SWEAR IT.
LOOK! I CAN SHOW YOU THE CONSTELLATION NOW.
SEE THE TWO DIAMONDS WITH THE BRIGHTEST STAR AT ITS TIP?
UH...NO. OH WAIT!
YEAH! I SEE IT.
WELL THAT'S OUR MYSTERIOUS LIZARD-DOG FRIEND.
GOODNIGHT, INOTU. YOU KNOW YOU MEAN THE WORLD TO ME, RIGHT?
YEAH. I DO. YOU DO TOO, BO.

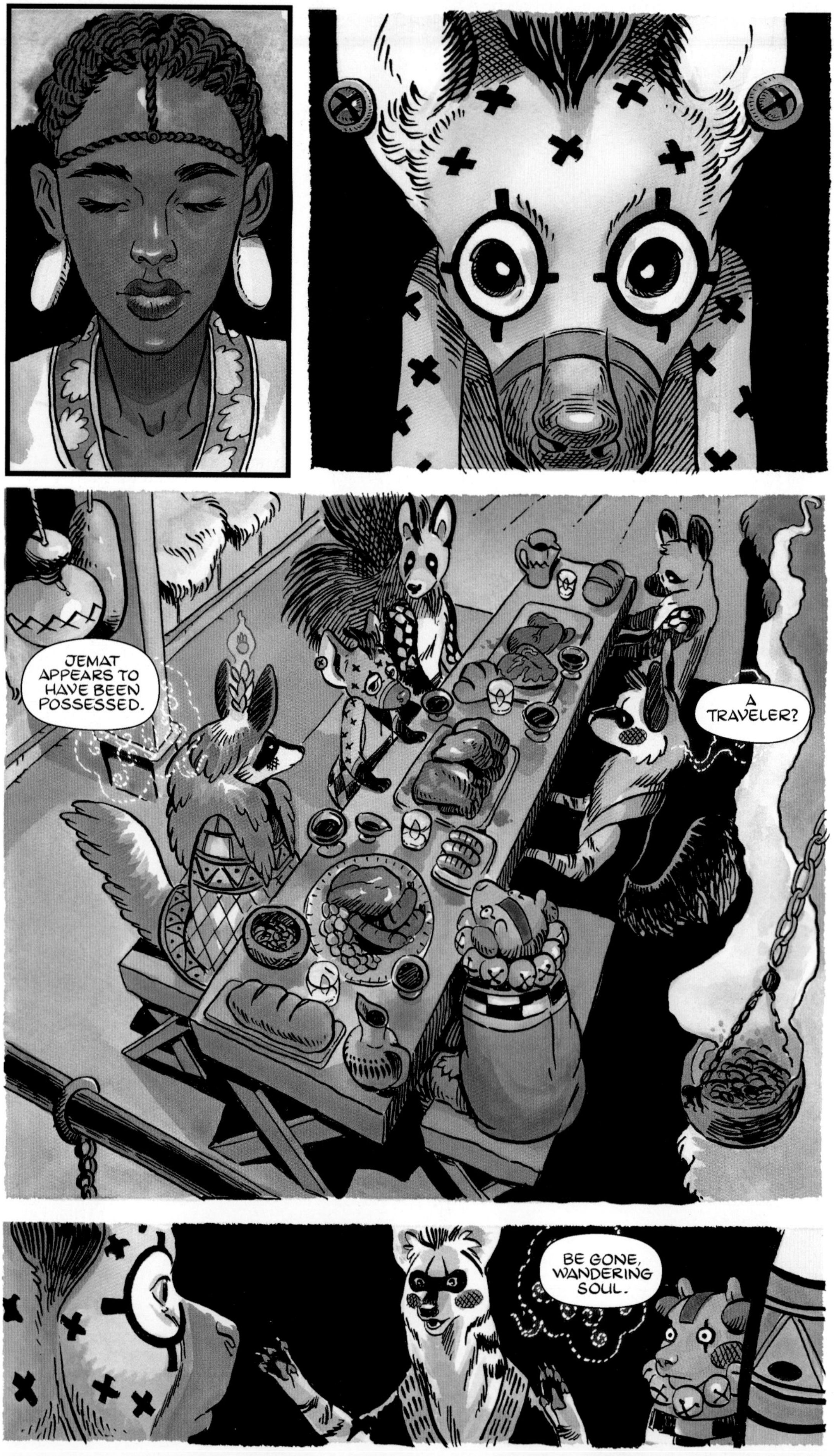
JEMAT APPEARS TO HAVE BEEN POSSESSED.
A TRAVELER?
BE GONE, WANDERING SOUL.

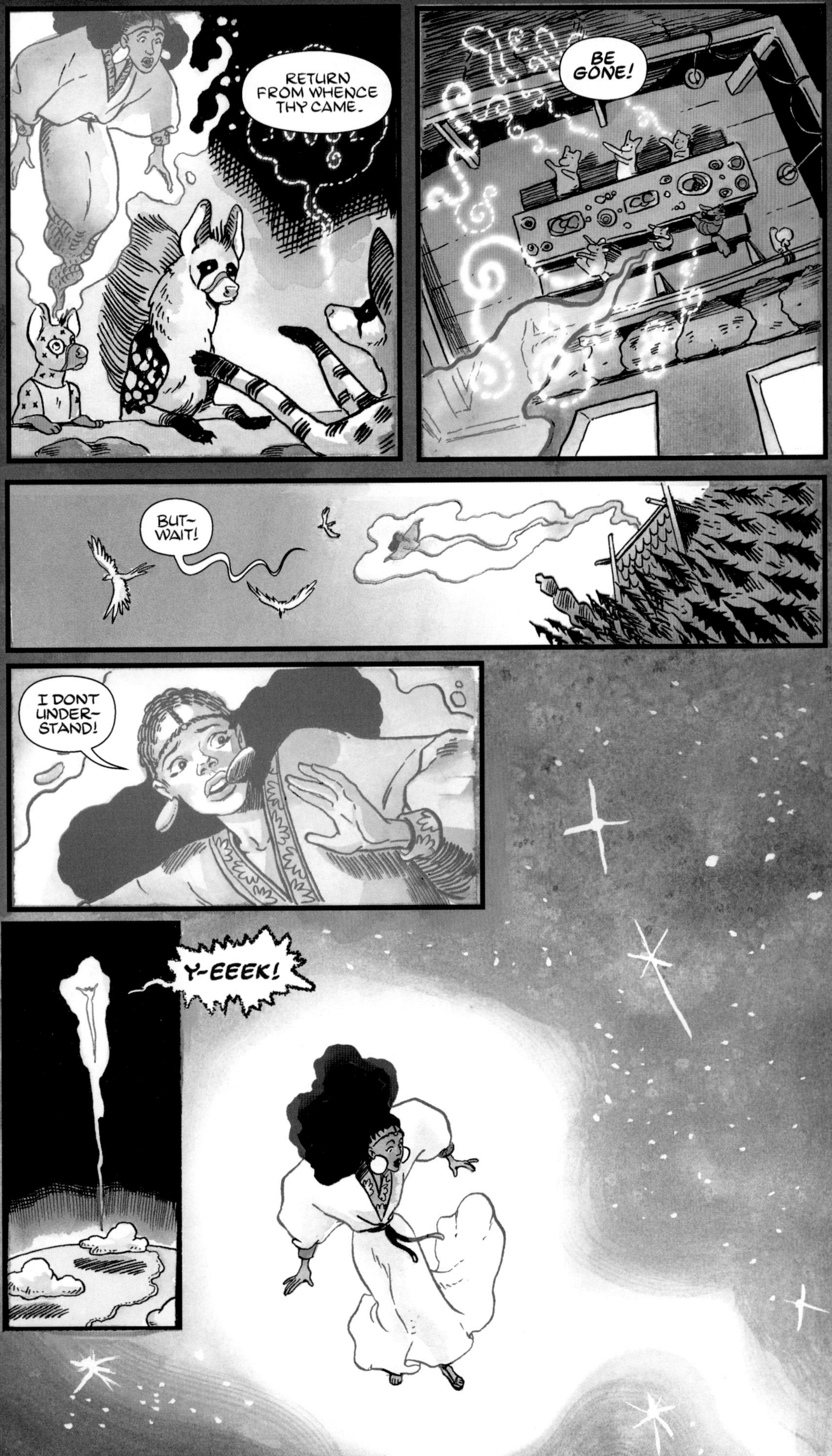
RETURN FROM WHENCE THY CAME.
BE GONE!
BUT— WAIT!
I DONT UNDER-STAND!
Y-EEEK!

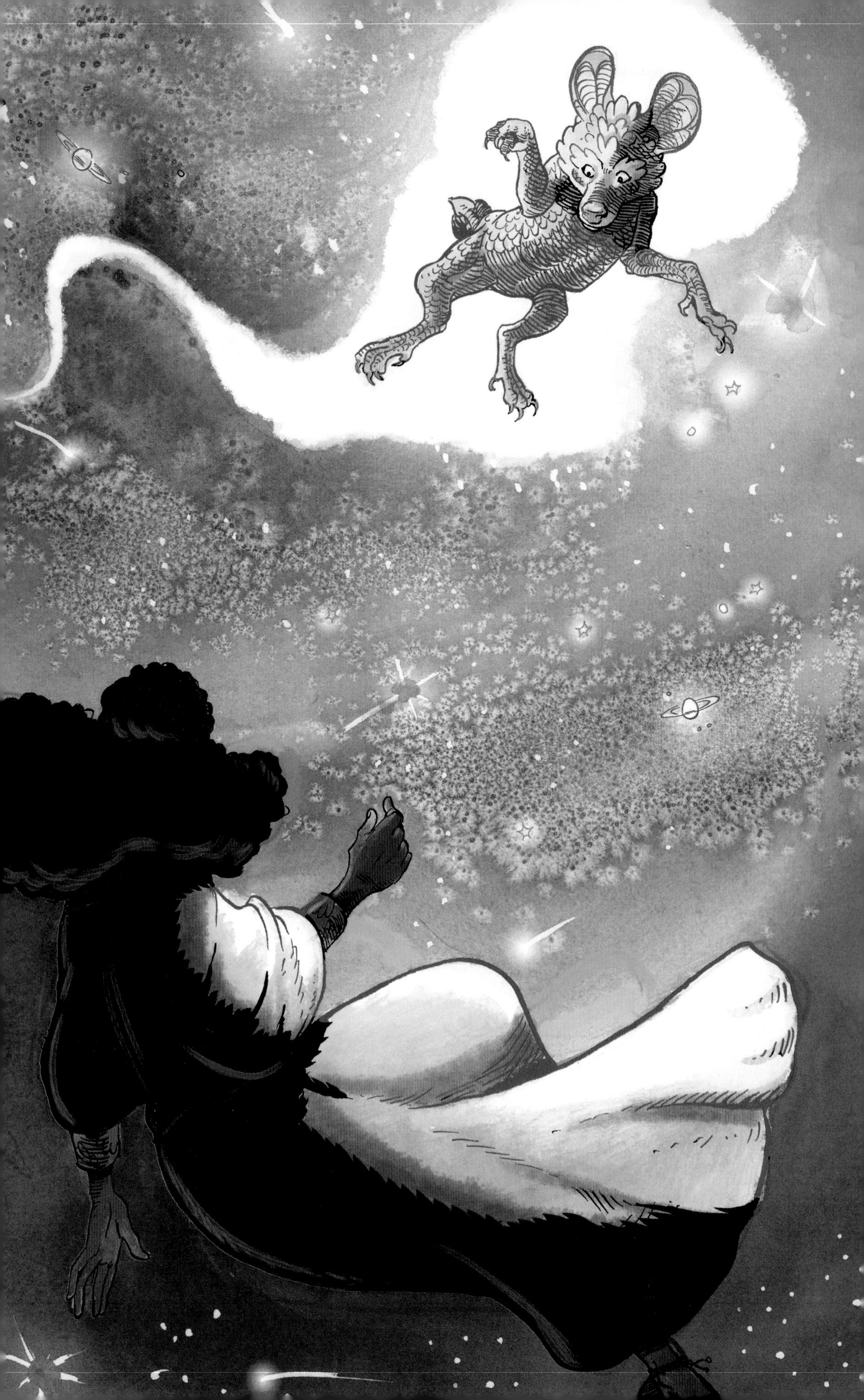

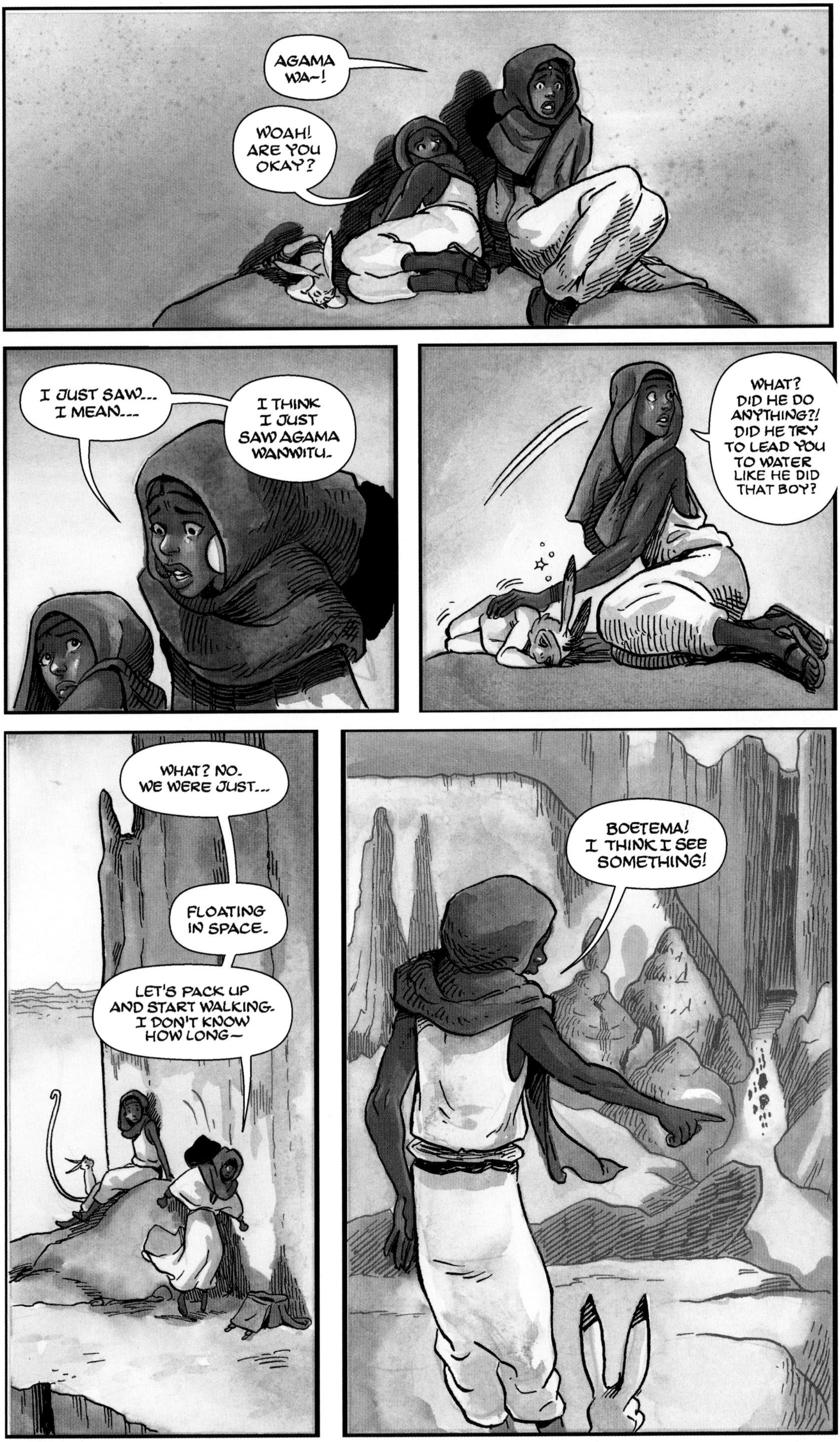
AGAMA WA-!
WOAH! ARE YOU OKAY?
I JUST SAW... I MEAN...
I THINK I JUST SAW AGAMA WANWITU.
WHAT? DID HE DO ANYTHING?! DID HE TRY TO LEAD YOU TO WATER LIKE HE DID THAT BOY?
WHAT? NO. WE WERE JUST...
FLOATING IN SPACE.
LET'S PACK UP AND START WALKING. I DON'T KNOW HOW LONG—
BOETEMA! I THINK I SEE SOMETHING!

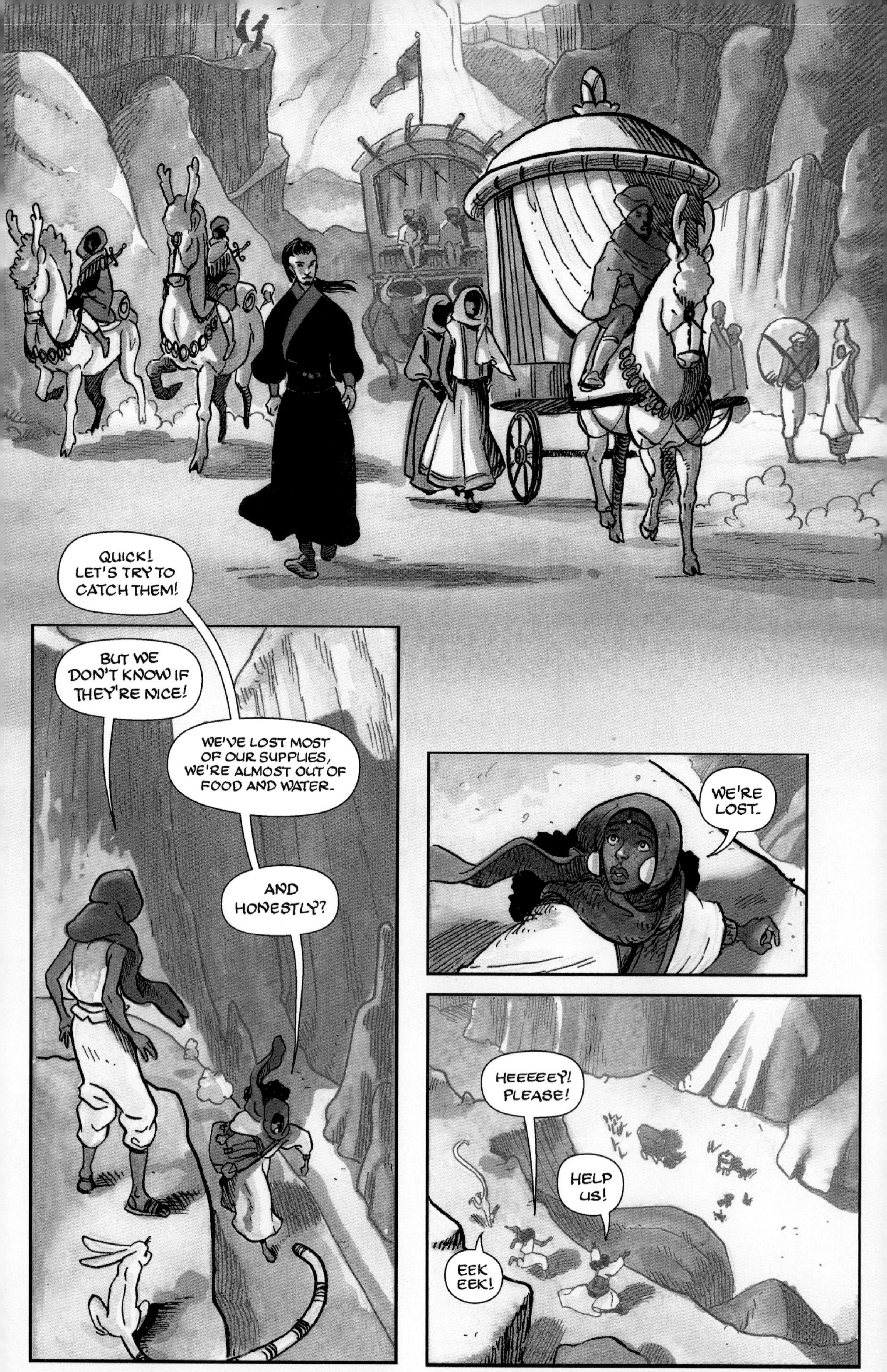
QUICK! LET'S TRY TO CATCH THEM!
BUT WE DON'T KNOW IF THEY'RE NICE!
WE'VE LOST MOST OF OUR SUPPLIES, WE'RE ALMOST OUT OF FOOD AND WATER.
AND HONESTLY?
WE'RE LOST.
HEEEEEY! PLEASE!
HELP US!
EEK EEK!

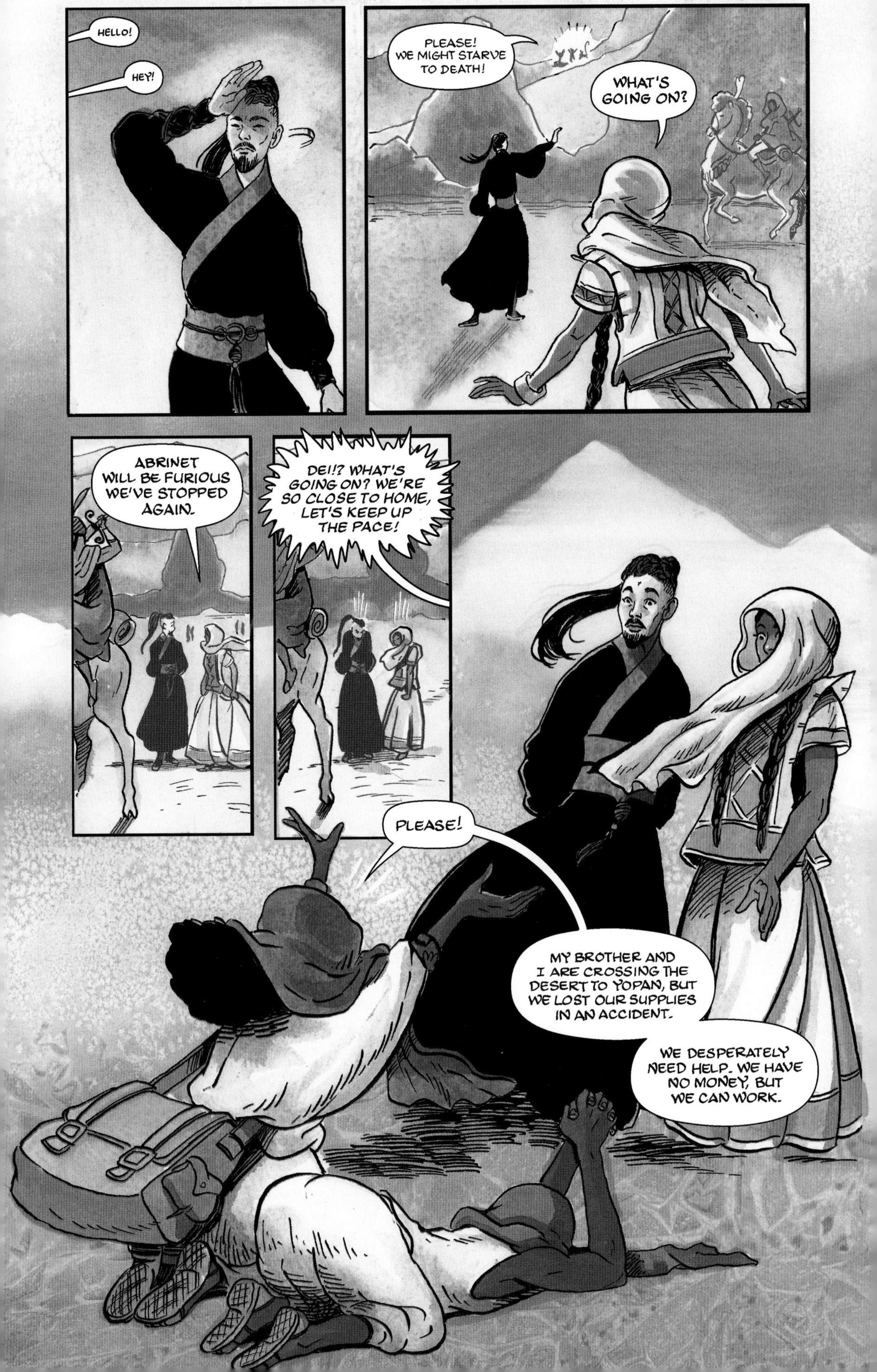
HELLO!
HEY!
PLEASE! WE MIGHT STARVE TO DEATH!
WHAT'S GOING ON?
ABRINET WILL BE FURIOUS WE'VE STOPPED AGAIN.
DEI!? WHAT'S GOING ON? WE'RE SO CLOSE TO HOME, LET'S KEEP UP THE PACE!
PLEASE!
MY BROTHER AND I ARE CROSSING THE DESERT TO YOPAN, BUT WE LOST OUR SUPPLIES IN AN ACCIDENT.
WE DESPERATELY NEED HELP. WE HAVE NO MONEY, BUT WE CAN WORK.

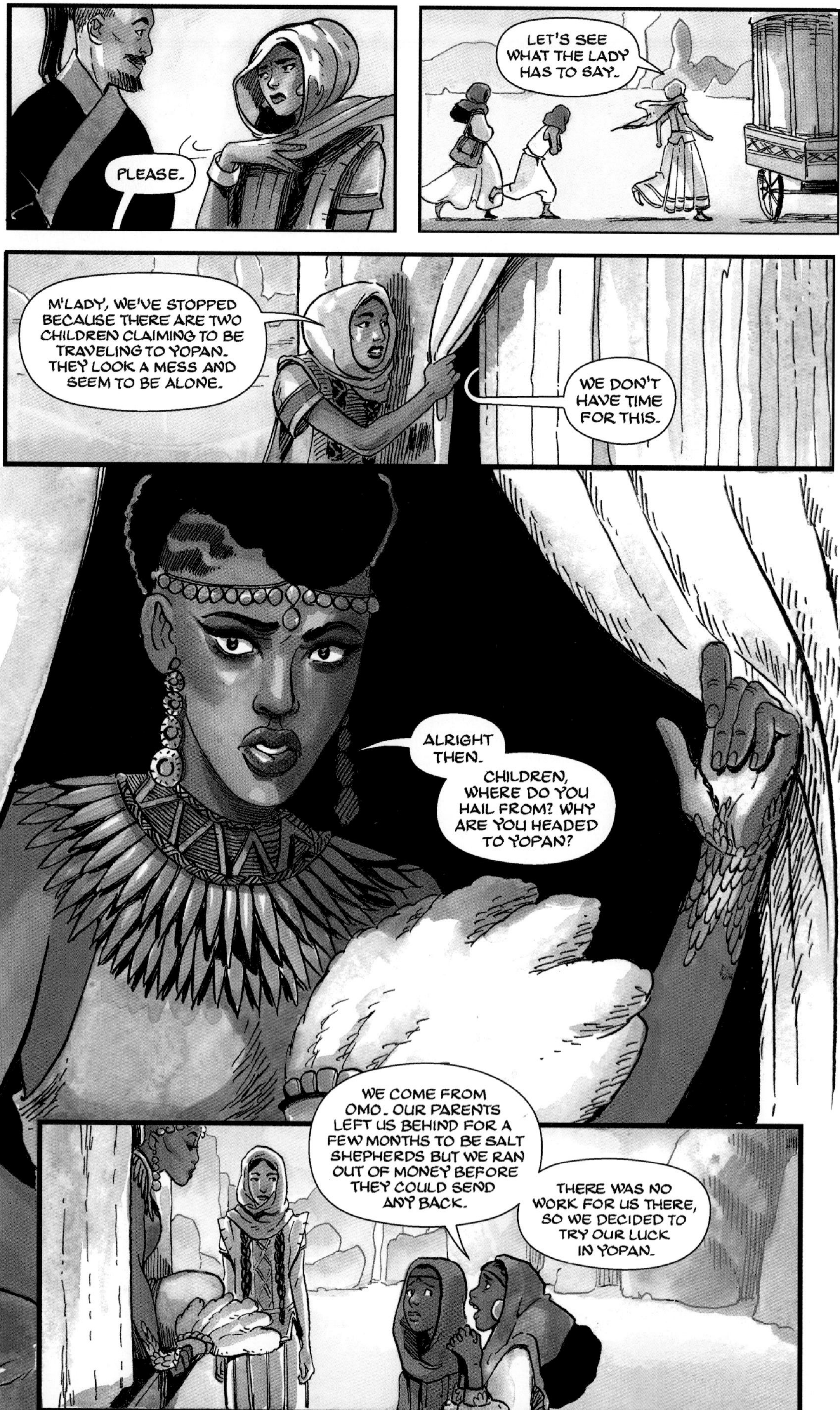
PLEASE.
LET'S SEE WHAT THE LADY HAS TO SAY.
M'LADY, WE'VE STOPPED BECAUSE THERE ARE TWO CHILDREN CLAIMING TO BE TRAVELING TO YOPAN. THEY LOOK A MESS AND SEEM TO BE ALONE.
WE DON'T HAVE TIME FOR THIS.
ALRIGHT THEN.
CHILDREN, WHERE DO YOU HAIL FROM? WHY ARE YOU HEADED TO YOPAN?
WE COME FROM OMO. OUR PARENTS LEFT US BEHIND FOR A FEW MONTHS TO BE SALT SHEPHERDS BUT WE RAN OUT OF MONEY BEFORE THEY COULD SEND ANY BACK.
THERE WAS NO WORK FOR US THERE, SO WE DECIDED TO TRY OUR LUCK IN YOPAN.

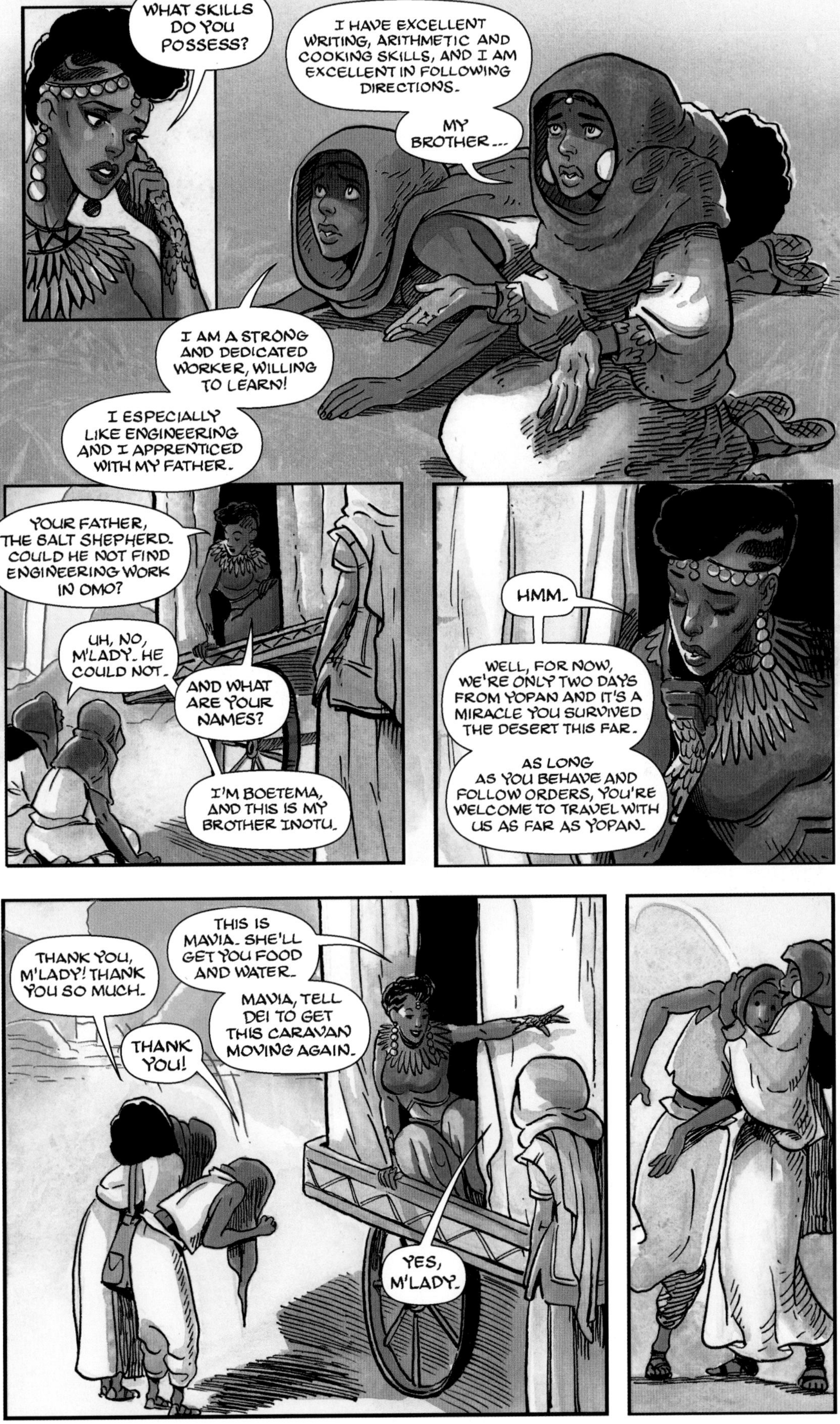
WHAT SKILLS DO YOU POSSESS?
I HAVE EXCELLENT WRITING, ARITHMETIC AND COOKING SKILLS, AND I AM EXCELLENT IN FOLLOWING DIRECTIONS.
MY BROTHER...
I AM A STRONG AND DEDICATED WORKER, WILLING TO LEARN!
I ESPECIALLY LIKE ENGINEERING AND I APPRENTICED WITH MY FATHER.
YOUR FATHER, THE SALT SHEPHERD. COULD HE NOT FIND ENGINEERING WORK IN OMO?
UH, NO, M'LADY. HE COULD NOT.
AND WHAT ARE YOUR NAMES?
I'M BOETEMA, AND THIS IS MY BROTHER INOTU.
HMM.
WELL, FOR NOW, WE'RE ONLY TWO DAYS FROM YOPAN AND IT'S A MIRACLE YOU SURVIVED THE DESERT THIS FAR.
AS LONG AS YOU BEHAVE AND FOLLOW ORDERS, YOU'RE WELCOME TO TRAVEL WITH US AS FAR AS YOPAN.
THANK YOU, M'LADY! THANK YOU SO MUCH.
THANK YOU!
THIS IS MAVIA. SHE'LL GET YOU FOOD AND WATER.
MAVIA, TELL DEI TO GET THIS CARAVAN MOVING AGAIN.
YES, M'LADY.

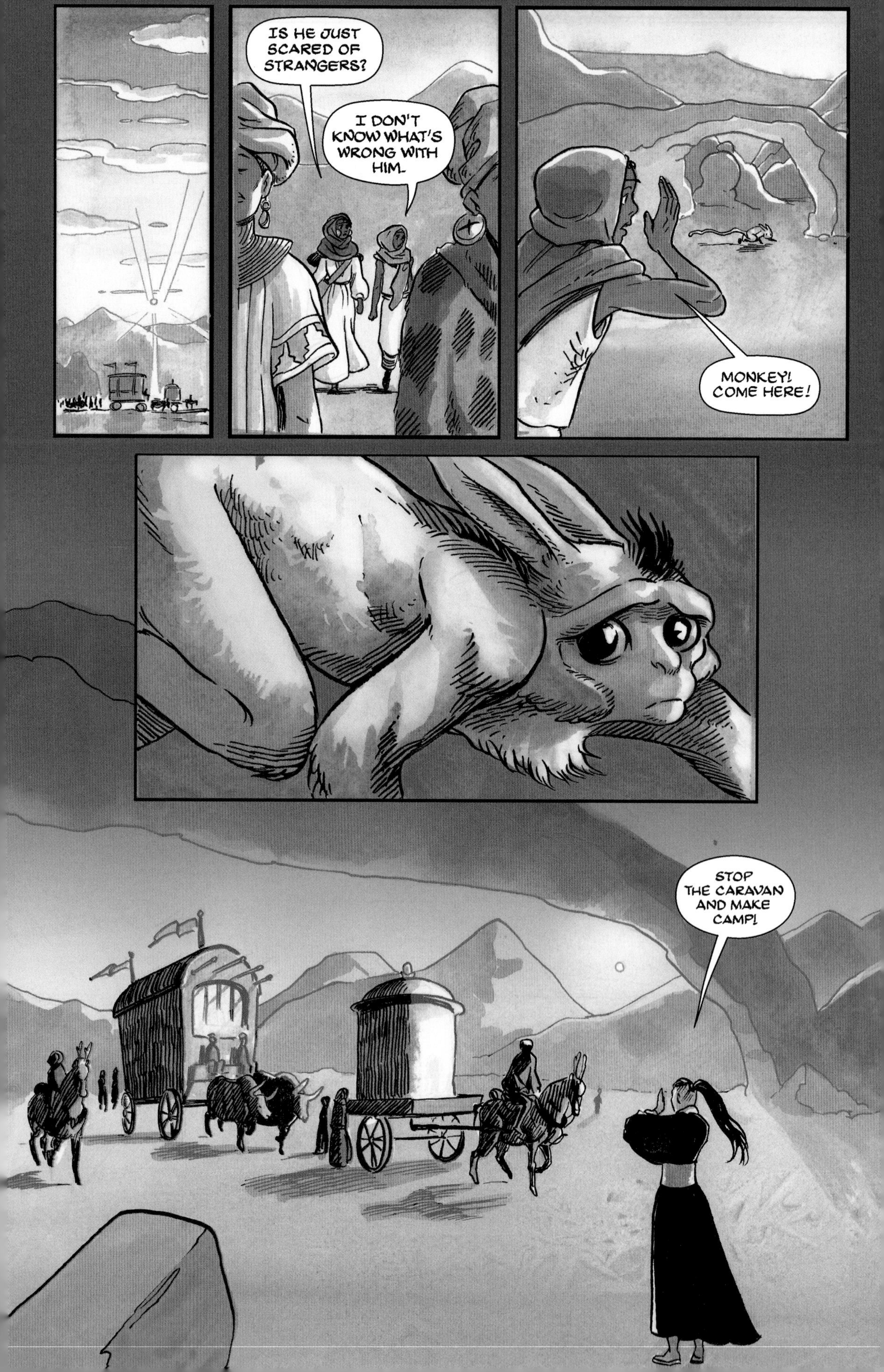
IS HE JUST SCARED OF STRANGERS?
I DON'T KNOW WHAT'S WRONG WITH HIM.
MONKEY! COME HERE!
STOP THE CARAVAN AND MAKE CAMP!

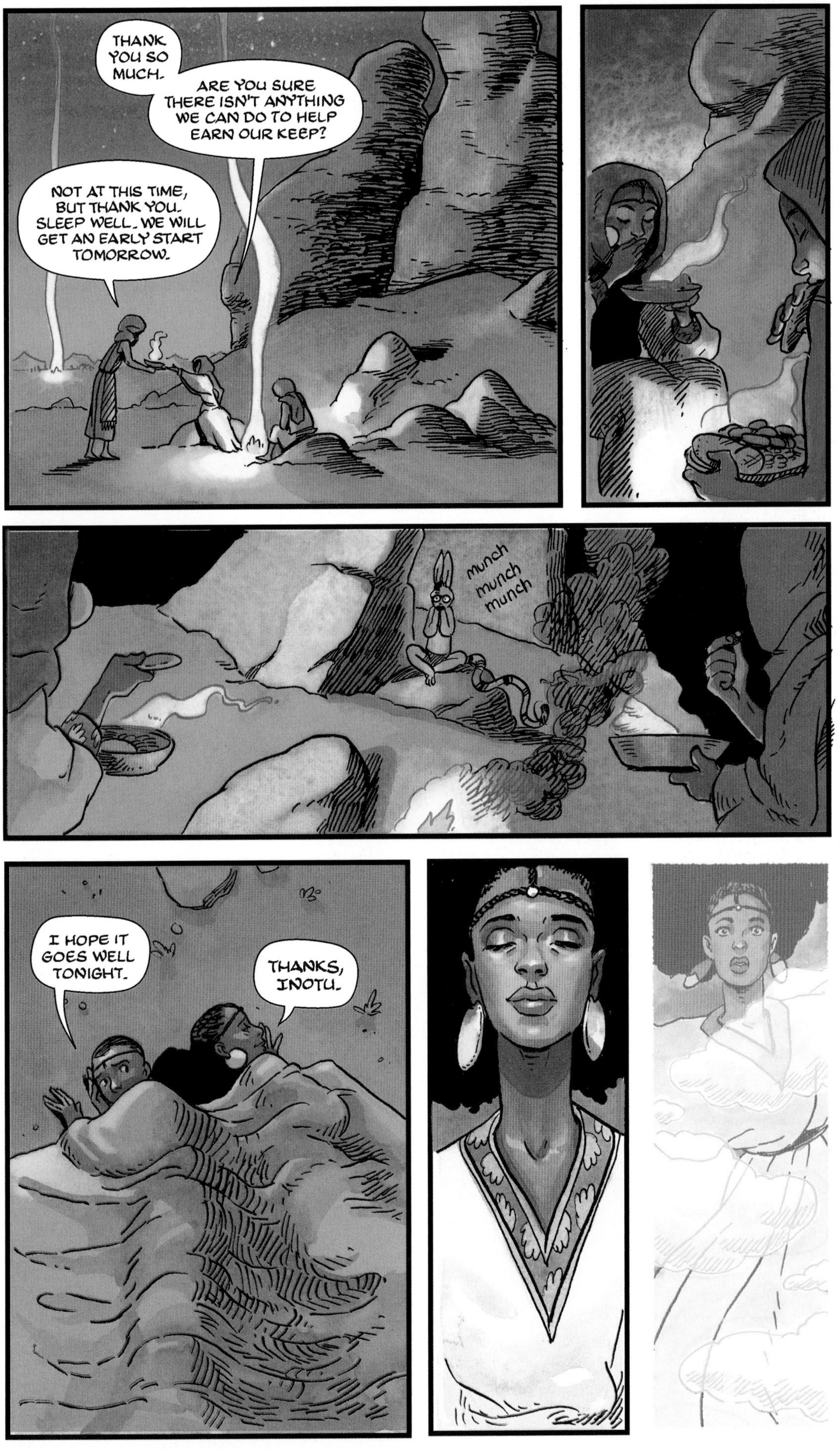
THANK YOU SO MUCH.
ARE YOU SURE THERE ISN'T ANYTHING WE CAN DO TO HELP EARN OUR KEEP?
NOT AT THIS TIME, BUT THANK YOU. SLEEP WELL. WE WILL GET AN EARLY START TOMORROW.
munch munch munch
I HOPE IT GOES WELL TONIGHT.
THANKS, INOTU.

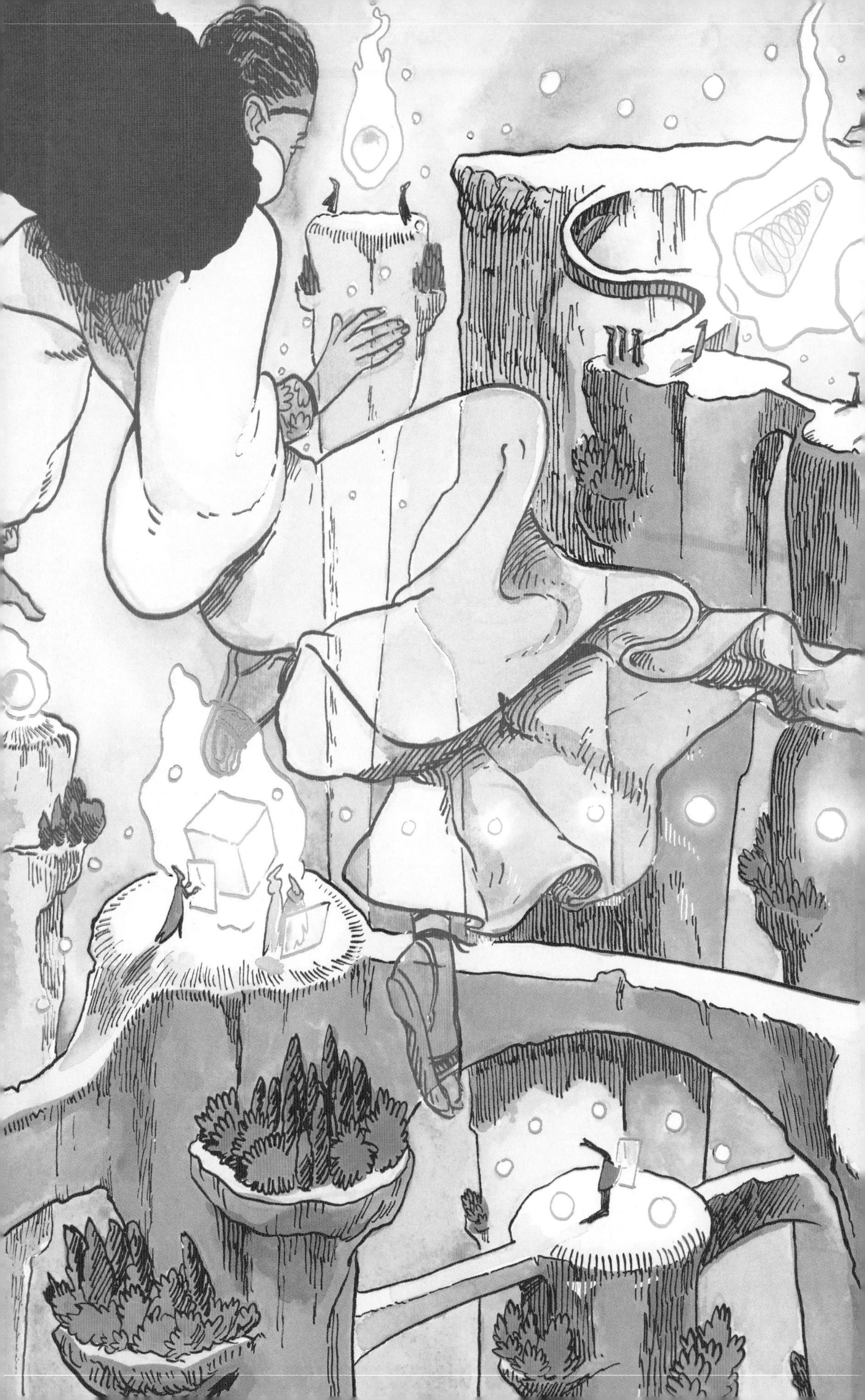

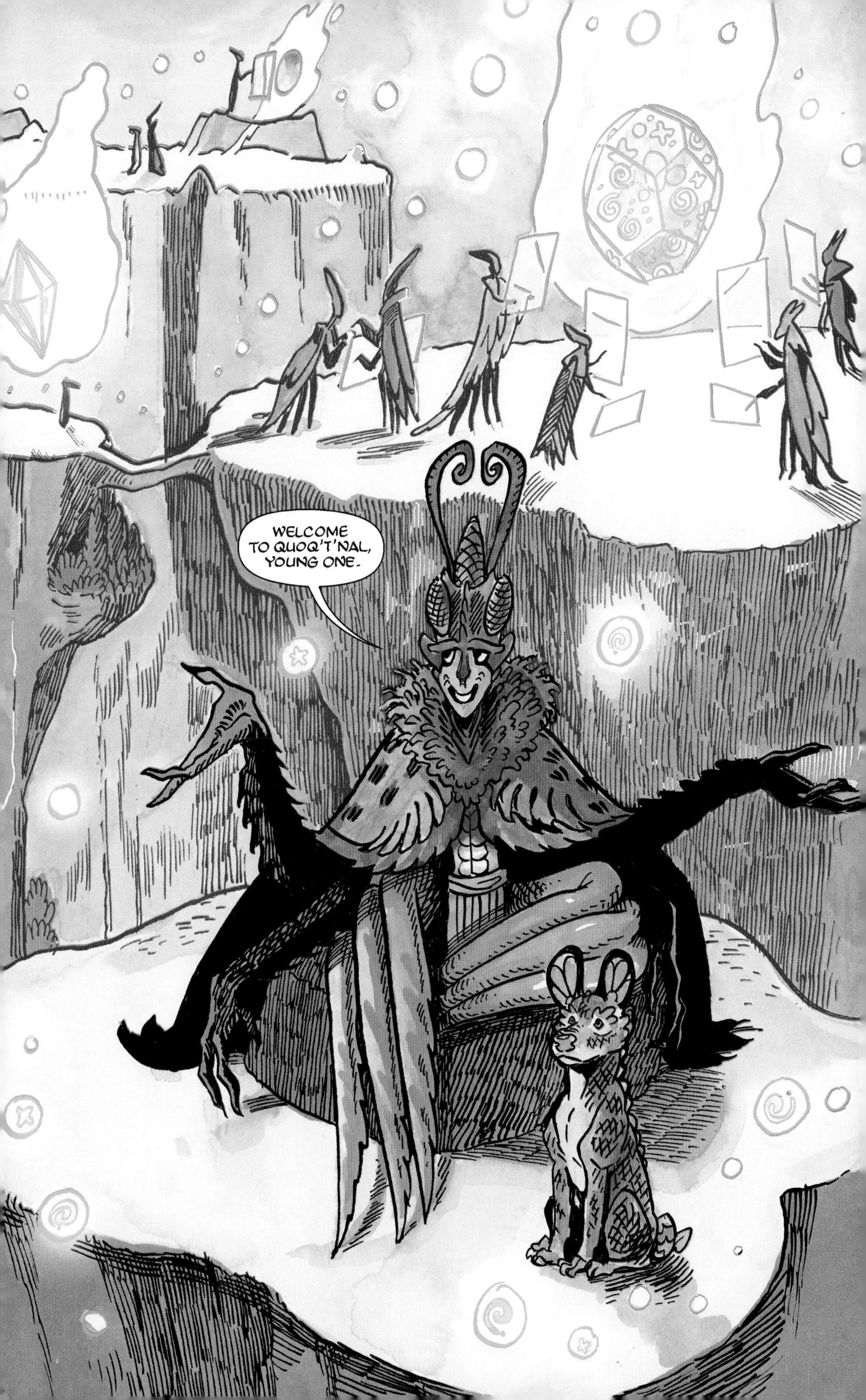
WELCOME TO QUOQ'T'NAL, YOUNG ONE.

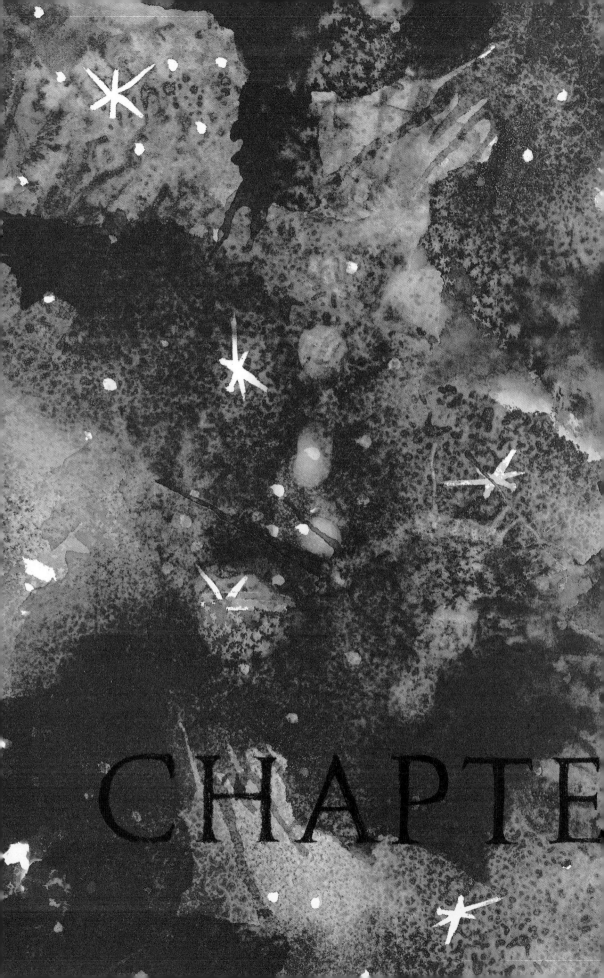

CHAPTE

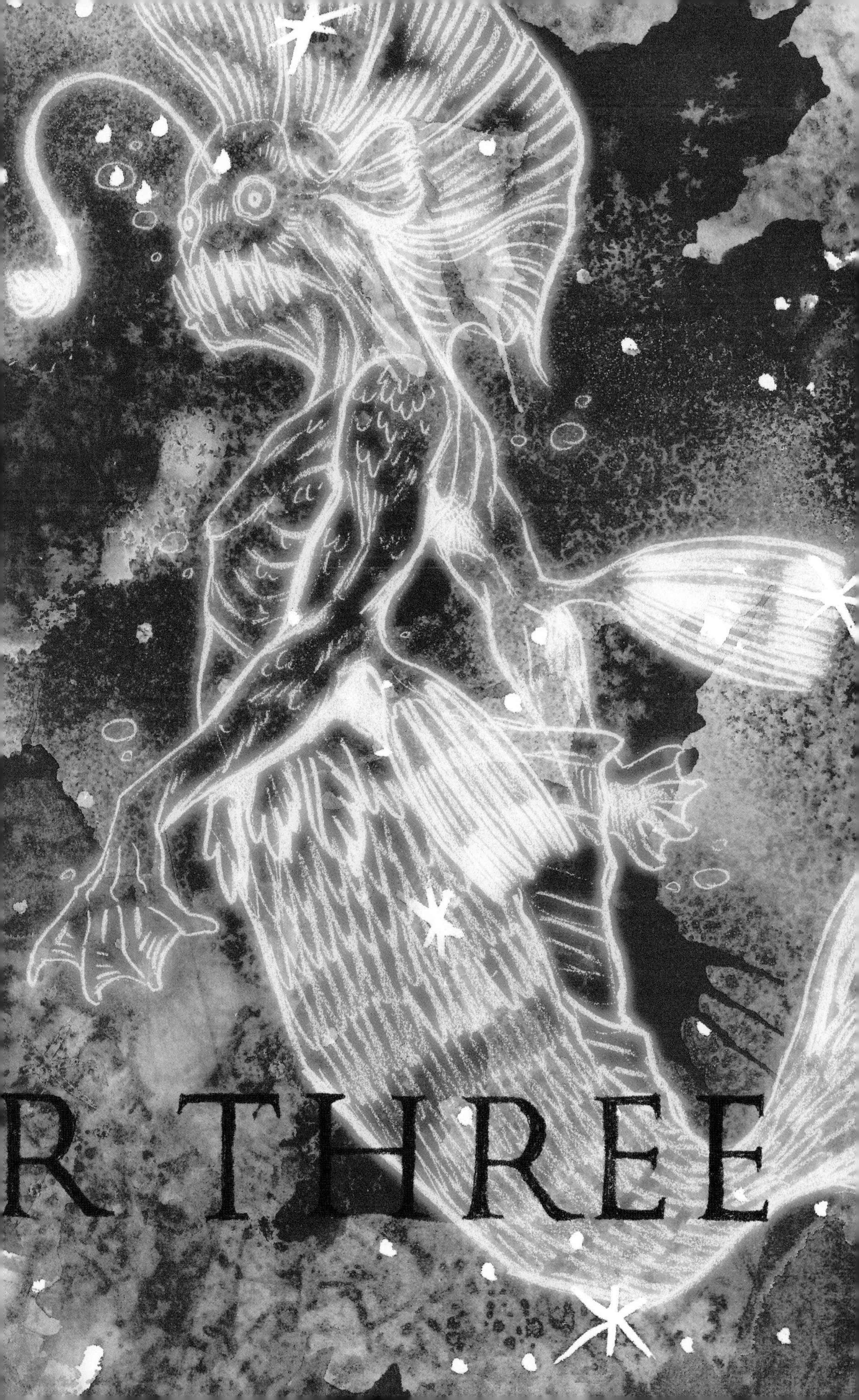
R THREE

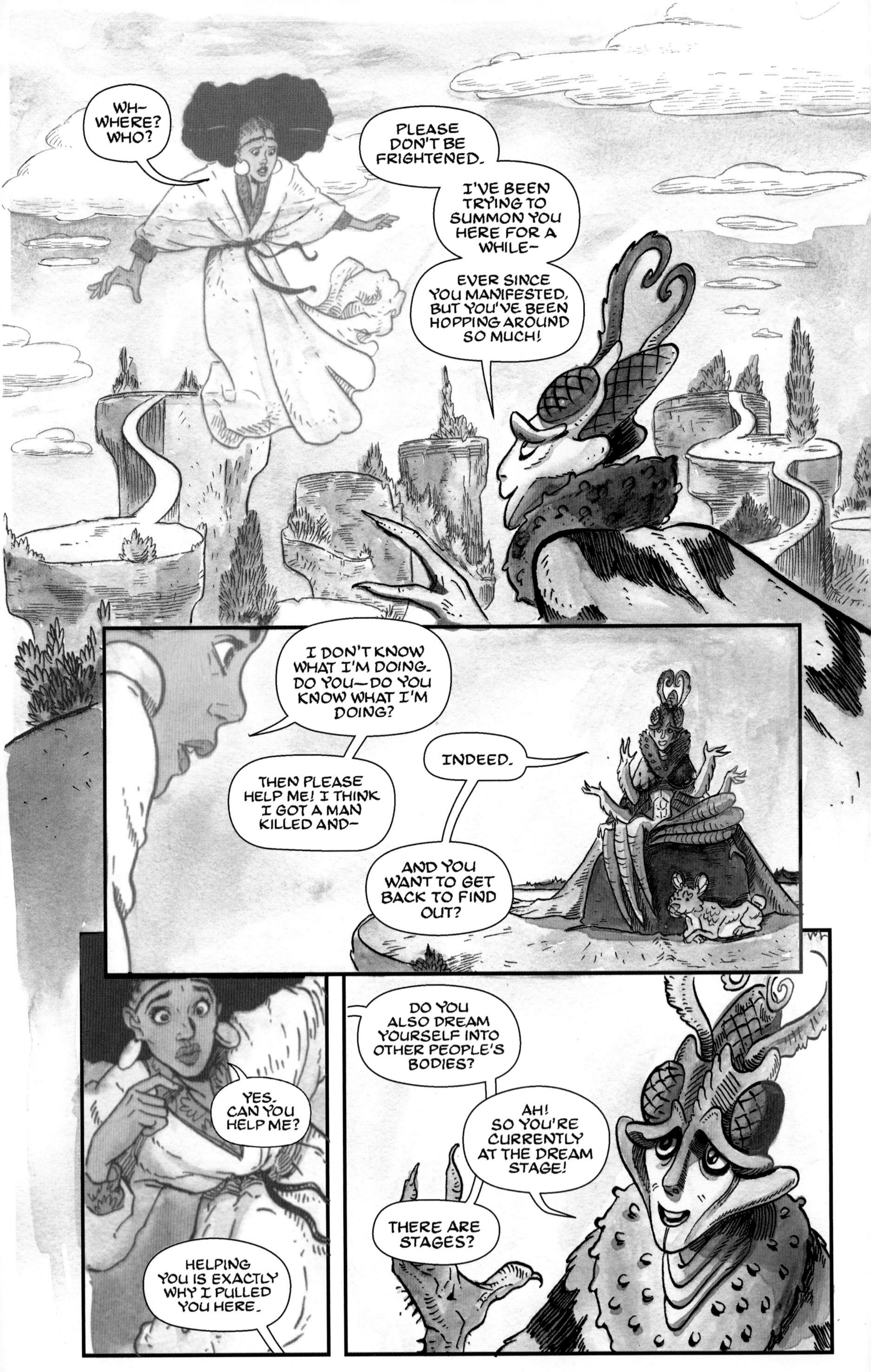
WH– WHERE? WHO?
PLEASE DON'T BE FRIGHTENED.
I'VE BEEN TRYING TO SUMMON YOU HERE FOR A WHILE–
EVER SINCE YOU MANIFESTED, BUT YOU'VE BEEN HOPPING AROUND SO MUCH!
I DON'T KNOW WHAT I'M DOING. DO YOU—DO YOU KNOW WHAT I'M DOING?
INDEED.
THEN PLEASE HELP ME! I THINK I GOT A MAN KILLED AND–
AND YOU WANT TO GET BACK TO FIND OUT?
DO YOU ALSO DREAM YOURSELF INTO OTHER PEOPLE'S BODIES?
YES. CAN YOU HELP ME?
HELPING YOU IS EXACTLY WHY I PULLED YOU HERE.
AH! SO YOU'RE CURRENTLY AT THE DREAM STAGE!
THERE ARE STAGES?

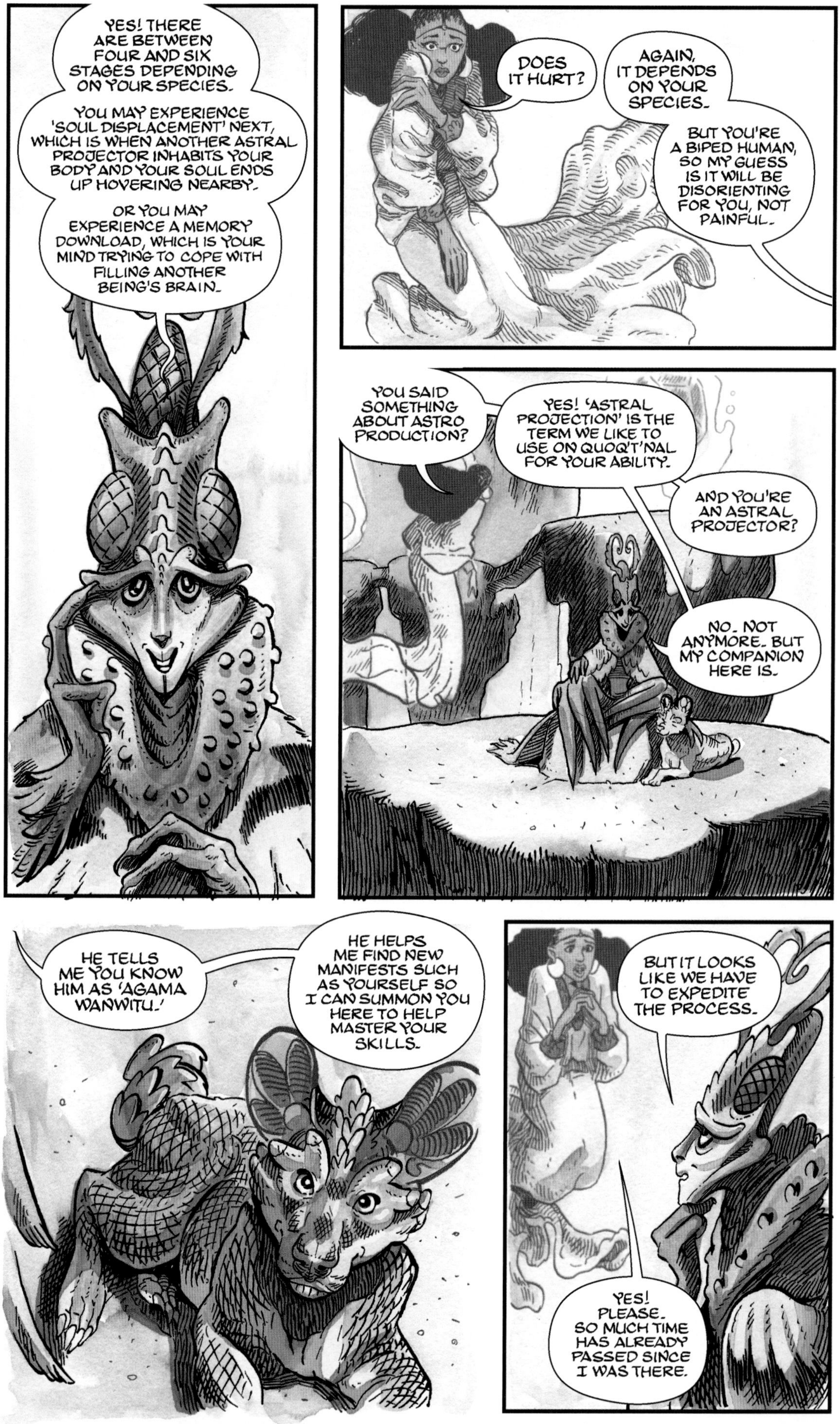
YES! THERE ARE BETWEEN FOUR AND SIX STAGES DEPENDING ON YOUR SPECIES.
YOU MAY EXPERIENCE 'SOUL DISPLACEMENT' NEXT, WHICH IS WHEN ANOTHER ASTRAL PROJECTOR INHABITS YOUR BODY AND YOUR SOUL ENDS UP HOVERING NEARBY.
OR YOU MAY EXPERIENCE A MEMORY DOWNLOAD, WHICH IS YOUR MIND TRYING TO COPE WITH FILLING ANOTHER BEING'S BRAIN.
DOES IT HURT?
AGAIN, IT DEPENDS ON YOUR SPECIES.
BUT YOU'RE A BIPED HUMAN, SO MY GUESS IS IT WILL BE DISORIENTING FOR YOU, NOT PAINFUL.
YOU SAID SOMETHING ABOUT ASTRO PRODUCTION?
YES! 'ASTRAL PROJECTION' IS THE TERM WE LIKE TO USE ON QUOQ'T'NAL FOR YOUR ABILITY.
AND YOU'RE AN ASTRAL PROJECTOR?
NO. NOT ANYMORE. BUT MY COMPANION HERE IS.
HE TELLS ME YOU KNOW HIM AS 'AGAMA WANWITU.'
HE HELPS ME FIND NEW MANIFESTS SUCH AS YOURSELF SO I CAN SUMMON YOU HERE TO HELP MASTER YOUR SKILLS.
BUT IT LOOKS LIKE WE HAVE TO EXPEDITE THE PROCESS.
YES! PLEASE. SO MUCH TIME HAS ALREADY PASSED SINCE I WAS THERE.

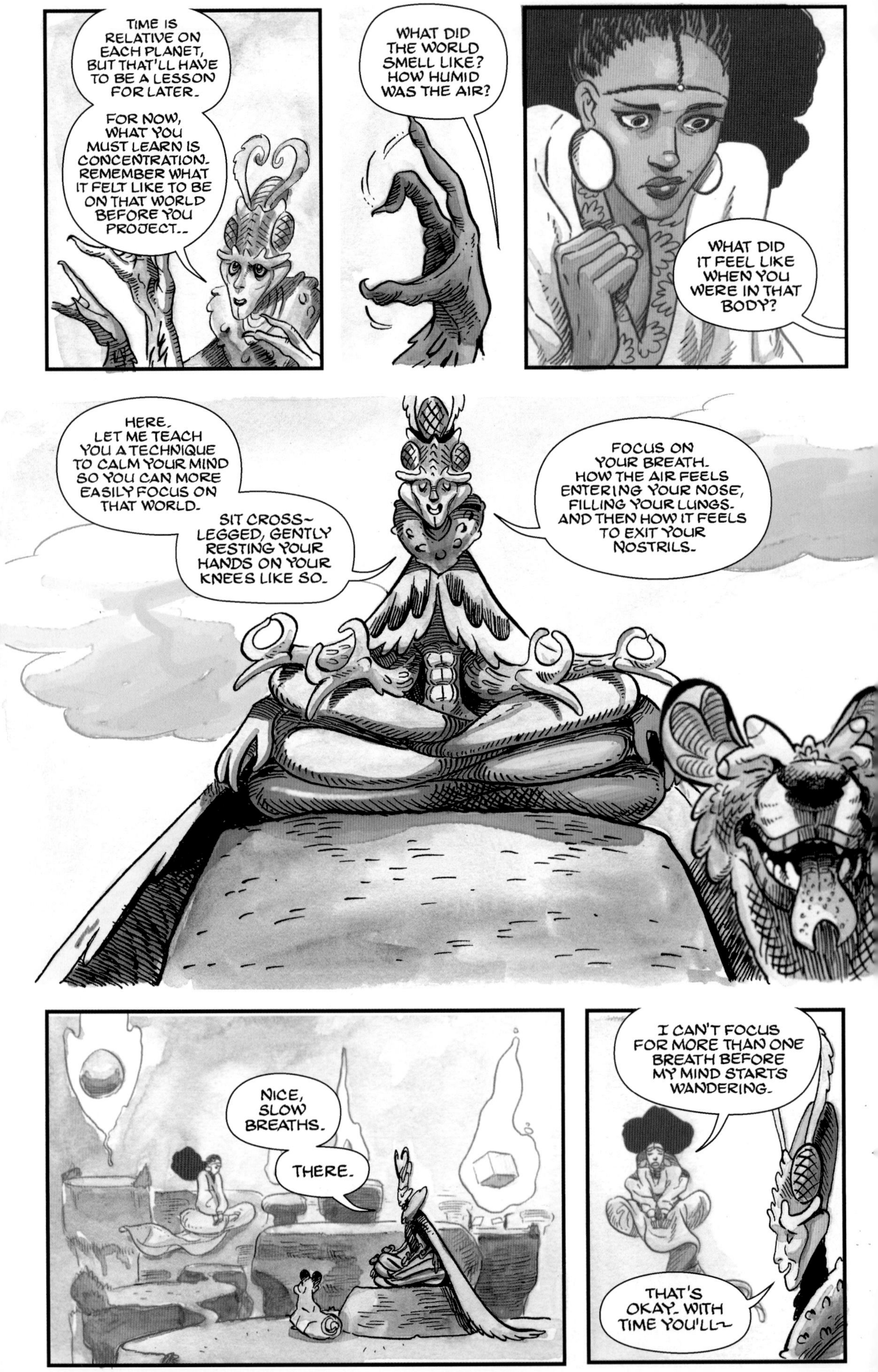
TIME IS RELATIVE ON EACH PLANET, BUT THAT'LL HAVE TO BE A LESSON FOR LATER.
FOR NOW, WHAT YOU MUST LEARN IS CONCENTRATION. REMEMBER WHAT IT FELT LIKE TO BE ON THAT WORLD BEFORE YOU PROJECT...
WHAT DID THE WORLD SMELL LIKE? HOW HUMID WAS THE AIR?
WHAT DID IT FEEL LIKE WHEN YOU WERE IN THAT BODY?
HERE. LET ME TEACH YOU A TECHNIQUE TO CALM YOUR MIND SO YOU CAN MORE EASILY FOCUS ON THAT WORLD.
SIT CROSS-LEGGED, GENTLY RESTING YOUR HANDS ON YOUR KNEES LIKE SO.
FOCUS ON YOUR BREATH. HOW THE AIR FEELS ENTERING YOUR NOSE, FILLING YOUR LUNGS. AND THEN HOW IT FEELS TO EXIT YOUR NOSTRILS.
NICE, SLOW BREATHS.
THERE.
I CAN'T FOCUS FOR MORE THAN ONE BREATH BEFORE MY MIND STARTS WANDERING.
THAT'S OKAY. WITH TIME YOU'LL~

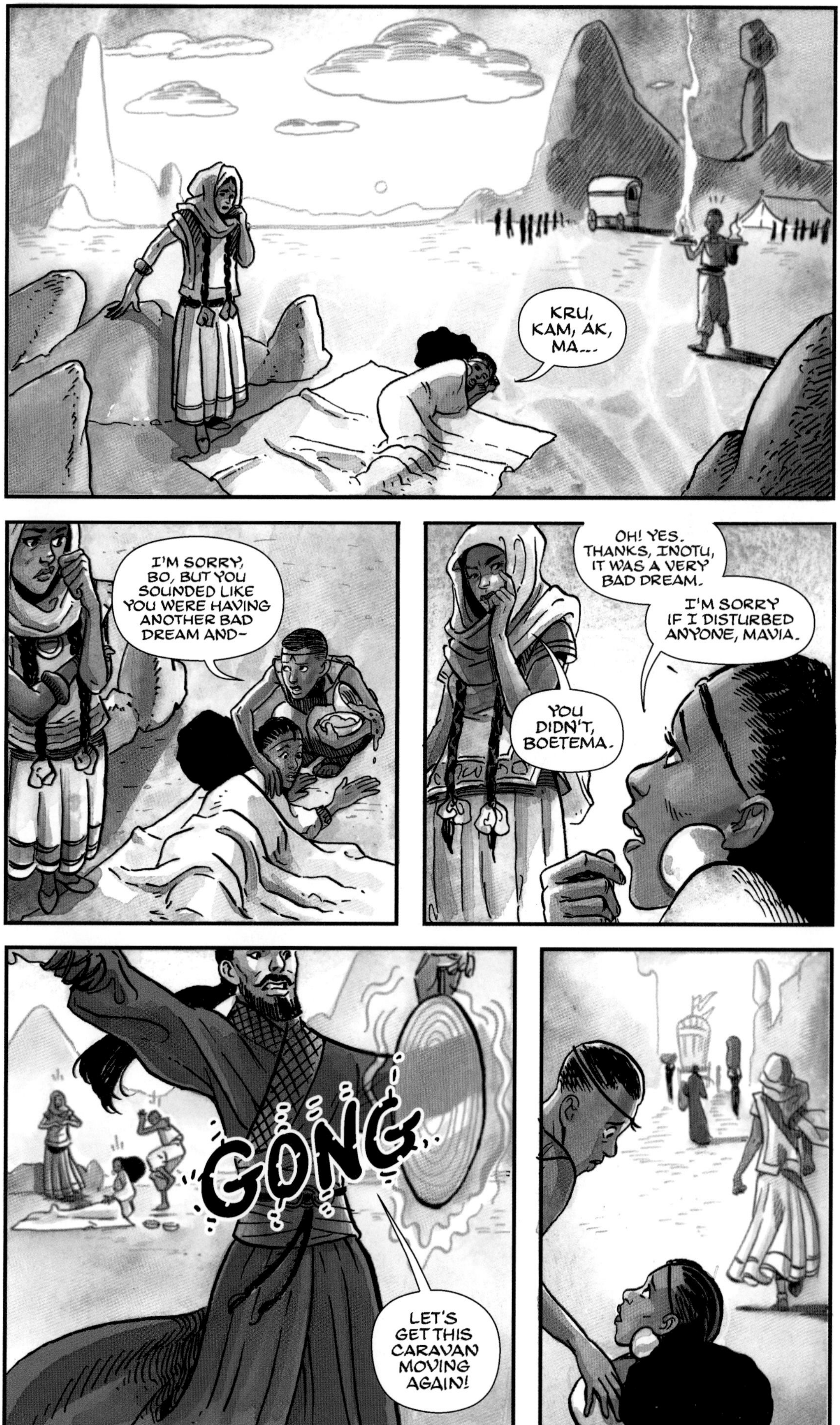
KRU, KAM, AK, MA...
I'M SORRY, BO, BUT YOU SOUNDED LIKE YOU WERE HAVING ANOTHER BAD DREAM AND-
OH! YES. THANKS, INOTU, IT WAS A VERY BAD DREAM.
I'M SORRY IF I DISTURBED ANYONE, MAVIA.
YOU DIDN'T, BOETEMA.
GONG
LET'S GET THIS CARAVAN MOVING AGAIN!

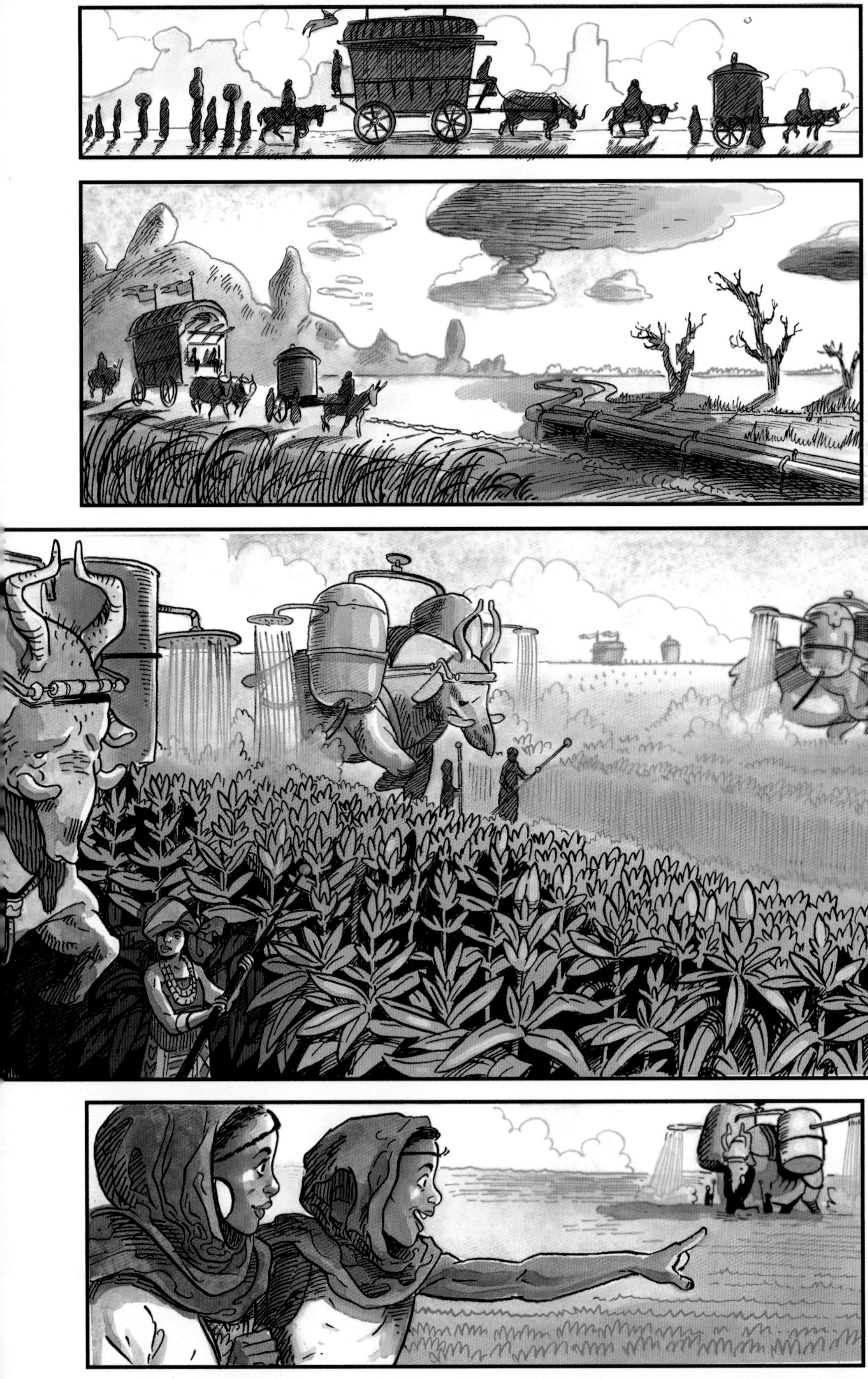

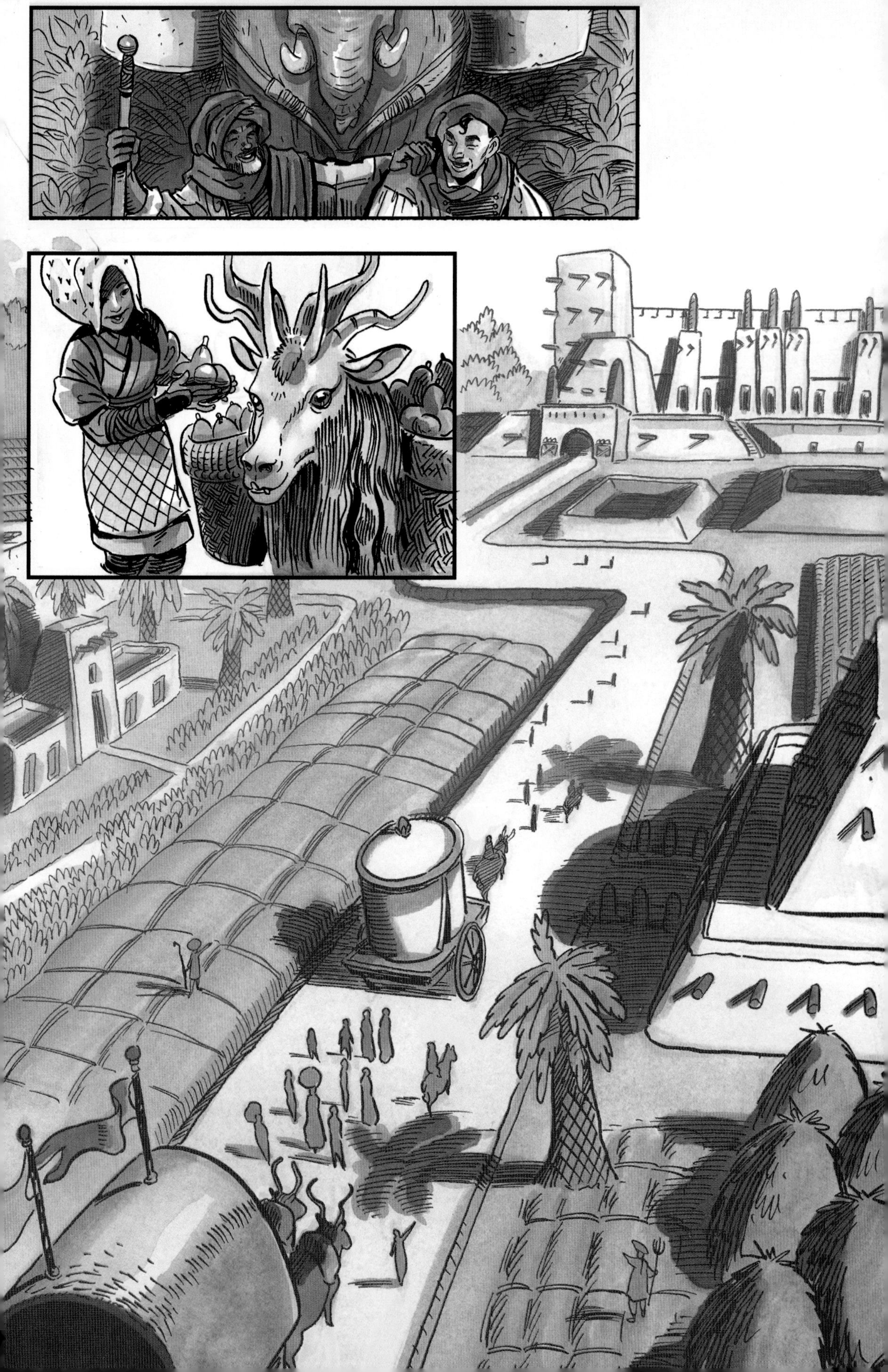

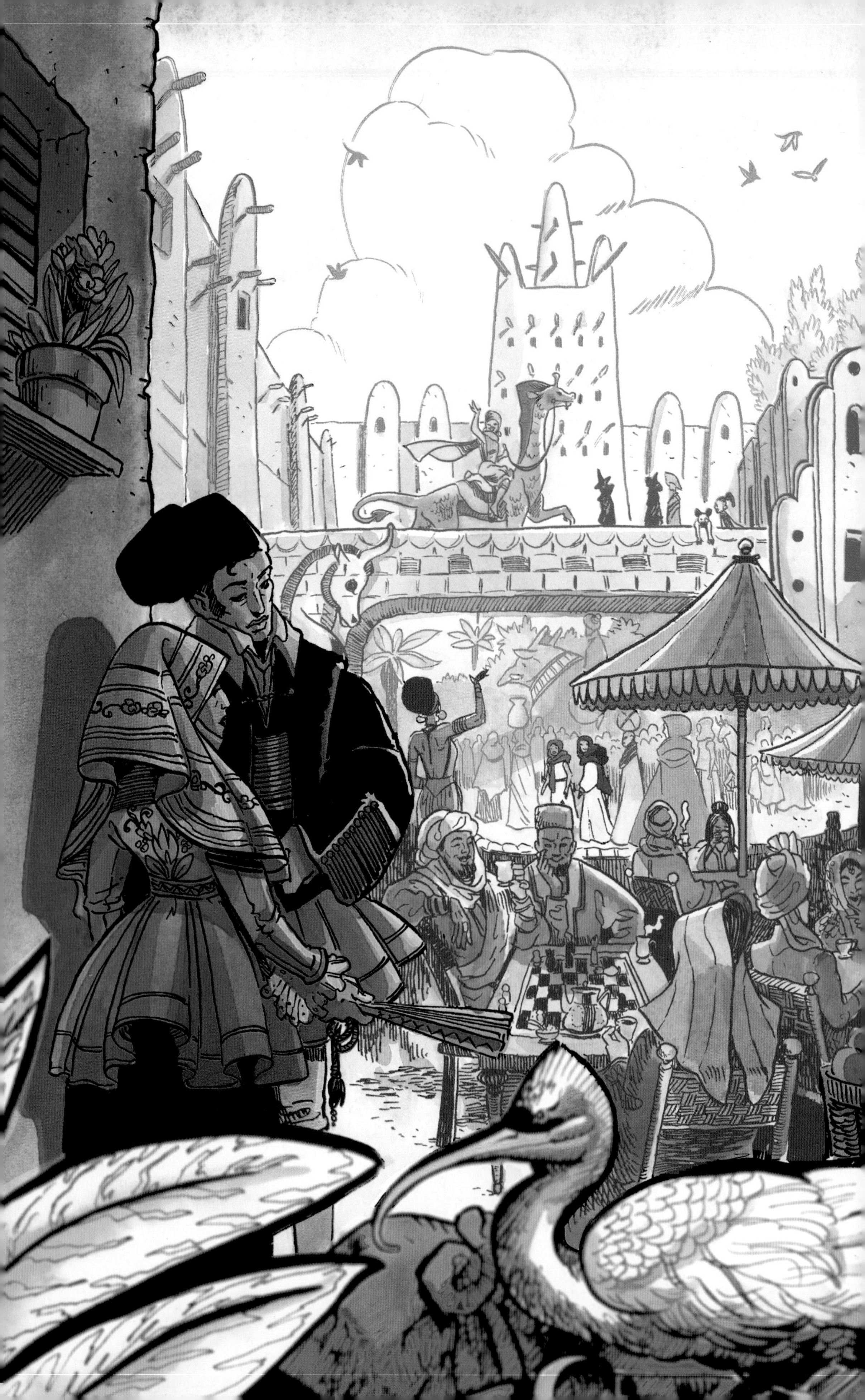

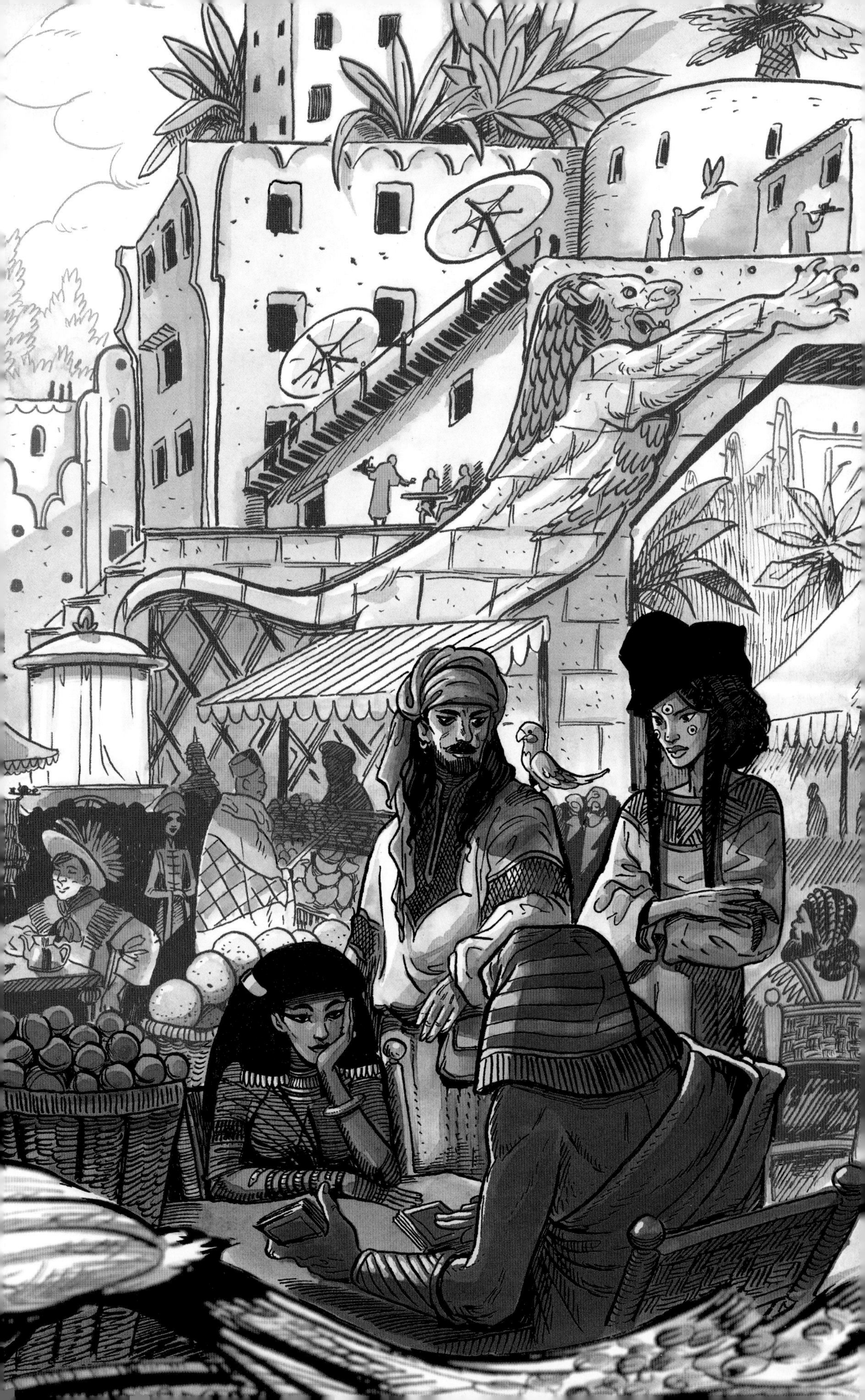

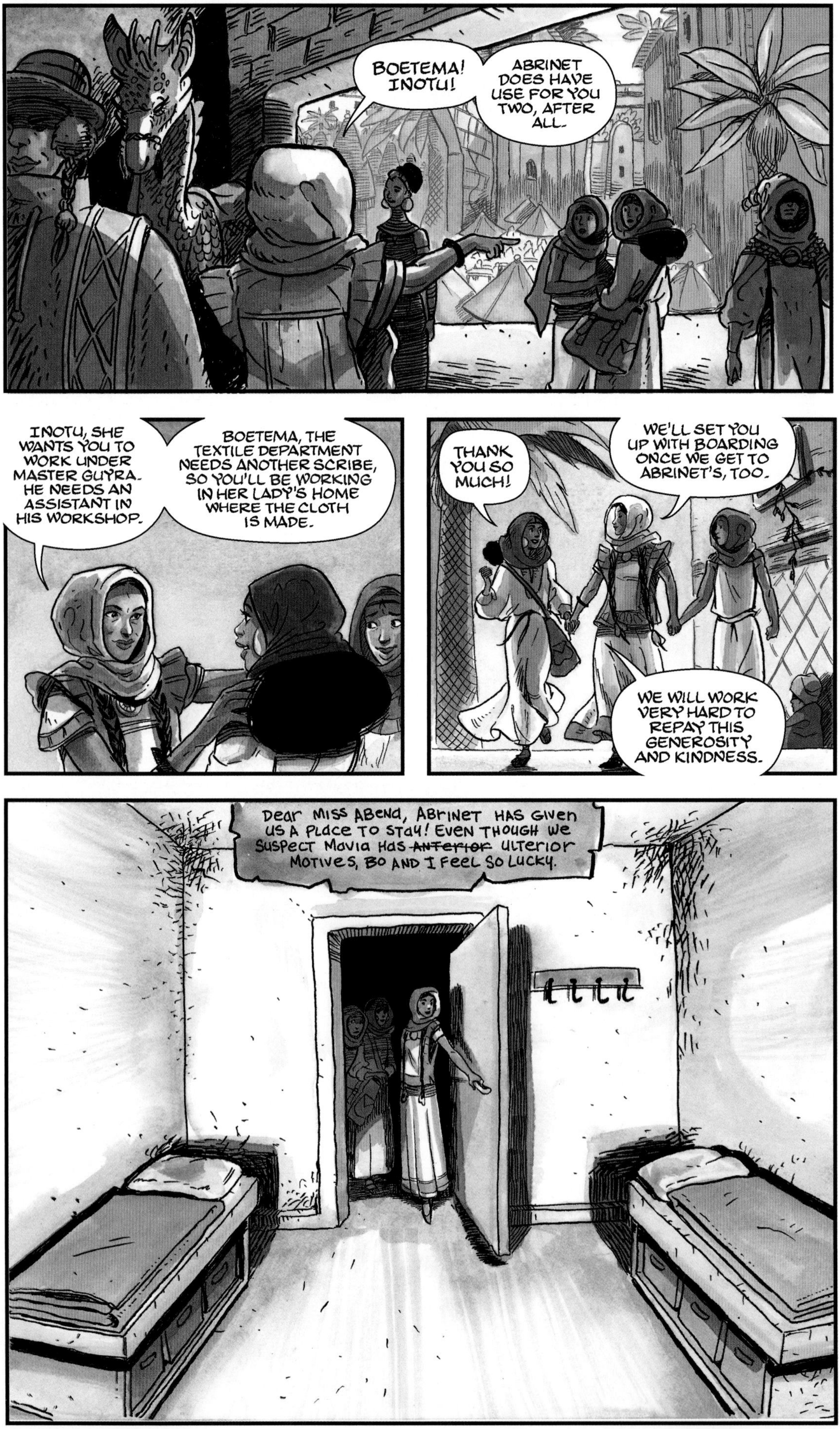
BOETEMA! INOTU!
ABRINET DOES HAVE USE FOR YOU TWO, AFTER ALL.
INOTU, SHE WANTS YOU TO WORK UNDER MASTER GUYRA. HE NEEDS AN ASSISTANT IN HIS WORKSHOP.
BOETEMA, THE TEXTILE DEPARTMENT NEEDS ANOTHER SCRIBE, SO YOU'LL BE WORKING IN HER LADY'S HOME WHERE THE CLOTH IS MADE.
THANK YOU SO MUCH!
WE'LL SET YOU UP WITH BOARDING ONCE WE GET TO ABRINET'S, TOO.
WE WILL WORK VERY HARD TO REPAY THIS GENEROSITY AND KINDNESS.
Dear Miss Abend, Abrinet has given us a place to stay! Even though we suspect Movia has ~~Anterior~~ ulterior motives, Bo and I feel so lucky.

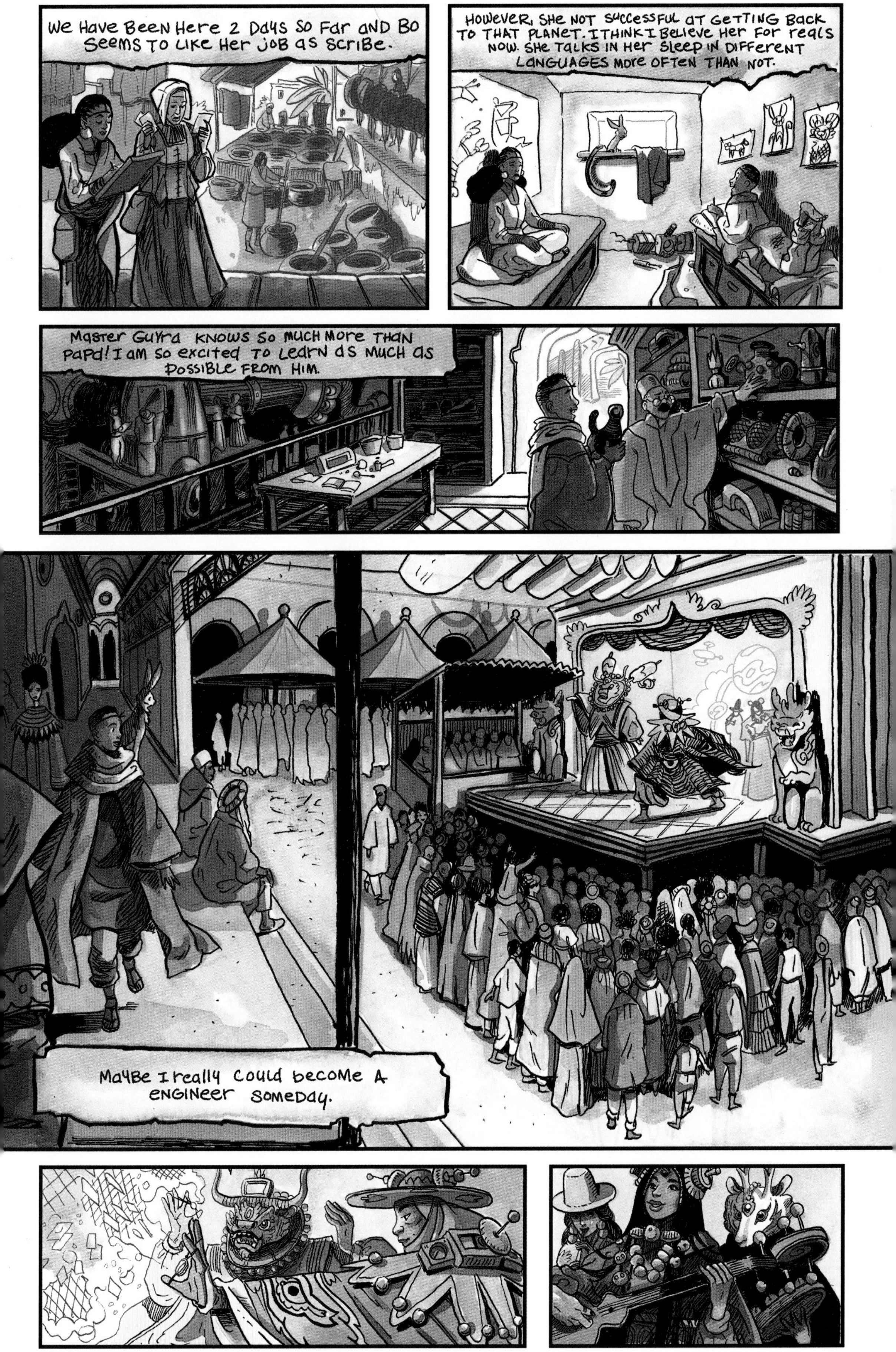
We Have Been Here 2 Days So Far and Bo Seems to Like Her job as scribe.
However, she not successful at getting back to that planet. I think I believe her for reals now. She talks in her sleep in different languages more often than not.
Master Guyra knows so much more than Papa! I am so excited to learn as much as possible from him.
Maybe I really could become a engineer someday.

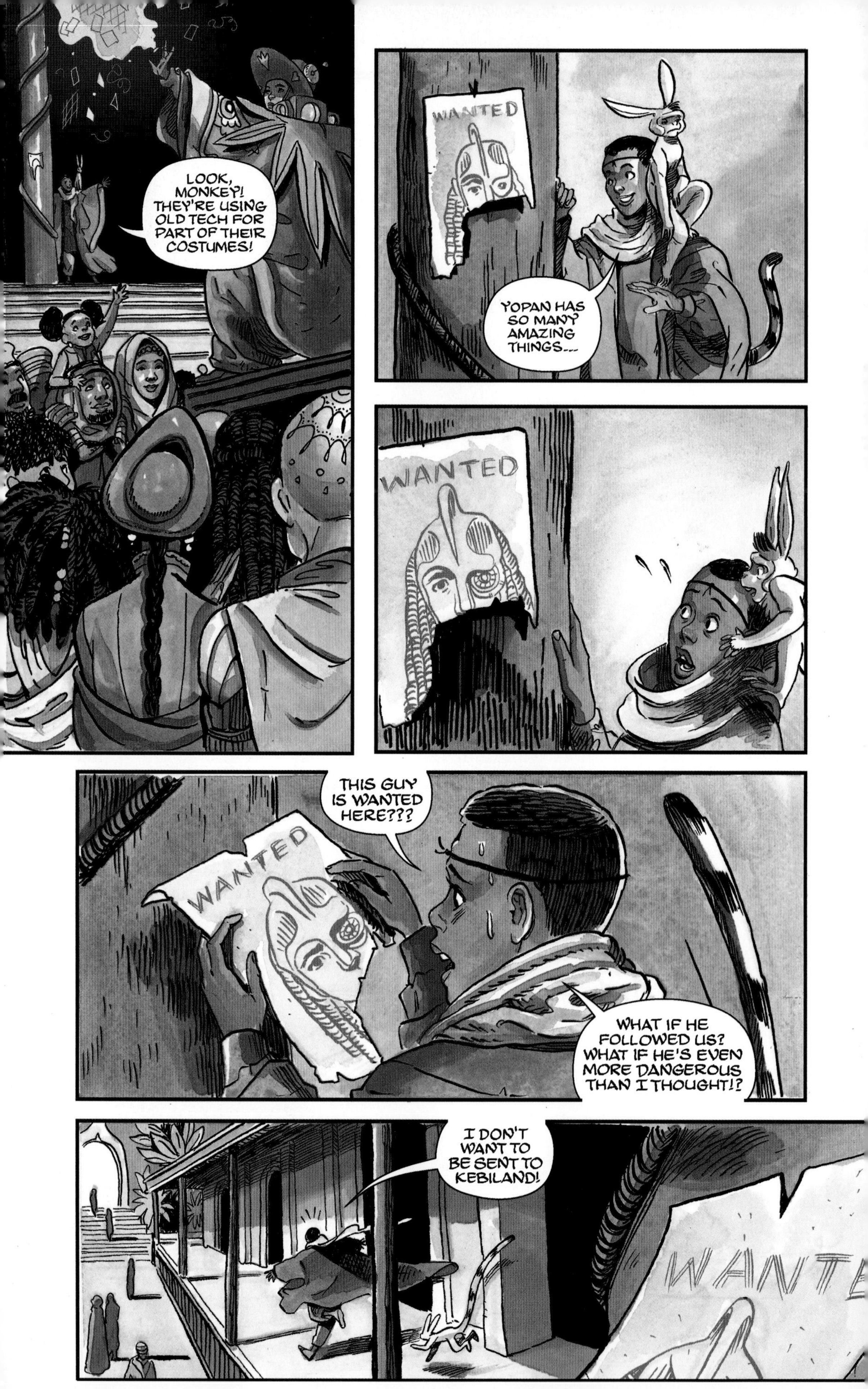
LOOK, MONKEY! THEY'RE USING OLD TECH FOR PART OF THEIR COSTUMES!
WANTED
YOPAN HAS SO MANY AMAZING THINGS...
WANTED
WANTED
THIS GUY IS WANTED HERE???
WHAT IF HE FOLLOWED US? WHAT IF HE'S EVEN MORE DANGEROUS THAN I THOUGHT!?
I DON'T WANT TO BE SENT TO KEBILAND!
WANTE

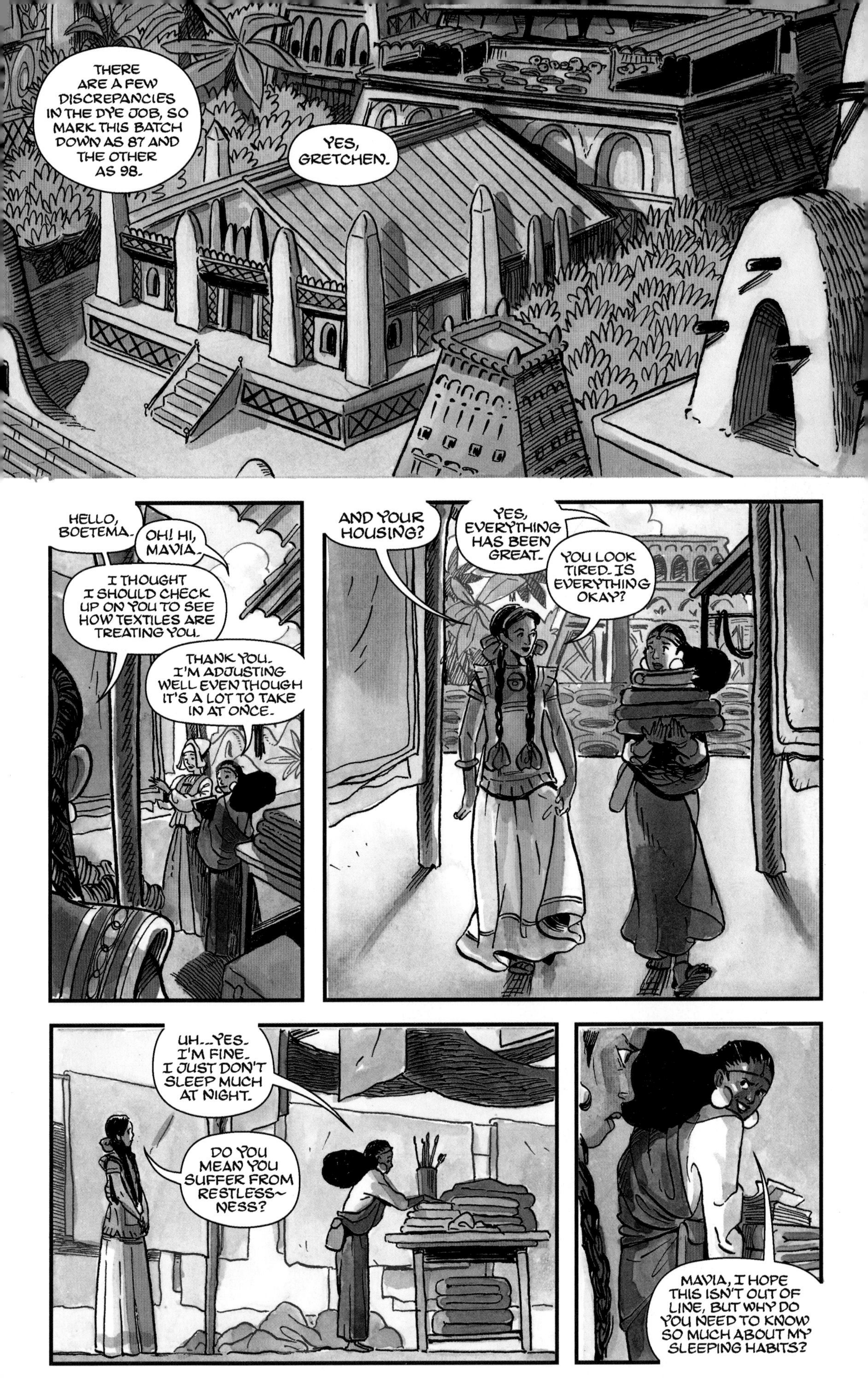
THERE ARE A FEW DISCREPANCIES IN THE DYE JOB, SO MARK THIS BATCH DOWN AS 87 AND THE OTHER AS 98.
YES, GRETCHEN.
HELLO, BOETEMA.
OH! HI, MAVIA.
I THOUGHT I SHOULD CHECK UP ON YOU TO SEE HOW TEXTILES ARE TREATING YOU.
THANK YOU. I'M ADJUSTING WELL EVEN THOUGH IT'S A LOT TO TAKE IN AT ONCE.
AND YOUR HOUSING?
YES, EVERYTHING HAS BEEN GREAT.
YOU LOOK TIRED. IS EVERYTHING OKAY?
UH... YES. I'M FINE. I JUST DON'T SLEEP MUCH AT NIGHT.
DO YOU MEAN YOU SUFFER FROM RESTLESS~NESS?
MAVIA, I HOPE THIS ISN'T OUT OF LINE, BUT WHY DO YOU NEED TO KNOW SO MUCH ABOUT MY SLEEPING HABITS?

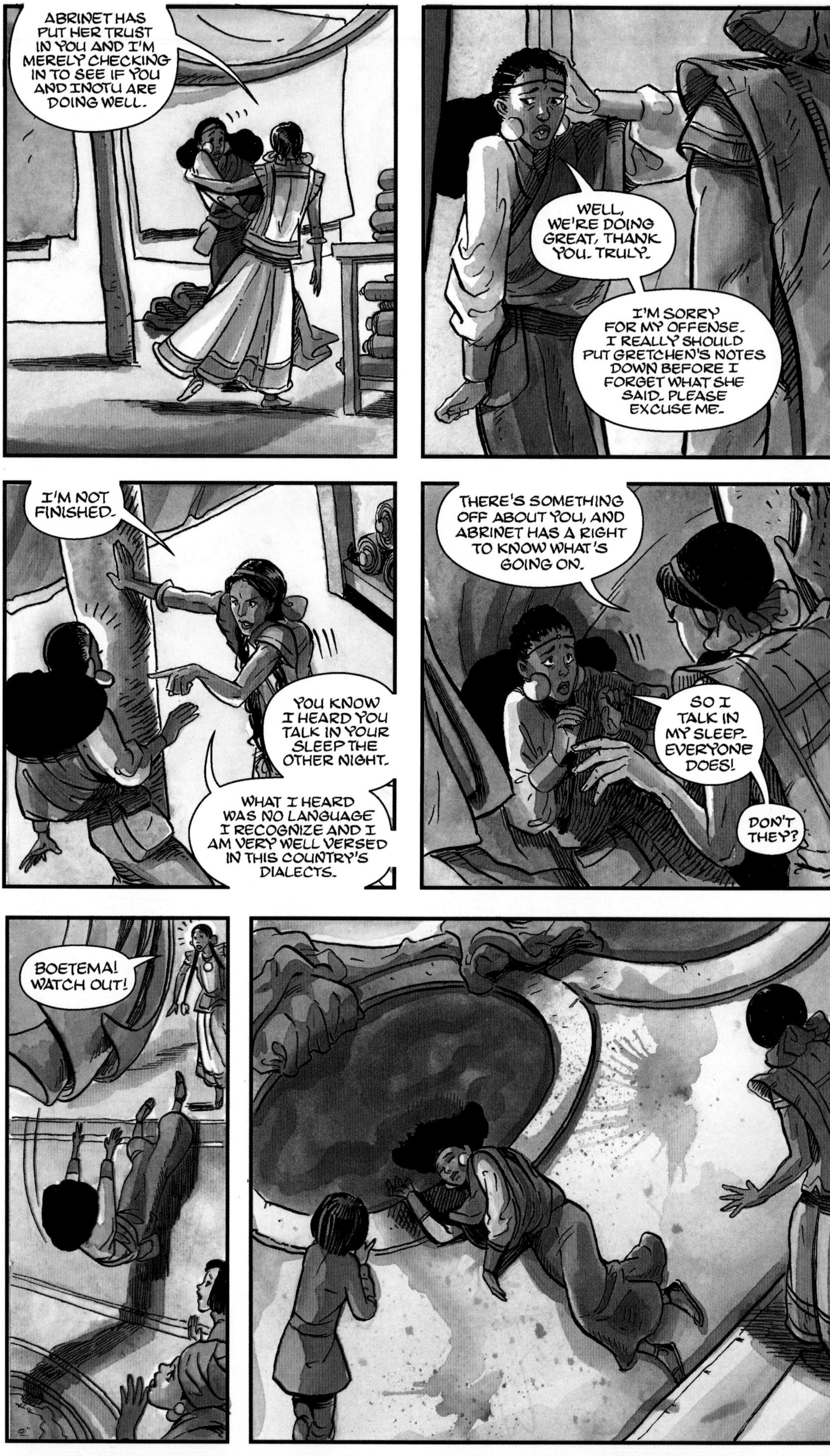
ABRINET HAS PUT HER TRUST IN YOU AND I'M MERELY CHECKING IN TO SEE IF YOU AND INOTU ARE DOING WELL.
WELL, WE'RE DOING GREAT, THANK YOU. TRULY.
I'M SORRY FOR MY OFFENSE. I REALLY SHOULD PUT GRETCHEN'S NOTES DOWN BEFORE I FORGET WHAT SHE SAID. PLEASE EXCUSE ME.
I'M NOT FINISHED.
YOU KNOW I HEARD YOU TALK IN YOUR SLEEP THE OTHER NIGHT.
WHAT I HEARD WAS NO LANGUAGE I RECOGNIZE AND I AM VERY WELL VERSED IN THIS COUNTRY'S DIALECTS.
THERE'S SOMETHING OFF ABOUT YOU, AND ABRINET HAS A RIGHT TO KNOW WHAT'S GOING ON.
SO I TALK IN MY SLEEP. EVERYONE DOES!
DON'T THEY?
BOETEMA! WATCH OUT!

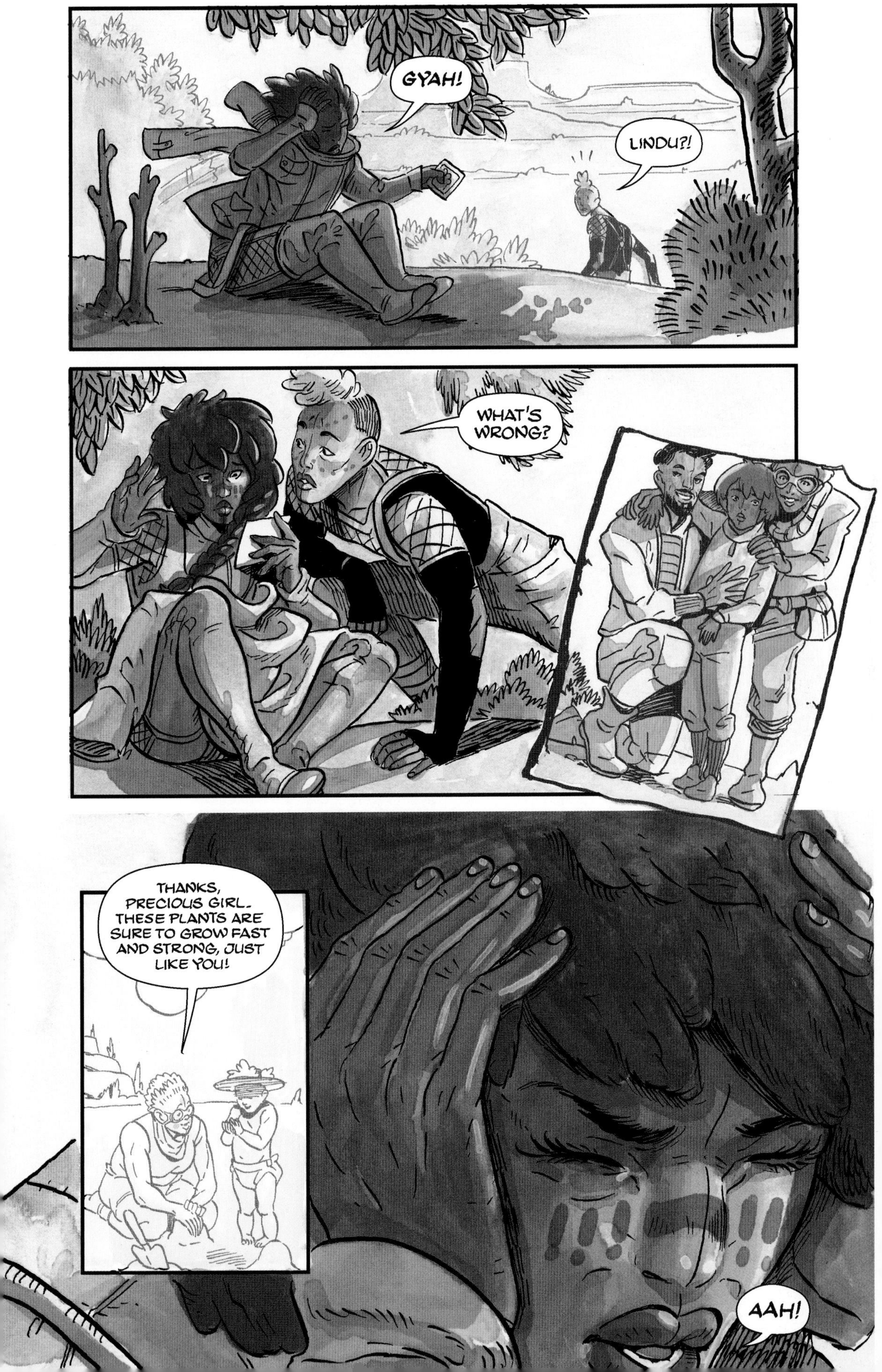
GYAH!
LINDU?!
WHAT'S WRONG?
THANKS, PRECIOUS GIRL. THESE PLANTS ARE SURE TO GROW FAST AND STRONG, JUST LIKE YOU!
AAH!

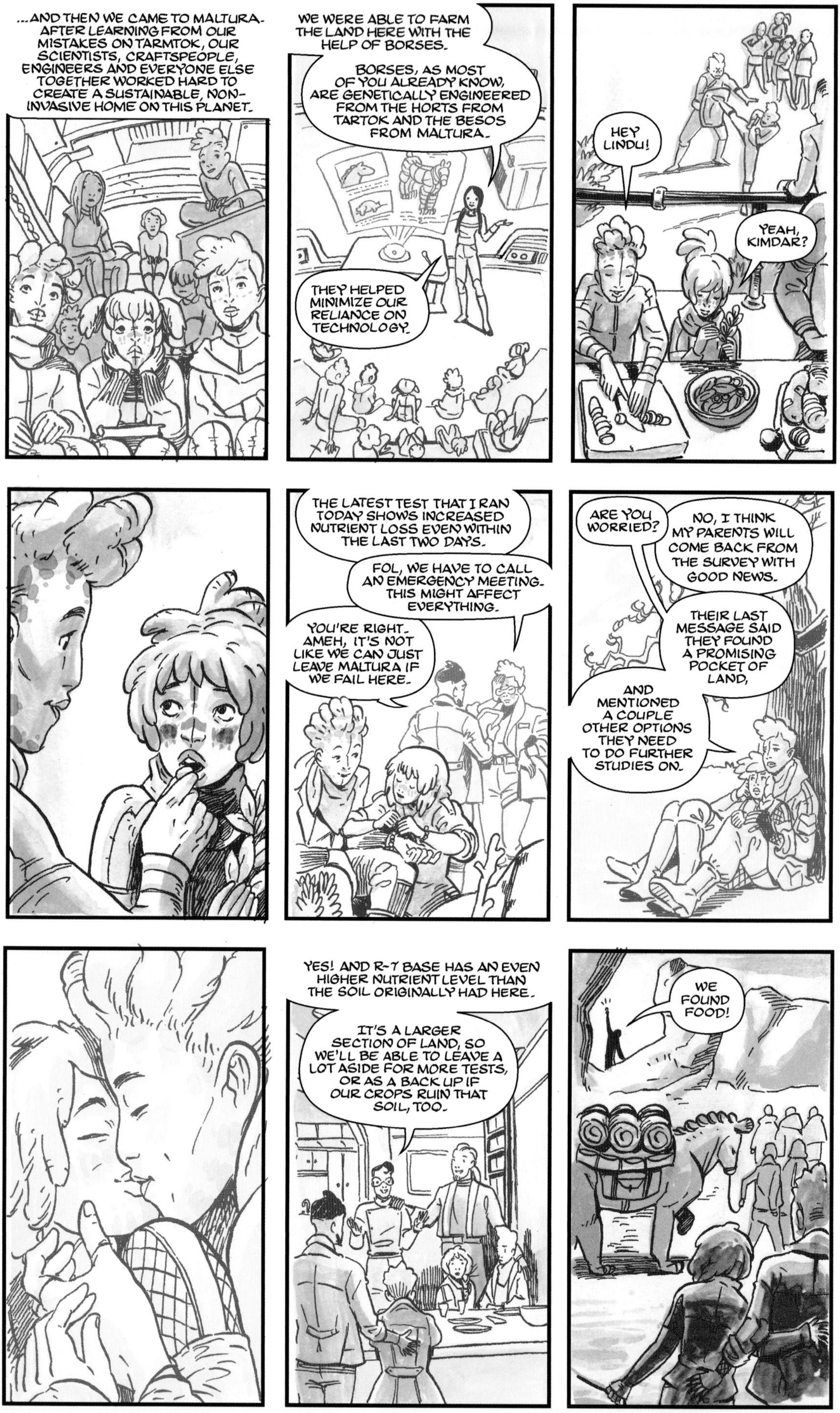
...AND THEN WE CAME TO MALTURA. AFTER LEARNING FROM OUR MISTAKES ON TARMTOK, OUR SCIENTISTS, CRAFTSPEOPLE, ENGINEERS AND EVERYONE ELSE TOGETHER WORKED HARD TO CREATE A SUSTAINABLE, NON-INVASIVE HOME ON THIS PLANET.
WE WERE ABLE TO FARM THE LAND HERE WITH THE HELP OF BORSES.
BORSES, AS MOST OF YOU ALREADY KNOW, ARE GENETICALLY ENGINEERED FROM THE HORTS FROM TARTOK AND THE BESOS FROM MALTURA.
THEY HELPED MINIMIZE OUR RELIANCE ON TECHNOLOGY.
HEY LINDU!
YEAH, KIMDAR?
THE LATEST TEST THAT I RAN TODAY SHOWS INCREASED NUTRIENT LOSS EVEN WITHIN THE LAST TWO DAYS.
FOL, WE HAVE TO CALL AN EMERGENCY MEETING. THIS MIGHT AFFECT EVERYTHING.
YOU'RE RIGHT. AMEH, IT'S NOT LIKE WE CAN JUST LEAVE MALTURA IF WE FAIL HERE.
ARE YOU WORRIED?
NO, I THINK MY PARENTS WILL COME BACK FROM THE SURVEY WITH GOOD NEWS.
THEIR LAST MESSAGE SAID THEY FOUND A PROMISING POCKET OF LAND,
AND MENTIONED A COUPLE OTHER OPTIONS THEY NEED TO DO FURTHER STUDIES ON.
YES! AND R-7 BASE HAS AN EVEN HIGHER NUTRIENT LEVEL THAN THE SOIL ORIGINALLY HAD HERE.
IT'S A LARGER SECTION OF LAND, SO WE'LL BE ABLE TO LEAVE A LOT ASIDE FOR MORE TESTS, OR AS A BACK UP IF OUR CROPS RUIN THAT SOIL, TOO.
WE FOUND FOOD!

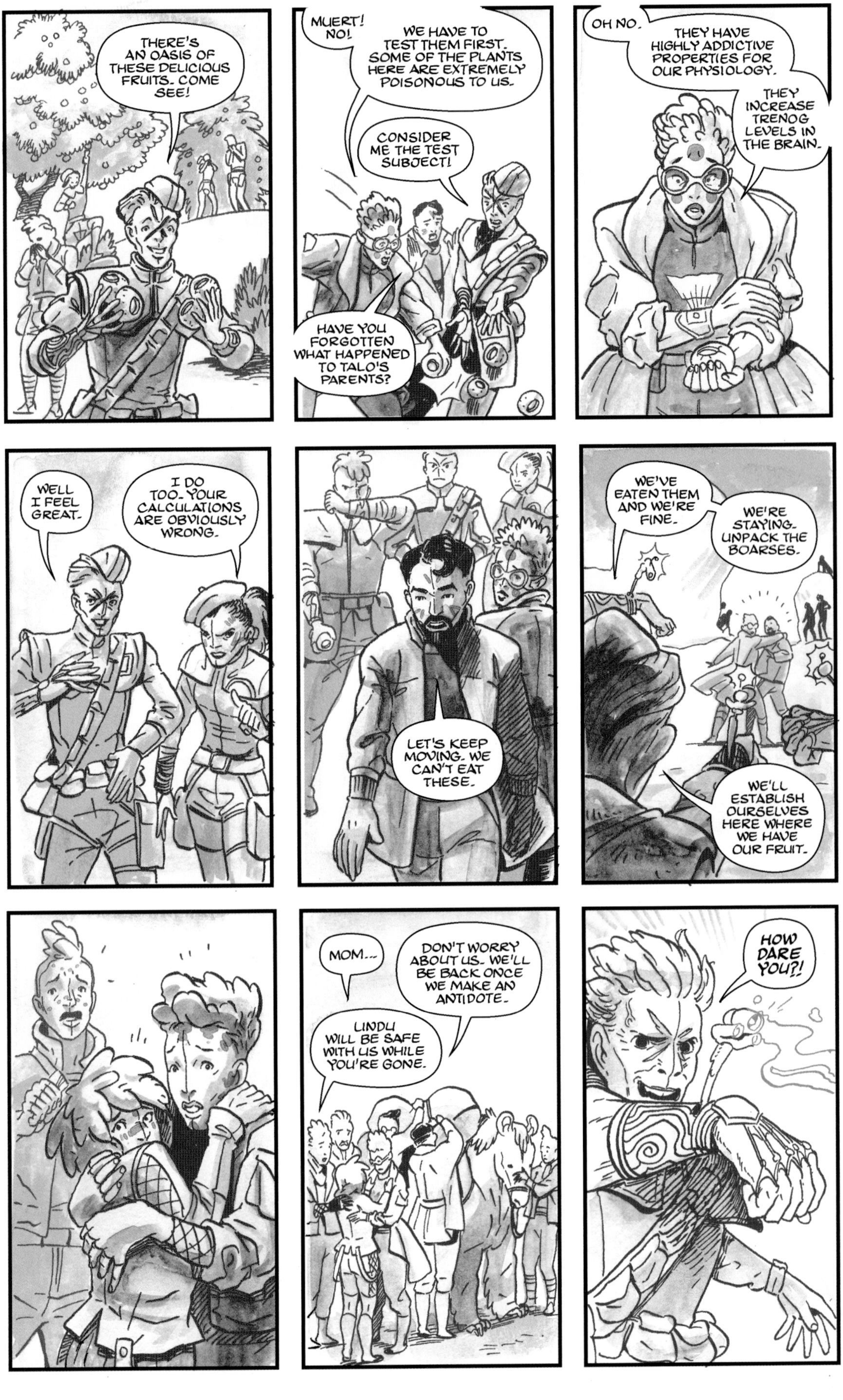
THERE'S AN OASIS OF THESE DELICIOUS FRUITS. COME SEE!
MUERT! NO!
WE HAVE TO TEST THEM FIRST. SOME OF THE PLANTS HERE ARE EXTREMELY POISONOUS TO US.
CONSIDER ME THE TEST SUBJECT!
HAVE YOU FORGOTTEN WHAT HAPPENED TO TALO'S PARENTS?
OH NO.
THEY HAVE HIGHLY ADDICTIVE PROPERTIES FOR OUR PHYSIOLOGY.
THEY INCREASE TRENOG LEVELS IN THE BRAIN.
WELL I FEEL GREAT.
I DO TOO. YOUR CALCULATIONS ARE OBVIOUSLY WRONG.
LET'S KEEP MOVING. WE CAN'T EAT THESE.
WE'VE EATEN THEM AND WE'RE FINE.
WE'RE STAYING. UNPACK THE BOARSES.
WE'LL ESTABLISH OURSELVES HERE WHERE WE HAVE OUR FRUIT.
MOM...
DON'T WORRY ABOUT US. WE'LL BE BACK ONCE WE MAKE AN ANTIDOTE.
LINDU WILL BE SAFE WITH US WHILE YOU'RE GONE.
HOW DARE YOU?!

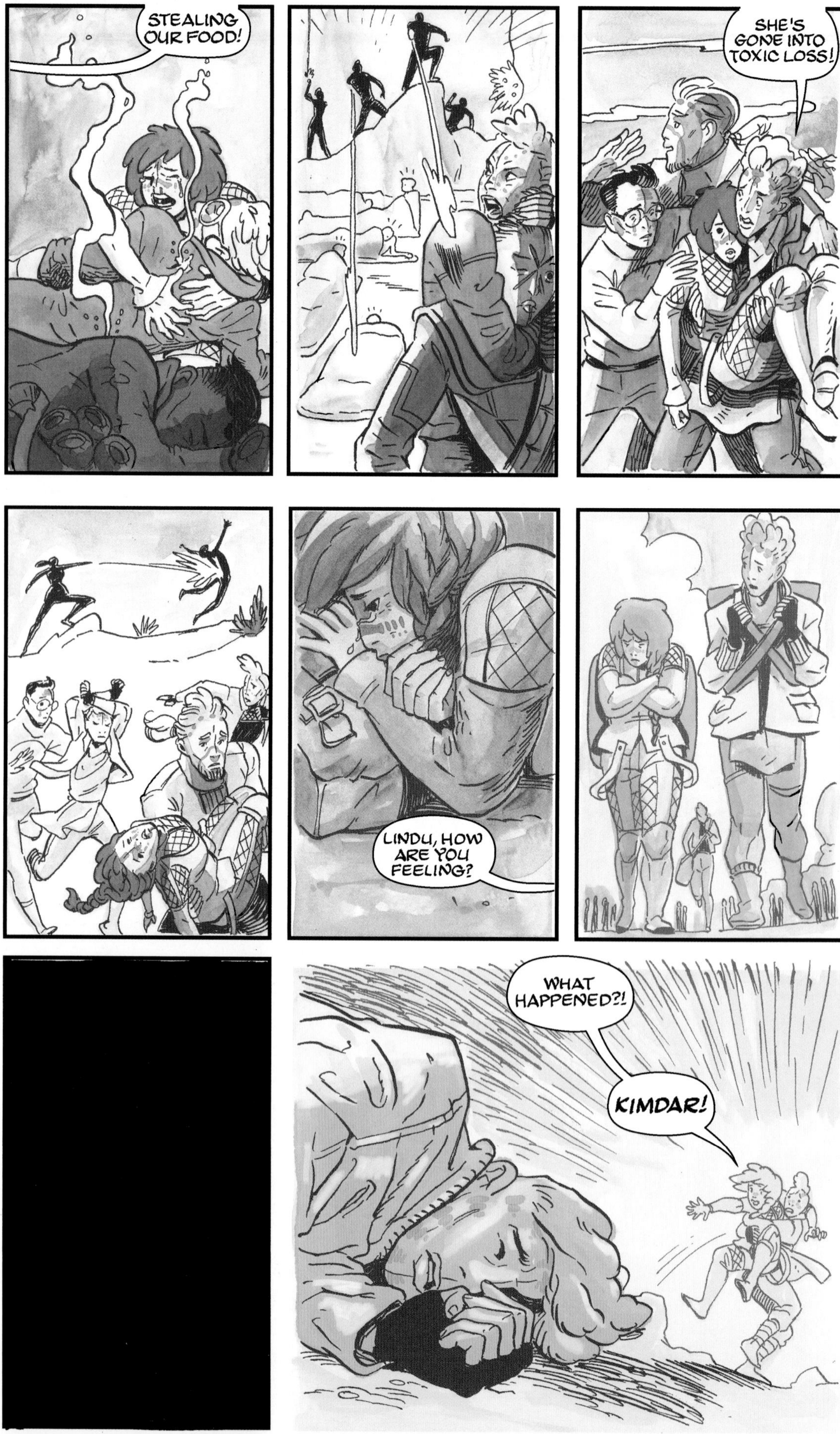
STEALING OUR FOOD!
SHE'S GONE INTO TOXIC LOSS!
LINDU, HOW ARE YOU FEELING?
WHAT HAPPENED?!
KIMDAR!

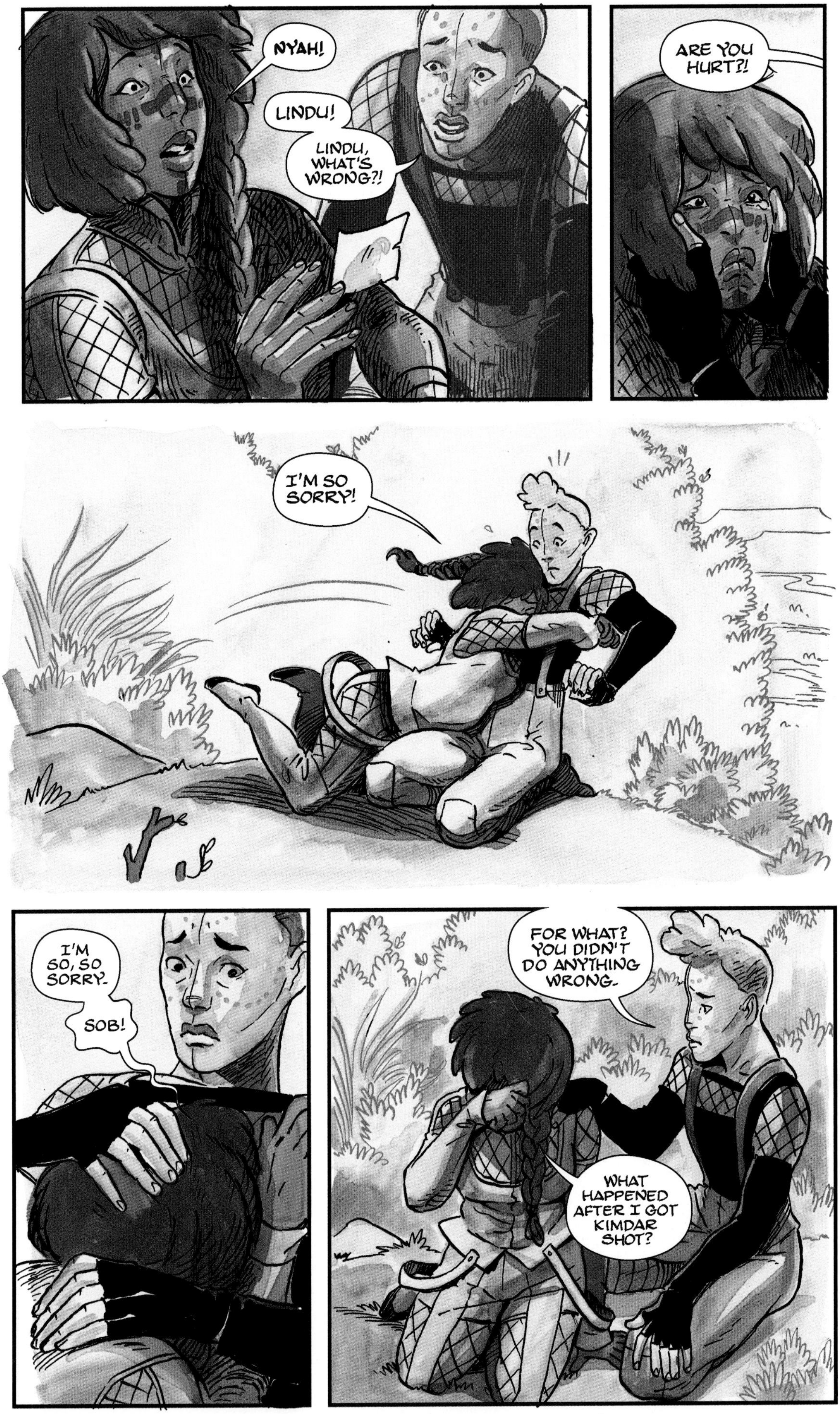
NYAH!
LINDU!
LINDU, WHAT'S WRONG?!
ARE YOU HURT?!
I'M SO SORRY!
I'M SO, SO SORRY.
SOB!
FOR WHAT? YOU DIDN'T DO ANYTHING WRONG.
WHAT HAPPENED AFTER I GOT KIMDAR SHOT?

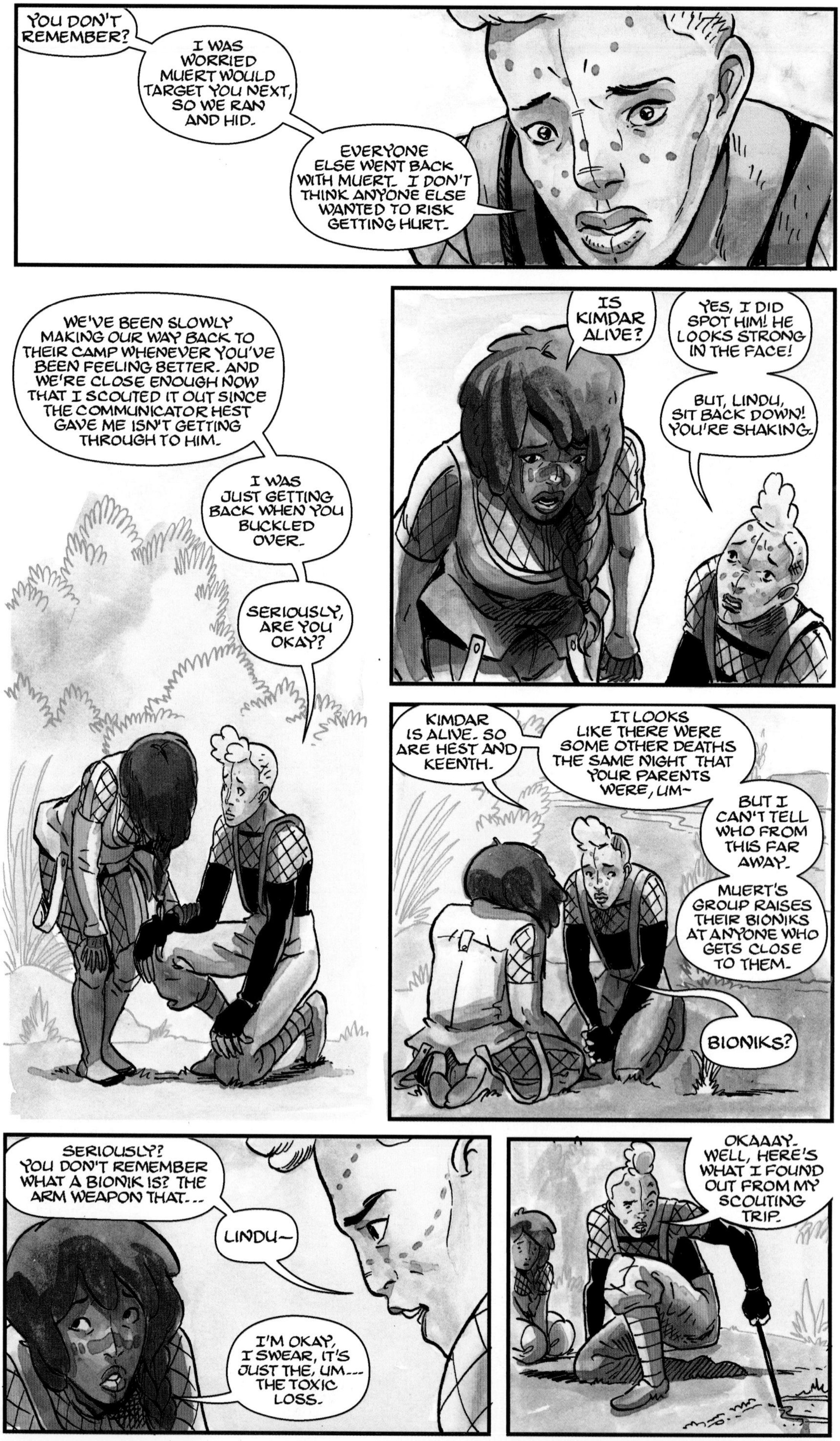

YOU DON'T REMEMBER?
I WAS WORRIED MUERT WOULD TARGET YOU NEXT, SO WE RAN AND HID.
EVERYONE ELSE WENT BACK WITH MUERT. I DON'T THINK ANYONE ELSE WANTED TO RISK GETTING HURT.
WE'VE BEEN SLOWLY MAKING OUR WAY BACK TO THEIR CAMP WHENEVER YOU'VE BEEN FEELING BETTER. AND WE'RE CLOSE ENOUGH NOW THAT I SCOUTED IT OUT SINCE THE COMMUNICATOR HEST GAVE ME ISN'T GETTING THROUGH TO HIM.
I WAS JUST GETTING BACK WHEN YOU BUCKLED OVER.
SERIOUSLY, ARE YOU OKAY?
IS KIMDAR ALIVE?
YES, I DID SPOT HIM! HE LOOKS STRONG IN THE FACE!
BUT, LINDU, SIT BACK DOWN! YOU'RE SHAKING.
KIMDAR IS ALIVE. SO ARE HEST AND KEENTH.
IT LOOKS LIKE THERE WERE SOME OTHER DEATHS THE SAME NIGHT THAT YOUR PARENTS WERE, UM--
BUT I CAN'T TELL WHO FROM THIS FAR AWAY.
MUERT'S GROUP RAISES THEIR BIONIKS AT ANYONE WHO GETS CLOSE TO THEM.
BIONIKS?
SERIOUSLY? YOU DON'T REMEMBER WHAT A BIONIK IS? THE ARM WEAPON THAT...
LINDU--
I'M OKAY, I SWEAR, IT'S JUST THE, UM... THE TOXIC LOSS.
OKAAAY. WELL, HERE'S WHAT I FOUND OUT FROM MY SCOUTING TRIP.

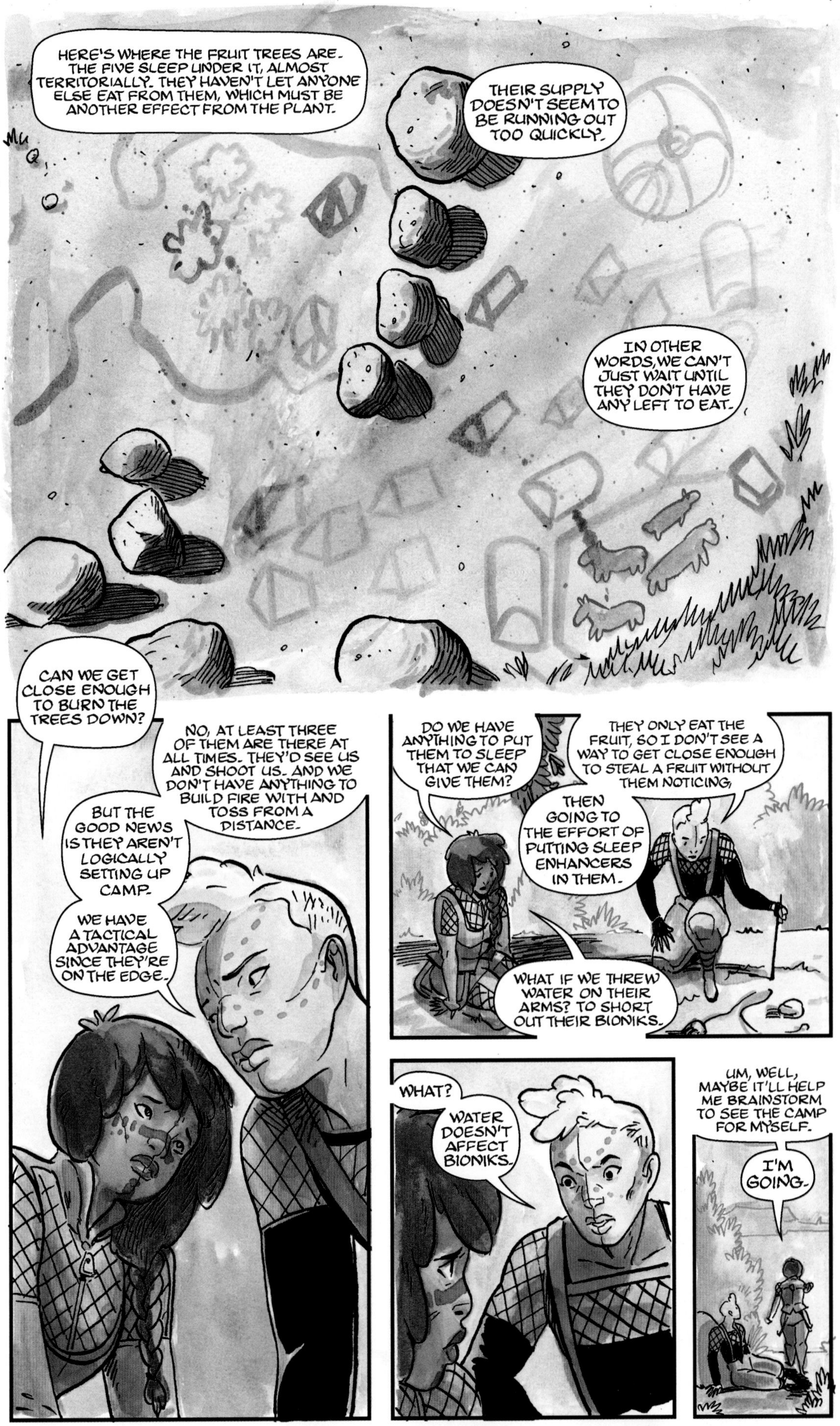
HERE'S WHERE THE FRUIT TREES ARE. THE FIVE SLEEP UNDER IT, ALMOST TERRITORIALLY. THEY HAVEN'T LET ANYONE ELSE EAT FROM THEM, WHICH MUST BE ANOTHER EFFECT FROM THE PLANT.
THEIR SUPPLY DOESN'T SEEM TO BE RUNNING OUT TOO QUICKLY.
IN OTHER WORDS, WE CAN'T JUST WAIT UNTIL THEY DON'T HAVE ANY LEFT TO EAT.
CAN WE GET CLOSE ENOUGH TO BURN THE TREES DOWN?
NO, AT LEAST THREE OF THEM ARE THERE AT ALL TIMES. THEY'D SEE US AND SHOOT US. AND WE DON'T HAVE ANYTHING TO BUILD FIRE WITH AND TOSS FROM A DISTANCE.
BUT THE GOOD NEWS IS THEY AREN'T LOGICALLY SETTING UP CAMP.
WE HAVE A TACTICAL ADVANTAGE SINCE THEY'RE ON THE EDGE.
DO WE HAVE ANYTHING TO PUT THEM TO SLEEP THAT WE CAN GIVE THEM?
THEY ONLY EAT THE FRUIT, SO I DON'T SEE A WAY TO GET CLOSE ENOUGH TO STEAL A FRUIT WITHOUT THEM NOTICING,
THEN GOING TO THE EFFORT OF PUTTING SLEEP ENHANCERS IN THEM.
WHAT IF WE THREW WATER ON THEIR ARMS? TO SHORT OUT THEIR BIONIKS.
WHAT?
WATER DOESN'T AFFECT BIONIKS.
UM, WELL, MAYBE IT'LL HELP ME BRAINSTORM TO SEE THE CAMP FOR MYSELF.
I'M GOING.

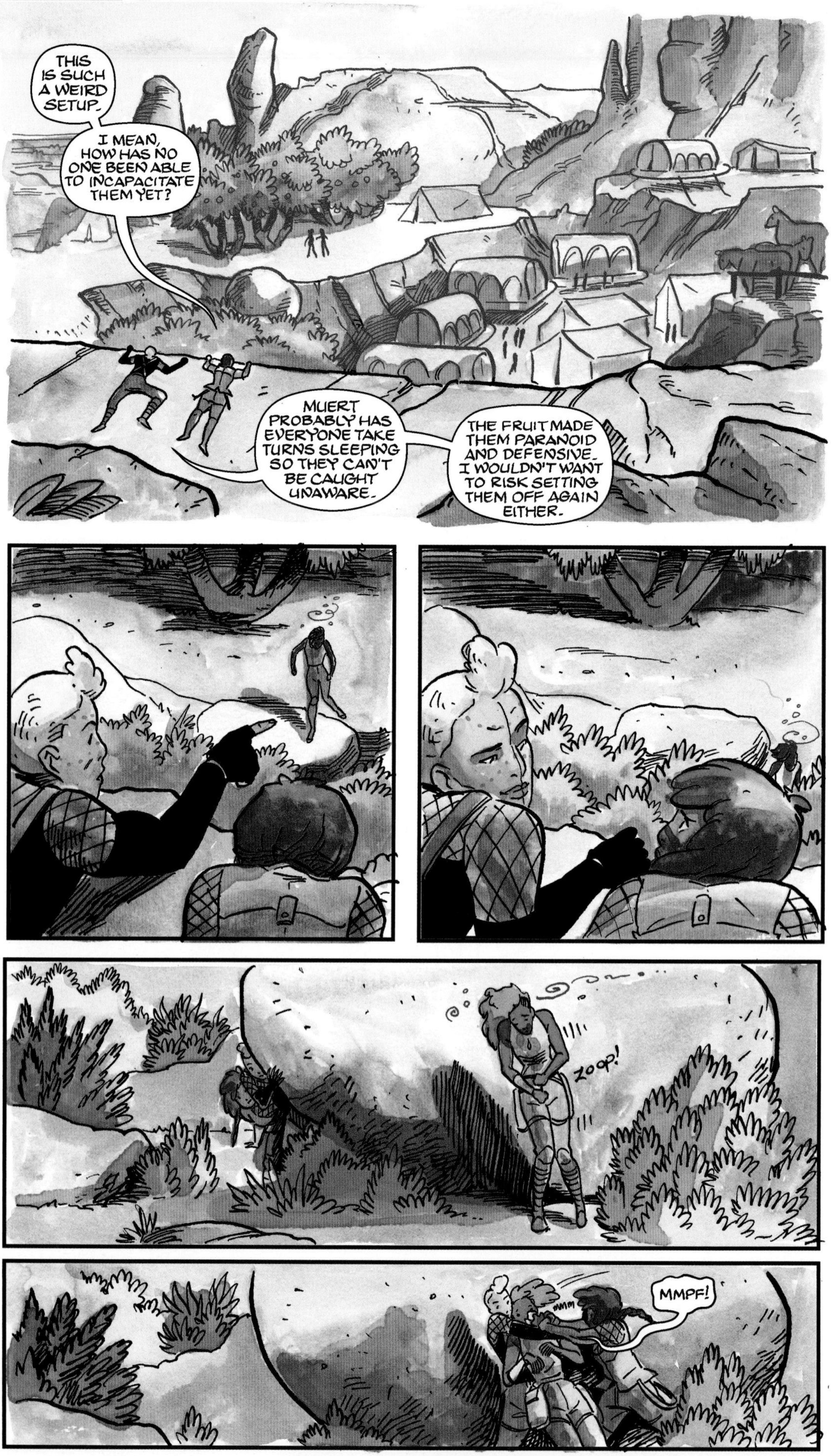
THIS IS SUCH A WEIRD SETUP.
I MEAN, HOW HAS NO ONE BEEN ABLE TO INCAPACITATE THEM YET?
MUERT PROBABLY HAS EVERYONE TAKE TURNS SLEEPING SO THEY CAN'T BE CAUGHT UNAWARE.
THE FRUIT MADE THEM PARANOID AND DEFENSIVE. I WOULDN'T WANT TO RISK SETTING THEM OFF AGAIN EITHER.
ZOOP!
MMPF!

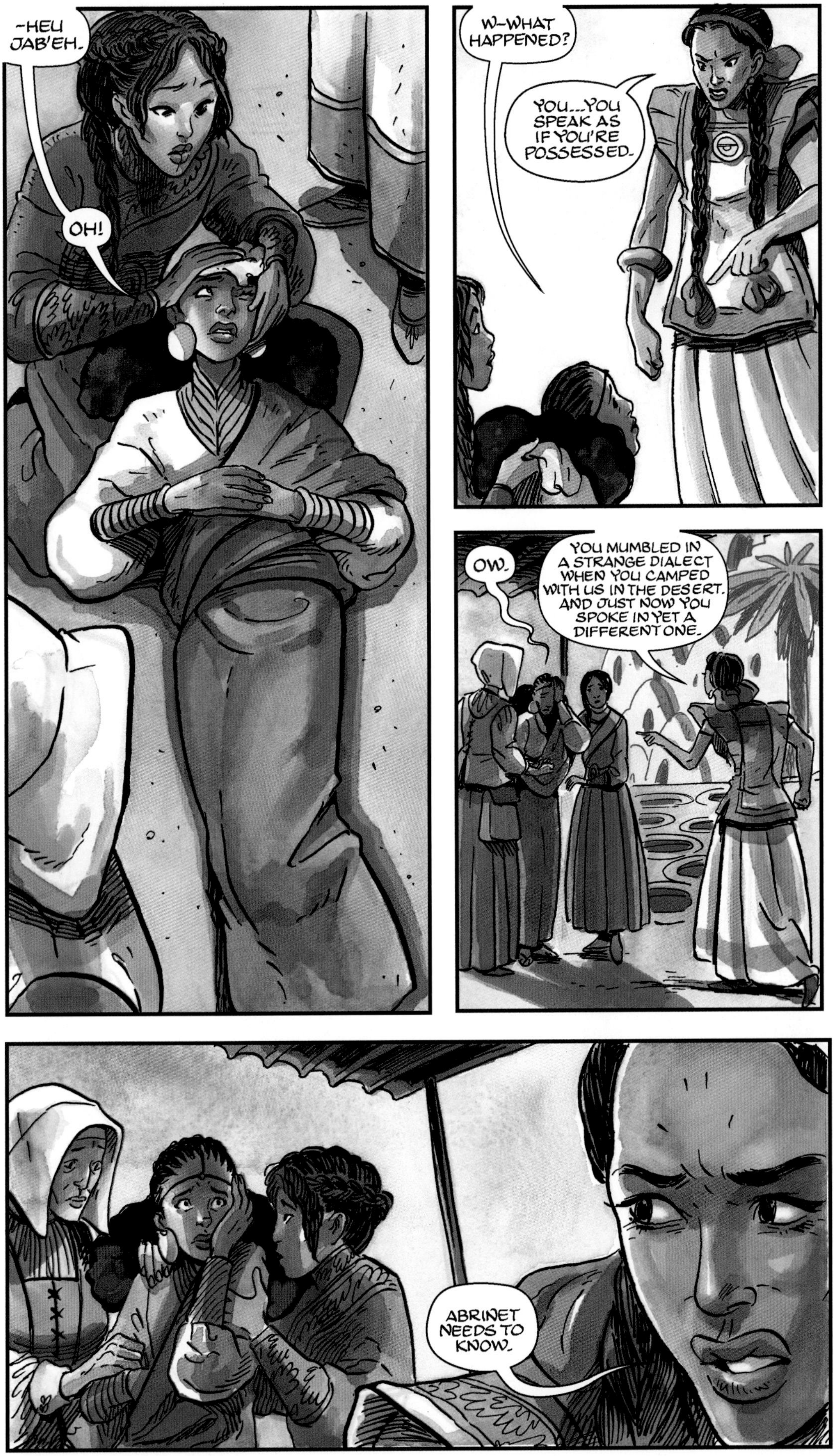
-HEY JAB'EH.
OH!
W-WHAT HAPPENED?
YOU...YOU SPEAK AS IF YOU'RE POSSESSED.
OW.
YOU MUMBLED IN A STRANGE DIALECT WHEN YOU CAMPED WITH US IN THE DESERT. AND JUST NOW YOU SPOKE IN YET A DIFFERENT ONE.
ABRINET NEEDS TO KNOW.

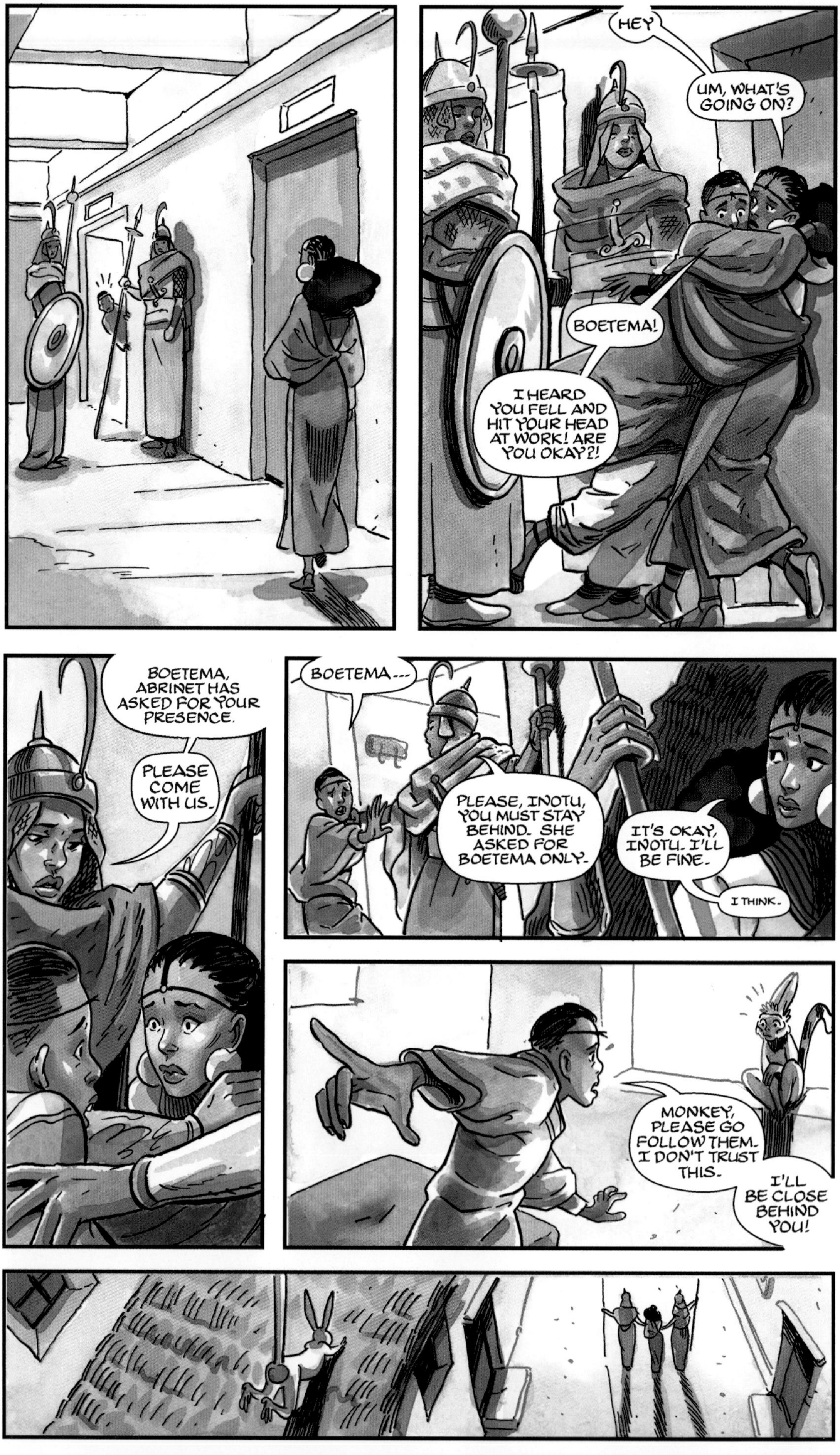
HEY
UM, WHAT'S GOING ON?
BOETEMA!
I HEARD YOU FELL AND HIT YOUR HEAD AT WORK! ARE YOU OKAY?!
BOETEMA, ABRINET HAS ASKED FOR YOUR PRESENCE.
PLEASE COME WITH US.
BOETEMA---
PLEASE, INOTU, YOU MUST STAY BEHIND. SHE ASKED FOR BOETEMA ONLY.
IT'S OKAY, INOTU. I'LL BE FINE.
I THINK.
MONKEY, PLEASE GO FOLLOW THEM. I DON'T TRUST THIS.
I'LL BE CLOSE BEHIND YOU!

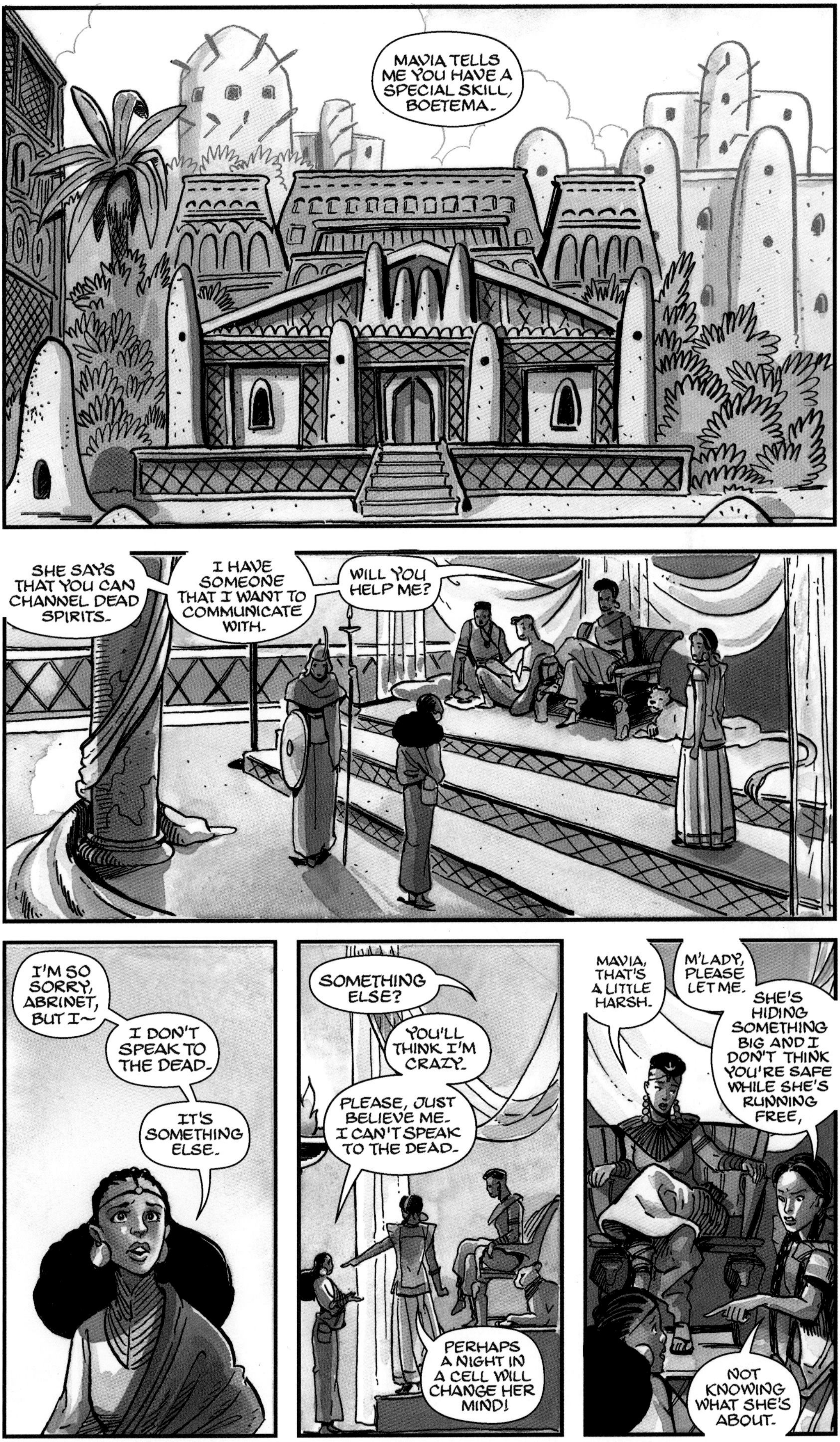
MAVIA TELLS ME YOU HAVE A SPECIAL SKILL, BOETEMA.
SHE SAYS THAT YOU CAN CHANNEL DEAD SPIRITS.
I HAVE SOMEONE THAT I WANT TO COMMUNICATE WITH.
WILL YOU HELP ME?
I'M SO SORRY, ABRINET, BUT I~
I DON'T SPEAK TO THE DEAD.
IT'S SOMETHING ELSE.
SOMETHING ELSE?
YOU'LL THINK I'M CRAZY.
PLEASE, JUST BELIEVE ME. I CAN'T SPEAK TO THE DEAD.
PERHAPS A NIGHT IN A CELL WILL CHANGE HER MIND!
MAVIA, THAT'S A LITTLE HARSH.
M'LADY, PLEASE LET ME.
SHE'S HIDING SOMETHING BIG AND I DON'T THINK YOU'RE SAFE WHILE SHE'S RUNNING FREE,
NOT KNOWING WHAT SHE'S ABOUT.

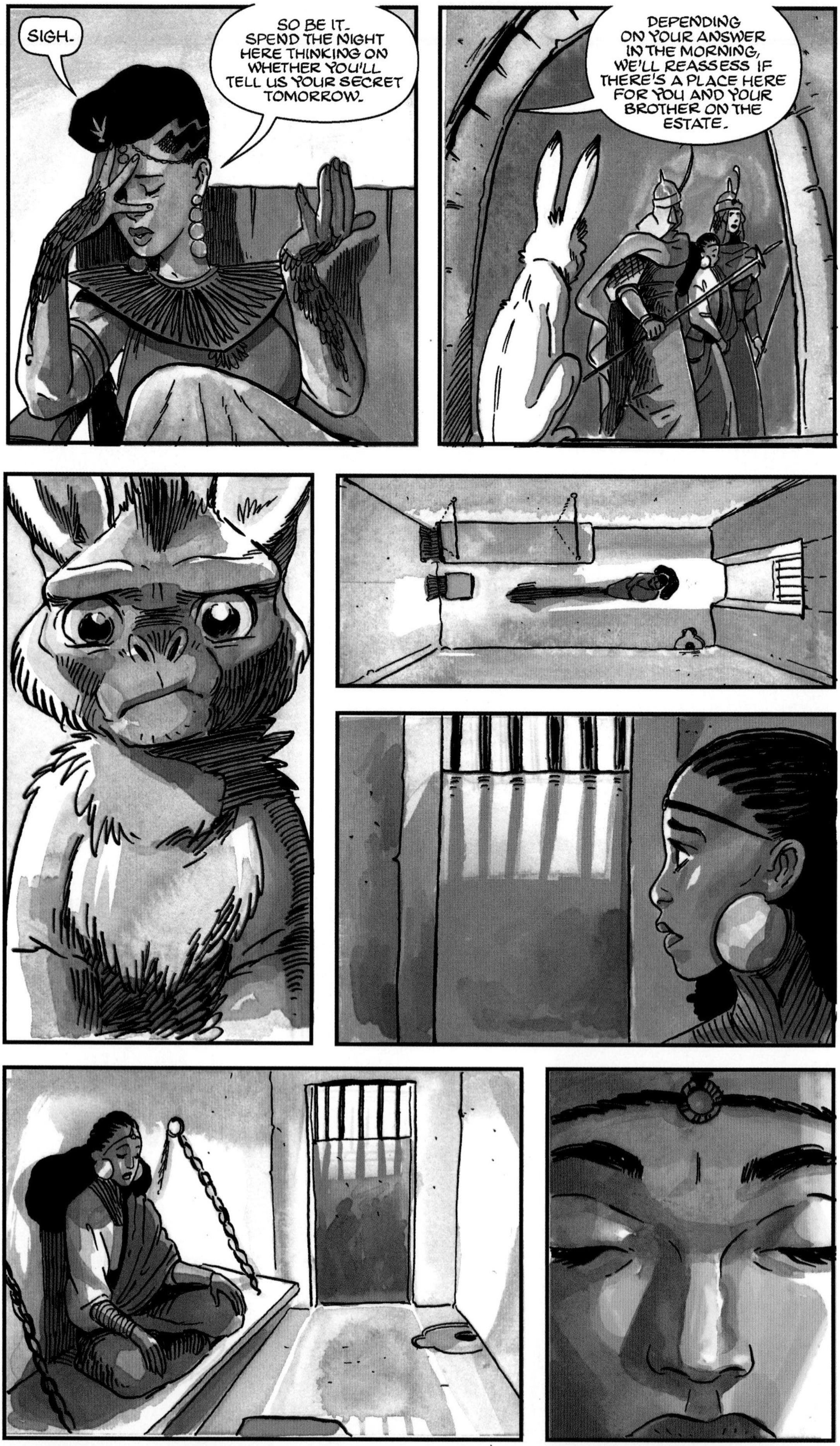
SIGH.
SO BE IT. SPEND THE NIGHT HERE THINKING ON WHETHER YOU'LL TELL US YOUR SECRET TOMORROW.
DEPENDING ON YOUR ANSWER IN THE MORNING, WE'LL REASSESS IF THERE'S A PLACE HERE FOR YOU AND YOUR BROTHER ON THE ESTATE.

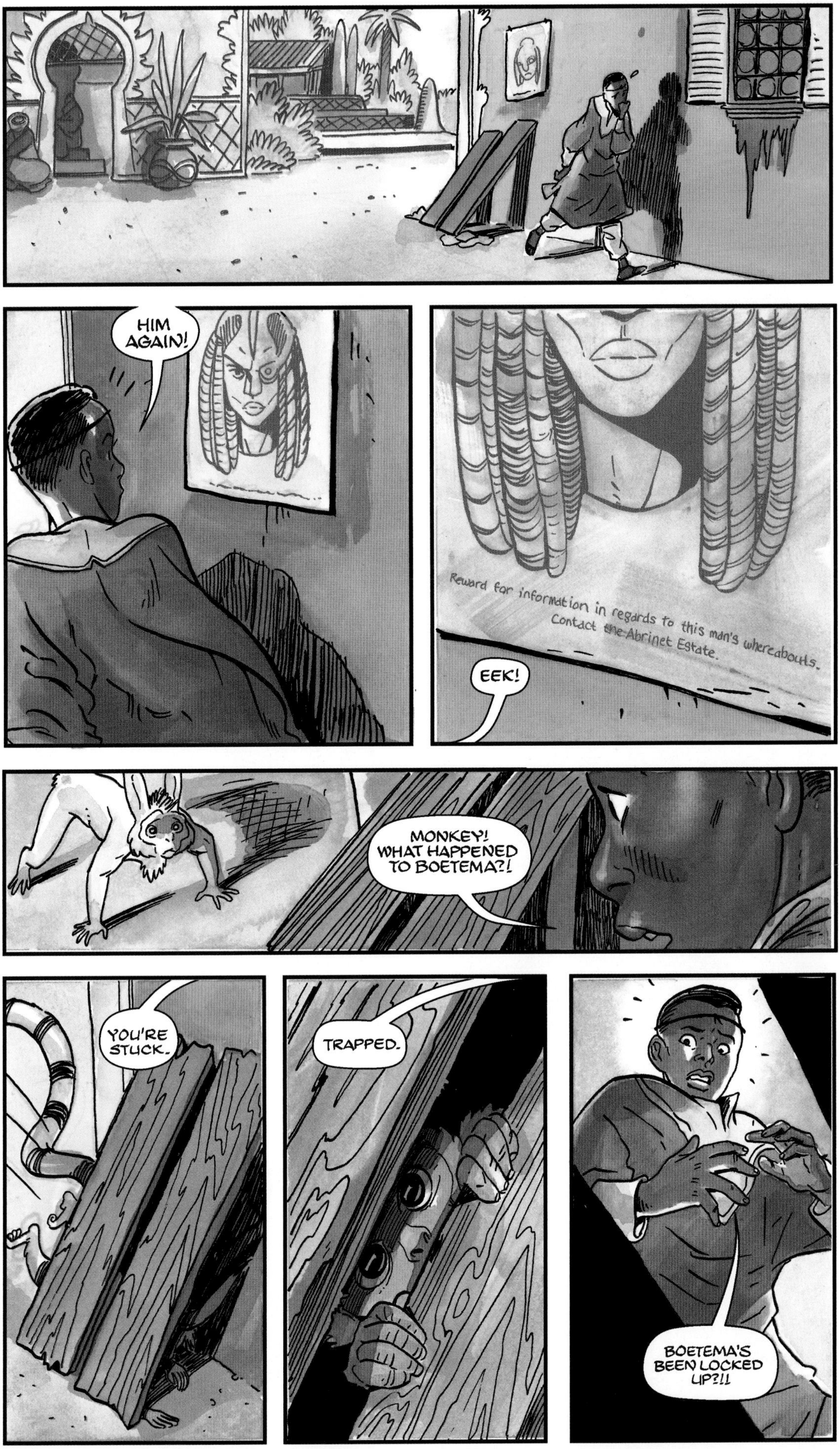
HIM AGAIN!
Reward for information in regards to this man's whereabouts.
Contact the Abrinet Estate.
EEK!
MONKEY! WHAT HAPPENED TO BOETEMA?!
YOU'RE STUCK.
TRAPPED.
BOETEMA'S BEEN LOCKED UP?!!

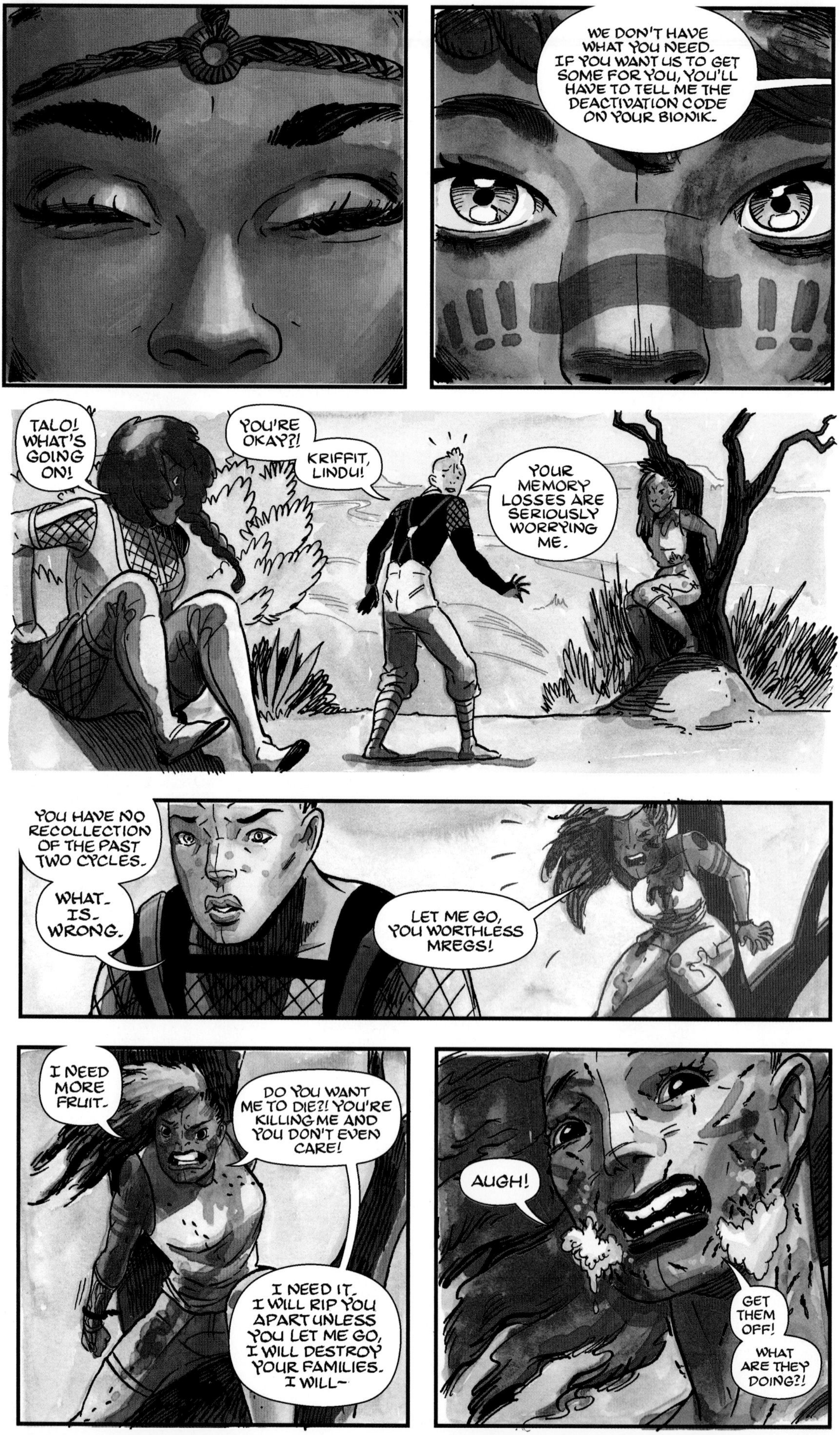
WE DON'T HAVE WHAT YOU NEED. IF YOU WANT US TO GET SOME FOR YOU, YOU'LL HAVE TO TELL ME THE DEACTIVATION CODE ON YOUR BIONIK.
TALO! WHAT'S GOING ON!
YOU'RE OKAY?!
KRIFFIT, LINDU!
YOUR MEMORY LOSSES ARE SERIOUSLY WORRYING ME.
YOU HAVE NO RECOLLECTION OF THE PAST TWO CYCLES.
WHAT. IS. WRONG.
LET ME GO, YOU WORTHLESS MREGS!
I NEED MORE FRUIT.
DO YOU WANT ME TO DIE?! YOU'RE KILLING ME AND YOU DON'T EVEN CARE!
I NEED IT. I WILL RIP YOU APART UNLESS YOU LET ME GO, I WILL DESTROY YOUR FAMILIES. I WILL--
AUGH!
GET THEM OFF!
WHAT ARE THEY DOING?!

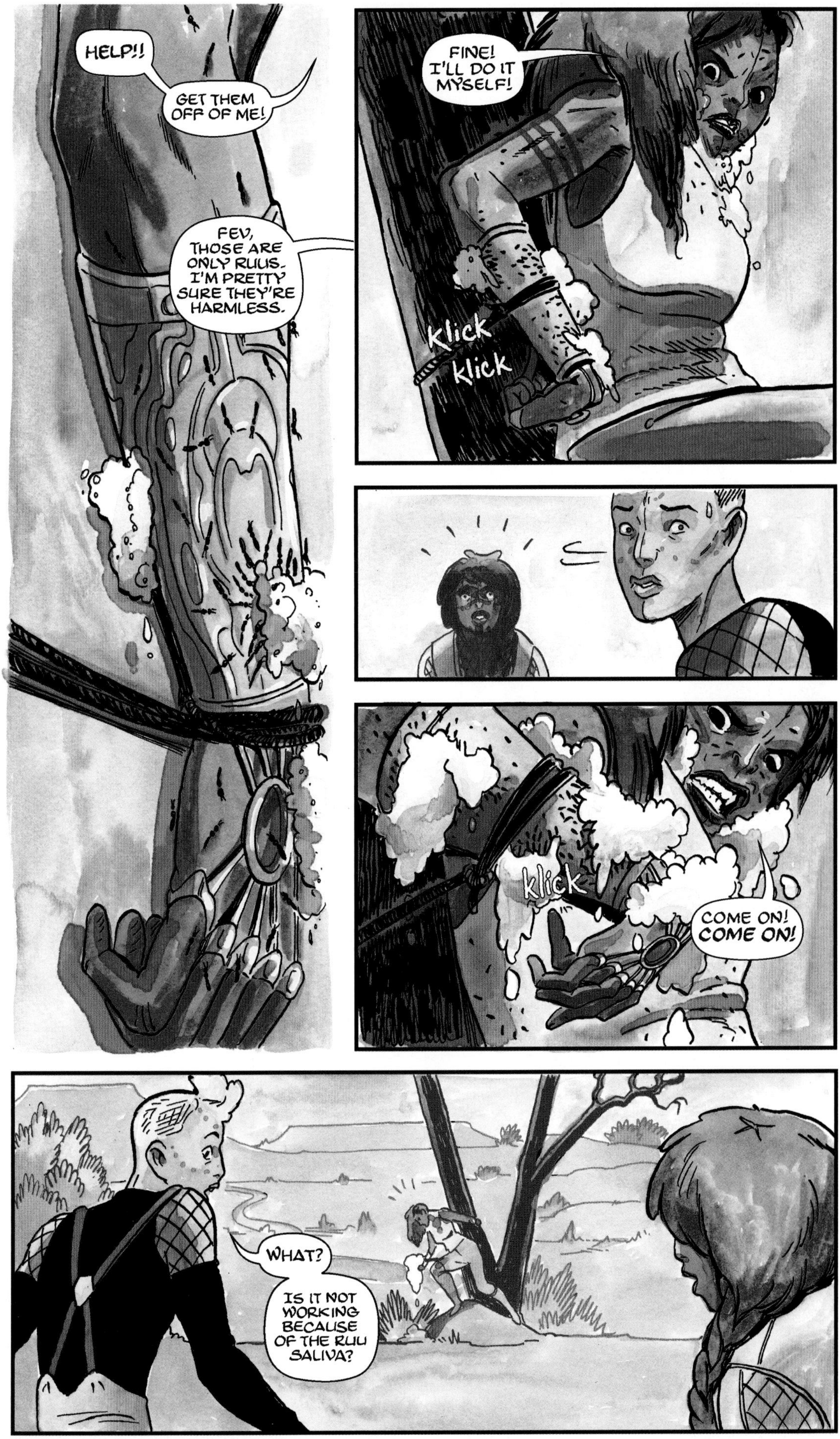
HELP!!
GET THEM OFF OF ME!
FEV, THOSE ARE ONLY RUUS. I'M PRETTY SURE THEY'RE HARMLESS.
FINE! I'LL DO IT MYSELF!
klick
klick
klick
COME ON! COME ON!
WHAT?
IS IT NOT WORKING BECAUSE OF THE RUU SALIVA?

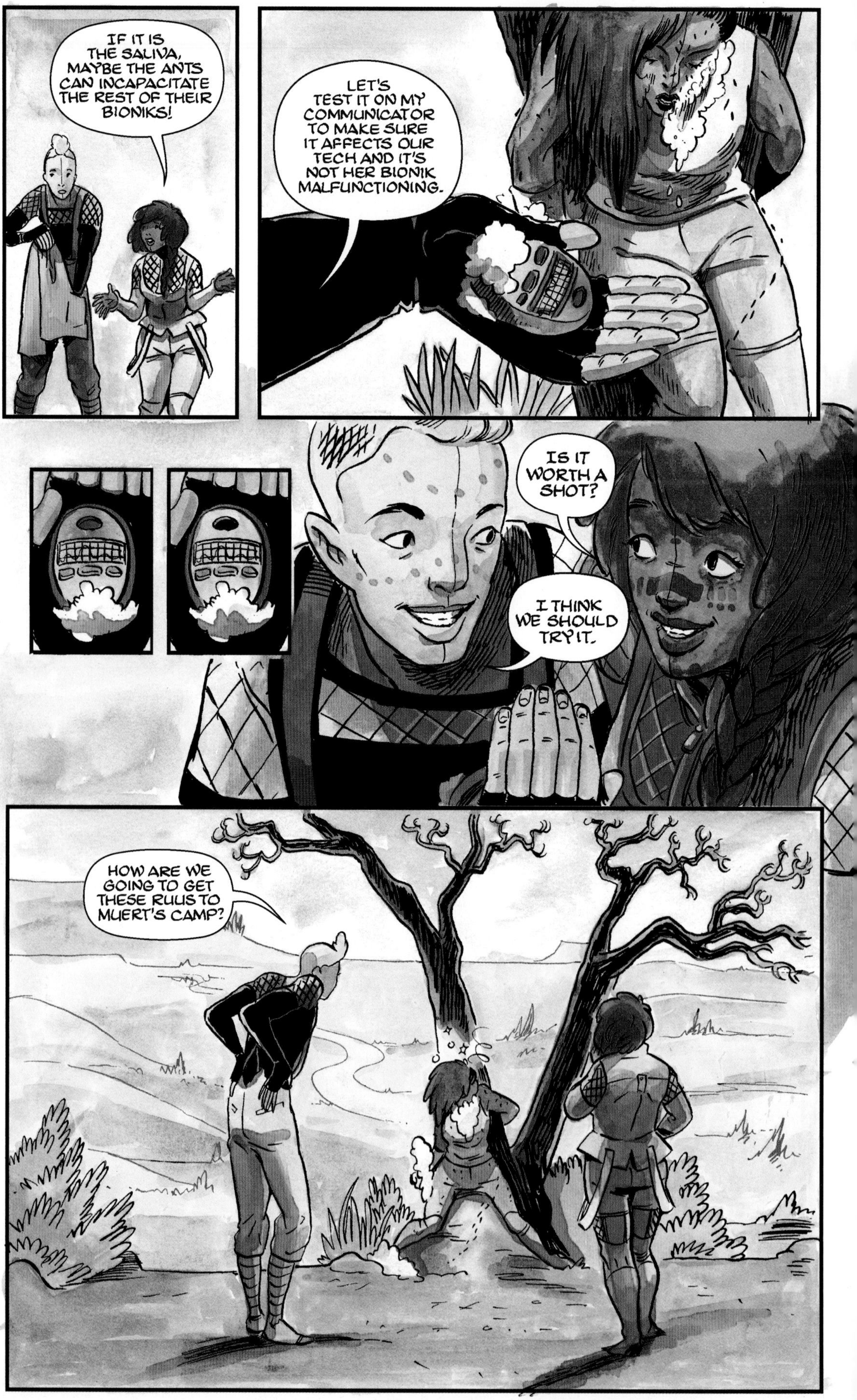
IF IT IS THE SALIVA, MAYBE THE ANTS CAN INCAPACITATE THE REST OF THEIR BIONIKS!
LET'S TEST IT ON MY COMMUNICATOR TO MAKE SURE IT AFFECTS OUR TECH AND IT'S NOT HER BIONIK MALFUNCTIONING.
IS IT WORTH A SHOT?
I THINK WE SHOULD TRY IT.
HOW ARE WE GOING TO GET THESE RUUS TO MUERT'S CAMP?

I HAVE INFORMATION REGARDING THIS PERSON.

PLEASE, MAY I SPEAK WITH ABRINET?

UH, THAT'S NOT HOW IT WORKS.

YOU HAVE TO TALK TO HER DEPUTY.

I'LL TAKE HIM.

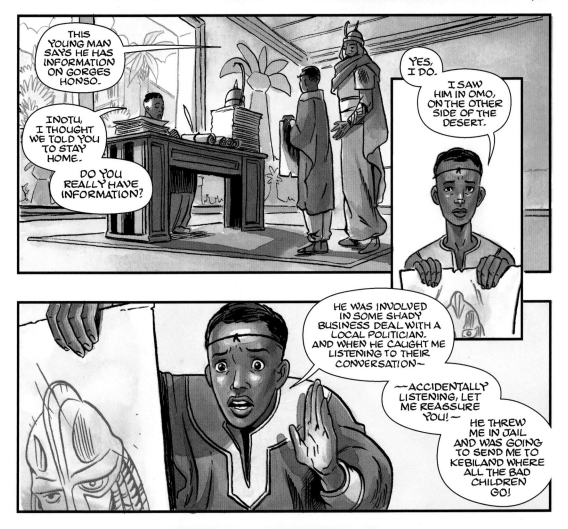

THIS YOUNG MAN SAYS HE HAS INFORMATION ON GORGES HONSO.

INOTU, I THOUGHT WE TOLD YOU TO STAY HOME.

DO YOU REALLY HAVE INFORMATION?

YES, I DO.

I SAW HIM IN OMO, ON THE OTHER SIDE OF THE DESERT.

HE WAS INVOLVED IN SOME SHADY BUSINESS DEAL WITH A LOCAL POLITICIAN. AND WHEN HE CAUGHT ME LISTENING TO THEIR CONVERSATION~

~ACCIDENTALLY LISTENING, LET ME REASSURE YOU!~

HE THREW ME IN JAIL AND WAS GOING TO SEND ME TO KEBILAND WHERE ALL THE BAD CHILDREN GO!

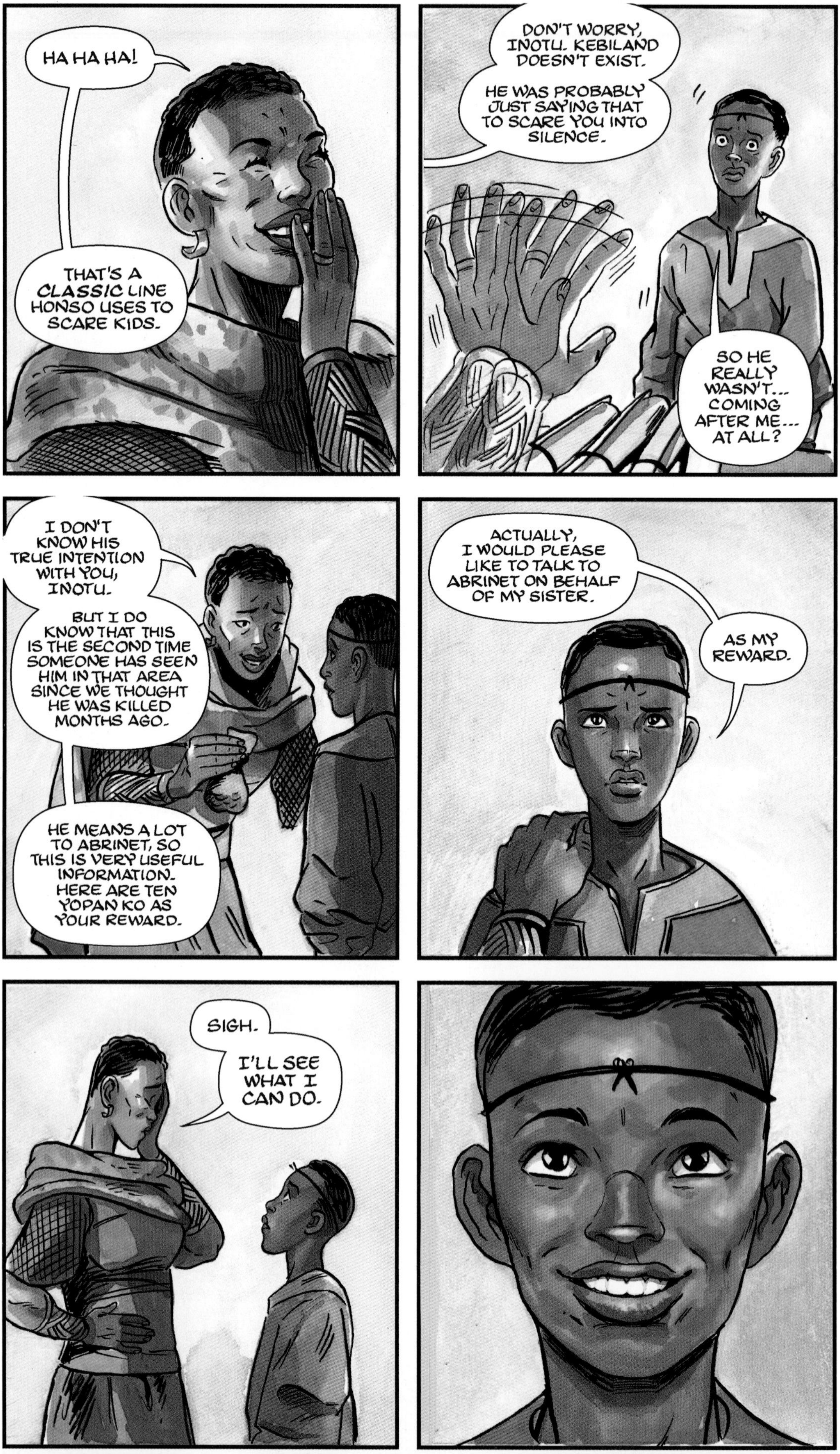
HA HA HA!
THAT'S A *CLASSIC* LINE HONSO USES TO SCARE KIDS.
DON'T WORRY, INOTU. KEBILAND DOESN'T EXIST.
HE WAS PROBABLY JUST SAYING THAT TO SCARE YOU INTO SILENCE.
SO HE REALLY WASN'T... COMING AFTER ME... AT ALL?
I DON'T KNOW HIS TRUE INTENTION WITH YOU, INOTU.
BUT I DO KNOW THAT THIS IS THE SECOND TIME SOMEONE HAS SEEN HIM IN THAT AREA SINCE WE THOUGHT HE WAS KILLED MONTHS AGO.
HE MEANS A LOT TO ABRINET, SO THIS IS VERY USEFUL INFORMATION. HERE ARE TEN YOPAN KO AS YOUR REWARD.
ACTUALLY, I WOULD PLEASE LIKE TO TALK TO ABRINET ON BEHALF OF MY SISTER.
AS MY REWARD.
SIGH.
I'LL SEE WHAT I CAN DO.

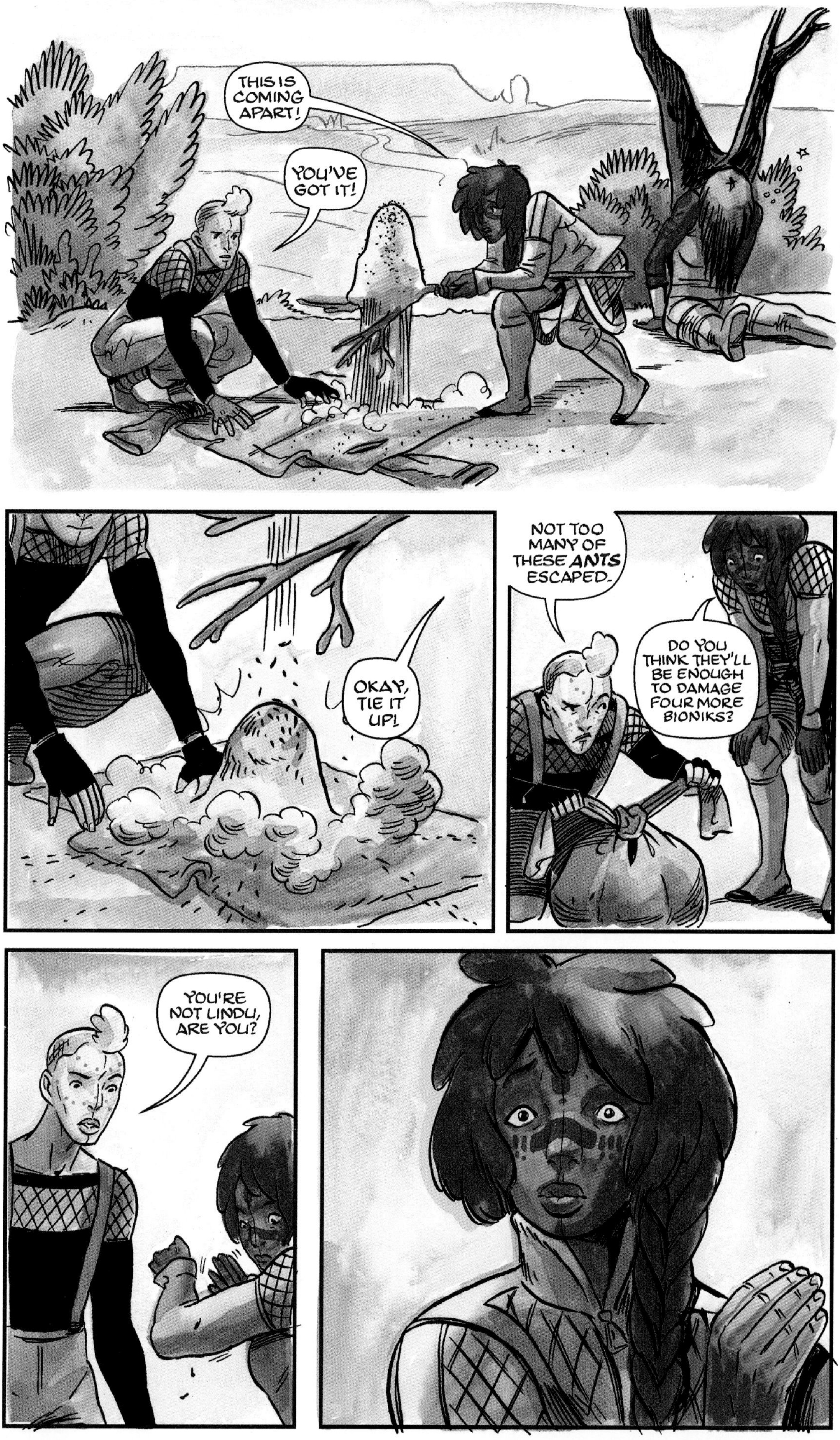
THIS IS COMING APART!
YOU'VE GOT IT!
OKAY, TIE IT UP!
NOT TOO MANY OF THESE ANTS ESCAPED.
DO YOU THINK THEY'LL BE ENOUGH TO DAMAGE FOUR MORE BIONIKS?
YOU'RE NOT LINDU, ARE YOU?

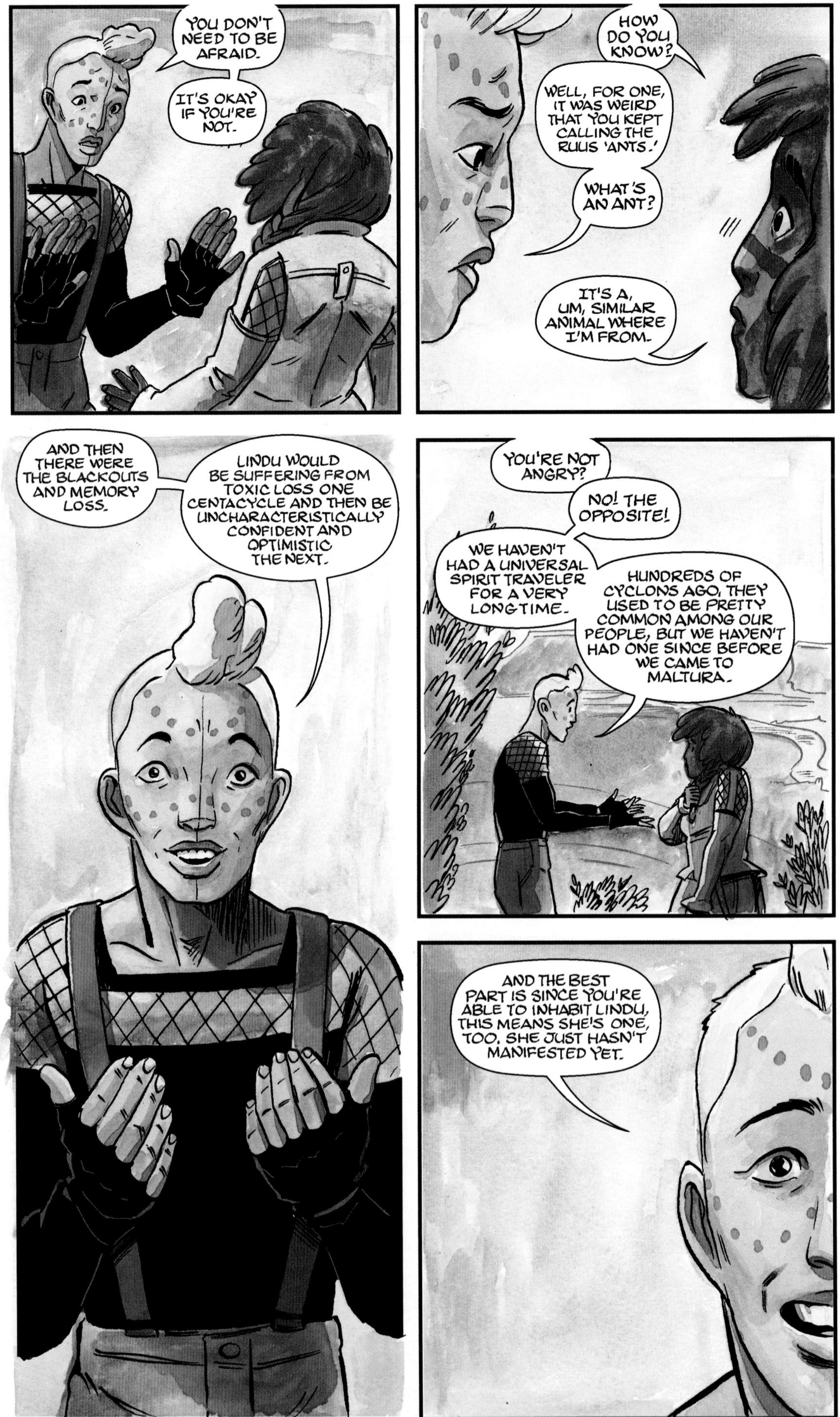
YOU DON'T NEED TO BE AFRAID.
IT'S OKAY IF YOU'RE NOT.
HOW DO YOU KNOW?
WELL, FOR ONE, IT WAS WEIRD THAT YOU KEPT CALLING THE RUUS 'ANTS.'
WHAT'S AN ANT?
IT'S A, UM, SIMILAR ANIMAL WHERE I'M FROM.
AND THEN THERE WERE THE BLACKOUTS AND MEMORY LOSS.
LINDU WOULD BE SUFFERING FROM TOXIC LOSS ONE CENTACYCLE AND THEN BE UNCHARACTERISTICALLY CONFIDENT AND OPTIMISTIC THE NEXT.
YOU'RE NOT ANGRY?
NO! THE OPPOSITE!
WE HAVEN'T HAD A UNIVERSAL SPIRIT TRAVELER FOR A VERY LONG TIME.
HUNDREDS OF CYCLONS AGO, THEY USED TO BE PRETTY COMMON AMONG OUR PEOPLE, BUT WE HAVEN'T HAD ONE SINCE BEFORE WE CAME TO MALTURA.
AND THE BEST PART IS SINCE YOU'RE ABLE TO INHABIT LINDU, THIS MEANS SHE'S ONE, TOO. SHE JUST HASN'T MANIFESTED YET.

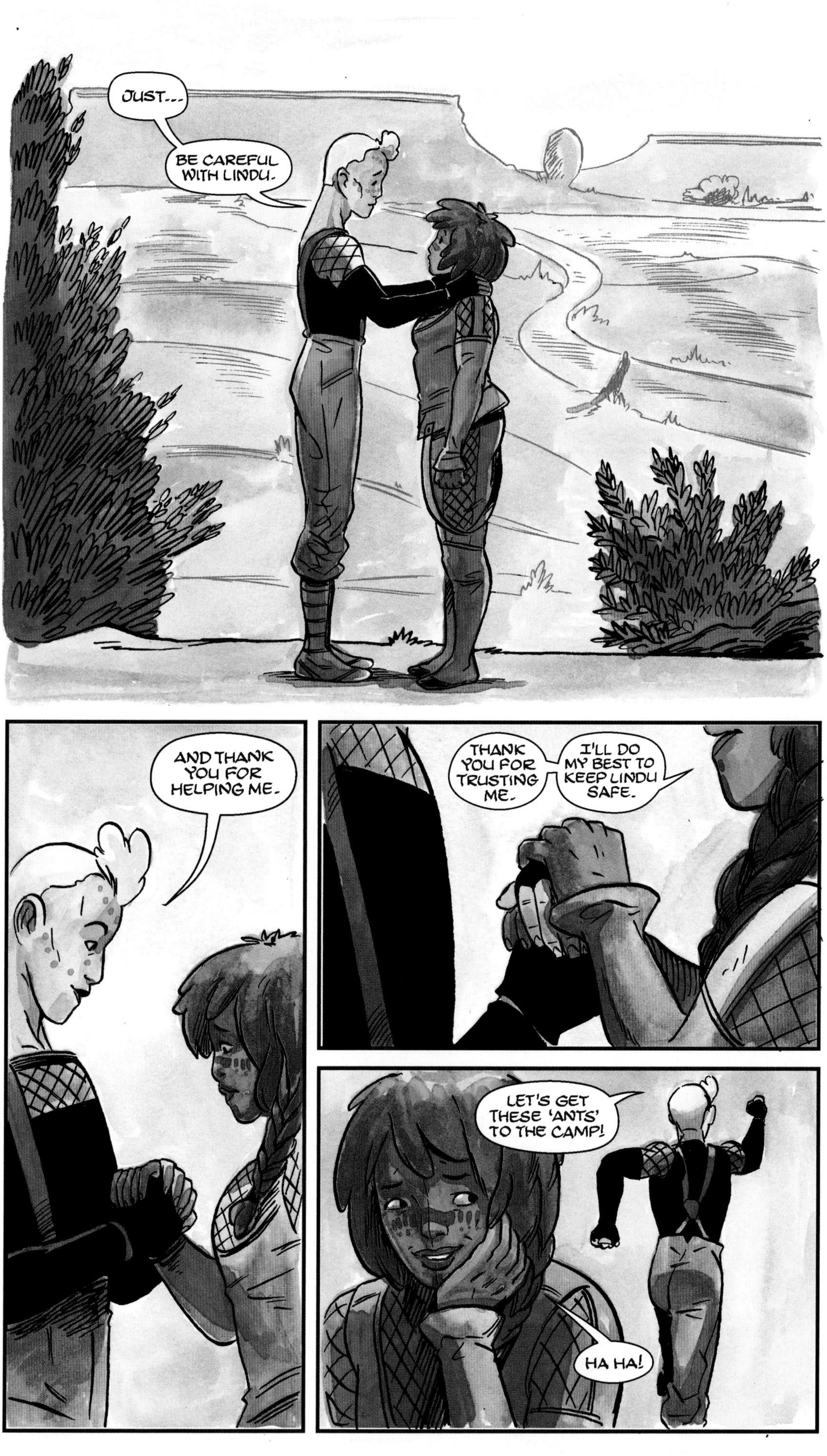
JUST...
BE CAREFUL WITH LINDU.
AND THANK YOU FOR HELPING ME.
THANK YOU FOR TRUSTING ME.
I'LL DO MY BEST TO KEEP LINDU SAFE.
LET'S GET THESE 'ANTS' TO THE CAMP!
HA HA!

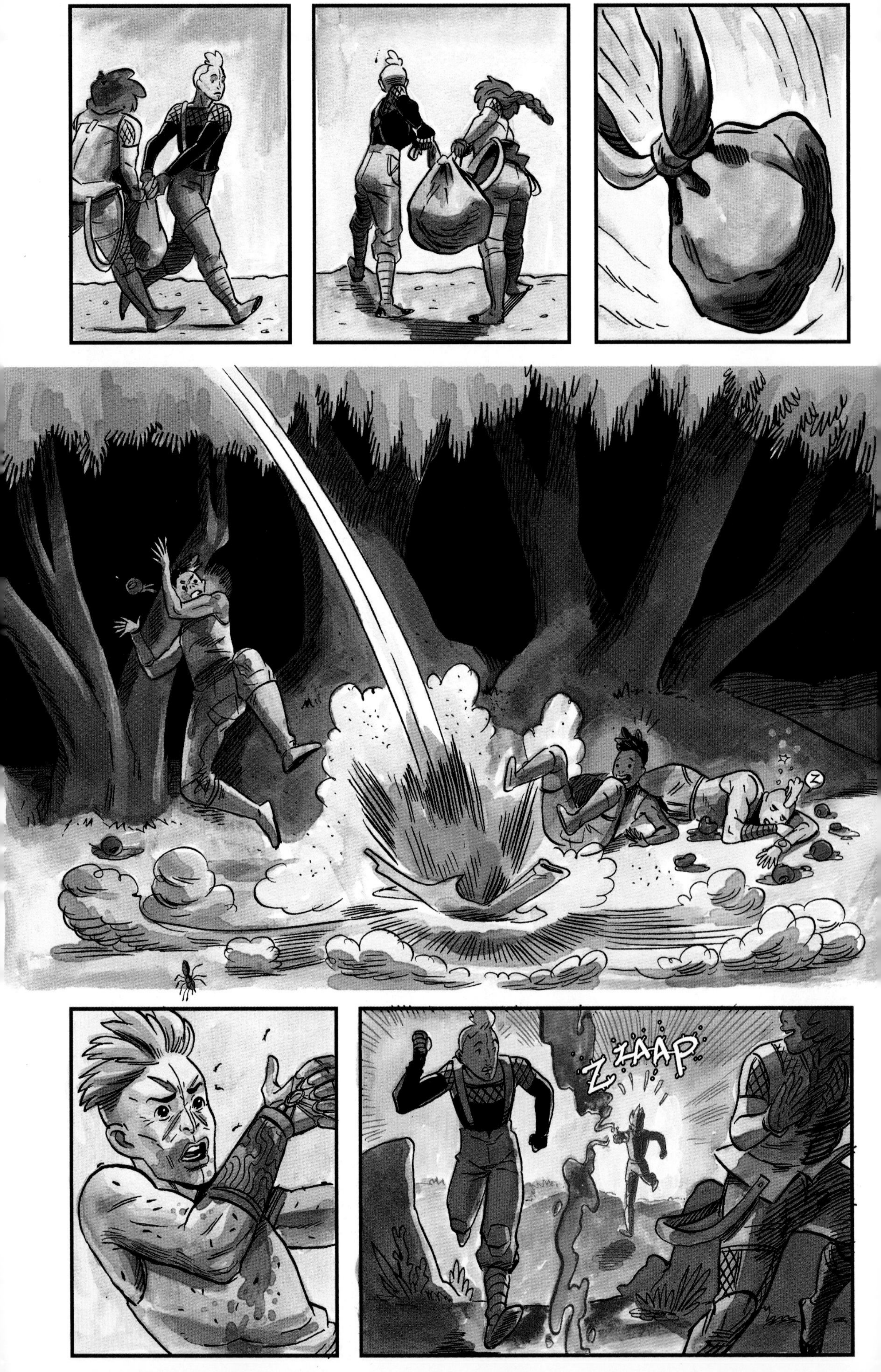
ZZAAP

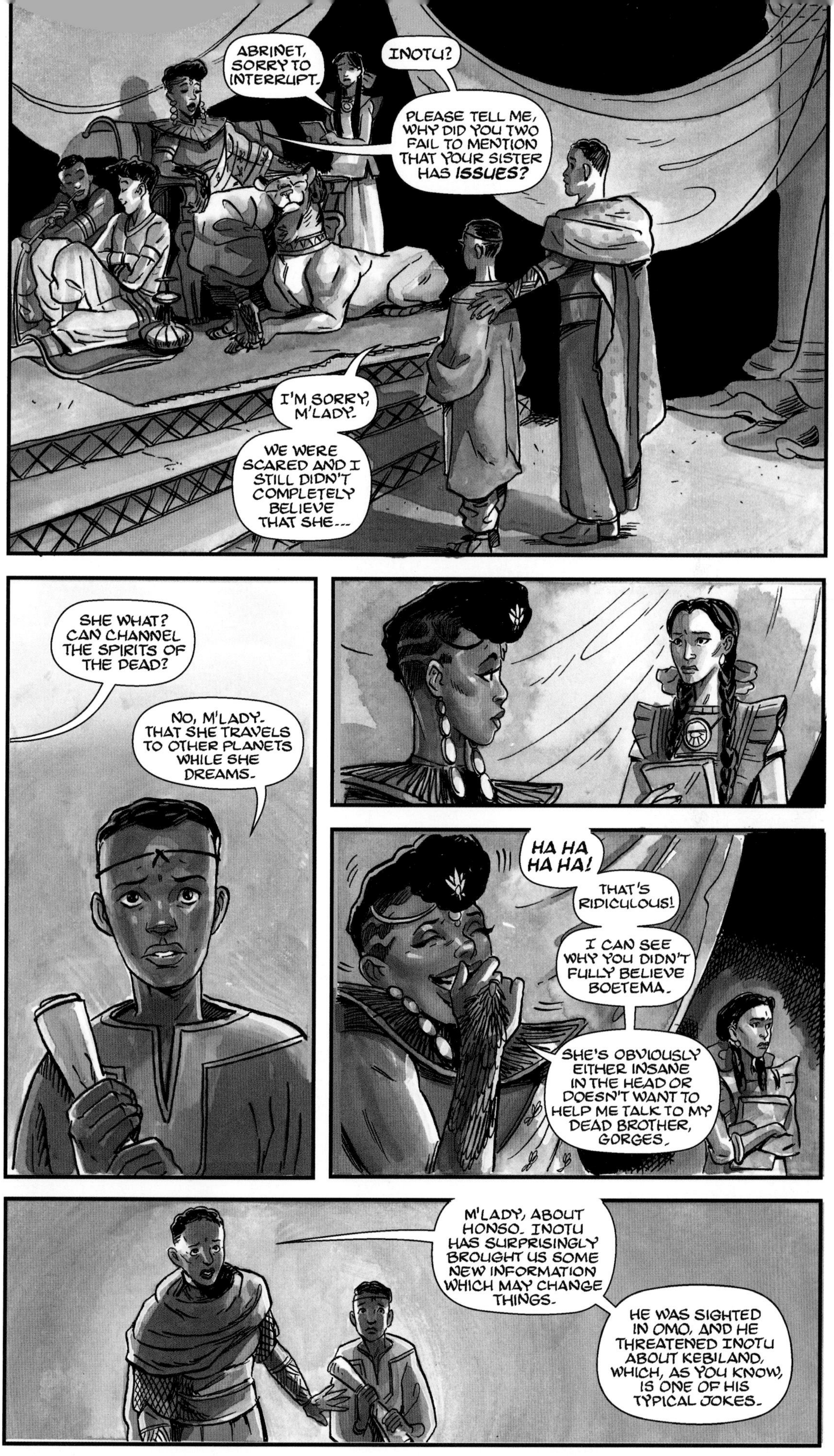
ABRINET, SORRY TO INTERRUPT.
INOTU?
PLEASE TELL ME, WHY DID YOU TWO FAIL TO MENTION THAT YOUR SISTER HAS ISSUES?
I'M SORRY, M'LADY.
WE WERE SCARED AND I STILL DIDN'T COMPLETELY BELIEVE THAT SHE...
SHE WHAT? CAN CHANNEL THE SPIRITS OF THE DEAD?
NO, M'LADY. THAT SHE TRAVELS TO OTHER PLANETS WHILE SHE DREAMS.
HA HA HA HA!
THAT'S RIDICULOUS!
I CAN SEE WHY YOU DIDN'T FULLY BELIEVE BOETEMA.
SHE'S OBVIOUSLY EITHER INSANE IN THE HEAD OR DOESN'T WANT TO HELP ME TALK TO MY DEAD BROTHER, GORGES.
M'LADY, ABOUT HONSO. INOTU HAS SURPRISINGLY BROUGHT US SOME NEW INFORMATION WHICH MAY CHANGE THINGS.
HE WAS SIGHTED IN OMO, AND HE THREATENED INOTU ABOUT KEBILAND, WHICH, AS YOU KNOW, IS ONE OF HIS TYPICAL JOKES.

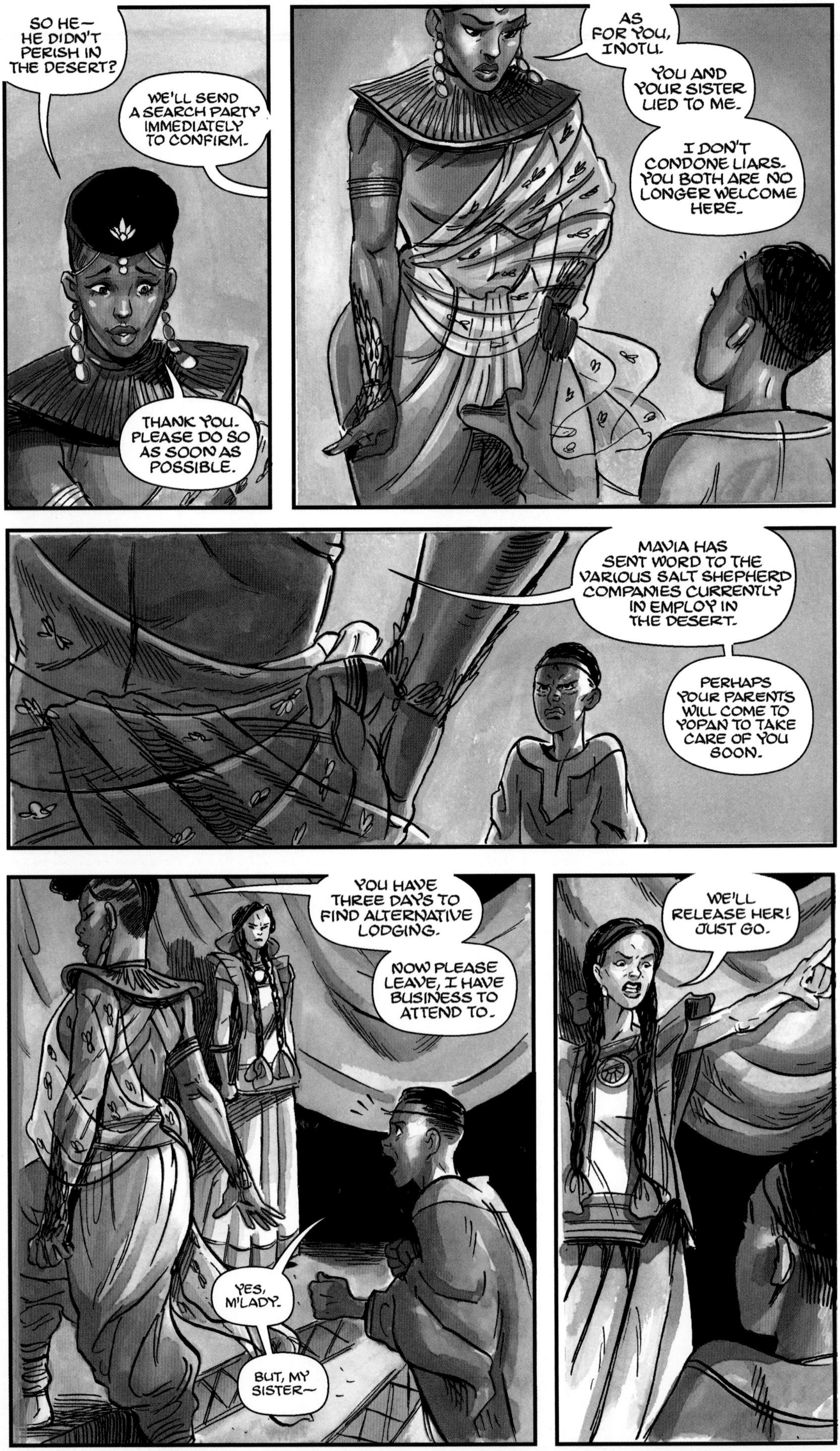
SO HE— HE DIDN'T PERISH IN THE DESERT?
WE'LL SEND A SEARCH PARTY IMMEDIATELY TO CONFIRM.
THANK YOU. PLEASE DO SO AS SOON AS POSSIBLE.
AS FOR YOU, INOTU.
YOU AND YOUR SISTER LIED TO ME.
I DON'T CONDONE LIARS. YOU BOTH ARE NO LONGER WELCOME HERE.
MAVIA HAS SENT WORD TO THE VARIOUS SALT SHEPHERD COMPANIES CURRENTLY IN EMPLOY IN THE DESERT.
PERHAPS YOUR PARENTS WILL COME TO YOPAN TO TAKE CARE OF YOU SOON.
YOU HAVE THREE DAYS TO FIND ALTERNATIVE LODGING.
NOW PLEASE LEAVE, I HAVE BUSINESS TO ATTEND TO.
YES, M'LADY.
BUT, MY SISTER—
WE'LL RELEASE HER! JUST GO.

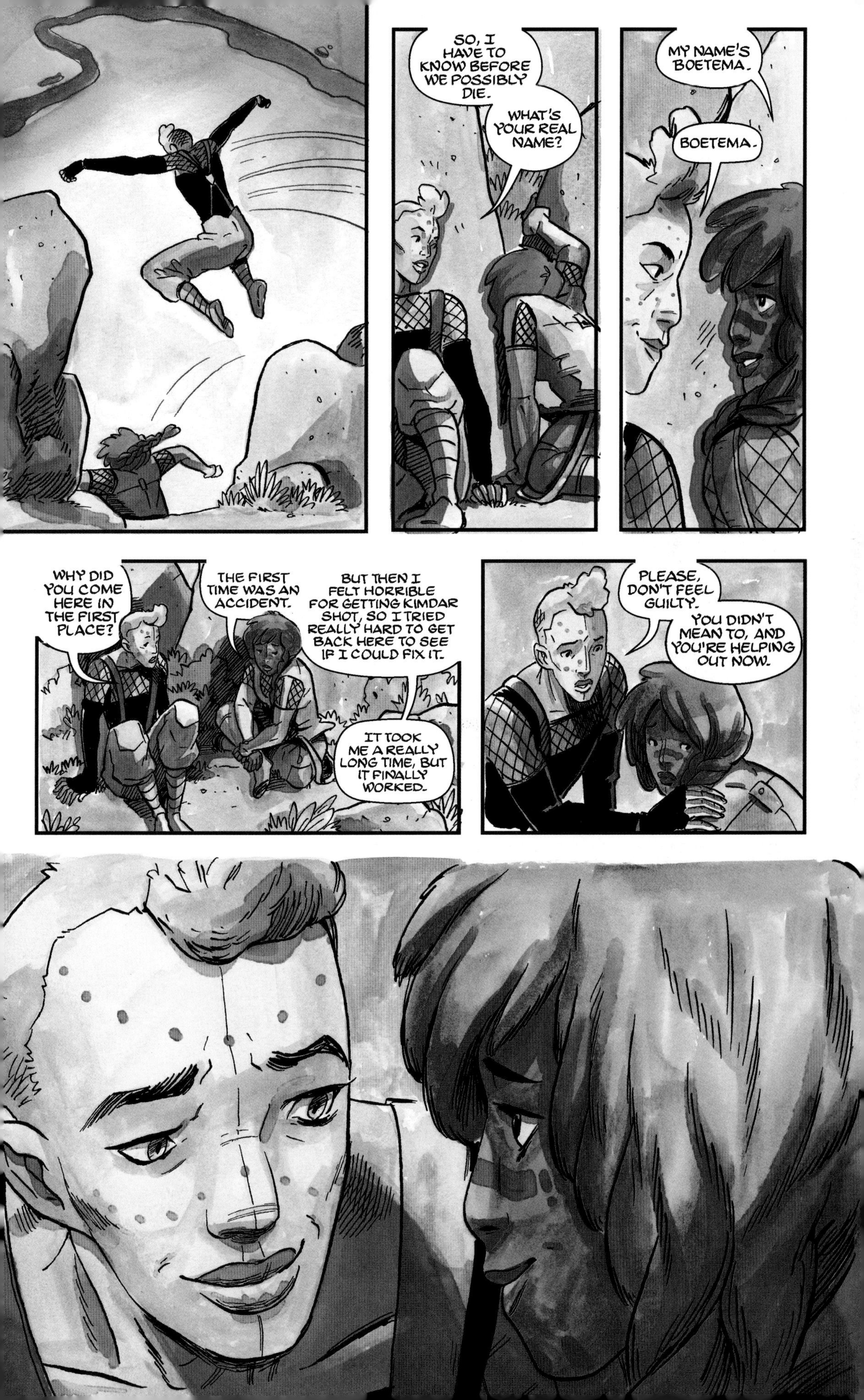
SO, I HAVE TO KNOW BEFORE WE POSSIBLY DIE.
WHAT'S YOUR REAL NAME?
MY NAME'S BOETEMA.
BOETEMA.
WHY DID YOU COME HERE IN THE FIRST PLACE?
THE FIRST TIME WAS AN ACCIDENT.
BUT THEN I FELT HORRIBLE FOR GETTING KIMDAR SHOT, SO I TRIED REALLY HARD TO GET BACK HERE TO SEE IF I COULD FIX IT.
IT TOOK ME A REALLY LONG TIME, BUT IT FINALLY WORKED.
PLEASE, DON'T FEEL GUILTY.
YOU DIDN'T MEAN TO, AND YOU'RE HELPING OUT NOW.

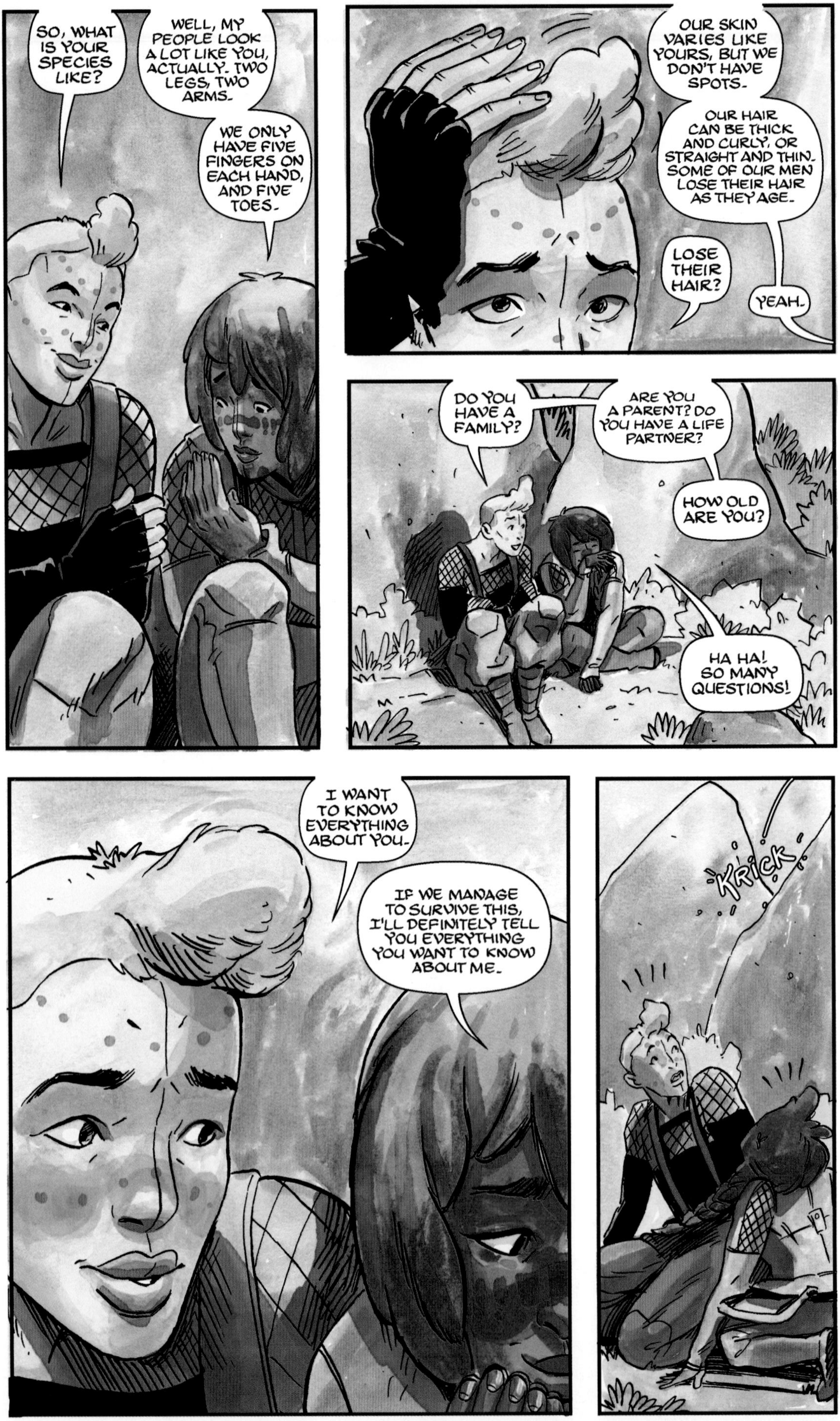
SO, WHAT IS YOUR SPECIES LIKE?
WELL, MY PEOPLE LOOK A LOT LIKE YOU, ACTUALLY. TWO LEGS, TWO ARMS.
WE ONLY HAVE FIVE FINGERS ON EACH HAND, AND FIVE TOES.
OUR SKIN VARIES LIKE YOURS, BUT WE DON'T HAVE SPOTS.
OUR HAIR CAN BE THICK AND CURLY, OR STRAIGHT AND THIN. SOME OF OUR MEN LOSE THEIR HAIR AS THEY AGE.
LOSE THEIR HAIR?
YEAH.
DO YOU HAVE A FAMILY?
ARE YOU A PARENT? DO YOU HAVE A LIFE PARTNER?
HOW OLD ARE YOU?
HA HA! SO MANY QUESTIONS!
I WANT TO KNOW EVERYTHING ABOUT YOU.
IF WE MANAGE TO SURVIVE THIS, I'LL DEFINITELY TELL YOU EVERYTHING YOU WANT TO KNOW ABOUT ME.
KRICK

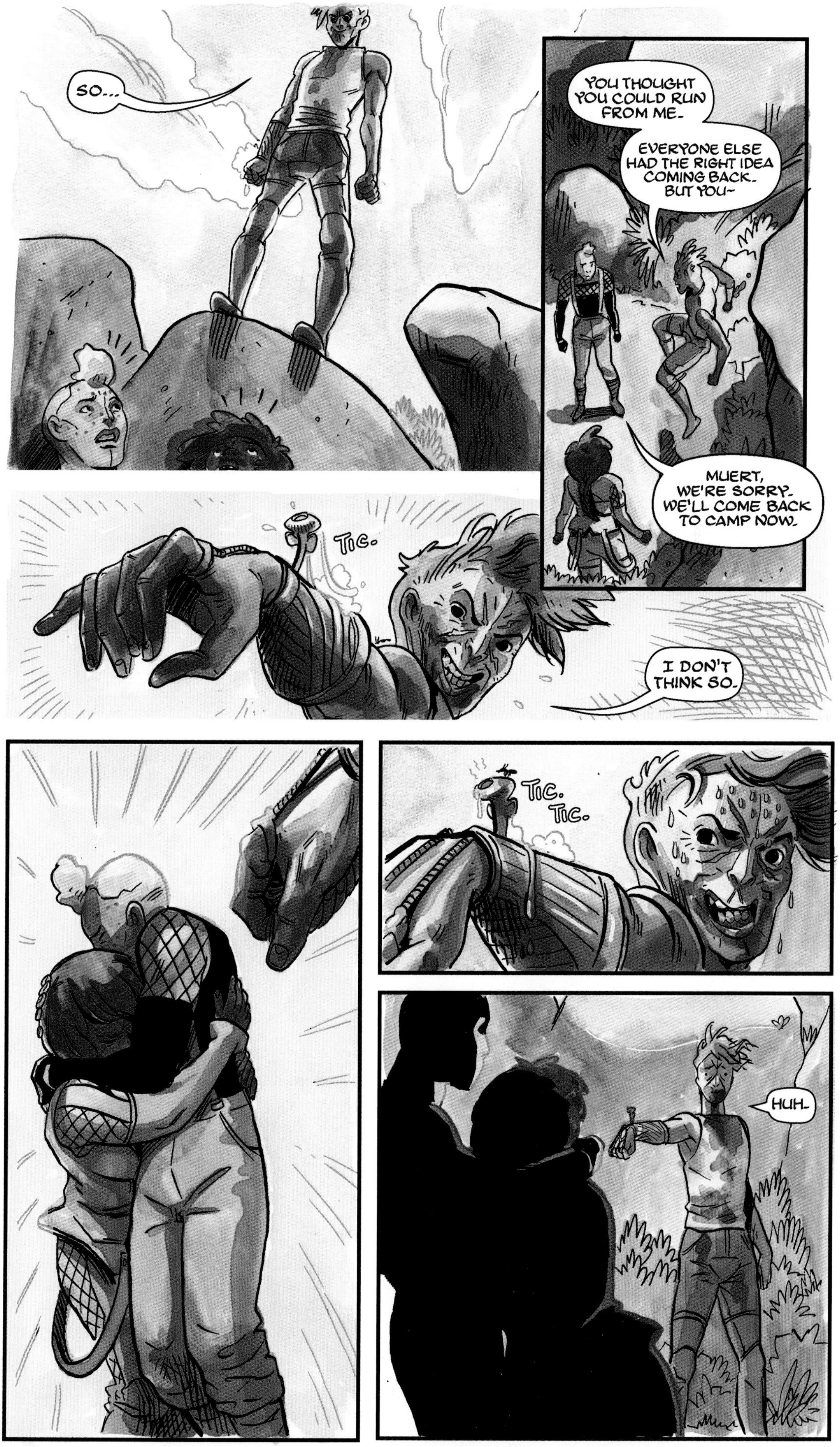
SO...
YOU THOUGHT YOU COULD RUN FROM ME.
EVERYONE ELSE HAD THE RIGHT IDEA COMING BACK. BUT YOU-
MUERT, WE'RE SORRY. WE'LL COME BACK TO CAMP NOW.
TIC.
I DON'T THINK SO.
TIC. TIC.
HUH.

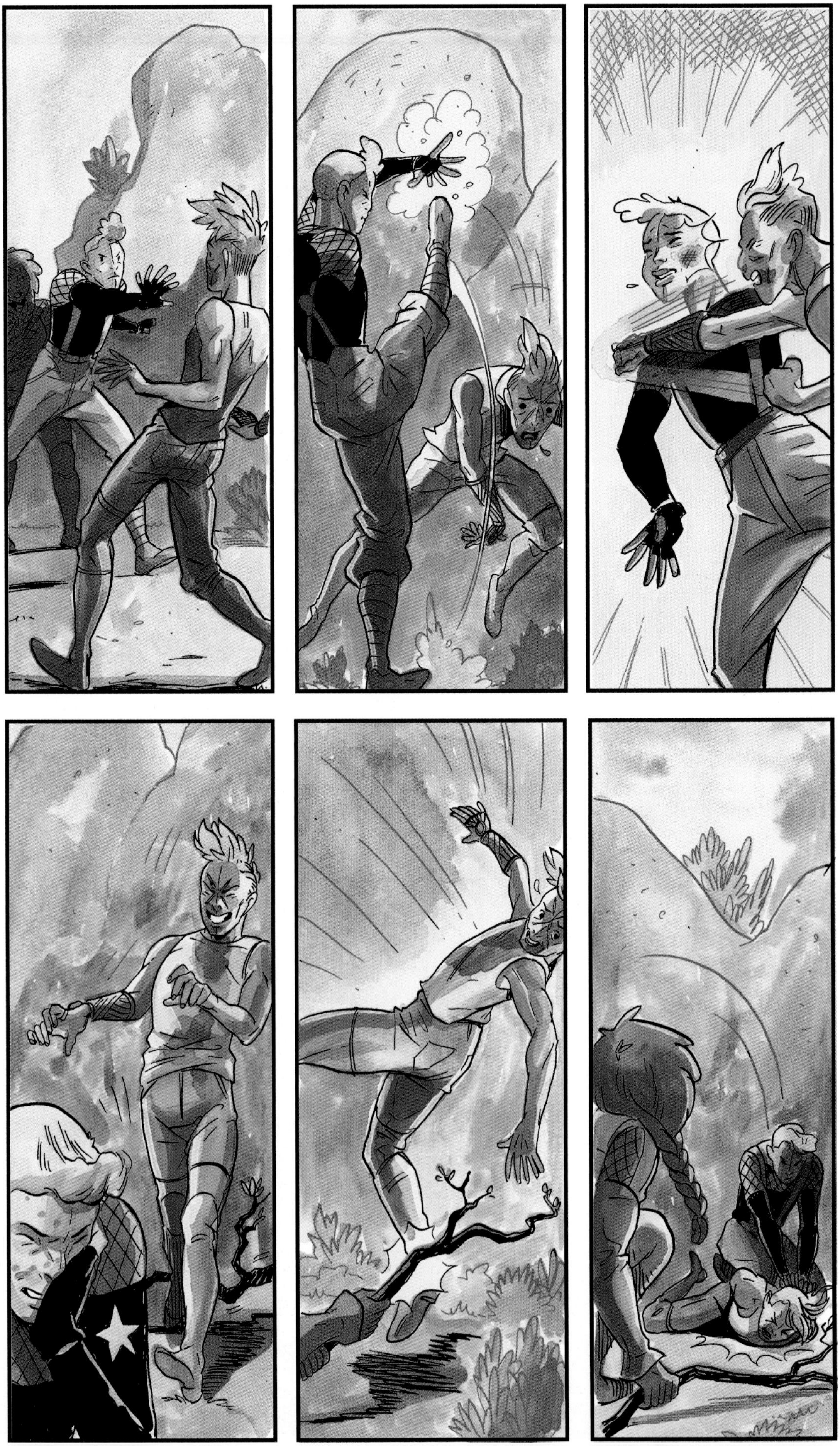

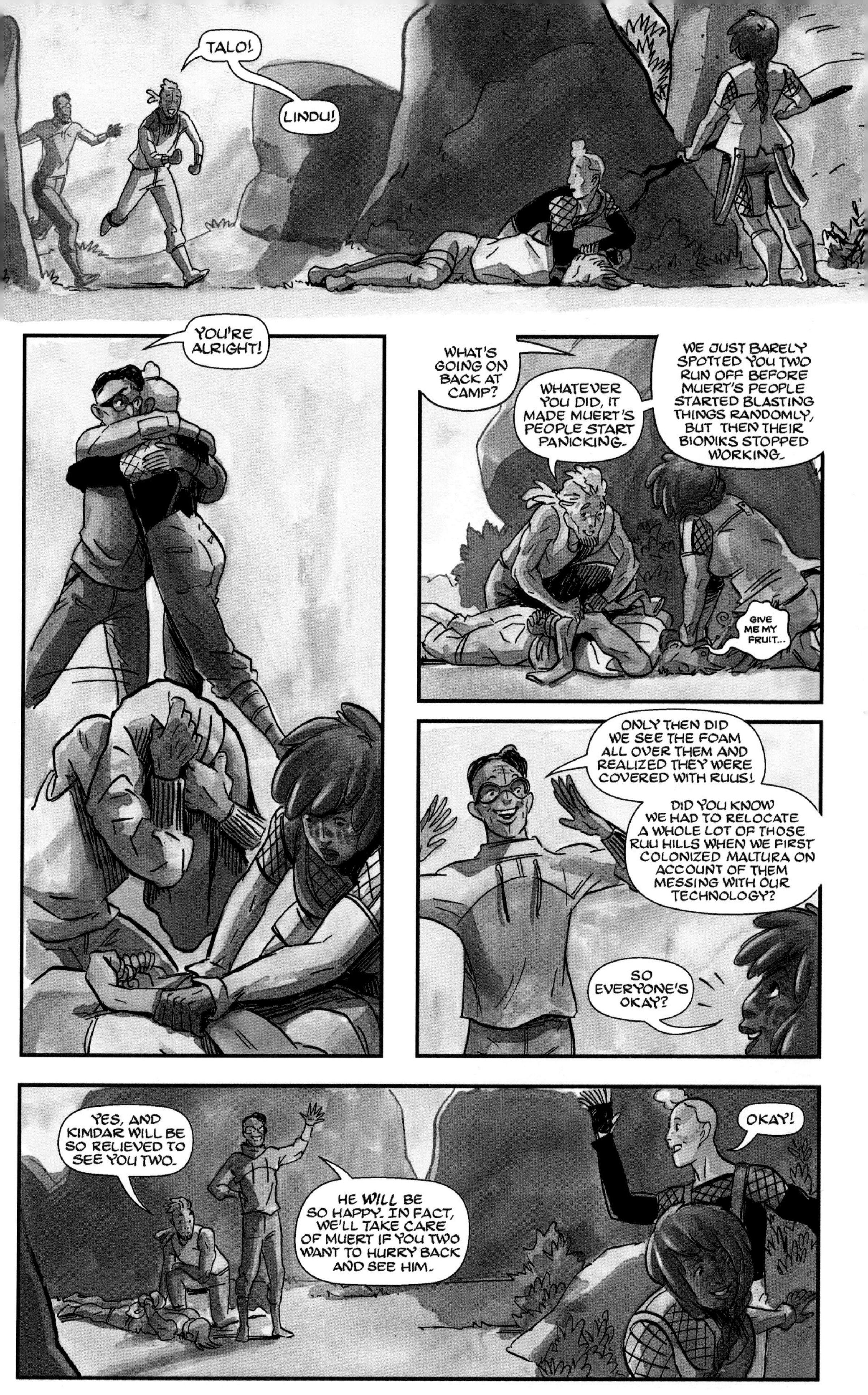
TALO!
LINDU!
YOU'RE ALRIGHT!
WHAT'S GOING ON BACK AT CAMP?
WHATEVER YOU DID, IT MADE MUERT'S PEOPLE START PANICKING.
WE JUST BARELY SPOTTED YOU TWO RUN OFF BEFORE MUERT'S PEOPLE STARTED BLASTING THINGS RANDOMLY, BUT THEN THEIR BIONIKS STOPPED WORKING.
GIVE ME MY FRUIT...
ONLY THEN DID WE SEE THE FOAM ALL OVER THEM AND REALIZED THEY WERE COVERED WITH RUUS!
DID YOU KNOW WE HAD TO RELOCATE A WHOLE LOT OF THOSE RUU HILLS WHEN WE FIRST COLONIZED MALTURA ON ACCOUNT OF THEM MESSING WITH OUR TECHNOLOGY?
SO EVERYONE'S OKAY?
YES, AND KIMDAR WILL BE SO RELIEVED TO SEE YOU TWO.
HE WILL BE SO HAPPY. IN FACT, WE'LL TAKE CARE OF MUERT IF YOU TWO WANT TO HURRY BACK AND SEE HIM.
OKAY!

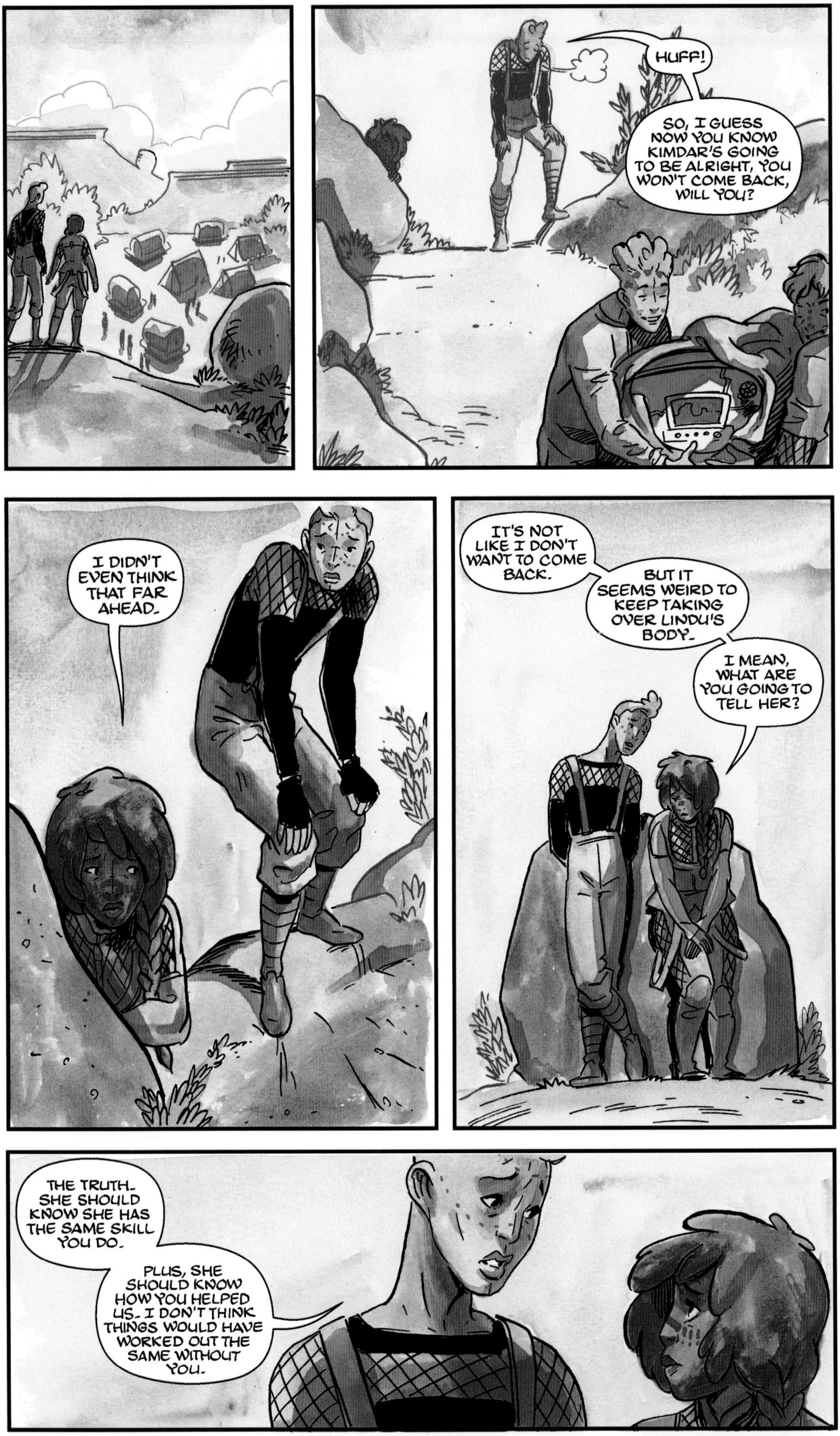
HUFF!
SO, I GUESS NOW YOU KNOW KIMDAR'S GOING TO BE ALRIGHT, YOU WON'T COME BACK, WILL YOU?
I DIDN'T EVEN THINK THAT FAR AHEAD.
IT'S NOT LIKE I DON'T WANT TO COME BACK.
BUT IT SEEMS WEIRD TO KEEP TAKING OVER LINDU'S BODY.
I MEAN, WHAT ARE YOU GOING TO TELL HER?
THE TRUTH. SHE SHOULD KNOW SHE HAS THE SAME SKILL YOU DO.
PLUS, SHE SHOULD KNOW HOW YOU HELPED US. I DON'T THINK THINGS WOULD HAVE WORKED OUT THE SAME WITHOUT YOU.

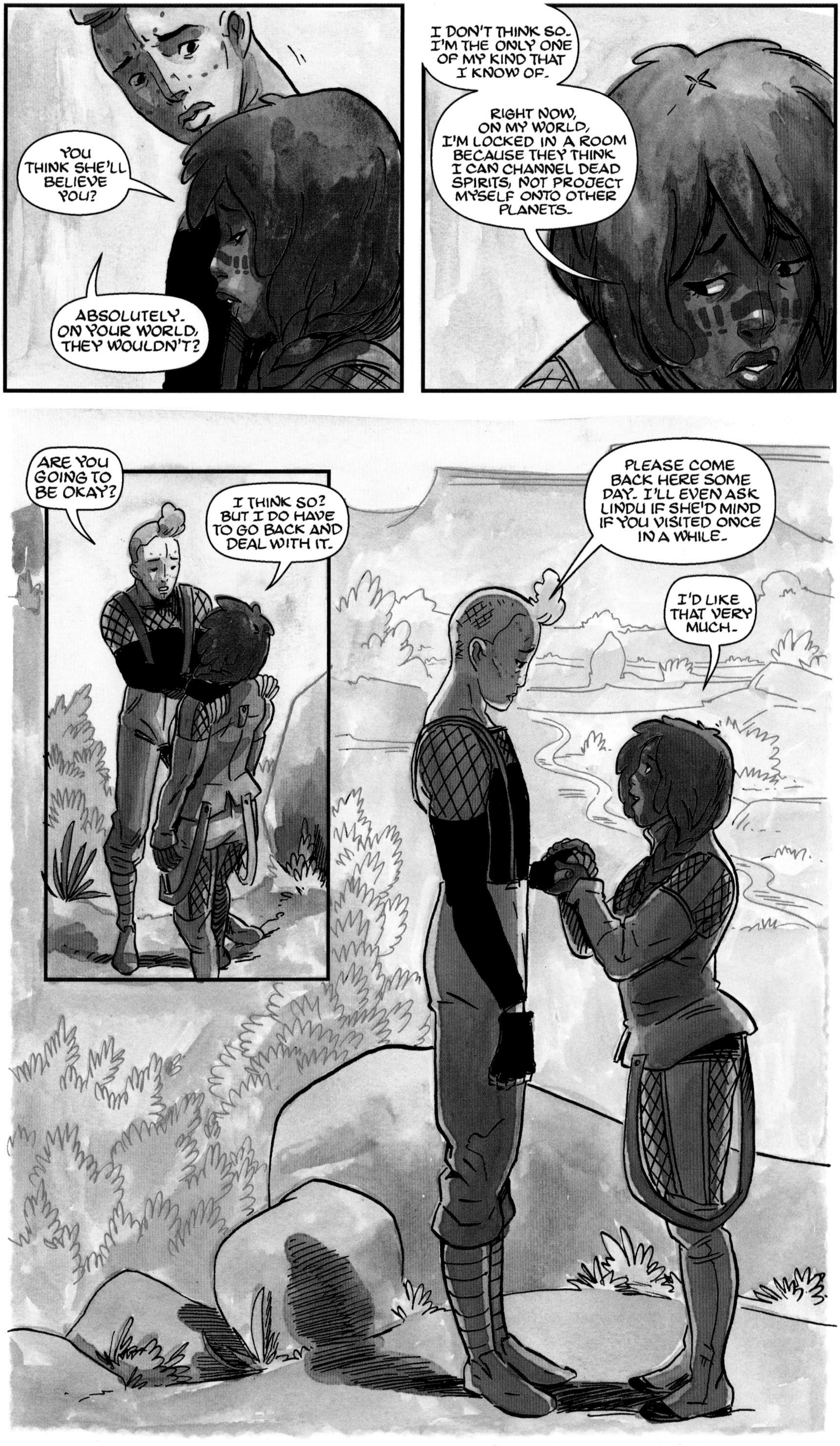
YOU THINK SHE'LL BELIEVE YOU?
ABSOLUTELY. ON YOUR WORLD, THEY WOULDN'T?
I DON'T THINK SO. I'M THE ONLY ONE OF MY KIND THAT I KNOW OF.
RIGHT NOW, ON MY WORLD, I'M LOCKED IN A ROOM BECAUSE THEY THINK I CAN CHANNEL DEAD SPIRITS, NOT PROJECT MYSELF ONTO OTHER PLANETS.
ARE YOU GOING TO BE OKAY?
I THINK SO? BUT I DO HAVE TO GO BACK AND DEAL WITH IT.
PLEASE COME BACK HERE SOME DAY. I'LL EVEN ASK LINDU IF SHE'D MIND IF YOU VISITED ONCE IN A WHILE.
I'D LIKE THAT VERY MUCH.

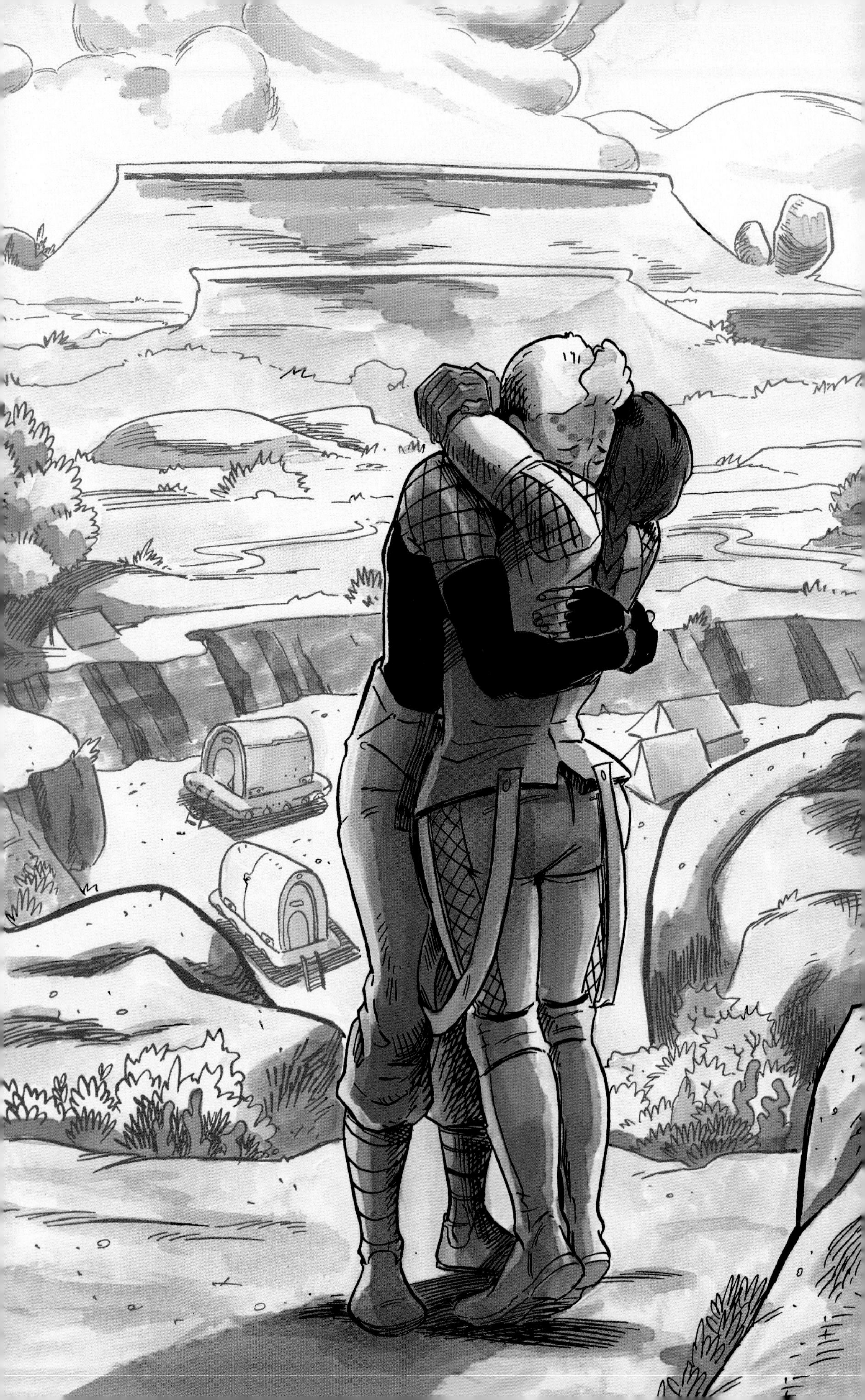

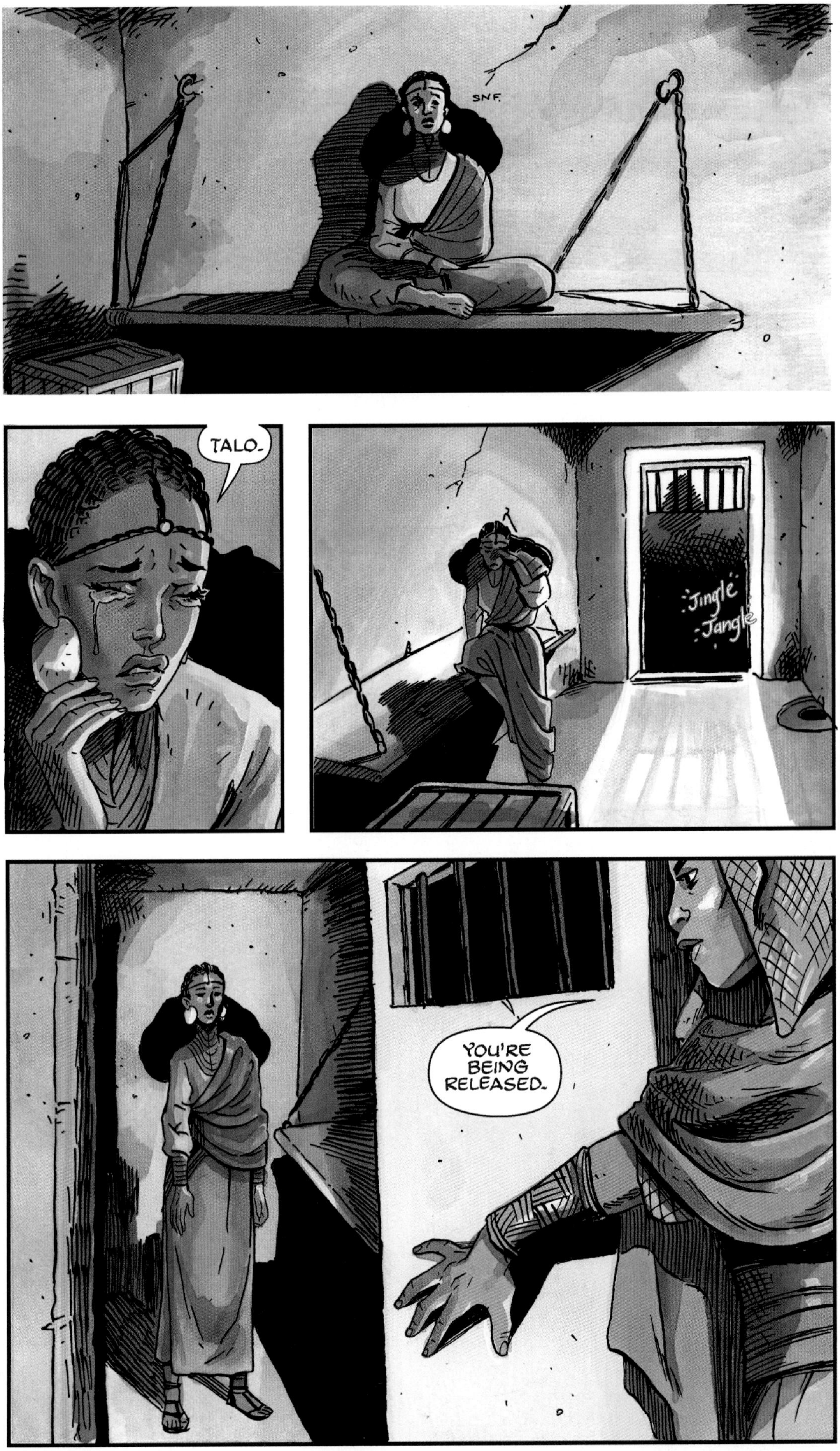
SNF.
TALO.
Jingle
Jangle
YOU'RE BEING RELEASED.

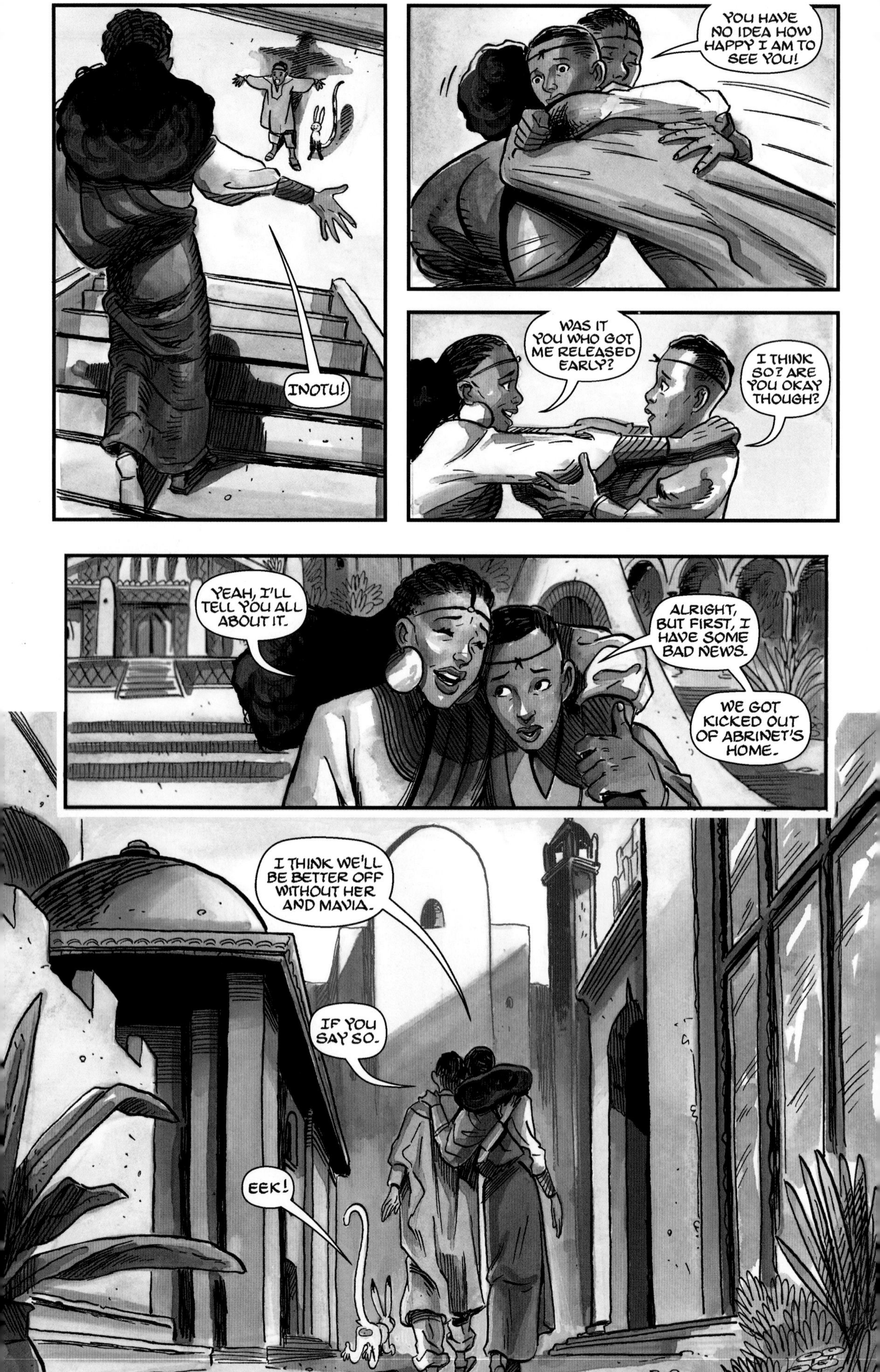
INOTU!
YOU HAVE NO IDEA HOW HAPPY I AM TO SEE YOU!
WAS IT YOU WHO GOT ME RELEASED EARLY?
I THINK SO? ARE YOU OKAY THOUGH?
YEAH, I'LL TELL YOU ALL ABOUT IT.
ALRIGHT, BUT FIRST, I HAVE SOME BAD NEWS.
WE GOT KICKED OUT OF ABRINET'S HOME.
I THINK WE'LL BE BETTER OFF WITHOUT HER AND MAVIA.
IF YOU SAY SO.
EEK!

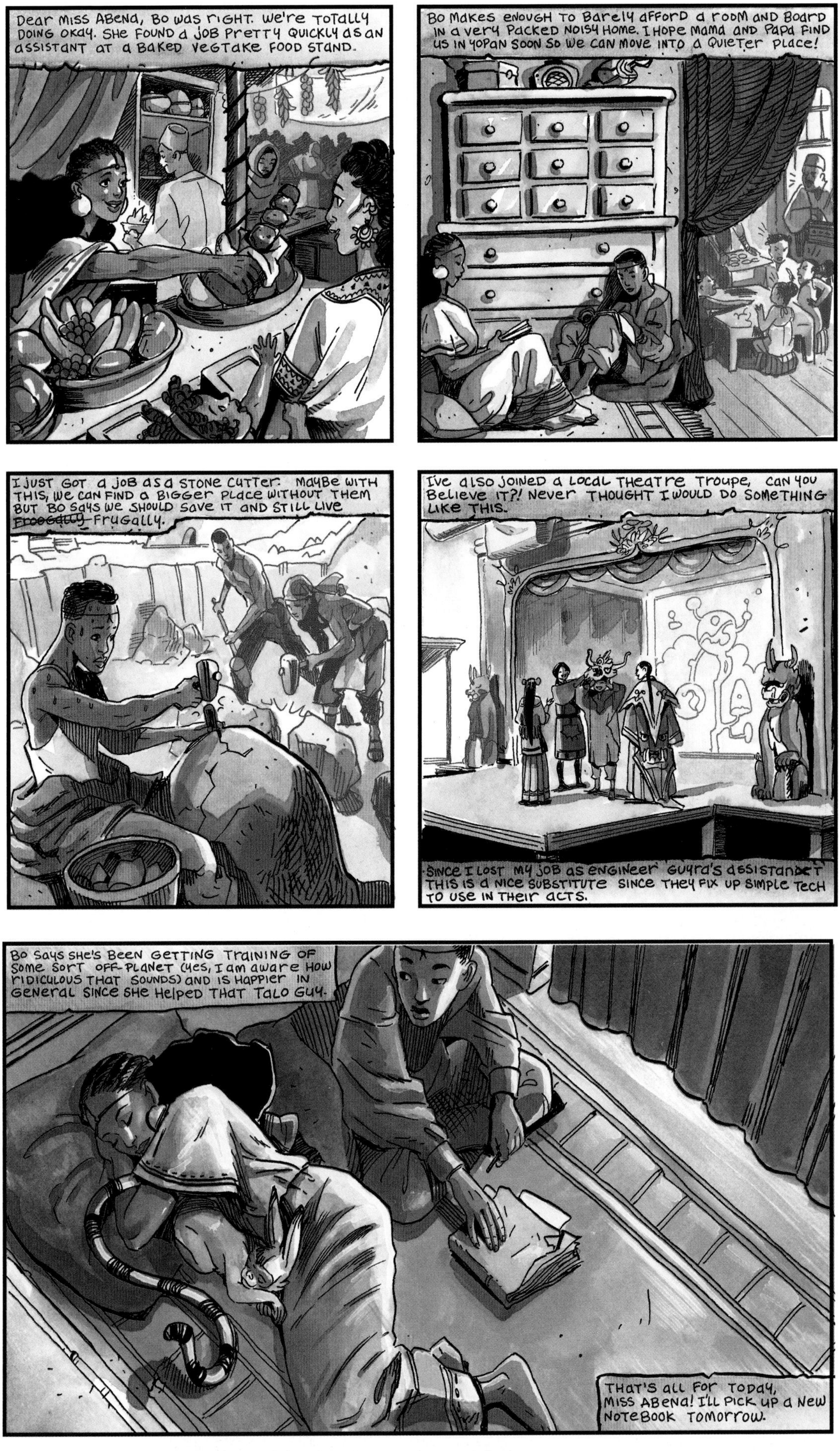
Dear Miss Abena, Bo was right. We're totally doing okay. She found a job pretty quickly as an assistant at a baked vegtake food stand.
Bo makes enough to barely afford a room and board in a very packed noisy home. I hope Mama and Papa find us in Yopan soon so we can move into a quieter place!
I just got a job as a stone cutter. Maybe with this, we can find a bigger place without them but Bo says we should save it and still live ~~Froogally~~ frugally.
I've also joined a local theatre troupe, can you believe it?! Never thought I would do something like this.
Since I lost my job as engineer Guyra's assistant this is a nice substitute since they fix up simple tech to use in their acts.
Bo says she's been getting training of some sort off-planet (yes, I am aware how ridiculous that sounds) and is happier in general since she helped that Talo guy.
That's all for today, Miss Abena! I'll pick up a new notebook tomorrow.

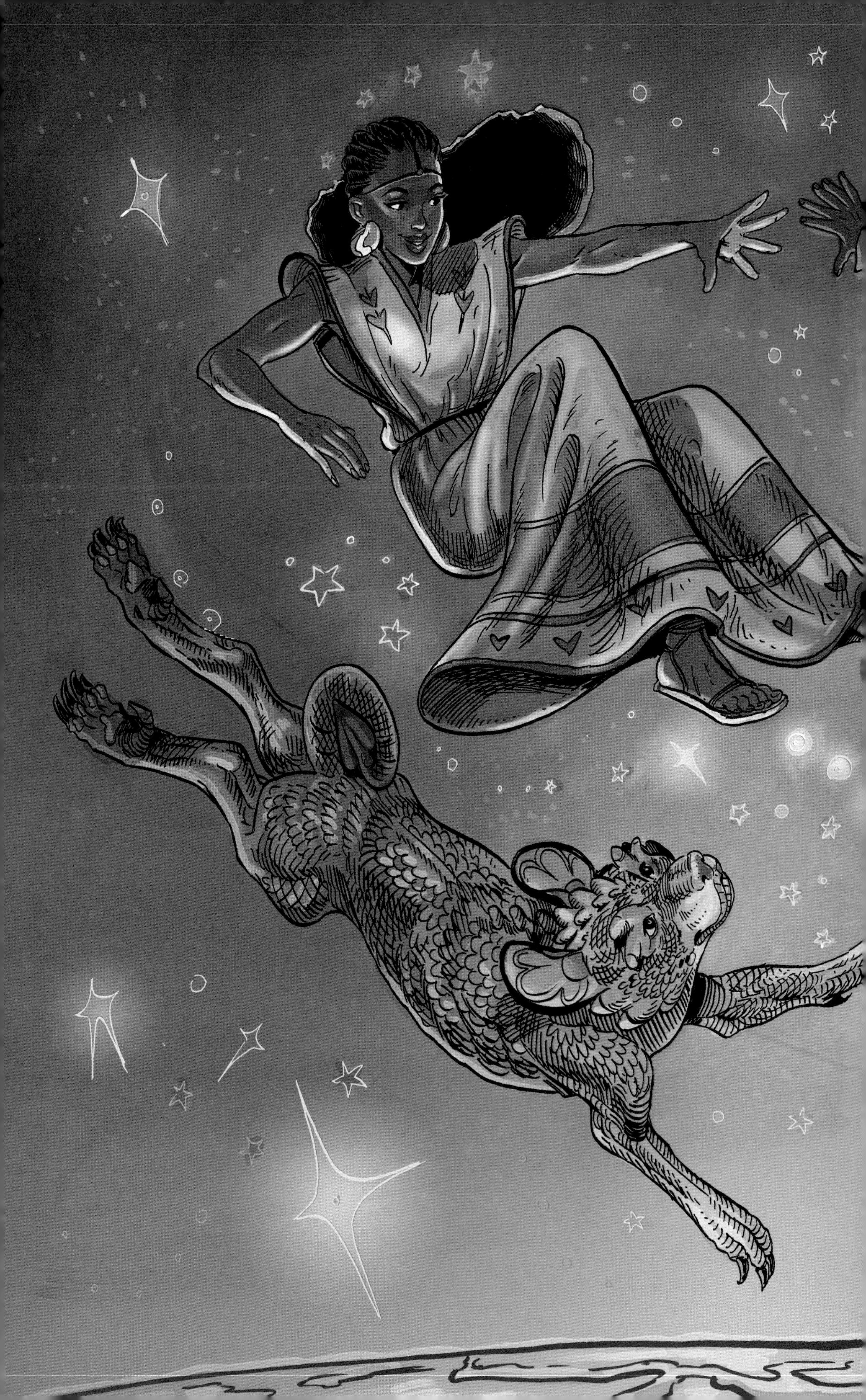

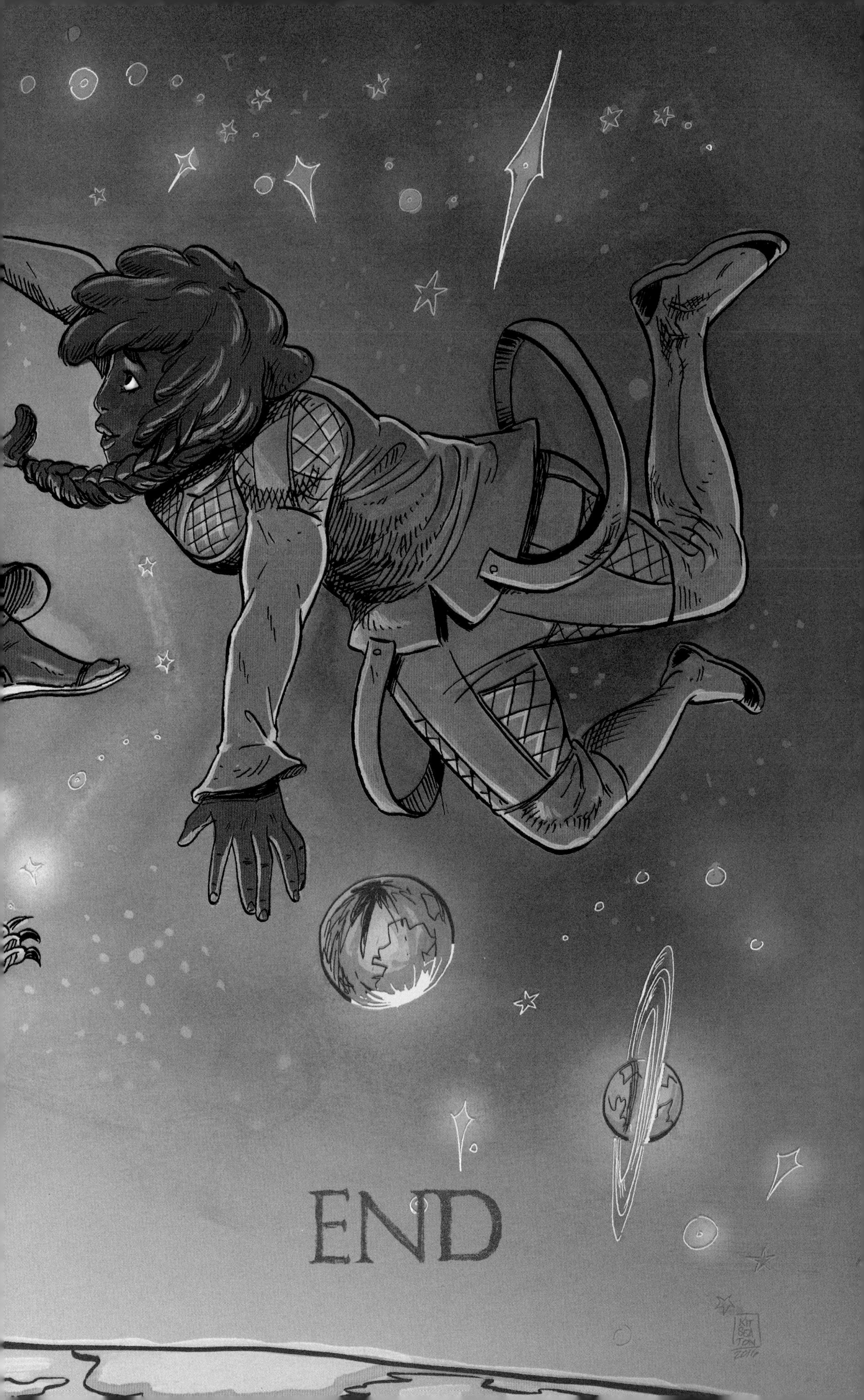
END

TO EVERY
DAYDREAMER
ON YOUR WORLD
AND OURS.

-KIT AND LEILA

EXTRAS

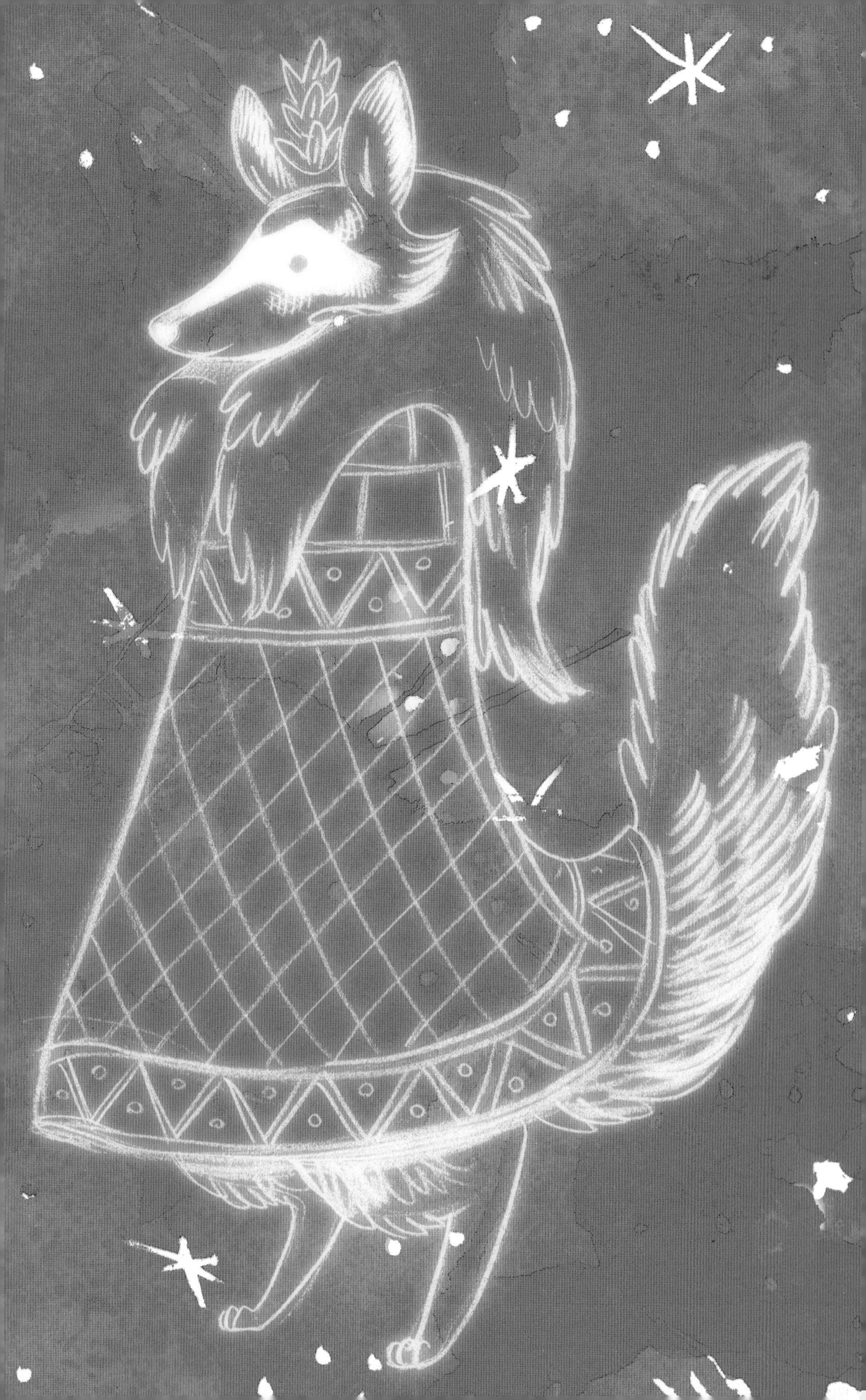

Kit and Leila had a lot of email correspondences during the project. Here are some of their communications paired with designs and process shots.

3/19/15 **Kit:** Got a few drawings for Boetema here. Let me know what you think, and if you would like to give some direction. I'll try to get some done for Inotu tomorrow. Cheers!

Leila: Holy moley, Kit. HOLY MOLEEYYYY!!!!!!!!!!!!!!!!!!!!!!!GVHRIwuyt4wpn97y-fAFT*&YEgpbm035tvywariuhfhui!!!!!!!!!!!!

THESE ARE PERFECT! Absolutely perfect! I can't believe how cool these are! Uh, so yeah, you nailed it. It's weirdly exactly how I was picturing her in my head. How did you do that? Are you psychic? Are you a magician? You're a magician AREN'T YOU??!!!

3/26/15 **Kit:** I had time to squeeze in a drawing this morning, so I thought I'd send it your way. :)

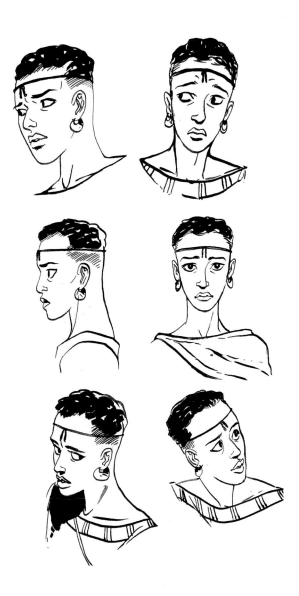

Leila: So rad!!!!!!! Love this! The only thing that seems weird to me is that he looks older than I imagine. I don't know it that's because of his hair or his facial features, but he's supposed to be two years younger than Boetema. What do you think? Otherwise, great! His clothing and body stance are great!

Kit: Thanks! Those are good points, I've been thinking about that myself. He's about Pantalone's age from Eve of All Saints. I'll keep sketching, glad the clothing is working. :)

Kit: Took another whack at it. Proportions on the full figure is a little short in the torso and legs, so I gotta work on that. Other thoughts?

Leila: Ooo! I think this is closer. Did you also make his forehead bigger? Because younger people typically have more pronounced foreheads and I think it's working. Now that I see this other version of him shorter and stalkier, I like his other body type better and believe he should still be tall and thin, but his younger features would best be expressed in his facial features and body language. What do you think of it all? Thanks so much for sending these over and kicking butt on designs!

Kit: I think so, I did give him a larger forehead and set his eyes wider and a bit larger. I agree, I don't like the proportions in this drawing. I think I was trying to do a down-shot here and it isn't working. I'll make him lankier. Like a string bean that hasn't grown into his body yet.

LINDU

KIMDAR

4/20/15 **Leila:** I had some free time just now to start figuring out Manga studio, and I decided to do a quick sketch of what I was envisioning the cat creatures to look like. You totally don't have to stay true to this, because I'm super interested to see what you imagine them looking like in your head. But in case you were drawing blanks! I made the tail kind of rat inspired and only put 3 digits on each paw. Maybe I should have made the face more human? Can't wait to see your design!!

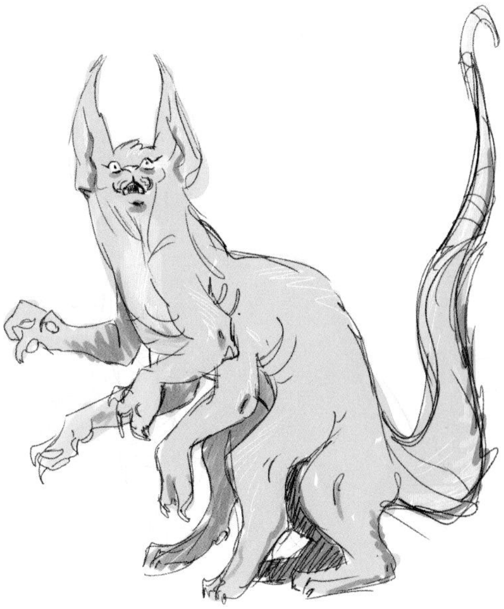

Kit: Omigosh. Look at 'im. He's so cute!

Kit's sketches of Gremsha of Clan Fustol and Inotu's friend, Abena:

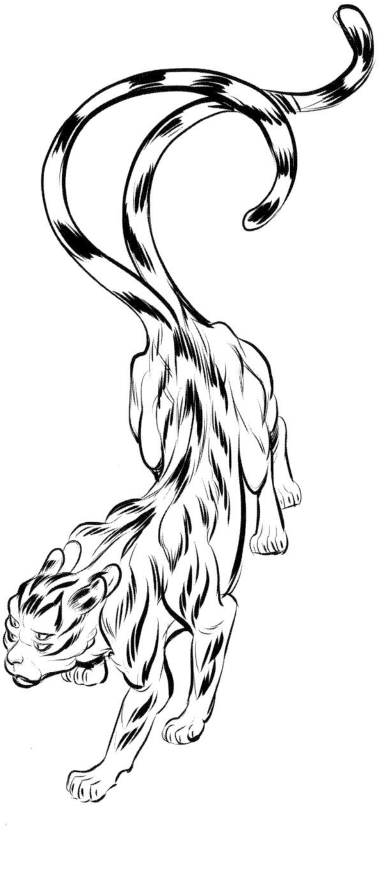

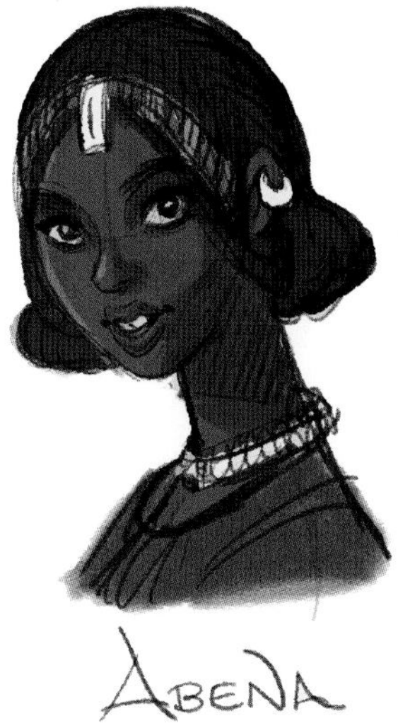
ABENA

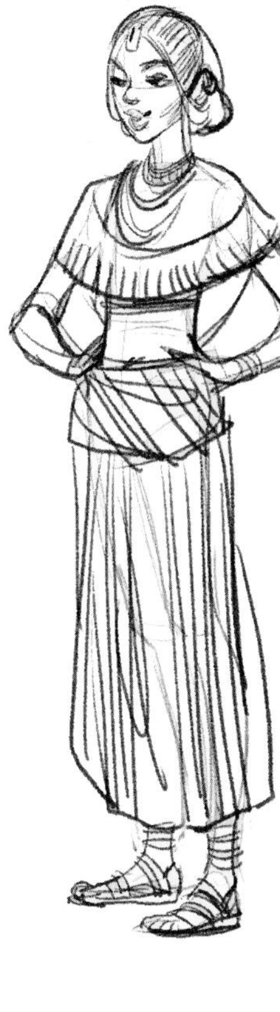

6/8/15 **Leila:** Here are some sketches of Agama Wanwitu, the animal and the constellation. Both are up for visual changes as you see fit.

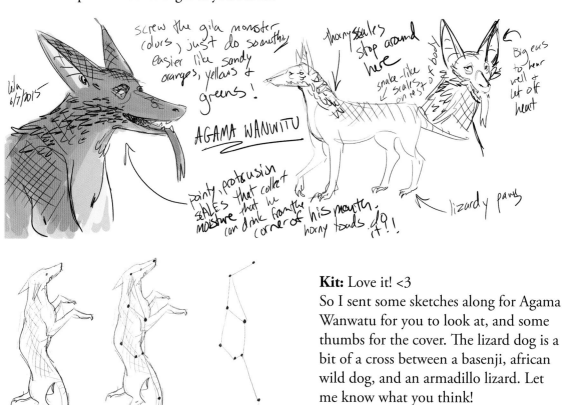

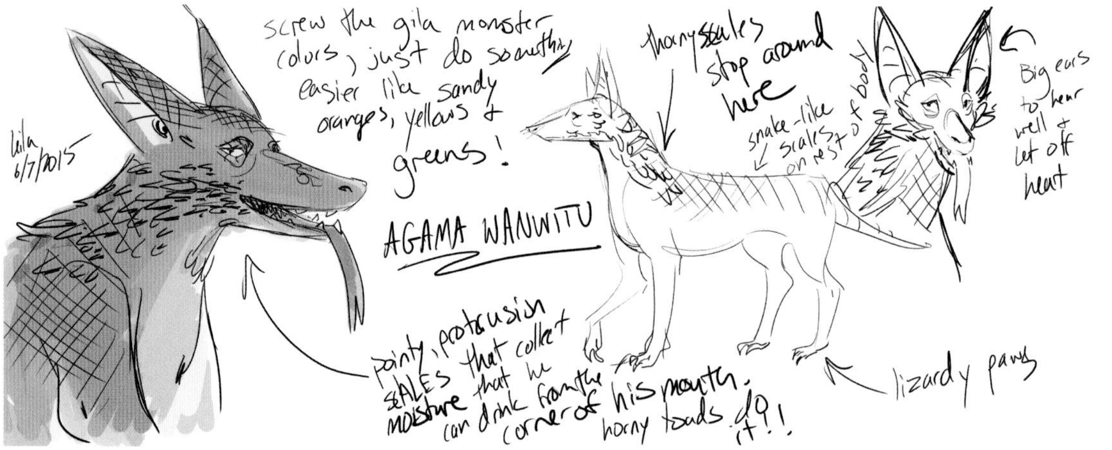
Leila
6/7/2015
screw the gila monster colors, just do something easier like sandy oranges, yellows & greens!
AGAMA WANWITU
thorny scales stop around here
snake-like scales on rest of body
Big ears to hear well & let off heat
pointy, protrusion SCALES that collect MOISTURE that he can drink from the corner of his mouth. horny toads do it?!
lizardy paws

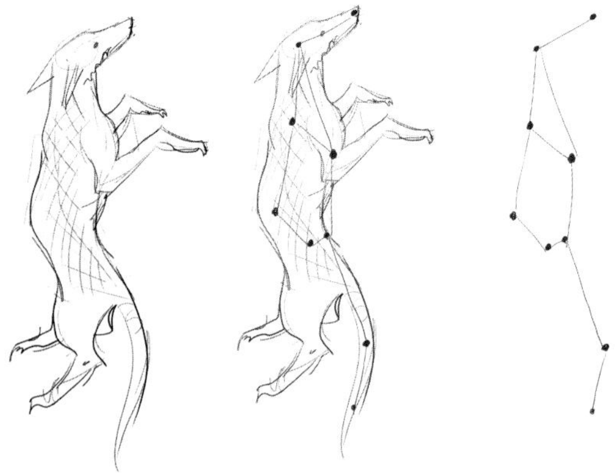

Kit: Love it! <3
So I sent some sketches along for Agama Wanwatu for you to look at, and some thumbs for the cover. The lizard dog is a bit of a cross between a basenji, african wild dog, and an armadillo lizard. Let me know what you think!

Leila: Agama Wanwitu is perfect!! You nailed 'im! love love love love

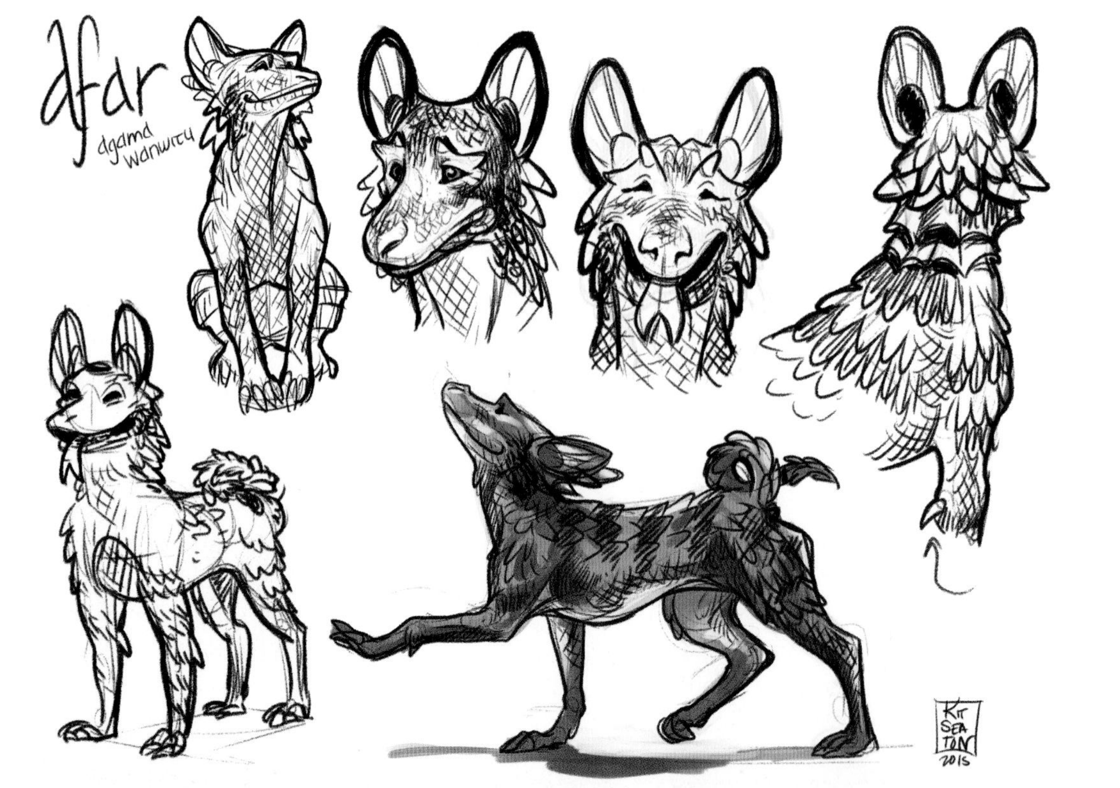
afar
agama wanwitu
KIT SEATON 2015

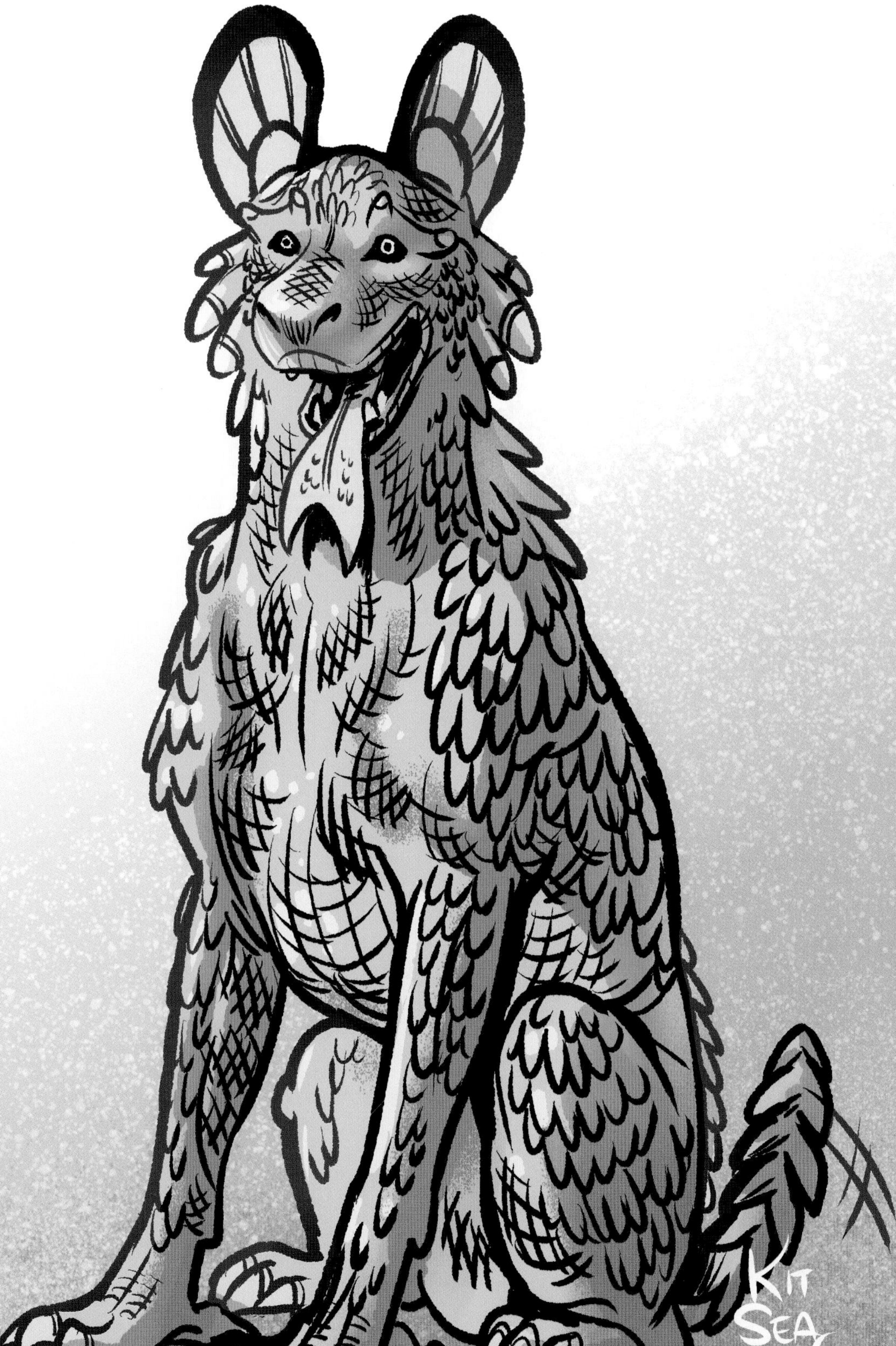
KIT
SEA
TON

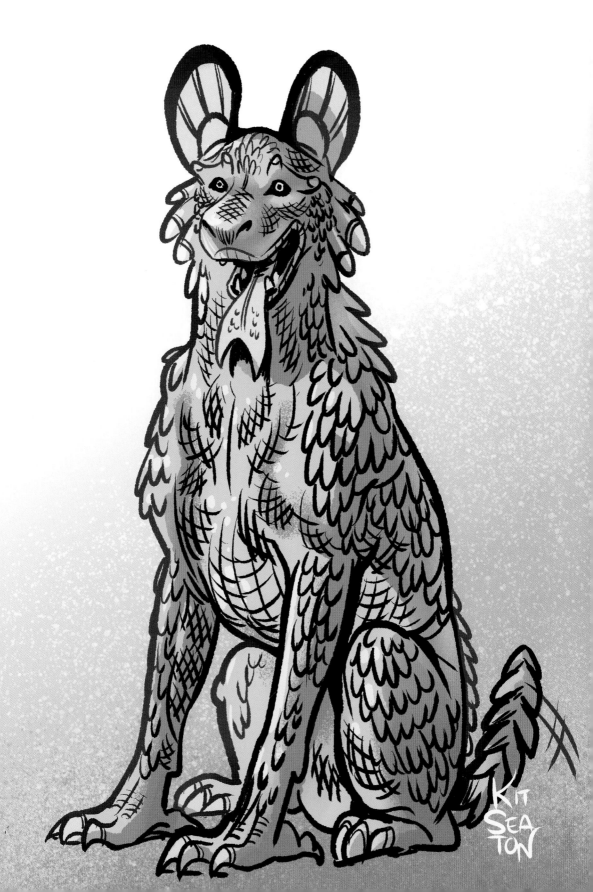

Kit's cover sketches:

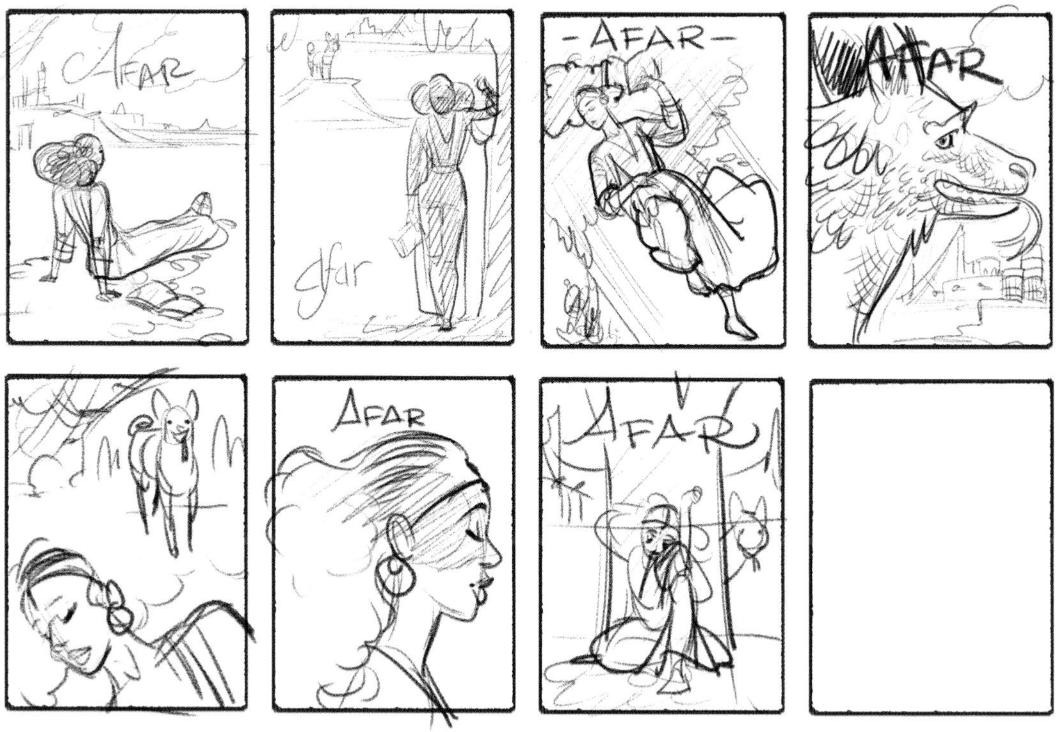
AFAR
AFAR
AFAR
AFAR
AFAR
AFAR

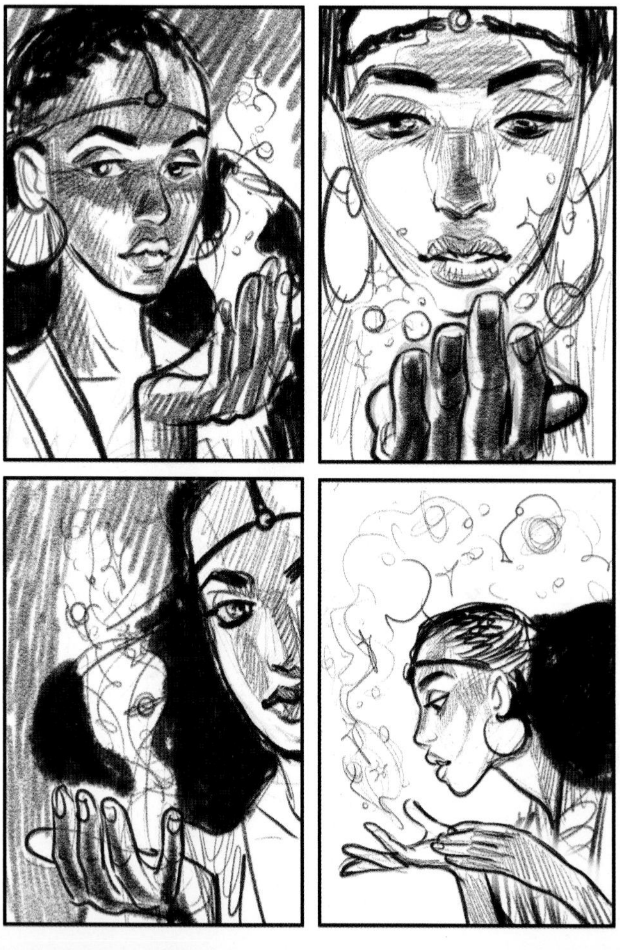

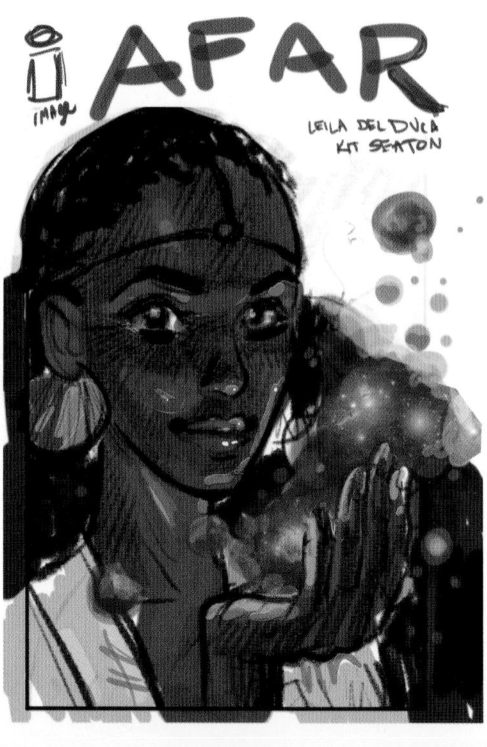
AFAR
LEILA DEL DUCA
KIT SEATON

03/01/16 **Kit:** Some Afar Chapter 2 sketches. Mostly some props and things, thought you'd like to see.

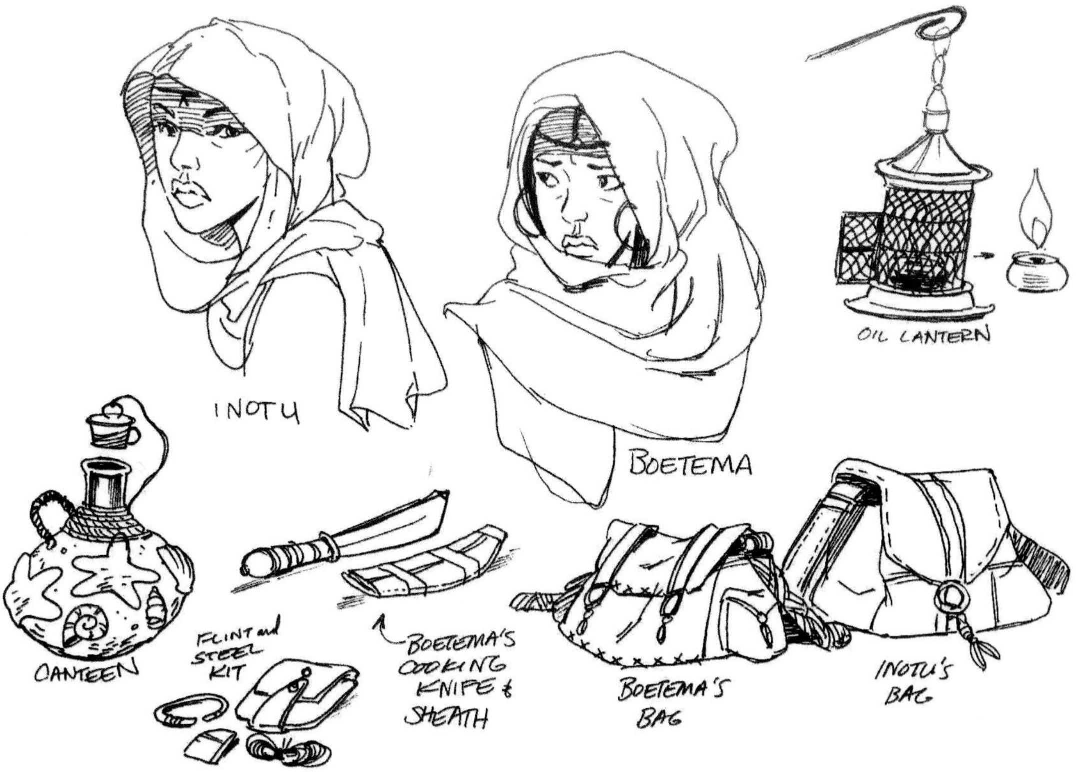
INOTU
BOETEMA
OIL LANTERN
CANTEEN
FLINT and STEEL KIT
BOETEMA'S COOKING KNIFE & SHEATH
BOETEMA'S BAG
INOTU'S BAG

Leila: Oh my god, yes!! These look perfect!! Looking over the thumbnails here in a second. Thanks!

11/25/15 **Kit:** ha! Six fingers. Inigo Montoya would have a helluva time finding the man who killed his father on this planet.

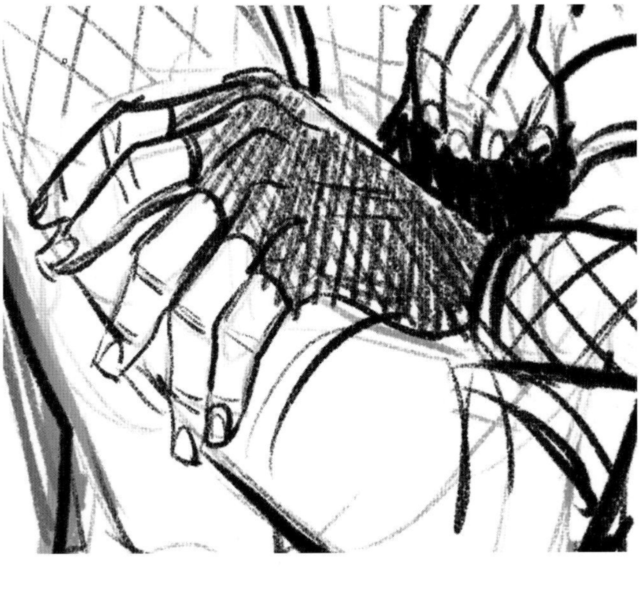

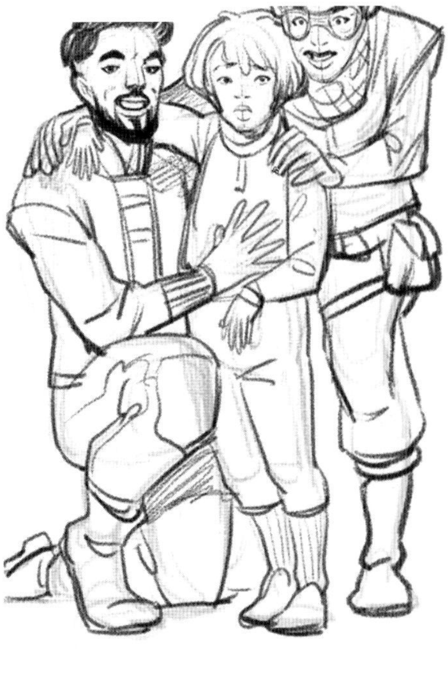

6/5/16 **Kit:** Hey, I threw together some designs for these creatures and wanted to see what you thought. As I was looking for reference I found other wild dogs, so I incorporated some of them to get some individuality. Let me know if this is a good direction. :>

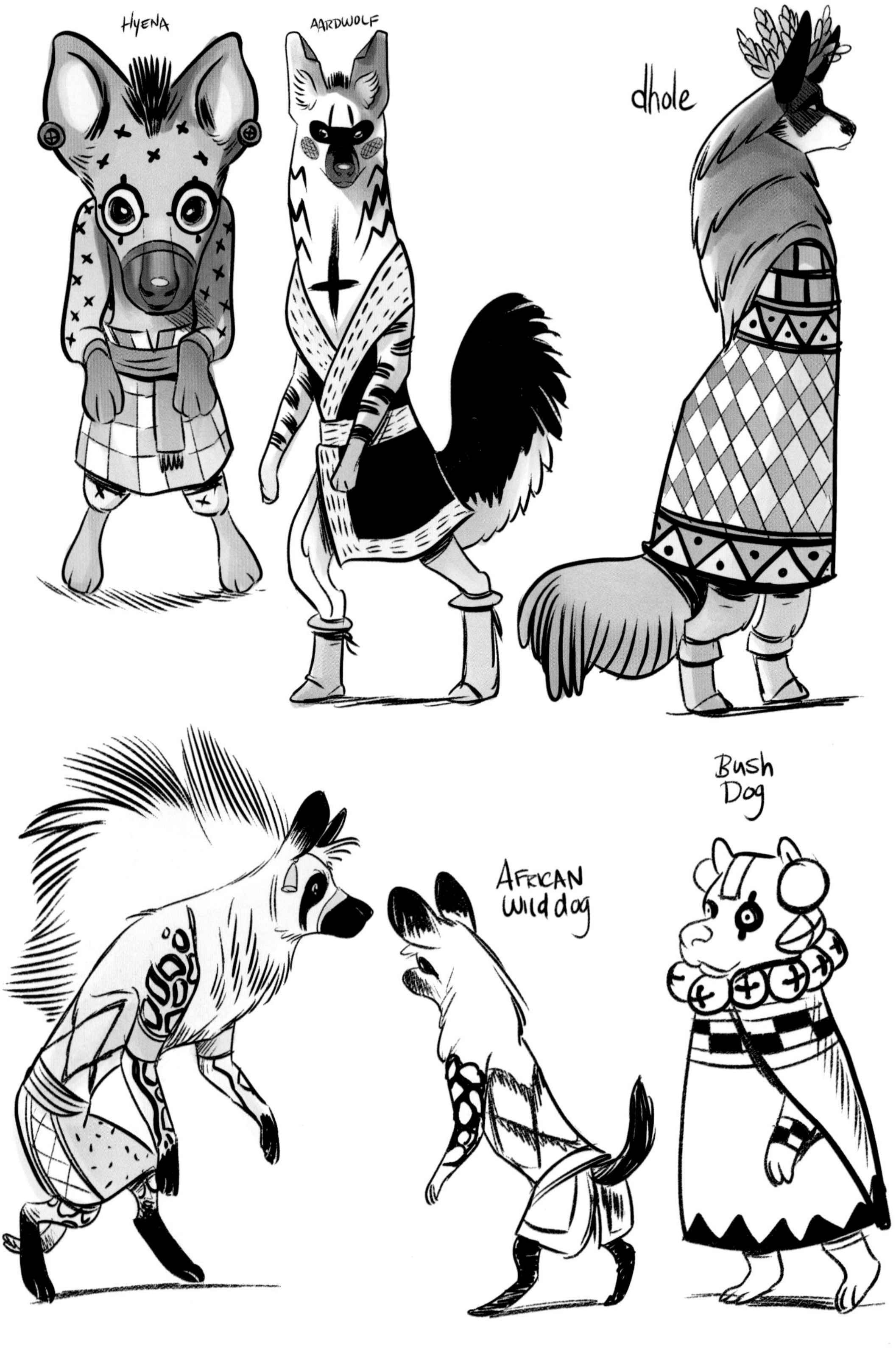
HYENA
AARDWOLF
dhole
Bush Dog
AFRICAN Wild dog

Leila: YYYEEEEEEESSSSSSSSSSSSSSSSS!!!!!!!!!!!!!! THIS IS THE PERFECT DIRECTION!

6/7/16 **Kit:** Here are some character designs for Mavia and Dei.

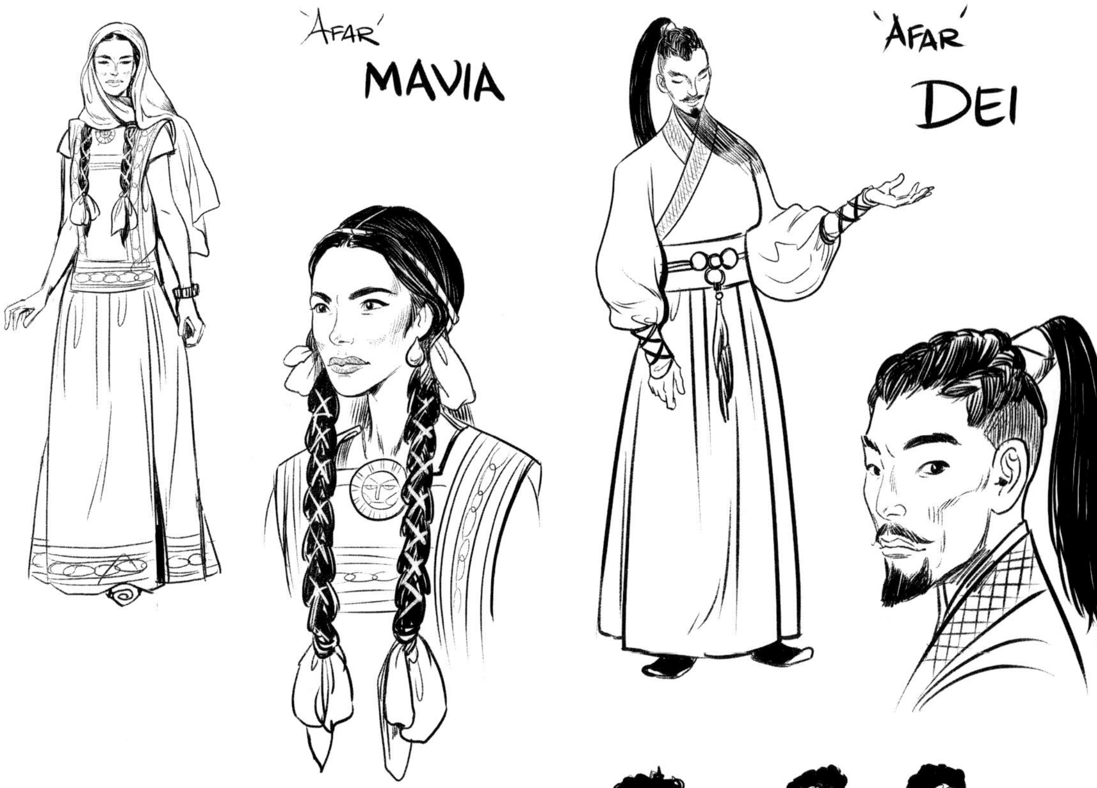

'Afar'
MAVIA
'Afar'
DEI

Leila: Dei's design is perfect!!!!! Nailed it. Mavia is great, too. POYFECT all around!! Thanks, Kit.

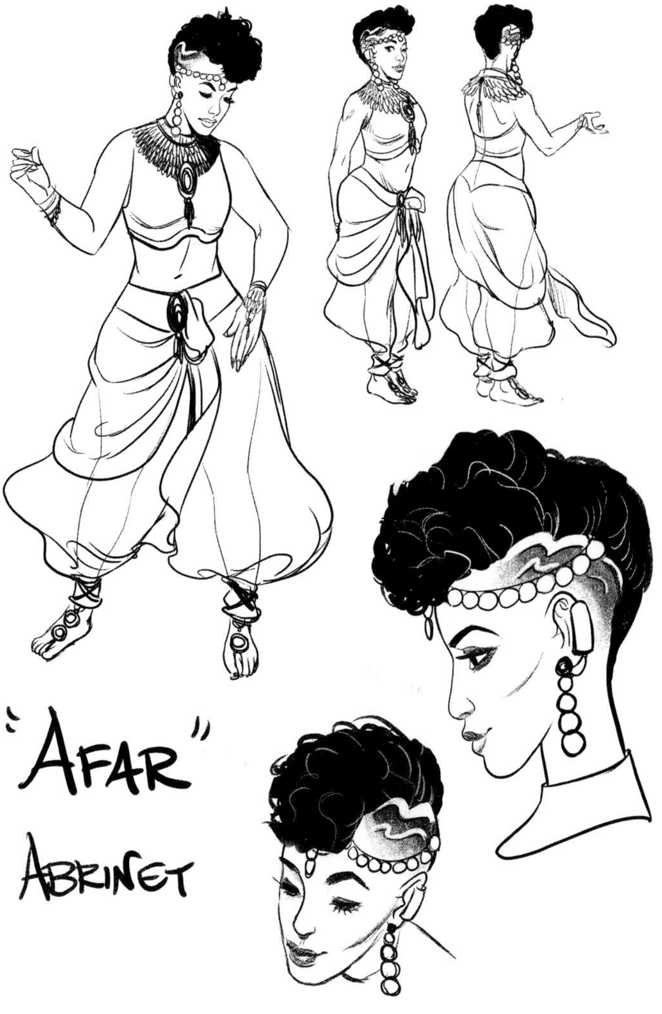

"Afar"
Abrinet

7/9/16 **Kit:** Hi Leila, here's a couple more pages and a character design to approve. Sorry it took a little longer than usual! D:

Leila: Abrinet's design is KILLER! I love it!! She's so incredible!!

7/7/16 **Leila:** Hey Kit! I didn't get all of my sketches for you done, but I'll keep working on them tomorrow and Saturday so you get them asap. In the meantime, here's what I have along with the final script! Please let me know what you think. For now, I have the Yopan double page spread, Abrinet's estate, the saliva ant effect, Muert's camp, and page 101's concepts sketched out for you and attached to this email.

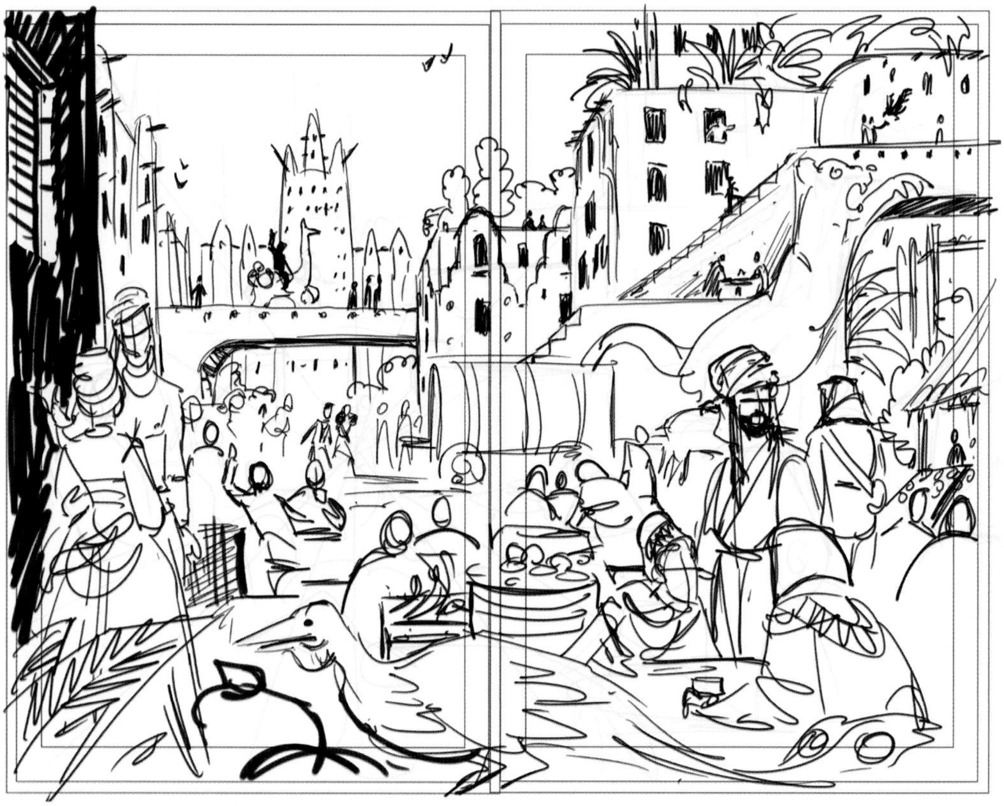

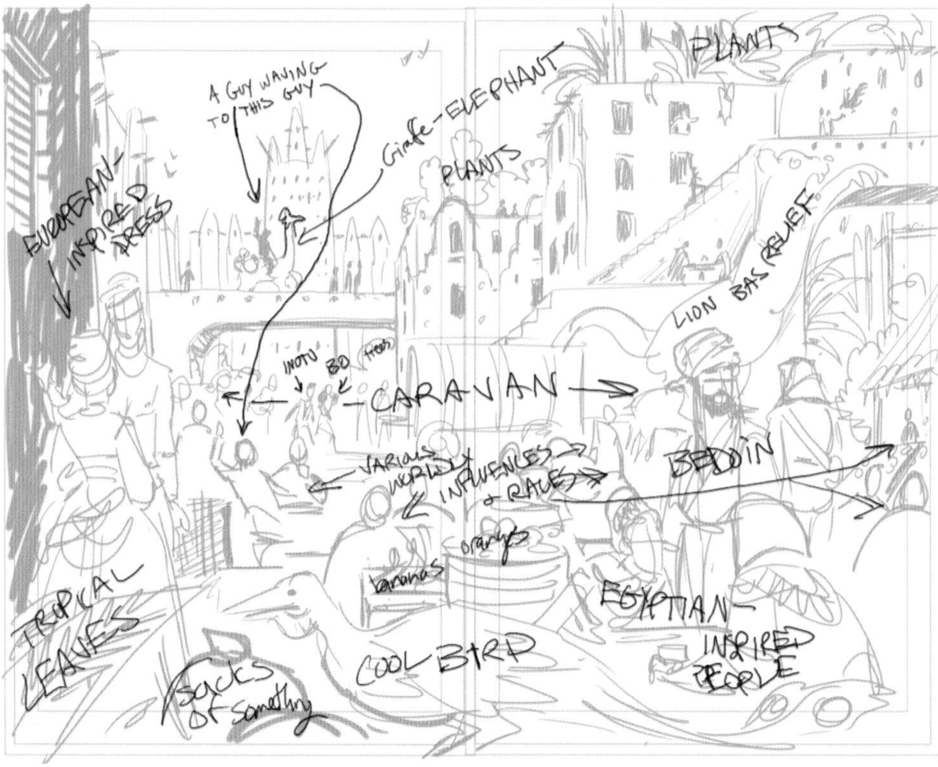
PLANTS
A GUY WAVING TO THIS GUY
Girafe-ELEPHANT
PLANTS
EUROPEAN-INSPIRED DRESS
LION BAS RELIEF
CARAVAN
VARIOUS WORLD INFLUENCES + RACES
BEDOIN
bananas
oranges
TROPICAL LEAVES
EGYPTIAN-INSPIRED PEOPLE
COOL BIRD
SACKS OF something

Kit: Awesome! Thank you Leila! I will look these over and let you know if I have any questions. I should have this last set of pages wrapped up and sent off to you for review in the next day or two. Then I can power through layouts. Congrats on finishing the script! You did it!

7/17/16 **Kit:** Here's this double page spread! Let me know what you think. Your thumbnail was a big help, I mostly just went with what you gave me here.

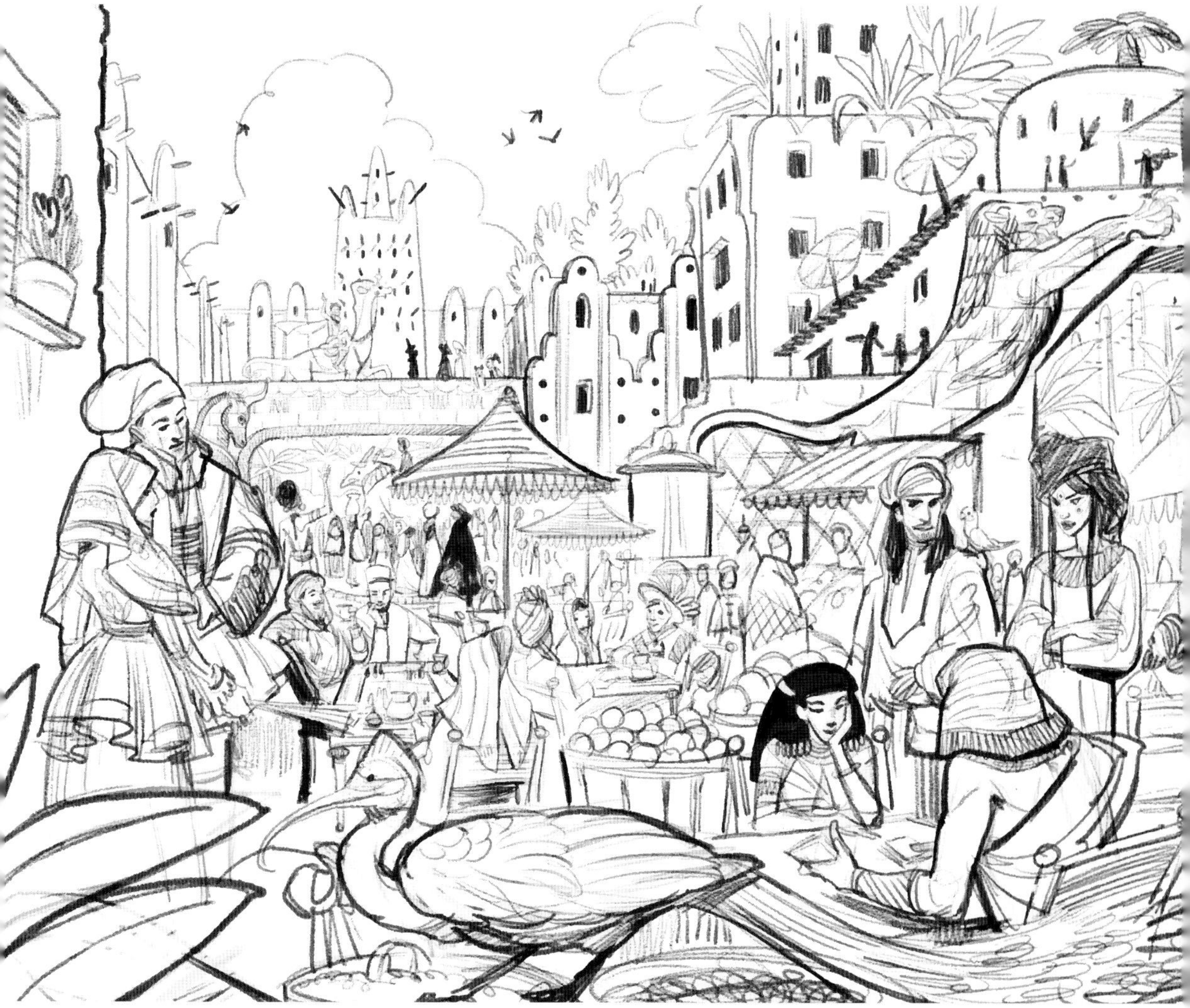

Leila: LOVE THIS
LOVE LOVE LOVE LOVE LOVE LOVE LOVE LOVE LOVE LOVE LOVE LOVE
LOVE LOVE LOVE LOVE LOVE LOVE LOVE LOVE LOVE LOVE LOVE LOVE
LOVE LOVE LOVE LOVE LOVE LOVE LOVE LOVE LOVE LOVE LOVE LOVE
LOVE LOVE LOVE LOVE LOVE LOVE LOVE LOVE LOVE LOVE LOVE LOVE
LOVE LOVE LOVE LOVE LOVE LOVE LOVE LOVE LOVE LOVE LOVE LOVE
LOVE LOVE LOVE LOVE LOVE LOVE LOVE LOVE THIS
IT'S PERFECT AND WONDERFUL AND BEAUTIFUL IN EVERY WAY

Leila sketches for Kit as reference:

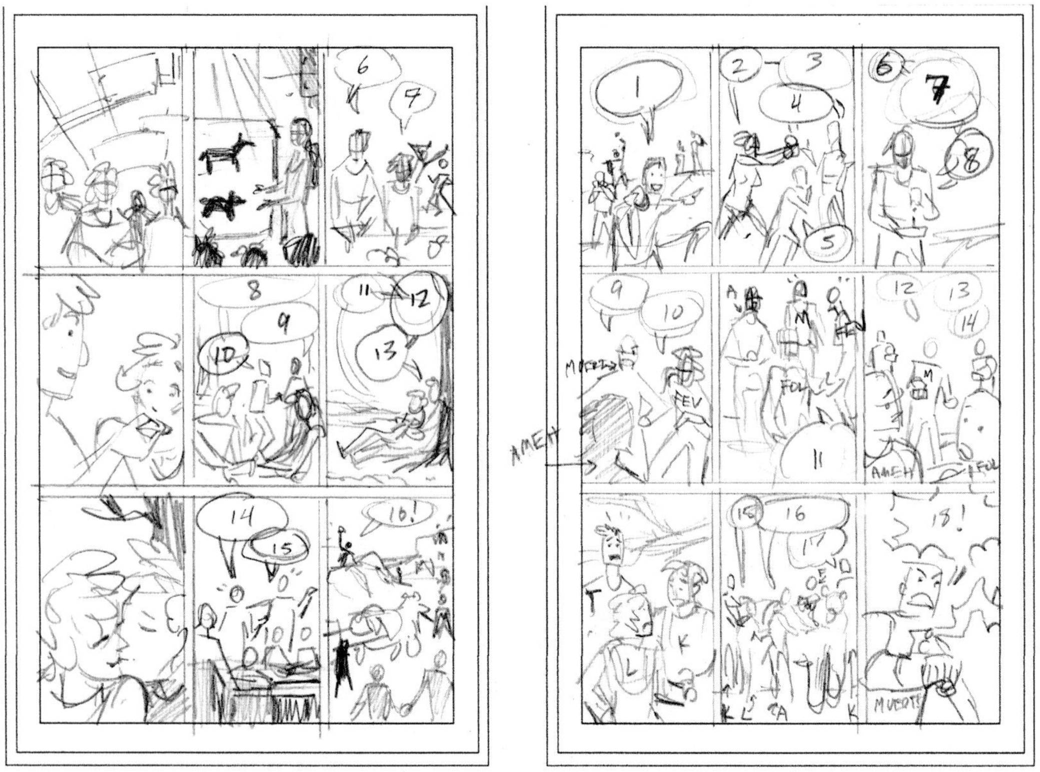
AMEH

Kit's merperson sketches for Chapter 1:

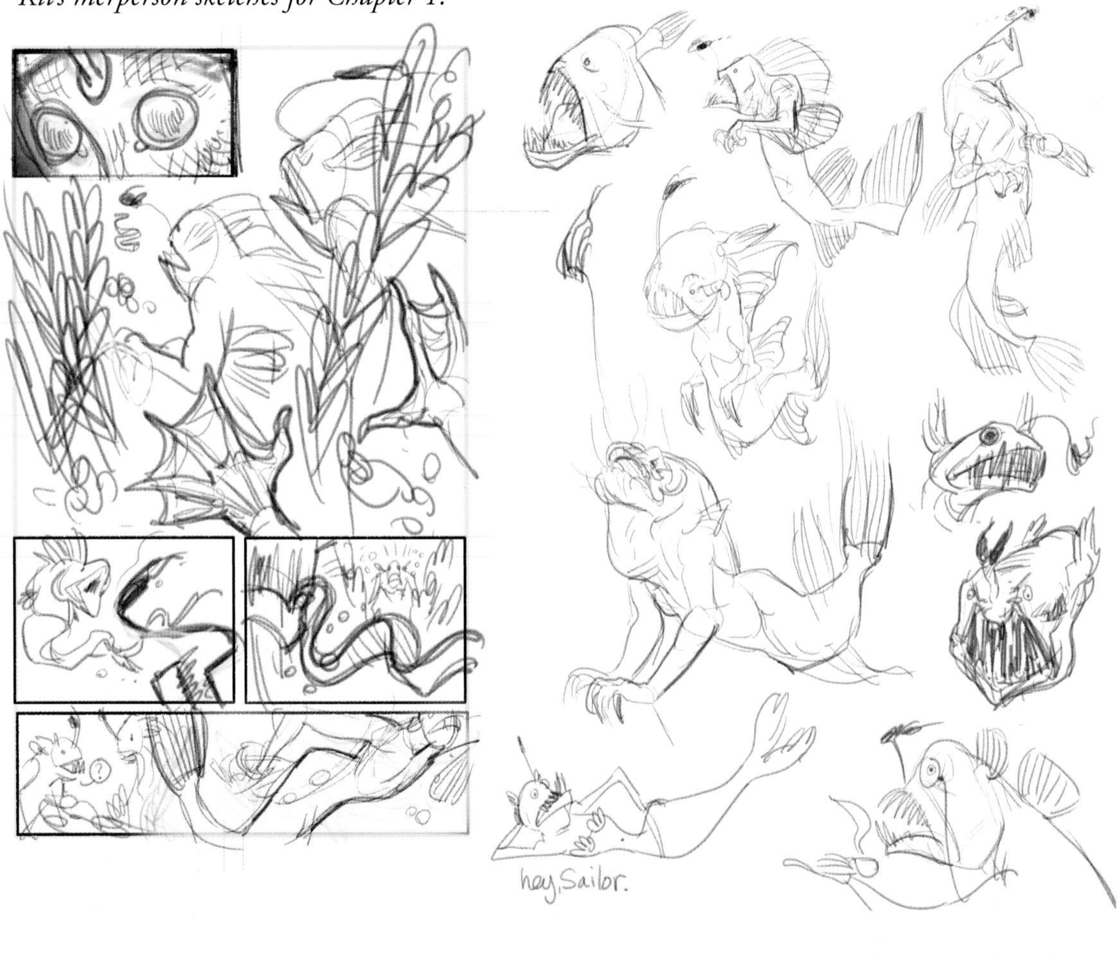
hey, Sailor.

- BOETEMA -

AGAMA WANWITU

- MONKEY -

The following two pages were a pull-out poster Kit made
that was featured in *Image+ Magazine*, Issue 2.

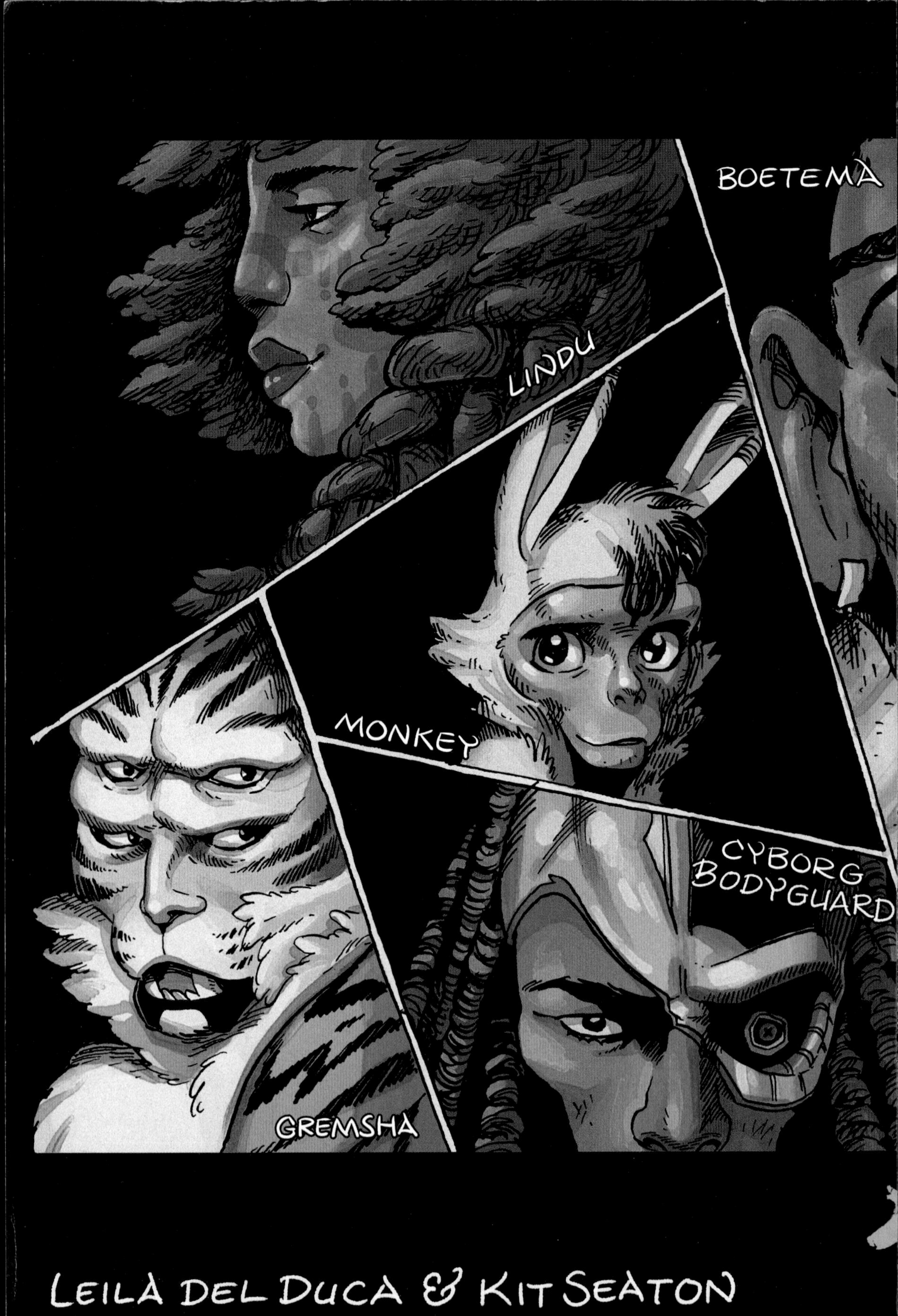
BOETEMA
LINDU
MONKEY
CYBORG BODYGUARD
GREMSHA

LEILA DEL DUCA & KIT SEATON

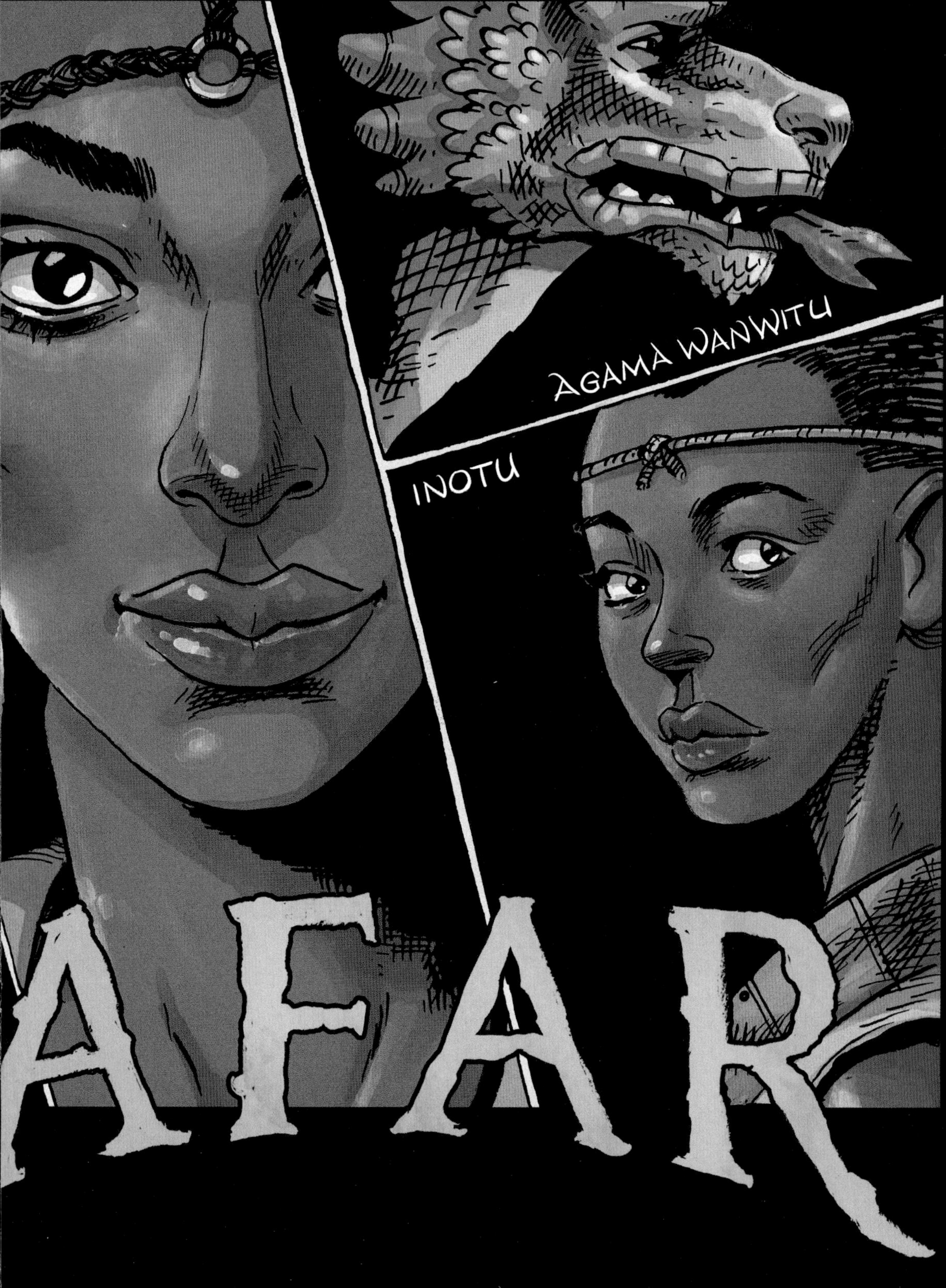
AGAMA WANWITU
INOTU
AFAR

~INOTU~

~MONKEY~

~ LINDU ~

~ MISS ABENA ~

~ SIMSOL ~

LEILA DEL DUCA is a comic book artist and illustrator currently drawing SHUTTER with Image Comics. Based in Portland, Oregon, Leila has worked on various projects including THE WICKED + THE DIVINE, SCARLET WITCH, AMERICAN VAMPIRE and THE PANTHEON PROJECT. Her client list includes Image Comics, Vertigo, Marvel, Oni Press, IDW, BOOM!, and *National Geographic*. During her free time, she dabbles in music, raw food exploration, reading, and staring off into space. AFAR is her first graphic novel as a writer.

KIT SEATON is a cartoonist and illustrator based in Savannah Georgia, and a professor in the Sequential Art department at Savannah College of Art and Design. Kit has previously worked as a theatrical director, costume designer, and comics colorist. She began creating webcomics in 2011, collaborating with author and playwright George Herman on two series: EVE OF ALL SAINTS and OTTO THE ODD AND THE DRAGON KING. Kit is currently working with her sister Cat Seaton on NORROWAY, a webcomic adaptation of a Scottish fairy tale.

TANEKA STOTTS is a queer little tumbleweed that stopped rolling somewhere in Portland, Oregon. After spending quite a few years as a spoken word artist, Taneka's focus shifted to comics, a medium full of collaboration and imagination. Taneka now writes the webcomics FULL CIRCLE, LOVE CIRCUITS, and DEJA BREW. Taneka has edited a few comics anthologies including, most recently, the award-winning BEYOND: THE QUEER SCI-FI AND FANTASY COMIC ANTHOLOGY and ELEMENTS: FIRE for Beyond Press, which she co-founded. Taneka is currently working on BEYOND 2: THE QUEER POST-APOCALYPTIC AND URBAN FANTASY COMIC ANTHOLOGY with Sfé R. Monster.

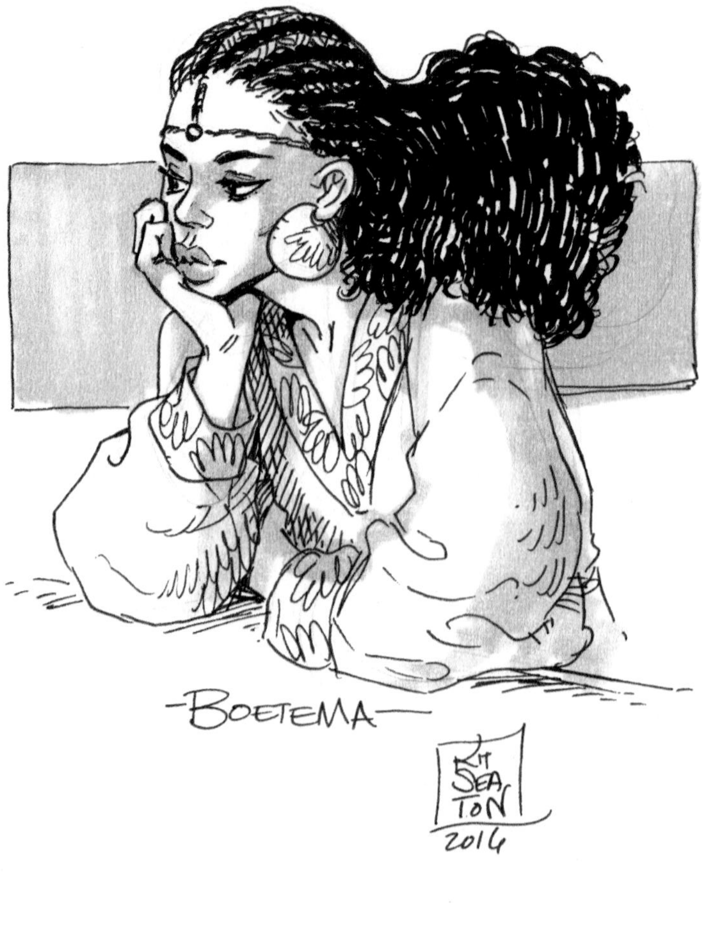
-BOETEMA-
KIT SEATON
2014